50 World's Greatest Horror Stories

FP CLASSICS

Reprint 2021

FINGERPRINT! CLASSICS
An imprint of Prakash Books India Pvt. Ltd.

113/A, Darya Ganj,
New Delhi-110 002
Tel: (011) 2324 7062 – 65, Fax: (011) 2324 6975
Email: info@prakashbooks.com/sales@prakashbooks.com

facebook www.facebook.com/fingerprintpublishing
twitter www.twitter.com/FingerprintP
www.fingerprintpublishing.com

ISBN: 978 93 8905 315 9

Processed & printed in India

The fact that that there might be something unknown out there, something we can never fully understand, is unnerving to acknowledge. It might be a being, a presence, or something else entirely, but this fact is believed in by people since time immemorial. And this fact has been used to concoct stories around the unknown, the horrible. Even today, when people go camping in the woods, it is common to sit around a fire telling spooky tales of the people lost in that very place, rumoured to roam around at night . . . looking to take the living with them . . .

Good horror stories freak people out, but they are also entertaining and fun to read. Whether you believe in ghosts or think it's all in the mind, this collection of fifty of the world's greatest horror stories would surely keep you up at night. Showing you the impossible, the tragic, and the grotesque, these stories are not for the faint-hearted.

And we all know that all of us, at times, love a good scare. The horrible and the fearful is as much alluring as it is frightening. So here is a spine-chilling collection that brings you face to face with ghosts, spirits, killers, supernatural beings, vampires, and many other such monstrosities. From classic horror stories, such as Edgar Allan Poe's 'Tell-Tale Heart' where madness plays a pivotal role, Bram Stoker's 'Dracula's Guest' which features the famous vampire Count Dracula, and Grimm Brothers' 'The Singing Bone' in which human remains are used to fish out a killer, to relatively lesser-known but equally terrifying stories, this edition is a must-have for horror fiction lovers. So, close the curtains, lock the door, and prepare to be scared stiff.

Contents

ANONYMOUS

1

Daniel Crowley and the Ghosts

There lived a man in Cork whose name was Daniel Crowley. He was a coffin-maker by trade, and had a deal of coffins laid by, so that his apprentice might sell them when himself was not at home.

A messenger came to Daniel Crowley's shop one day and told him that there was a man dead at the end of the town, and to send up a coffin for him, or to make one.

Daniel Crowley took down a coffin, put it on a donkey cart, drove to the wake house, went in and told the people of the house that the coffin was there for them. The corpse was laid out on a table in a room next to the kitchen. Five or six women were keeping watch around it; many people were in the kitchen. Daniel Crowley was asked to sit down and commence to shorten the night: that is, to tell stories, amuse himself and others. A tumbler of punch was brought, and he promised to do the best he could.

He began to tell stories and shorten the night. A second glass of punch was brought to him, and he went on telling tales. There was a man at the wake who sang a song: after him another was found, and then another. Then the people asked Daniel Crowley to sing, and he did. The song that he sang was of another nation. He sang about the good people, the fairies. The song pleased the company, they desired him to sing again, and he did not refuse.

Daniel Crowley pleased the company so much with his two songs that a woman who had three daughters wanted to make a match for one of them, and get Daniel Crowley as a husband for her. Crowley was a bachelor, well on in years, and had never thought of marrying.

The mother spoke of the match to a woman sitting next to her. The woman shook her head, but the mother said:

"If he takes one of my daughters I'll be glad, for he has money laid by. Do you go and speak to him, but say nothing of me at first."

The woman went to Daniel Crowley then, and told him that she had a fine, beautiful girl in view, and that now was his time to get a good wife; he'd never have such a chance again.

Crowley rose up in great anger. "There isn't a woman wearing clothes that I'd marry," said he. "There isn't a woman born that could bring me to make two halves of my loaf for her."

The mother was insulted now and forgot herself. She began to abuse Crowley.

"Bad luck to you, you hairy little scoundrel," said she, "you might be a grandfather to my child. You are not fit to clean the shoes on her feet. You have only dead people for company day and night; 'tis by them you make your living."

"Oh, then," said Daniel Crowley, "I'd prefer the dead to the living any day if all the living were like you. Besides, I have nothing against the dead. I am getting employment by them and not by the living, for 'tis the dead that want coffins."

"Bad luck to you, 'tis with the dead you ought to be and not with the living; 'twould be fitter for you to go out of this altogether and go to your dead people."

"I'd go if I knew how to go to them," said Crowley.

"Why not invite them to supper?" retorted the woman.

He rose up then, went out, and called:

"Men, women, children, soldiers, sailors, all people that I have ever made coffins for, I invite you tonight to my house, and I'll spend what is needed in giving a feast."

The people who were watching the dead man on the table saw him smile when he heard the invitation. They ran out of the room in a fright and out of the kitchen, and Daniel Crowley hurried away to his shop as fast as ever his donkey could carry him. On the way he came to a public-house and, going in, bought a pint bottle of whiskey, put it in his pocket, and drove on.

The workshop was locked and the shutters down when he left that evening, but when he came near he saw that all the windows were shining with light, and he was in dread that the building was burning or that robbers were in it. When right there Crowley slipped into a corner of the building opposite, to know could he see what was happening, and soon he saw crowds of men, women, and children walking toward his shop and going in, but none coming out. He was hiding some time when a man tapped him on the shoulder and asked, "Is it here you are, and we waiting for you? 'Tis a shame to treat company this way. Come now."

Crowley went with the man to the shop, and as he passed the threshold he saw a great gathering of people. Some were neighbours, people he had known in the past. All were dancing, singing, amusing themselves. He was not long looking on when a man came up to him and said:

"You seem not to know me, Daniel Crowley."

"I don't know you," said Crowley. "How could I?"

"You might then, and you ought to know me, for I am the first man you made a coffin for, and 'twas I gave you the first start in business."

Soon another came up, a lame man: "Do you know me, Daniel Crowley?"

"I do not."

"I am your cousin, and it isn't long since I died."

"Oh, now I know you well, for you are lame. In God's name," said Crowley to the cousin, "how am I to get these people out o' this. What time is it?"

"'Tis early yet, it's hardly eleven o'clock, man."

Crowley wondered that it was so early.

"Receive them kindly," said the cousin; "be good to them, make merriment as you can."

"I have no money with me to get food or drink for them; 'tis night now, and all places are closed," answered Crowley.

"Well, do the best you can," said the cousin.

The fun and dancing went on, and while Daniel Crowley was looking around, examining everything, he saw a woman in the far-off corner. She took no part in the amusement, but seemed very shy in herself.

"Why is that woman so shy—she seems to be afraid?" asked he of the cousin. "And why doesn't she dance and make merry like others?"

"Oh, 'tis not long since she died, and you gave the coffin, as she had no means of paying for it. She is in dread you'll ask her for the money, or let the company know that she didn't pay," said the cousin.

The best dancer they had was a piper by the name of John Reardon from the city of Cork. The fiddler was one John Healy. Healy brought no fiddle with him, but he made one, and the way he made it was to take off what flesh he had on his body. He rubbed up and down on his own ribs, each rib having a different note, and he made the loveliest music that Daniel Crowley had ever heard. After that the whole company followed his example. All threw off what flesh they had on them and began to dance jigs and hornpipes in their bare bones. When by chance they struck against one another in dancing, you'd think it was Brandon Mountain that was striking Mount Eagle, with the noise that was in it.

Daniel Crowley plucked up all his courage to know, could he live through the night, but still he thought daylight would never come. There was one man, John Sullivan, that he noticed especially. This man had married twice in his life, and with him came the two women. Crowley saw him taking out the second wife to dance a breakdown, and the two danced so well that the company were delighted, and all the skeletons had their mouths open, laughing. He danced and knocked so much merriment out of them all that his first wife, who was at the end of the house, became jealous and very mad altogether. She ran down to where he was and told him she had a better right to dance with him than the second wife.

"That's not the truth for you," said the second wife; "I have a better right than you. When he married me you were a dead woman and he was free, and, besides, I'm a better dancer than what you are, and I will dance with him whether you like it or not."

"Hold your tongue!" screamed the first wife. "Sure, you couldn't come to this feast tonight at all but for the loan of another woman's shinbones."

Sullivan looked at his two wives, and asked the second one:

"Isn't it your own shinbones you have?"

"No, they are borrowed. I borrowed a neighbouring woman's shins from her, and 'tis those I have with me tonight."

"Who is the owner of the shinbones you have under you?" asked the husband.

"They belong to one Catherine Murray. She hadn't a very good name in life."

"But why didn't you come on your own feet?"

"Oh, I wasn't good myself in life, and I was put under a penalty, and the penalty is that whenever there is a feast or a ball I cannot go to it unless I am able to borrow a pair of shins."

Sullivan was raging when he found that the shinbones he had been dancing with belonged to a third woman, and she not the best, and he gave a slap to the wife that sent her spinning into a corner.

The woman had relations among the skeletons present, and they were angry when they saw the man strike their friend. 'We'll never let that go with him," said they. "We must knock satisfaction out of Sullivan!"

The woman's friends rose up, and, as there were no clubs or weapons, they pulled off their left arms and began to slash and strike with them in terrible fashion. There was an awful battle in one minute.

While this was going on Daniel Crowley was standing below at the end of the room, cold and hungry, not knowing but he'd be killed. As Sullivan was trying to dodge the blows sent against him he got as far as Daniel Crowley, and stepped on his toe without knowing it; Crowley got vexed and gave Sullivan a blow with his fist that drove the head from him, and sent it flying to the opposite corner.

When Sullivan saw his head flying off from the blow he ran, and, catching it, aimed a blow at Daniel Crowley with the head, and aimed so truly that he knocked him under the bench; then, having him at a disadvantage, Sullivan hurried to the bench and began to strangle him. He squeezed his throat and held him so firmly between the bench and the floor that the man lost his senses, and couldn't remember a thing more.

When Daniel Crowley came to himself in the morning his apprentice found him stretched under the bench with an empty bottle under his arm. He was bruised and pounded. His throat was sore where Sullivan had squeezed it; he didn't know how the company broke up, nor when his guests went away.

AMBROSE BIERCE

(1842-c.1914)

2

An Occurrence at Owl Creek Bridge

I

A man stood upon a railroad bridge in northern Alabama, looking down into the swift water twenty feet below. The man's hands were behind his back, the wrists bound with a cord. A rope closely encircled his neck. It was attached to a stout cross-timber above his head and the slack fell to the level of his knees. Some loose boards laid upon the ties supporting the rails of the railway supplied a footing for him and his executioners—two private soldiers of the Federal army, directed by a sergeant who in civil life may have been a deputy sheriff. At a short remove upon the same temporary platform was an officer in the uniform of his rank, armed. He was a captain. A sentinel at each end of the bridge stood with his rifle in the position known as 'support,' that is to say, vertical in front of the left shoulder, the hammer resting on the forearm thrown straight across the chest—a formal and unnatural position, enforcing an erect carriage of the body. It did not appear to be the duty of these two men to know what was occurring at the center of the bridge; they merely blockaded the two ends of the foot planking that traversed it.

lines; my wife and little ones are still beyond the invader's farthest advance."

As these thoughts, which have here to be set down in words, were flashed into the doomed man's brain rather than evolved from it the captain nodded to the sergeant. The sergeant stepped aside.

II

Peyton Farquhar was a well to do planter, of an old and highly respected Alabama family. Being a slave owner and like other slave owners a politician, he was naturally an original secessionist and ardently devoted to the Southern cause. Circumstances of an imperious nature, which it is unnecessary to relate here, had prevented him from taking service with that gallant army which had fought the disastrous campaigns ending with the fall of Corinth, and he chafed under the inglorious restraint, longing for the release of his energies, the larger life of the soldier, the opportunity for distinction. That opportunity, he felt, would come, as it comes to all in wartime. Meanwhile he did what he could. No service was too humble for him to perform in the aid of the South, no adventure too perilous for him to undertake if consistent with the character of a civilian who was at heart a soldier, and who in good faith and without too much qualification assented to at least a part of the frankly villainous dictum that all is fair in love and war.

One evening while Farquhar and his wife were sitting on a rustic bench near the entrance to his grounds, a gray-clad soldier rode up to the gate and asked for a drink of water. Mrs. Farquhar was only too happy to serve him with her own white hands. While she was fetching the water her husband approached the dusty horseman and inquired eagerly for news from the front.

"The Yanks are repairing the railroads," said the man, "and are getting ready for another advance. They have reached the Owl Creek bridge, put it in order and built a stockade on the north bank. The commandant has issued an order, which is posted everywhere, declaring that any civilian caught interfering with the railroad, its bridges, tunnels, or trains will be summarily hanged. I saw the order."

"How far is it to the Owl Creek bridge?" Farquhar asked.

"About thirty miles."

"Is there no force on this side of the creek?"

"Only a picket post half a mile out, on the railroad, and a single sentinel at this end of the bridge."

"Suppose a man—a civilian and student of hanging—should elude the picket post and perhaps get the better of the sentinel," said Farquhar, smiling, "what could he accomplish?"

The soldier reflected. "I was there a month ago," he replied. "I observed that the flood of last winter had lodged a great quantity of driftwood against the wooden pier at this end of the bridge. It is now dry and would burn like tinder."

The lady had now brought the water, which the soldier drank. He thanked her ceremoniously, bowed to her husband and rode away. An hour later, after nightfall, he repassed the plantation, going northward in the direction from which he had come. He was a Federal scout.

III

As Peyton Farquhar fell straight downward through the bridge he lost consciousness and was as one already dead. From this state he was awakened—ages later, it seemed to him—by the pain of a sharp pressure upon his throat, followed by a sense of suffocation. Keen, poignant agonies seemed to shoot from his neck downward through every fiber of his body and limbs. These pains appeared to flash along well defined lines of ramification and to beat with an inconceivably rapid periodicity. They seemed like streams of pulsating fire heating him to an intolerable temperature. As to his head, he was conscious of nothing but a feeling of fullness—of congestion. These sensations were unaccompanied by thought. The intellectual part of his nature was already effaced; he had power only to feel, and feeling was torment. He was conscious of motion. Encompassed in a luminous cloud, of which he was now merely the fiery heart, without material substance, he swung through unthinkable arcs of oscillation, like a vast pendulum. Then all at once, with terrible suddenness, the light about him shot upward with the noise of a loud splash; a frightful roaring was in his ears, and all was cold and dark. The power of thought was restored; he knew that the rope had broken and he had fallen into the stream. There was no additional strangulation; the noose about his neck was already suffocating him and kept the water from his lungs. To die of hanging at the bottom of a river!—the idea seemed to him ludicrous. He opened his eyes in the darkness and saw above him a gleam of light, but how distant, how inaccessible! He was still sinking, for the light became fainter and fainter until it was a mere glimmer. Then it began to grow and brighten, and he knew that he was rising toward the surface—knew it with reluctance, for he was now very comfortable. "To be hanged and drowned," he thought, "that is not so bad; but I do not wish to be shot. No; I will not be shot; that is not fair."

He was not conscious of an effort, but a sharp pain in his wrist apprised him that he was trying to free his hands. He gave the struggle his attention, as an idler might observe the feat of a juggler, without interest in the outcome. What splendid effort!—what magnificent, what superhuman strength! Ah, that was a fine endeavour! Bravo! The cord fell away; his arms parted and floated upward, the hands dimly seen on each side in the growing light. He watched them with a new interest as first one and then the other pounced upon the noose at his neck. They tore it away and thrust it fiercely aside, its undulations resembling those of a water snake. "Put it back, put it back!" He thought he shouted these words to his hands, for the undoing of the noose had been succeeded by the direst pang that he had yet experienced. His neck ached horribly; his brain was on fire, his heart, which had been fluttering faintly, gave a great leap, trying to force itself out at his mouth. His whole body was racked and wrenched with an insupportable anguish! But his disobedient hands gave no heed to the command. They beat the water vigorously with quick, downward strokes, forcing him to the surface. He felt his head emerge; his eyes were blinded by the sunlight; his chest expanded convulsively, and with a supreme and crowning agony his lungs engulfed a great draught of air, which instantly he expelled in a shriek!

He was now in full possession of his physical senses. They were, indeed, preternaturally keen and alert. Something in the awful disturbance of his organic system had so exalted and refined them that they made record of things never before perceived. He felt the ripples upon his face and heard their separate sounds as they struck. He looked at the forest on the bank of the stream, saw the individual trees, the leaves and the veining of each leaf—he saw the very insects upon them: the locusts, the brilliant bodied flies, the gray spiders stretching their webs from twig to twig. He noted the prismatic colours in all the dewdrops upon a million blades of grass. The humming of the gnats that danced above the eddies of the stream, the beating of the dragon flies' wings, the strokes of the water spiders' legs, like oars which had lifted their boat—all these made audible music. A fish slid along beneath his eyes and he heard the rush of its body parting the water.

He had come to the surface facing down the stream; in a moment the visible world seemed to wheel slowly round, himself the pivotal point, and he saw the bridge, the fort, the soldiers upon the bridge, the captain, the sergeant, the two privates, his executioners. They were in silhouette against the blue sky. They shouted and gesticulated, pointing at him. The captain had drawn his pistol, but did not fire; the others were unarmed. Their movements were grotesque and horrible, their forms gigantic.

Suddenly he heard a sharp report and something struck the water smartly within a few inches of his head, spattering his face with spray. He heard a second report, and saw one of the sentinels with his rifle at his shoulder, a light cloud of blue smoke rising from the muzzle. The man in the water saw the eye of the man on the bridge gazing into his own through the sights of the rifle. He observed that it was a gray eye and remembered having read that gray eyes were keenest, and that all famous marksmen had them. Nevertheless, this one had missed.

A counter-swirl had caught Farquhar and turned him half round; he was again looking at the forest on the bank opposite the fort. The sound of a clear, high voice in a monotonous singsong now rang out behind him and came across the water with a distinctness that pierced and subdued all other sounds, even the beating of the ripples in his ears. Although no soldier, he had frequented camps enough to know the dread significance of that deliberate, drawling, aspirated chant; the lieutenant on shore was taking a part in the morning's work. How coldly and pitilessly—with what an even, calm intonation, presaging, and enforcing tranquility in the men—with what accurately measured interval fell those cruel words:

"Company! . . . Attention! . . . Shoulder arms! . . . Ready! . . . Aim! . . . Fire!"

Farquhar dived—dived as deeply as he could. The water roared in his ears like the voice of Niagara, yet he heard the dull thunder of the volley and, rising again toward the surface, met shining bits of metal, singularly flattened, oscillating slowly downward. Some of them touched him on the face and hands, then fell away, continuing their descent. One lodged between his collar and neck; it was uncomfortably warm and he snatched it out.

As he rose to the surface, gasping for breath, he saw that he had been a long time under water; he was perceptibly farther downstream—nearer to safety. The soldiers had almost finished reloading; the metal ramrods flashed all at once in the sunshine as they were drawn from the barrels, turned in the air, and thrust into their sockets. The two sentinels fired again, independently and ineffectually.

The hunted man saw all this over his shoulder; he was now swimming vigorously with the current. His brain was as energetic as his arms and legs; he thought with the rapidity of lightning:

"The officer," he reasoned, "will not make that martinet's error a second time. It is as easy to dodge a volley as a single shot. He has probably already given the command to fire at will. God help me, I cannot dodge them all!"

An appalling splash within two yards of him was followed by a loud, rushing sound, DIMINUENDO, which seemed to travel back through the air to the fort and died in an explosion which stirred the very river to its deeps! A rising sheet of water curved over him, fell down upon him, blinded him, strangled him! The cannon had taken a hand in the game. As he shook his head free from the commotion of the smitten water he heard the deflected shot humming through the air ahead, and in an instant it was cracking and smashing the branches in the forest beyond.

"They will not do that again," he thought; "the next time they will use a charge of grape. I must keep my eye upon the gun; the smoke will apprise me—the report arrives too late; it lags behind the missile. That is a good gun."

Suddenly he felt himself whirled round and round—spinning like a top. The water, the banks, the forests, the now distant bridge, fort and men, all were commingled and blurred. Objects were represented by their colours only; circular horizontal streaks of colour—that was all he saw. He had been caught in a vortex and was being whirled on with a velocity of advance and gyration that made him giddy and sick. In few moments he was flung upon the gravel at the foot of the left bank of the stream—the southern bank—and behind a projecting point which concealed him from his enemies. The sudden arrest of his motion, the abrasion of one of his hands on the gravel, restored him, and he wept with delight. He dug his fingers into the sand, threw it over himself in handfuls and audibly blessed it. It looked like diamonds, rubies, emeralds; he could think of nothing beautiful which it did not resemble. The trees upon the bank were giant garden plants; he noted a definite order in their arrangement, inhaled the fragrance of their blooms. A strange roseate light shone through the spaces among their trunks and the wind made in their branches the music of Aeolian harps. He had not wish to perfect his escape—he was content to remain in that enchanting spot until retaken.

A whiz and a rattle of grapeshot among the branches high above his head roused him from his dream. The baffled cannoneer had fired him a random farewell. He sprang to his feet, rushed up the sloping bank, and plunged into the forest.

All that day he traveled, laying his course by the rounding sun. The forest seemed interminable; nowhere did he discover a break in it, not even a woodman's road. He had not known that he lived in so wild a region. There was something uncanny in the revelation.

By nightfall he was fatigued, footsore, famished. The thought of his wife and children urged him on. At last he found a road which led him in what he knew to be the right direction. It was as wide and straight as a city street, yet it seemed untraveled. No fields bordered it, no dwelling anywhere. Not so much as the barking of a dog suggested human habitation. The black bodies of the trees formed a straight wall on both sides, terminating on the horizon in a point, like a diagram in a lesson in perspective. Overhead, as he looked up through this rift in the wood, shone great golden stars looking unfamiliar and grouped in strange constellations. He was sure they were arranged in some order which had a secret and malign significance. The wood on either side was full of singular noises, among which—once, twice, and again—he distinctly heard whispers in an unknown tongue.

His neck was in pain and lifting his hand to it found it horribly swollen. He knew that it had a circle of black where the rope had bruised it. His eyes felt congested; he could no longer close them. His tongue was swollen with thirst; he relieved its fever by thrusting it forward from between his teeth into the cold air. How softly the turf had carpeted the untraveled avenue—he could no longer feel the roadway beneath his feet!

Doubtless, despite his suffering, he had fallen asleep while walking, for now he sees another scene—perhaps he has merely recovered from a delirium. He stands at the gate of his own home. All is as he left it, and all bright and beautiful in the morning sunshine. He must have traveled the entire night. As he pushes open the gate and passes up the wide white walk, he sees a flutter of female garments; his wife, looking fresh and cool and sweet, steps down from the veranda to meet him. At the bottom of the steps she stands waiting, with a smile of ineffable joy, an attitude of matchless grace and dignity. Ah, how beautiful she is! He springs forwards with extended arms. As he is about to clasp her he feels a stunning blow upon the back of the neck; a blinding white light blazes all about him with a sound like the shock of a cannon—then all is darkness and silence!

Peyton Farquhar was dead; his body, with a broken neck, swung gently from side to side beneath the timbers of the Owl Creek bridge.

3

Beyond the Wall

Many years ago, on my way from Hong Kong to New York, I passed a week in San Francisco. A long time had gone by since I had been in that city, during which my ventures in the Orient had prospered beyond my hope; I was rich and could afford to revisit my own country to renew my friendship with such of the companions of my youth as still lived and remembered me with the old affection. Chief of these, I hoped, was Mohun Dampier, an old schoolmate with whom I had held a desultory correspondence which had long ceased, as is the way of correspondence between men. You may have observed that the indisposition to write a merely social letter is in the ratio of the square of the distance between you and your correspondent. It is a law.

I remembered Dampier as a handsome, strong young fellow of scholarly tastes, with an aversion to work and a marked indifference to many of the things that the world cares for, including wealth, of which, however, he had inherited enough to put him beyond the reach of want. In his family, one of the oldest and most aristocratic in the country, it was, I think, a matter of pride that no member of it had ever been in trade nor politics, nor suffered any kind of distinction. Mohun was a trifle sentimental, and had in him a singular element of superstition, which led him to the study of all manner of occult subjects, although his sane mental health safeguarded him against fantastic and perilous faiths. He made daring incursions into the realm of the unreal without renouncing his residence in the partly surveyed and charted region of what we are pleased to call certitude.

The night of my visit to him was stormy. The Californian winter was on, and the incessant rain plashed in the deserted streets, or, lifted by irregular gusts of wind, was hurled against the houses with incredible fury. With no small difficulty my cabman found the right place, away out toward the ocean beach, in a sparsely populated suburb. The dwelling, a rather ugly one, apparently, stood in the center of its grounds, which as nearly as I could make out in the gloom were destitute of either flowers or grass. Three or four trees, writhing and moaning in the torment of the tempest, appeared to be trying to escape from their dismal environment and take the chance of finding a better one out at sea. The house was a two-story brick structure with a tower, a story higher, at one corner. In a window of that was the only visible light. Something in the appearance of the place made me shudder, a performance that may have been assisted by a rill of rain-water down my back as I scuttled to cover in the doorway.

In answer to my note apprising him of my wish to call, Dampier had written, "Don't ring—open the door and come up." I did so. The staircase was dimly lighted by a single gas-jet at the top of the second flight. I managed to reach the landing without disaster and entered by an open door into the lighted square room of the tower. Dampier came forward in gown and slippers to receive me, giving me the greeting that I wished, and if I had held a thought that it might more fitly have been accorded me at the front door the first look at him dispelled any sense of his inhospitality.

He was not the same. Hardly past middle age, he had gone gray and had acquired a pronounced stoop. His figure was thin and angular, his face deeply lined, his complexion dead-white, without a touch of colour. His eyes, unnaturally large, glowed with a fire that was almost uncanny.

He seated me, proffered a cigar, and with grave and obvious sincerity assured me of the pleasure that it gave him to meet me. Some unimportant conversation followed, but all the while I was dominated by a melancholy sense of the great change in him. This he must have perceived, for he suddenly said with a bright enough smile, "You are disappointed in me—*non sum qualis eram.*"

I hardly knew what to reply, but managed to say: "Why, really, I don't know: your Latin is about the same."

He brightened again. "No," he said, "being a dead language, it grows in appropriateness. But please have the patience to wait: where I am going there is perhaps a better tongue. Will you care to have a message in it?"

The smile faded as he spoke, and as he concluded he was looking into my eyes with a gravity that distressed me. Yet I would not surrender myself to his mood, nor permit him to see how deeply his prescience of death affected me.

"I fancy that it will be long," I said, "before human speech will cease to serve our need; and then the need, with its possibilities of service, will have passed."

He made no reply, and I too was silent, for the talk had taken a dispiriting turn, yet I knew not how to give it a more agreeable character. Suddenly, in a pause of the storm, when the dead silence was almost startling by contrast with the previous uproar, I heard a gentle tapping, which appeared to come from the wall behind my chair. The sound was such as might have been made by a human hand, not as upon a door by one asking admittance, but rather, I thought, as an agreed signal, an assurance of someone's presence in an adjoining room; most of us, I fancy, have had more experience of such communications than we should care to relate. I glanced at Dampier. If possibly there was something of amusement in the look he did not observe it. He appeared to have forgotten my presence, and was staring at the wall behind me with an expression in his eyes that I am unable to name, although my memory of it is as vivid today as was my sense of it then. The situation was embarrassing; I rose to take my leave. At this he seemed to recover himself.

"Please be seated," he said; "it is nothing—no one is there."

But the tapping was repeated, and with the same gentle, slow insistence as before.

"Pardon me," I said, "it is late. May I call tomorrow?"

He smiled—a little mechanically, I thought. "It is very delicate of you," said he, "but quite needless. Really, this is the only room in the tower, and no one is there. At least—" He left the sentence incomplete, rose, and threw up a window, the only opening in the wall from which the sound seemed to come. "See."

Not clearly knowing what else to do I followed him to the window and looked out. A street-lamp some little distance away gave enough light through the murk of the rain that was again falling in torrents to make it entirely plain that 'no one was there.' In truth there was nothing but the sheer blank wall of the tower.

Dampier closed the window and signing me to my seat resumed his own.

The incident was not in itself particularly mysterious; any one of a dozen explanations was possible (though none has occurred to me), yet it impressed me strangely, the more, perhaps, from my friend's effort to reassure me, which seemed to dignify it with a certain significance and importance. He had proved that no one was there, but in that fact lay all the interest; and he proffered no explanation. His silence was irritating and made me resentful.

"My good friend," I said, somewhat ironically, I fear, "I am not disposed to question your right to harbor as many spooks as you find agreeable to your taste and consistent with your notions of companionship; that is no business of mine. But being just a plain man of affairs, mostly of this world, I find spooks needless to my peace and comfort. I am going to my hotel, where my fellow-guests are still in the flesh."

It was not a very civil speech, but he manifested no feeling about it. "Kindly remain," he said. "I am grateful for your presence here. What you have heard tonight I believe myself to have heard twice before. Now I *know* it was no illusion. That is much to me—more than you know. Have a fresh cigar and a good stock of patience while I tell you the story."

The rain was now falling more steadily, with a low, monotonous susurration, interrupted at long intervals by the sudden slashing of the boughs of the trees as the wind rose and failed. The night was well advanced, but both sympathy and curiosity held me a willing listener to my friend's monologue, which I did not interrupt by a single word from beginning to end.

"Ten years ago," he said, "I occupied a ground-floor apartment in one of a row of houses, all alike, away at the other end of the town, on what we call Rincon Hill. This had been the best quarter of San Francisco, but had fallen into neglect and decay, partly because the primitive character of its domestic architecture no longer suited the maturing tastes of our wealthy citizens, partly because certain public improvements had made a wreck of it. The row of dwellings in one of which I lived stood a little way back from the street, each having a miniature garden, separated from its neighbours by low iron fences and bisected with mathematical precision by a box-bordered gravel walk from gate to door.

"One morning as I was leaving my lodging I observed a young girl entering the adjoining garden on the left. It was a warm day in June, and she was lightly gowned in white. From her shoulders hung a broad straw hat profusely decorated with flowers and wonderfully beribboned in the fashion of the time. My attention was not long held by the exquisite simplicity of her costume, for no one could look at her face and think of anything earthly. Do not fear; I shall not profane it by description; it was beautiful exceedingly. All that I had ever seen or dreamed of loveliness was in that matchless living picture by the hand of the Divine Artist. So deeply did it move me that, without a thought of the impropriety of the act, I unconsciously bared my head, as a devout Catholic or well-bred Protestant uncovers before an image of the Blessed Virgin. The maiden showed no displeasure; she merely turned her glorious dark eyes upon me with a look that made me catch my breath, and without other recognition of my act passed into the house. For a moment I stood motionless, hat in hand, painfully conscious of my rudeness, yet so dominated by the emotion inspired by that vision of incomparable beauty that my penitence was less poignant than it should have been. Then I went my way, leaving my heart behind.

In the natural course of things I should probably have remained away until nightfall, but by the middle of the afternoon I was back in the little garden, affecting an interest in the few foolish flowers that I had never before observed. My hope was vain; she did not appear.

"To a night of unrest succeeded a day of expectation and disappointment, but on the day after, as I wandered aimlessly about the neighbourhood, I met her. Of course I did not repeat my folly of uncovering, nor venture by even so much as too long a look to manifest an interest in her; yet my heart was beating audibly. I trembled and consciously coloured as she turned her big black eyes upon me with a look of obvious recognition entirely devoid of boldness or coquetry.

"I will not weary you with particulars; many times afterward I met the maiden, yet never either addressed her or sought to fix her attention. Nor did I take any action toward making her acquaintance. Perhaps my forbearance, requiring so supreme an effort of self-denial, will not be entirely clear to you. That I was heels over head in love is true, but who can overcome his habit of thought, or reconstruct his character?

"I was what some foolish persons are pleased to call, and others, more foolish, are pleased to be called—an aristocrat; and despite her beauty, her charms and graces, the girl was not of my class. I had learned her name—which it is needless to speak—and something of her family. She was an orphan, a dependent niece of the impossible elderly fat woman in whose lodging-house she lived. My income was small and I lacked the talent for marrying; it is perhaps a gift. An alliance with that family would condemn me to its manner of life, part me from my books and studies, and in a social sense reduce me to the ranks. It is easy to deprecate such considerations as these and I have not retained myself for the defense. Let judgment be entered against me, but in strict justice all my ancestors for generations should be made co-defendants and I be permitted to plead in mitigation of punishment the imperious mandate of heredity. To a mésalliance of that kind every globule of my ancestral blood spoke in opposition. In brief, my tastes, habits, instinct, with whatever of reason my love had left me—all fought against it. Moreover, I was an irreclaimable sentimentalist, and found a subtle charm in an impersonal and spiritual relation which acquaintance might vulgarize and marriage would certainly dispel. No woman, I argued, is what this lovely creature seems. Love is a delicious dream; why should I bring about my own awakening?

"The course dictated by all this sense and sentiment was obvious. Honour, pride, prudence, preservation of my ideals—all commanded me to go away, but for that I was too weak. The utmost that I could do by a mighty effort of will was to cease meeting the girl, and that I did. I even avoided the chance encounters of the garden, leaving my lodging only when I knew that she had gone to her music lessons, and returning after nightfall. Yet all the while I was as one in a trance, indulging the most fascinating fancies and ordering my entire intellectual life in accordance with my dream. Ah, my friend, as one whose actions have a traceable relation to reason, you cannot know the fool's paradise in which I lived.

"One evening the devil put it into my head to be an unspeakable idiot. By apparently careless and purposeless questioning I learned from my gossipy landlady that the young woman's bedroom adjoined my own, a party-wall between. Yielding to a sudden and coarse impulse I gently rapped on the wall. There was no response, naturally, but I was in no mood to accept a rebuke. A madness was upon me and I repeated the folly, the offense, but again ineffectually, and I had the decency to desist.

"An hour later, while absorbed in some of my infernal studies, I heard, or thought I heard, my signal answered. Flinging down my books I sprang to the wall and as steadily as my beating heart would permit gave three slow taps upon it. This time the response was distinct, unmistakable: one, two, three—an exact repetition of my signal. That was all I could elicit, but it was enough—too much.

"The next evening, and for many evenings afterward, that folly went on, I always having 'the last word.' During the whole period I was deliriously happy, but with the perversity of my nature I persevered in my resolution not to see her. Then, as I should have expected, I got no further answers. 'She is disgusted,'

I said to myself, 'with what she thinks my timidity in making no more definite advances'; and I resolved to seek her and make her acquaintance and—what? I did not know, nor do I now know, what might have come of it. I know only that I passed days and days trying to meet her, and all in vain; she was invisible as well as inaudible. I haunted the streets where we had met, but she did not come. From my window I watched the garden in front of her house, but she passed neither in nor out. I fell into the deepest dejection, believing that she had gone away, yet took no steps to resolve my doubt by inquiry of my landlady, to whom, indeed, I had taken an unconquerable aversion from her having once spoken of the girl with less of reverence than I thought befitting.

"There came a fateful night. Worn out with emotion, irresolution and despondency, I had retired early and fallen into such sleep as was still possible to me. In the middle of the night something—some malign power bent upon the wrecking of my peace forever—caused me to open my eyes and sit up, wide awake and listening intently for I knew not what. Then I thought I heard a faint tapping on the wall—the mere ghost of the familiar signal. In a few moments it was repeated: one, two, three—no louder than before, but addressing a sense alert and strained to receive it. I was about to reply when the Adversary of Peace again intervened in my affairs with a rascally suggestion of retaliation. She had long and cruelly ignored me; now I would ignore her. Incredible fatuity—may God forgive it! All the rest of the night I lay awake, fortifying my obstinacy with shameless justifications and—listening.

"Late the next morning, as I was leaving the house, I met my landlady, entering.

"'Good morning, Mr. Dampier,' she said. 'Have you heard the news?'

"I replied in words that I had heard no news; in manner, that I did not care to hear any. The manner escaped her observation.

"'About the sick young lady next door,' she babbled on. 'What! You did not know? Why, she has been ill for weeks. And now—'

"I almost sprang upon her. 'And now,' I cried, 'now what?'

"'She is dead.'

"That is not the whole story. In the middle of the night, as I learned later, the patient, awakening from a long stupor after a week of delirium, had asked—it was her last utterance—that her bed be moved to the opposite side of the room. Those in attendance had thought the request a vagary of her delirium, but had complied. And there the poor passing soul had exerted its failing will to restore a broken connection—a golden thread of sentiment between its innocence and a monstrous baseness owning a blind, brutal allegiance to the Law of Self.

"What reparation could I make? Are there masses that can be said for the repose of souls that are abroad such nights as this—spirits 'blown about by the viewless winds'—coming in the storm and darkness with signs and portents, hints of memory and presages of doom?

"This is the third visitation. On the first occasion I was too skeptical to do more than verify by natural methods the character of the incident; on the second, I responded to the signal after it had been several times repeated, but without result. Tonight's recurrence completes the 'fatal triad' expounded by Parapelius Necromantius. There is no more to tell."

When Dampier had finished his story I could think of nothing relevant that I cared to say, and to question him would have been a hideous impertinence. I rose and bade him good night in a way to convey to him a sense of my sympathy, which he silently acknowledged by a pressure of the hand. That night, alone with his sorrow and remorse, he passed into the Unknown.

4

The Moonlit Road

I—Statement of Joel Hetman, Jr.

I am the most unfortunate of men. Rich, respected, fairly well-educated and of sound health—with many other advantages usually valued by those having them and coveted by those who have them not—I sometimes think that I should be less unhappy if they had been denied me, for then the contrast between my outer and my inner life would not be continually demanding a painful attention. In the stress of privation and the need of effort I might sometimes forget the somber secret ever baffling the conjecture that it compels.

I am the only child of Joel and Julia Hetman. The one was a well-to-do country gentleman, the other a beautiful and accomplished woman to whom he was passionately attached with what I now know to have been a jealous and exacting devotion. The family home was a few miles from Nashville, Tennessee, a large, irregularly built dwelling of no particular order of architecture, a little way off the road, in a park of trees and shrubbery.

At the time of which I write I was nineteen years old, a student at Yale. One day I received a telegram from my father of such urgency that in compliance with its unexplained demand I left at once for home. At the railway station in Nashville a distant relative awaited me to apprise me of the reason for my recall: my mother had been barbarously murdered—why and by whom none could conjecture, but the circumstances were these: My father had gone to Nashville, intending to return the next afternoon. Something prevented his accomplishing the business in hand, so he returned on the same night, arriving just before the dawn. In his testimony before the coroner he explained that having no latchkey and not caring to disturb the sleeping servants, he had, with no clearly defined intention, gone round to the rear of the house. As he turned an angle of the building, he heard a sound as of a door gently closed, and saw in the darkness, indistinctly, the figure of a man, which instantly disappeared among the trees of the lawn. A hasty pursuit and brief search of the grounds in the belief that the trespasser was some one secretly visiting a servant proving fruitless, he entered at the unlocked door and mounted the stairs to my mother's chamber. Its door was open, and stepping into black darkness he fell headlong over some heavy object on the floor. I may spare myself the details; it was my poor mother, dead of strangulation by human hands!

Nothing had been taken from the house, the servants had heard no sound, and excepting those terrible finger-marks upon the dead woman's throat—dear God! that I might forget them!—no trace of the assassin was ever found.

I gave up my studies and remained with my father, who, naturally, was greatly changed. Always of a sedate, taciturn disposition, he now fell into so deep a dejection that nothing could hold his attention, yet anything—a footfall, the sudden closing of a door—aroused in him a fitful interest; one might have called it an apprehension. At any small surprise of the senses he would start visibly and sometimes turn pale, then relapse into a melancholy apathy deeper than before. I suppose he was what is called a 'nervous wreck.' As to me, I was younger then than now—there is much in that. Youth is Gilead, in which is balm for every wound. Ah, that I might again dwell in that enchanted land! Unacquainted with grief, I knew not how to appraise my bereavement; I could not rightly estimate the strength of the stroke.

One night, a few months after the dreadful event, my father and I walked home from the city. The full moon was about three hours above the eastern horizon; the entire countryside had the solemn stillness of a summer night; our footfalls and the ceaseless song of the katydids were the only sound aloof. Black shadows of bordering trees lay athwart the road, which, in the short reaches between, gleamed a ghostly white. As we approached the gate to our dwelling, whose front was in shadow, and in which no light shone, my father suddenly stopped and clutched my arm, saying, hardly above his breath:

"God! God! What is that?"

"I hear nothing," I replied.

"But see—see!" he said, pointing along the road, directly ahead.

I said: "Nothing is there. Come, father, let us go in—you are ill."

He had released my arm and was standing rigid and motionless in the center of the illuminated roadway, staring like one bereft of sense. His face in the moonlight showed a pallor and fixity inexpressibly distressing. I pulled gently at his sleeve, but he had forgotten my existence. Presently he began to retire backward, step by step, never for an instant removing his eyes from what he saw, or thought he saw. I turned half round to follow, but stood irresolute. I do not recall any feeling of fear, unless a sudden chill was its physical manifestation. It seemed as if an icy wind had touched my face and enfolded my body from head to foot; I could feel the stir of it in my hair.

At that moment my attention was drawn to a light that suddenly streamed from an upper window of the house: one of the servants, awakened by what mysterious premonition of evil who can say, and in obedience to an impulse that she was never able to name, had lit a lamp. When I turned to look for my father he was gone, and in all the years that have passed no whisper of his fate has come across the borderland of conjecture from the realm of the unknown.

II—Statement of Caspar Grattan

Today I am said to live; tomorrow, here in this room, will lie a senseless shape of clay that all too long was I. If anyone lift the cloth from the face of that unpleasant thing it will be in gratification of a mere morbid curiosity. Some, doubtless, will go further and inquire, "Who was he?" In this writing I supply the only answer that I am able to make—Caspar Grattan. Surely, that should be enough. The name has served my small need for more than twenty years of a life of unknown length. True, I gave it to myself, but lacking another I had the right. In this world one must have a name; it prevents confusion, even when it does not establish identity. Some, though, are known by numbers, which also seem inadequate distinctions.

One day, for illustration, I was passing along a street of a city, far from here, when I met two men in uniform, one of whom, half pausing and looking curiously into my face, said to his companion, "That man looks like 767." Something in the number seemed familiar and horrible. Moved by an uncontrollable impulse, I sprang into a side street and ran until I fell exhausted in a country lane.

I have never forgotten that number, and always it comes to memory attended by gibbering obscenity, peals of joyless laughter, the clang of iron doors. So I say a name, even if self-bestowed, is better than a number. In the register of the potter's field I shall soon have both. What wealth!

Of him who shall find this paper I must beg a little consideration. It is not the history of my life; the knowledge to write that is denied me. This is only a record of broken and apparently unrelated memories, some of them as distinct and sequent as brilliant beads upon a thread, others remote and strange, having the character of crimson dreams with interspaces blank and black—witch-fires glowing still and red in a great desolation.

Standing upon the shore of eternity, I turn for a last look landward over the course by which I came. There are twenty years of footprints fairly distinct, the impressions of bleeding feet. They lead through poverty and pain, devious and unsure, as of one staggering beneath a burden—

Remote, unfriended, melancholy, slow.

Ah, the poet's prophecy of Me—how admirable, how dreadfully admirable!

Backward beyond the beginning of this via dolorosa—this epic of suffering with episodes of sin—I see nothing clearly; it comes out of a cloud. I know that it spans only twenty years, yet I am an old man.

One does not remember one's birth—one has to be told. But with me it was different; life came to me full-handed and dowered me with all my faculties and powers. Of a previous existence I know no more than others, for all have stammering intimations that may be memories and may be dreams. I know only that my first consciousness was of maturity in body and mind—a consciousness accepted without surprise or conjecture. I merely found myself walking in a forest, half-clad, footsore, unutterably weary and hungry. Seeing a farmhouse, I approached and asked for food, which was given me by one who inquired my name. I did not know, yet knew that all had names. Greatly embarrassed, I retreated, and night coming on, lay down in the forest and slept.

The next day I entered a large town which I shall not name. Nor shall I recount further incidents of the life that is now to end—a life of wandering, always and everywhere haunted by an overmastering sense of crime in punishment of wrong and of terror in punishment of crime. Let me see if I can reduce it to narrative.

I seem once to have lived near a great city, a prosperous planter, married to a woman whom I loved and distrusted. We had, it sometimes seems, one child, a youth of brilliant parts and promise. He is at all times a vague figure, never clearly drawn, frequently altogether out of the picture.

One luckless evening it occurred to me to test my wife's fidelity in a vulgar, commonplace way familiar to everyone who has acquaintance with the literature of fact and fiction. I went to the city, telling my wife that I should be absent until the following afternoon. But I returned before daybreak and went to the rear of the house, purposing to enter by a door with which I had secretly so tampered that it would seem to lock, yet not actually fasten.

As I approached it, I heard it gently open and close, and saw a man steal away into the darkness. With murder in my heart, I sprang after him, but he had vanished without even the bad luck of identification. Sometimes now I cannot even persuade myself that it was a human being.

Crazed with jealousy and rage, blind and bestial with all the elemental passions of insulted manhood, I entered the house and sprang up the stairs to the door of my wife's chamber. It was closed, but having tampered with its lock also, I easily entered and despite the black darkness soon stood by the side of her bed. My groping hands told me that although disarranged it was unoccupied.

"She is below," I thought, "and terrified by my entrance has evaded me in the darkness of the hall."

With the purpose of seeking her I turned to leave the room, but took a wrong direction—the right one! My foot struck her, cowering in a corner of the room. Instantly my hands were at her throat, stifling a shriek, my knees were upon her struggling body; and there in the darkness, without a word of accusation or reproach, I strangled her till she died!

There ends the dream. I have related it in the past tense, but the present would be the fitter form, for again and again the somber tragedy reenacts itself in my consciousness—over and over I lay the plan, I suffer the confirmation, I redress the wrong. Then all is blank; and afterward the rains beat against the grimy window-panes, or the snows fall upon my scant attire, the wheels rattle in the squalid streets where my life lies in poverty and mean employment. If there is ever sunshine I do not recall it; if there are birds they do not sing.

There is another dream, another vision of the night. I stand among the shadows in a moonlit road. I am aware of another presence, but whose I cannot rightly determine. In the shadow of a great dwelling I catch the gleam of white garments; then the figure of a woman confronts me in the road—my murdered wife! There is death in the face; there are marks upon the throat. The eyes are fixed on mine with an infinite gravity which is not reproach, nor hate, nor menace, nor anything less terrible than recognition.

Before this awful apparition I retreat in terror—a terror that is upon me as I write. I can no longer rightly shape the words. See! they—

Now I am calm, but truly there is no more to tell: the incident ends where it began—in darkness and in doubt.

Yes, I am again in control of myself: 'the captain of my soul.' But that is not respite; it is another stage and phase of expiation. My penance, constant in degree, is mutable in kind: one of its variants is tranquillity. After all, it is only a life-sentence. 'To Hell for life'—that is a foolish penalty: the culprit chooses the duration of his punishment. Today my term expires.

To each and all, the peace that was not mine.

III—Statement of the Late Julia Hetman, Through the Medium Bayrolles

I had retired early and fallen almost immediately into a peaceful sleep, from which I awoke with that indefinable sense of peril which is, I think, a common experience in that other, earlier life. Of its unmeaning character, too, I was entirely persuaded, yet that did not banish it. My husband, Joel Hetman, was away from home; the servants slept in another part of the house. But these were familiar conditions; they had never before distressed me. Nevertheless, the strange terror grew so insupportable that conquering my reluctance to move I sat up and lit the lamp at my bedside. Contrary to my expectation this gave me no relief; the light seemed rather an added danger, for I reflected that it would shine out under the door, disclosing my presence to whatever evil thing might lurk outside. You that are still in the flesh, subject to horrors of the imagination, think what a monstrous fear that must be which seeks in darkness security from malevolent existences of the night. That is to spring to close quarters with an unseen enemy—the strategy of despair!

Extinguishing the lamp I pulled the bed-clothing about my head and lay trembling and silent, unable to shriek, forgetful to pray. In this pitiable state I must have lain for what you call hours—with us there are no hours, there is no time.

At last it came—a soft, irregular sound of footfalls on the

stairs! They were slow, hesitant, uncertain, as of something that did not see its way; to my disordered reason all the more terrifying for that, as the approach of some blind and mindless malevolence to which is no appeal. I even thought that I must have left the hall lamp burning and the groping of this creature proved it a monster of the night. This was foolish and inconsistent with my previous dread of the light, but what would you have? Fear has no brains; it is an idiot. The dismal witness that it bears and the cowardly counsel that it whispers are unrelated. We know this well, we who have passed into the Realm of Terror, who skulk in eternal dusk among the scenes of our former lives, invisible even to ourselves and one another, yet hiding forlorn in lonely places; yearning for speech with our loved ones, yet dumb, and as fearful of them as they of us. Sometimes the disability is removed, the law suspended: by the deathless power of love or hate we break the spell—we are seen by those whom we would warn, console, or punish. What form we seem to them to bear we know not; we know only that we terrify even those whom we most wish to comfort, and from whom we most crave tenderness and sympathy.

Forgive, I pray you, this inconsequent digression by what was once a woman. You who consult us in this imperfect way—you do not understand. You ask foolish questions about things unknown and things forbidden. Much that we know and could impart in our speech is meaningless in yours. We must communicate with you through a stammering intelligence in that small fraction of our language that you yourselves can speak. You think that we are of another world. No, we have knowledge of no world but yours, though for us it holds no sunlight, no warmth, no music, no laughter, no song of birds, nor any companionship. O God! what a thing it is to be a ghost, cowering and shivering in an altered world, a prey to apprehension and despair!

No, I did not die of fright: the Thing turned and went away. I heard it go down the stairs, hurriedly, I thought, as if itself in sudden fear. Then I rose to call for help. Hardly had my shaking hand found the doorknob when—merciful heaven!—I heard it returning. Its footfalls as it remounted the stairs were rapid, heavy and loud; they shook the house. I fled to an angle of the wall and crouched upon the floor. I tried to pray. I tried to call the name of my dear husband. Then I heard the door thrown open. There was an interval of unconsciousness, and when I revived I felt a strangling clutch upon my throat—felt my arms feebly beating against something that bore me backward—felt my tongue thrusting itself from between my teeth! And then I passed into this life.

No, I have no knowledge of what it was. The sum of what we knew at death is the measure of what we know afterward of all that went before. Of this existence we know many things, but no new light falls upon any page of that; in memory is written all of it that we can read. Here are no heights of truth overlooking the confused landscape of that dubitable domain. We still dwell in the Valley of the Shadow, lurk in its desolate places, peering from brambles and thickets at its mad, malign inhabitants. How should we have new knowledge of that fading past?

What I am about to relate happened on a night. We know when it is night, for then you retire to your houses and we can venture from our places of concealment to move unafraid about our old homes, to look in at the windows, even to enter and gaze upon your faces as you sleep. I had lingered long near the dwelling where I had been so cruelly changed to what I am, as we do while any that we love or hate remain. Vainly I had sought some method of manifestation, some way to make my continued existence and my great love and poignant pity understood by my husband and son. Always if they slept they would wake, or if in my desperation I dared approach them when they were awake, would turn toward me the terrible eyes of the living, frightening me by the glances that I sought from the purpose that I held.

On this night I had searched for them without success, fearing to find them; they were nowhere in the house, nor about the moonlit lawn. For, although the sun is lost to us forever, the moon, full-orbed or slender, remains to us. Sometimes it shines by night, sometimes by day, but always it rises and sets, as in that other life.

I left the lawn and moved in the white light and silence along the road, aimless and sorrowing. Suddenly I heard the voice of my poor husband in exclamations of astonishment, with that of my son in reassurance and dissuasion; and there by the shadow of a group of trees they stood—near, so near! Their faces were toward me, the eyes of the elder man fixed upon mine. He saw me—at last, at last, he saw me! In the consciousness of that, my terror fled as a cruel dream. The death-spell was broken: Love had conquered Law! Mad with exultation I shouted—I MUST have shouted, "He sees, he sees: he will understand!" Then, controlling myself, I moved forward, smiling and consciously beautiful, to offer myself to his arms, to comfort him with endearments, and, with my son's hand in mine, to speak words that should restore the broken bonds between the living and the dead.

Alas! alas! his face went white with fear, his eyes were as those of a hunted animal. He backed away from me, as I advanced, and at last turned and fled into the wood—whither, it is not given to me to know.

To my poor boy, left doubly desolate, I have never been able to impart a sense of my presence. Soon he, too, must pass to this Life Invisible and be lost to me forever.

5

The Damned Thing

I

By the light of a tallow candle, which had been placed on one end of a rough table, a man was reading something written in a book. It was an old account book, greatly worn; and the writing was not, apparently, very legible, for the man sometimes held the page close to the flame of the candle to get a stronger light upon it. The shadow of the book would then throw into obscurity a half of the room, darkening a number of faces and figures; for besides the reader, eight other men were present. Seven of them sat against the rough log walls, silent and motionless, and, the room being small, not very far from the table. By extending an arm any one of them could have touched the eighth man, who lay on the table, face upward, partly covered by a sheet, his arms at his sides. He was dead.

The man with the book was not reading aloud, and no one spoke; all seemed to be waiting for something to occur; the dead man only was without expectation. From the blank darkness outside came in, through the aperture that served for a window, all the ever unfamiliar noises of night in the wilderness—the long, nameless note of a distant coyote; the stilly pulsing thrill of tireless insects in trees; strange cries of night birds, so different from those of the birds of day; the drone of great blundering beetles, and all that mysterious chorus of small sounds that seem always to have been but half heard when they have suddenly ceased, as if conscious of an indiscretion. But nothing of all this was noted in that company; its members were not overmuch addicted to idle interest in matters of no practical importance; that was obvious in every line of their rugged faces—obvious even in the dim light of the single candle. They were evidently men of the vicinity—farmers and woodmen.

The person reading was a trifle different; one would have said of him that he was of the world, worldly, albeit there was that in his attire which attested a certain fellowship with the organisms of his environment. His coat would hardly have passed muster in San Francisco: his footgear was not of urban origin, and the hat that lay by him on the floor (he was the only one uncovered) was such that if one had considered it as an article of mere personal adornment he would have missed its meaning. In countenance the man was rather prepossessing, with just a hint of sternness; though that he may have assumed or cultivated, as appropriate to one in authority. For he was a coroner. It was by virtue of his office that he had possession of the book in which he was reading; it had been found among the dead man's effects—in his cabin, where the inquest was now taking place.

When the coroner had finished reading he put the book into his breast pocket. At that moment the door was pushed open and a young man entered. He, clearly, was not of mountain birth and breeding: he was clad as those who dwell in cities. His clothing was dusty, however, as from travel. He had, in fact, been riding hard to attend the inquest.

The coroner nodded; no one else greeted him.

"We have waited for you," said the coroner. "It is necessary to have done with this business tonight."

The young man smiled. "I am sorry to have kept you," he said. "I went away, not to evade your summons, but to post to my newspaper an account of what I suppose I am called back to relate."

The coroner smiled.

"The account that you posted to your newspaper," he said, "differs probably from that which you will give here under oath."

"That," replied the other, rather hotly and with a visible flush, "is as you choose. I used manifold paper and have a copy of what I sent. It was not written as news, for it is incredible, but as fiction. It may go as a part of my testimony under oath."

"But you say it is incredible."

"That is nothing to you, sir, if I also swear that it is true."

The coroner was apparently not greatly affected by the young man's manifest resentment. He was silent for some moments, his eyes upon the floor. The men about the sides of the cabin talked in whispers, but seldom withdrew their gaze from the face of the corpse. Presently the coroner lifted his eyes and said: "We will resume the inquest."

The men removed their hats. The witness was sworn.

"What is your name?" the coroner asked.

"William Harker."

"Age?"

"Twenty-seven."

"You knew the deceased, Hugh Morgan?"

"Yes."

"You were with him when he died?"

"Near him."

"How did that happen—your presence, I mean?"

"I was visiting him at this place to shoot and fish. A part of my purpose, however, was to study him, and his odd, solitary way of life. He seemed a good model for a character in fiction. I sometimes write stories."

"I sometimes read them."

"Thank you."

"Stories in general—not yours."

Some of the jurors laughed. Against a sombre background

humour shows high lights. Soldiers in the intervals of battle laugh easily, and a jest in the death chamber conquers by surprise.

"Relate the circumstances of this man's death," said the coroner. "You may use any notes or memoranda that you please."

The witness understood. Pulling a manuscript from his breast pocket he held it near the candle, and turning the leaves until he found the passage that he wanted, began to read.

II

". . . The sun had hardly risen when we left the house. We were looking for quail, each with a shotgun, but we had only one dog. Morgan said that our best ground was beyond a certain ridge that he pointed out, and we crossed it by a trail through the *chaparral.* On the other side was comparatively level ground, thickly covered with wild oats. As we emerged from the *chaparral*, Morgan was but a few yards in advance. Suddenly, we heard, at a little distance to our right, and partly in front, a noise as of some animal thrashing about in the bushes, which we could see were violently agitated.

"'We've started a deer,' I said. 'I wish we had brought a rifle.'

"Morgan, who had stopped and was intently watching the agitated chaparral, said nothing, but had cocked both barrels of his gun, and was holding it in readiness to aim. I thought him a trifle excited, which surprised me, for he had a reputation for exceptional coolness, even in moments of sudden and imminent peril.

"'O, come!' I said. 'You are not going to fill up a deer with quail-shot, are you?'

"Still he did not reply; but, catching a sight of his face as he turned it slightly toward me, I was struck by the pallor of it. Then I understood that we had serious business on hand, and my first conjecture was that we had 'jumped' a grizzly. I advanced to Morgan's side, cocking my piece as I moved.

"The bushes were now quiet, and the sounds had ceased, but Morgan was as attentive to the place as before.

"'What is it? What the devil is it?' I asked.

"'That Damned Thing!' he replied, without turning his head. His voice was husky and unnatural. He trembled visibly.

"I was about to speak further, when I observed the wild oats near the place of the disturbance moving in the most inexplicable way. I can hardly describe it. It seemed as if stirred by a streak of wind, which not only bent it, but pressed it down—crushed it so that it did not rise, and this movement was slowly prolonging itself directly toward us.

"Nothing that I had ever seen had affected me so strangely as this unfamiliar and unaccountable phenomenon, yet I am unable to recall any sense of fear. I remember—and tell it here because, singularly enough, I recollected it then—that once, in looking carelessly out of an open window, I momentarily mistook a small tree close at hand for one of a group of larger trees at a little distance away. It looked the same size as the others, but, being more distinctly and sharply defined in mass and detail, seemed out of harmony with them. It was a mere falsification of the law of aerial perspective, but it startled, almost terrified me. We so rely upon the orderly operation of familiar natural laws that any seeming suspension of them is noted as a menace to our safety, a warning of unthinkable calamity. So now the apparently causeless movement of the herbage, and the slow, undeviating approach of the line of disturbance were distinctly disquieting. My companion appeared actually frightened, and I could hardly credit my senses when I saw him suddenly throw his gun to his shoulders and fire both barrels at the agitated grass! Before the smoke of the discharge had cleared away I heard a loud savage cry—a scream like that of a wild animal—and, flinging his gun upon the ground, Morgan sprang away and ran swiftly from the spot. At the same instant I was thrown violently to the ground by the impact of something unseen in the smoke—some soft, heavy substance that seemed thrown against me with great force.

"Before I could get upon my feet and recover my gun, which seemed to have been struck from my hands, I heard Morgan crying out as if in mortal agony, and mingling with his cries were such hoarse savage sounds as one hears from fighting dogs.

Inexpressibly terrified, I struggled to my feet and looked in the direction of Morgan's retreat; and may heaven in mercy spare me from another sight like that! At a distance of less than thirty yards was my friend, down upon one knee, his head thrown back at a frightful angle, hatless, his long hair in disorder and his whole body in violent movement from side to side, backward and forward. His right arm was lifted and seemed to lack the hand—at least, I could see none. The other arm was invisible. At times, as my memory now reports this extraordinary scene, I could discern but a part of his body; it was as if he had been partly blotted out—I can not otherwise express it—then a shifting of his position would bring it all into view again.

"All this must have occurred within a few seconds, yet in that time Morgan assumed all the postures of a determined wrestler vanquished by superior weight and strength. I saw nothing but him, and him not always distinctly. During the entire incident his shouts and curses were heard, as if through an enveloping uproar of such sounds of rage and fury as I had never heard from the throat of man or brute!

"For a moment only I stood irresolute, then, throwing down my gun, I ran forward to my friend's assistance. I had a vague belief that he was suffering from a fit or some form of convulsion. Before I could reach his side he was down and quiet. All sounds had ceased, but, with a feeling of such terror as even these awful events had not inspired, I now saw the same mysterious movement of the wild oats prolonging itself from the trampled area about the prostrate man toward the edge of a wood. It was only when it had reached the wood that I was able to withdraw my eyes and look at my companion. He was dead."

III

The coroner rose from his seat and stood beside the dead man. Lifting an edge of the sheet he pulled it away, exposing the entire body, altogether naked and showing in the candle light a clay-like yellow. It had, however, broad maculations of bluish-black, obviously caused by extravasated blood from contusions. The chest and sides looked as if they had been beaten with a bludgeon. There were dreadful lacerations; the skin was torn in strips and shreds.

The coroner moved round to the end of the table and undid a silk handkerchief, which had been passed under the chin and knotted on the top of the head. When the handkerchief was drawn away it exposed what had been the throat. Some of the jurors who had risen to get a better view repented their curiosity, and turned away their faces. Witness Harker went to the open window and leaned out across the sill, faint and sick. Dropping the handkerchief upon the dead man's neck, the coroner stepped to an angle of the room, and from a pile of clothing produced one garment after another, each of which he held up a moment for inspection. All were torn, and stiff with blood. The jurors did not make a closer inspection. They seemed rather uninterested. They had, in truth, seen all this before; the only thing that was new to them being Harker's testimony.

"Gentlemen," the coroner said, "we have no more evidence, I think. Your duty has been already explained to you; if there is nothing you wish to ask you may go outside and consider your verdict."

The foreman rose—a tall, bearded man of sixty, coarsely clad.

"I should like to ask one question, Mr. Coroner," he said. "What asylum did this yer last witness escape from?"

"Mr. Harker," said the coroner, gravely and tranquilly, "from what asylum did you last escape?"

Harker flushed crimson again, but said nothing, and the seven jurors rose and solemnly filed out of the cabin.

"If you have done insulting me, sir," said Harker, as soon as he and the officer were left alone with the dead man, "I suppose I am at liberty to go?"

"Yes."

Harker started to leave, but paused, with his hand on the door latch. The habit of his profession was strong in him—stronger than his sense of personal dignity. He turned about and said:

"The book that you have there—I recognize it as Morgan's

diary. You seemed greatly interested in it; you read in it while I was testifying. May I see it? The public would like—"

"The book will cut no figure in this matter," replied the official, slipping it into his coat pocket; "all the entries in it were made before the writer's death."

As Harker passed out of the house the jury reentered and stood about the table on which the now covered corpse showed under the sheet with sharp definition. The foreman seated himself near the candle, produced from his breast pocket a pencil and scrap of paper, and wrote rather laboriously the following verdict, which with various degrees of effort all signed:

"We, the jury, do find that the remains come to their death at the hands of a mountain lion, but some of us thinks, all the same, they had fits."

IV

In the diary of the late Hugh Morgan are certain interesting entries having, possibly, a scientific value as suggestions. At the inquest upon his body the book was not put in evidence; possibly the coroner thought it not worth while to confuse the jury. The date of the first of the entries mentioned can not be ascertained; the upper part of the leaf is torn away; the part of the entry remaining is as follows:

". . . would run in a half circle, keeping his head turned always toward the centre and again he would stand still, barking furiously. At last he ran away into the brush as fast as he could go. I thought at first that he had gone mad, but on returning to the house found no other alteration in his manner than what was obviously due to fear of punishment.

"Can a dog see with his nose? Do odours impress some olfactory centre with images of the thing emitting them? . . .

"Sept. 2—Looking at the stars last night as they rose above the crest of the ridge east of the house, I observed them successively disappear—from left to right. Each was eclipsed but an instant, and only a few at the same time, but along the entire length of the ridge all that were within a degree or two of the crest were blotted out. It was as if something had passed along between me and them; but I could not see it, and the stars were not thick enough to define its outline. Ugh! I don't like this . . ."

Several weeks' entries are missing, three leaves being torn from the book.

"Sept. 27—It has been about here again—I find evidences of its presence every day. I watched again all of last night in the same cover, gun in hand, double-charged with buckshot. In the morning the fresh footprints were there, as before. Yet I would have sworn that I did not sleep—indeed, I hardly sleep at all. It is terrible, insupportable! If these amazing experiences are real I shall go mad; if they are fanciful I am mad already.

"Oct. 3—I shall not go—it shall not drive me away. No, this is *my* house, my land. God hates a coward . . .

"Oct. 5—I can stand it no longer; I have invited Harker to pass a few weeks with me—he has a level head. I can judge from his manner if he thinks me mad.

"Oct. 7—I have the solution of the problem; it came to me last night—suddenly, as by revelation. How simple—how terribly simple!

"There are sounds that we can not hear. At either end of the scale are notes that stir no chord of that imperfect instrument, the human ear. They are too high or too grave. I have observed a flock of blackbirds occupying an entire treetop—the tops of several trees—and all in full song. Suddenly—in a moment—at absolutely the same instant—all spring into the air and fly away. How? They could not all see one another—whole treetops intervened. At no point could a leader have been visible to all. There must have been a signal of warning or command, high and shrill above the din, but by me unheard. I have observed, too, the same simultaneous flight when all were silent, among not only blackbirds, but other birds—quail, for example, widely separated by bushes—even on opposite sides of a hill.

"It is known to seamen that a school of whales basking or sporting on the surface of the ocean, miles apart, with the convexity of the earth between them, will sometimes dive at the same instant—all gone out of sight in a moment. The signal has been sounded—too grave for the ear of the sailor at the masthead and his comrades on the deck—who nevertheless feel its vibrations in the ship as the stones of a cathedral are stirred by the bass of the organ.

"As with sounds, so with colours. At each end of the solar spectrum the chemist can detect the presence of what are known as 'actinic' rays. They represent colours—integral colours in the composition of light—which we are unable to discern. The human eye is an imperfect instrument; its range is but a few octaves of the real 'chromatic scale' I am not mad; there are colours that we can not see.

"And, God help me! the Damned Thing is of such a colour!"

6
The Stranger

A man stepped out of the darkness into the little illuminated circle about our failing campfire and seated himself upon a rock.

"You are not the first to explore this region," he said, gravely.

Nobody controverted his statement; he was himself proof of its truth, for he was not of our party and must have been somewhere near when we camped. Moreover, he must have companions not far away; it was not a place where one would be living or traveling alone. For more than a week we had seen, besides ourselves and our animals, only such living things as rattlesnakes and horned toads. In an Arizona desert one does not long coexist with only such creatures as these: one must have pack animals, supplies, arms—'an outfit.' And all these imply comrades. It was perhaps a doubt as to what manner of men this unceremonious stranger's comrades might be, together with something in his words interpretable as a challenge, that caused every man of our half-dozen 'gentlemen adventurers' to rise to a sitting posture and lay his hand upon a weapon—an act signifying, in that time and place, a policy of expectation. The stranger gave the matter no attention and began again to speak in the same deliberate, uninflected monotone in which he had delivered his first sentence:

"Thirty years ago Ramon Gallegos, William Shaw, George W. Kent and Berry Davis, all of Tucson, crossed the Santa Catalina mountains and traveled due west, as nearly as the configuration of the country permitted. We were prospecting and it was our intention, if we found nothing, to push through to the Gila river at some point near Big Bend, where we understood there was a settlement. We had a good outfit but no guide—just Ramon Gallegos, William Shaw, George W. Kent and Berry Davis."

The man repeated the names slowly and distinctly, as if to fix them in the memories of his audience, every member of which was now attentively observing him, but with a slackened apprehension regarding his possible companions somewhere in the darkness that seemed to enclose us like a black wall; in the manner of this volunteer historian was no suggestion of an unfriendly purpose. His act was rather that of a harmless lunatic than an enemy. We were not so new to the country as not to know that the solitary life of many a plainsman had a tendency to develop eccentricities of conduct and character not always easily distinguishable from mental aberration. A man is like a tree: in a forest of his fellows he will grow as straight as his generic and individual nature permits; alone in the open, he yields to the deforming stresses and tortions that environ him. Some such thoughts were in my mind as I watched the man from the shadow of my hat, pulled low to shut out the firelight. A witless fellow, no doubt, but what could he be doing there in the heart of a desert?

Having undertaken to tell this story, I wish that I could describe the man's appearance; that would be a natural thing to do. Unfortunately, and somewhat strangely, I find myself unable to do so with any degree of confidence, for afterward no two of us agreed as to what he wore and how he looked; and when I try to set down my own impressions they elude me. Anyone can tell some kind of story; narration is one of the elemental powers of the race. But the talent for description is a gift.

Nobody having broken silence the visitor went on to say:

"This country was not then what it is now. There was not a ranch between the Gila and the Gulf. There was a little game here and there in the mountains, and near the infrequent water-holes grass enough to keep our animals from starvation. If we should be so fortunate as to encounter no Indians we might get through. But within a week the purpose of the expedition had altered from discovery of wealth to preservation of life. We had gone too far to go back, for what was ahead could be no worse than what was behind; so we pushed on, riding by night to avoid Indians and the intolerable heat, and concealing ourselves by day as best we could. Sometimes, having exhausted our supply of wild meat and emptied our casks, we were days without food or drink; then a water-hole or a shallow pool in the bottom of an arroyo so restored our strength and sanity that we were able to shoot some of the wild animals that sought it also. Sometimes it was a bear, sometimes an antelope, a coyote, a cougar—that was as God pleased; all were food.

"One morning as we skirted a mountain range, seeking a practicable pass, we were attacked by a band of Apaches who had followed our trail up a gulch—it is not far from here. Knowing that they outnumbered us ten to one, they took none of their usual cowardly precautions, but dashed upon us at a gallop, firing and yelling. Fighting was out of the question: we urged our feeble animals up the gulch as far as there was footing for a hoof, then threw ourselves out of our saddles and took to the chaparral on one of the slopes, abandoning our entire outfit to the enemy. But we retained our rifles, every man—Ramon Gallegos, William Shaw, George W. Kent and Berry Davis."

"Same old crowd," said the humorist of our party. He was an Eastern man, unfamiliar with the decent observances of social intercourse. A gesture of disapproval from our leader silenced him and the stranger proceeded with his tale:

"The savages dismounted also, and some of them ran up the gulch beyond the point at which we had left it, cutting off further retreat in that direction and forcing us on up the side. Unfortunately the chaparral extended only a short distance up the slope, and as we came into the open ground above we took the fire of a dozen rifles; but Apaches shoot badly when in a hurry, and God so willed it that none of us fell. Twenty yards up the slope, beyond the edge of the brush, were vertical cliffs, in which, directly in front of us, was a narrow opening. Into that we ran, finding ourselves in a cavern about as large as an ordinary room in a house. Here for a time we were safe: a single man with a repeating rifle could defend the entrance against all the Apaches in the land. But against hunger and thirst we had no defense. Courage we still had, but hope was a memory.

"Not one of those Indians did we afterward see, but by the smoke and glare of their fires in the gulch we knew that by day and by night they watched with ready rifles in the edge of the bush—knew that if we made a sortie not a man of us would live to take three steps into the open. For three days, watching in turn, we held out before our suffering became insupportable. Then—it was the morning of the fourth day—Ramon Gallegos said:

"'Senores, I know not well of the good God and what please him. I have live without religion, and I am not acquaint with that of you. Pardon, senores, if I shock you, but for me the time is come to beat the game of the Apache.'

"He knelt upon the rock floor of the cave and pressed his pistol against his temple. 'Madre de Dios,' he said, 'comes now the soul of Ramon Gallegos.'

"And so he left us—William Shaw, George W. Kent and Berry Davis.

"I was the leader: it was for me to speak.

"'He was a brave man,' I said—'he knew when to die, and how. It is foolish to go mad from thirst and fall by Apache bullets, or be skinned alive—it is in bad taste. Let us join Ramon Gallegos.'

"'That is right,' said William Shaw.

"'That is right,' said George W. Kent.

"I straightened the limbs of Ramon Gallegos and put a handkerchief over his face. Then William Shaw said: 'I should like to look like that—a little while.'

"And George W. Kent said that he felt that way, too.

"'It shall be so,' I said: 'the red devils will wait a week. William Shaw and George W. Kent, draw and kneel.'

"They did so and I stood before them.

"'Almighty God, our Father,' said I.

"'Almighty God, our Father,' said William Shaw.

"'Almighty God, our Father,' said George W. Kent.

"'Forgive us our sins,' said I.

"'Forgive us our sins,' said they.

"'And receive our souls.'

"'And receive our souls.'

"'Amen!'

"'Amen!'

"I laid them beside Ramon Gallegos and covered their faces."

There was a quick commotion on the opposite side of the campfire: one of our party had sprung to his feet, pistol in hand.

"And you!" he shouted—"YOU dared to escape?—You dare to be alive? You cowardly hound, I'll send you to join them if I hang for it!"

But with the leap of a panther the captain was upon him, grasping his wrist. "Hold it in, Sam Yountsey, hold it in!"

We were now all upon our feet—except the stranger, who sat motionless and apparently inattentive. Some one seized Yountsey's other arm.

"Captain," I said, "there is something wrong here. This fellow is either a lunatic or merely a liar—just a plain, every-day liar whom Yountsey has no call to kill. If this man was of that party it had five members, one of whom—probably himself—he has not named."

"Yes," said the captain, releasing the insurgent, who sat down, "there is something—unusual. Years ago four dead bodies of white men, scalped and shamefully mutilated, were found about the mouth of that cave. They are buried there; I have seen the graves—we shall all see them tomorrow."

The stranger rose, standing tall in the light of the expiring fire, which in our breathless attention to his story we had neglected to keep going.

"There were four," he said—"Ramon Gallegos, William Shaw, George W. Kent and Berry Davis."

With this reiterated roll-call of the dead he walked into the darkness and we saw him no more.

At that moment one of our party, who had been on guard, strode in among us, rifle in hand and somewhat excited.

"Captain," he said, "for the last half-hour three men have been standing out there on the mesa." He pointed in the direction taken by the stranger. "I could see them distinctly, for the moon is up, but as they had no guns and I had them covered with mine I thought it was their move. They have made none, but, damn it! they have got on to my nerves."

"Go back to your post, and stay till you see them again," said the captain. "The rest of you lie down again, or I'll kick you all into the fire."

The sentinel obediently withdrew, swearing, and did not return. As we were arranging our blankets the fiery Yountsey said: "I beg your pardon, Captain, but who the devil do you take them to be?"

"Ramon Gallegos, William Shaw and George W. Kent."

"But how about Berry Davis? I ought to have shot him."

"Quite needless; you couldn't have made him any deader. Go to sleep."

ANTON CHEKHOV

(1860-1904)

7

A Bad Business

"Who goes there?"

No answer. The watchman sees nothing, but through the roar of the wind and the trees distinctly hears someone walking along the avenue ahead of him. A March night, cloudy and foggy, envelopes the earth, and it seems to the watchman that the earth, the sky, and he himself with his thoughts are all merged together into something vast and impenetrably black. He can only grope his way.

"Who goes there?" the watchman repeats, and he begins to fancy that he hears whispering and smothered laughter. "Who's there?"

"It's I, friend . . ." answers an old man's voice.

"But who are you?"

"I . . . a traveller."

"What sort of traveller?" the watchman cries angrily, trying to disguise his terror by shouting. "What the devil do you want here? You go prowling about the graveyard at night, you ruffian!"

"You don't say it's a graveyard here?"

"Why, what else? Of course it's the graveyard! Don't you see it is?"

"O-o-oh . . . Queen of Heaven!" there is a sound of an old man sighing. "I see nothing, my good soul, nothing. Oh the darkness, the darkness! You can't see your hand before your face, it is dark, friend. O-o-oh . . ."

"But who are you?"

"I am a pilgrim, friend, a wandering man."

"The devils, the nightbirds . . . Nice sort of pilgrims! They are drunkards . . ." mutters the watchman, reassured by the tone and sighs of the stranger. "One's tempted to sin by you. They drink the day away and prowl about at night. But I fancy I heard you were not alone; it sounded like two or three of you."

"I am alone, friend, alone. Quite alone. O-o-oh our sins . . ."

The watchman stumbles up against the man and stops.

"How did you get here?" he asks.

"I have lost my way, good man. I was walking to the Mitrievsky Mill and I lost my way."

"Whew! Is this the road to Mitrievsky Mill? You sheepshead! For the Mitrievsky Mill you must keep much more to the left, straight out of the town along the high road. You have been drinking and have gone a couple of miles out of your way. You must have had a drop in the town."

"I did, friend . . . Truly I did; I won't hide my sins. But how am I to go now?"

"Go straight on and on along this avenue till you can go no farther, and then turn at once to the left and go till you have crossed the whole graveyard right to the gate. There will be a gate there . . . Open it and go with God's blessing. Mind you don't fall into the ditch. And when you are out of the graveyard you go all the way by the fields till you come out on the main road."

"God give you health, friend. May the Queen of Heaven save you and have mercy on you. You might take me along, good man! Be merciful! Lead me to the gate."

"As though I had the time to waste! Go by yourself!"

"Be merciful! I'll pray for you. I can't see anything; one can't see one's hand before one's face, friend . . . It's so dark, so dark! Show me the way, sir!"

"As though I had the time to take you about; if I were to play the nurse to everyone I should never have done."

"For Christ's sake, take me! I can't see, and I am afraid to go alone through the graveyard. It's terrifying, friend, it's terrifying; I am afraid, good man."

"There's no getting rid of you," sighs the watchman. "All right then, come along."

The watchman and the traveller go on together. They walk shoulder to shoulder in silence. A damp, cutting wind blows straight into their faces and the unseen trees murmuring and rustling scatter big drops upon them . . . The path is almost entirely covered with puddles.

"There is one thing passes my understanding," says the watchman after a prolonged silence—"how you got here. The gate's locked. Did you climb over the wall? If you did climb over the wall, that's the last thing you would expect of an old man."

"I don't know, friend, I don't know. I can't say myself how I got here. It's a visitation. A chastisement of the Lord. Truly a visitation, the evil one confounded me. So you are a watchman here, friend?"

"Yes."

"The only one for the whole graveyard?"

There is such a violent gust of wind that both stop for a minute. Waiting till the violence of the wind abates, the watchman answers:

"There are three of us, but one is lying ill in a fever and the other's asleep. He and I take turns about."

"Ah, to be sure, friend. What a wind! The dead must hear it! It howls like a wild beast! O-o-oh."

"And where do you come from?"

"From a distance, friend. I am from Vologda, a long way off. I go from one holy place to another and pray for people. Save me and have mercy upon me, O Lord."

The watchman stops for a minute to light his pipe. He stoops down behind the traveller's back and lights several matches. The gleam of the first match lights up for one instant a bit of the avenue on the right, a white tombstone with an angel, and a dark cross; the light of the second match, flaring up brightly and extinguished by the wind, flashes like lightning on the left side, and from the darkness nothing stands out but the angle of some sort of trellis; the third match throws light to right and to left, revealing the white tombstone, the dark cross, and the trellis round a child's grave.

"The departed sleep; the dear ones sleep!" the stranger mutters, sighing loudly. "They all sleep alike, rich and poor, wise and foolish, good and wicked. They are of the same value now. And they will sleep till the last trump. The Kingdom of Heaven and peace eternal be theirs."

"Here we are walking along now, but the time will come when we shall be lying here ourselves," says the watchman.

"To be sure, to be sure, we shall all. There is no man who will not die. O-o-oh. Our doings are wicked, our thoughts are deceitful! Sins, sins! My soul accursed, ever covetous, my belly greedy and lustful! I have angered the Lord and there is no salvation for me in this world and the next. I am deep in sins like a worm in the earth."

"Yes, and you have to die."

"You are right there."

"Death is easier for a pilgrim than for fellows like us," says the watchman.

"There are pilgrims of different sorts. There are the real ones who are God-fearing men and watch over their own souls, and there are such as stray about the graveyard at night and are a delight to the devils. . . Ye-es! There's one who is a pilgrim could give you a crack on the pate with an axe if he liked and knock the breath out of you."

"What are you talking like that for?"

"Oh, nothing . . . Why, I fancy here's the gate. Yes, it is. Open it, good man."

The watchman, feeling his way, opens the gate, leads the pilgrim out by the sleeve, and says:

"Here's the end of the graveyard. Now you must keep on through the open fields till you get to the main road. Only close here there will be the boundary ditch—don't fall in . . . And when you come out on to the road, turn to the right, and keep on till you reach the mill . . ."

"O-o-oh!" sighs the pilgrim after a pause, "and now I am thinking that I have no cause to go to Mitrievsky Mill . . . Why the devil should I go there? I had better stay a bit with you here, sir . . ."

"What do you want to stay with me for?"

"Oh . . . it's merrier with you! . . ."

"So you've found a merry companion, have you? You, pilgrim, are fond of a joke I see . . ."

"To be sure I am," says the stranger, with a hoarse chuckle. "Ah, my dear good man, I bet you will remember the pilgrim many a long year!"

"Why should I remember you?"

"Why I've got round you so smartly . . . Am I a pilgrim? I am not a pilgrim at all."

"What are you then?"

"A dead man . . . I've only just got out of my coffin . . . Do you remember Gubaryev, the locksmith, who hanged himself in carnival week? Well, I am Gubaryev himself! . . ."

"Tell us something else!"

The watchman does not believe him, but he feels all over such a cold, oppressive terror that he starts off and begins hurriedly feeling for the gate.

"Stop, where are you off to?" says the stranger, clutching him by the arm. "Aie, aie, aie . . . what a fellow you are! How can you leave me all alone?"

"Let go!" cries the watchman, trying to pull his arm away.

"Sto-op! I bid you stop and you stop. Don't struggle, you dirty dog! If you want to stay among the living, stop and hold your tongue till I tell you. It's only that I don't care to spill blood or you would have been a dead man long ago, you scurvy rascal . . . Stop!"

The watchman's knees give way under him. In his terror he shuts his eyes, and trembling all over huddles close to the wall. He would like to call out, but he knows his cries would not reach any living thing. The stranger stands beside him and holds him by the arm . . . Three minutes pass in silence.

"One's in a fever, another's asleep, and the third is seeing pilgrims on their way," mutters the stranger. "Capital watchmen, they are worth their salary! Ye-es, brother, thieves have always been cleverer than watchmen! Stand still, don't stir . . ."

Five minutes, ten minutes pass in silence. All at once the wind brings the sound of a whistle.

"Well, now you can go," says the stranger, releasing the watchman's arm. "Go and thank God you are alive!"

The stranger gives a whistle too, runs away from the gate, and the watchman hears him leap over the ditch.

With a foreboding of something very dreadful in his heart, the watchman, still trembling with terror, opens the gate irresolutely and runs back with his eyes shut.

At the turning into the main avenue he hears hurried footsteps, and someone asks him, in a hissing voice: "Is that you, Timofey? Where is Mitka?"

And after running the whole length of the main avenue he notices a little dim light in the darkness. The nearer he gets to the light the more frightened he is and the stronger his foreboding of evil.

"It looks as though the light were in the church," he thinks. "And how can it have come there? Save me and have mercy on me, Queen of Heaven! And that it is."

The watchman stands for a minute before the broken window and looks with horror towards the altar . . . A little wax candle which the thieves had forgotten to put out flickers in the wind that bursts in at the window and throws dim red patches of light on the vestments flung about and a cupboard overturned on the floor, on numerous footprints near the high altar and the altar of offerings.

A little time passes and the howling wind sends floating over the churchyard the hurried uneven clangs of the alarm-bell . . .

ARTHUR CONAN DOYLE

(1859-1930)

8

The Lord of Chateau Noir

It was in the days when the German armies had broken their way across France, and when the shattered forces of the young Republic had been swept away to the north of the Aisne and to the south of the Loire. Three broad streams of armed men had rolled slowly but irresistibly from the Rhine, now meandering to the north, now to the south, dividing, coalescing, but all uniting to form one great lake round Paris. And from this lake there welled out smaller streams—one to the north, one southward, to Orleans, and a third westward to Normandy. Many a German trooper saw the sea for the first time when he rode his horse girth-deep into the waves at Dieppe.

Black and bitter were the thoughts of Frenchmen when they saw this weal of dishonour slashed across the fair face of their country. They had fought and they had been overborne. That swarming cavalry, those countless footmen, the masterful guns—they had tried and tried to make head against them. In battalions their invaders were not to be beaten, but man to man, or ten to ten, they were their equals. A brave Frenchman might still make a single German rue the day that he had left his own bank of the

Rhine. Thus, unchronicled amid the battles and the sieges, there broke out another war, a war of individuals, with foul murder upon the one side and brutal reprisal on the other.

Colonel von Gramm, of the 24th Posen Infantry, had suffered severely during this new development. He commanded in the little Norman town of Les Andelys, and his outposts stretched amid the hamlets and farmhouses of the district round. No French force was within fifty miles of him, and yet morning after morning he had to listen to a black report of sentries found dead at their posts, or of foraging parties which had never returned. Then the colonel would go forth in his wrath, and farmsteadings would blaze and villages tremble; but next morning there was still that same dismal tale to be told. Do what he might, he could not shake off his invisible enemies. And yet it should not have been so hard, for, from certain signs in common, in the plan and in the deed, it was certain that all these outrages came from a single source.

Colonel von Gramm had tried violence, and it had failed. Gold might be more successful. He published it abroad over the countryside that 500frs. would be paid for information. There was no response. Then 800frs. The peasants were incorruptible. Then, goaded on by a murdered corporal, he rose to a thousand, and so bought the soul of Francois Rejane, farm labourer, whose Norman avarice was a stronger passion than his French hatred.

"You say that you know who did these crimes?" asked the Prussian colonel, eyeing with loathing the blue-bloused, rat-faced creature before him.

"Yes, colonel."

"And it was—?"

"Those thousand francs, colonel—"

"Not a sou until your story has been tested. Come! Who is it who has murdered my men?"

"It is Count Eustace of Chateau Noir."

"You lie!" cried the colonel, angrily. "A gentleman and a nobleman could not have done such crimes."

The peasant shrugged his shoulders. "It is evident to me that you do not know the count. It is this way, colonel. What I tell you is the truth, and I am not afraid that you should test it. The Count of Chateau Noir is a hard man, even at the best time he was a hard man. But of late he has been terrible. It was his son's death, you know. His son was under Douay, and he was taken, and then in escaping from Germany he met his death. It was the count's only child, and indeed we all think that it has driven him mad. With his peasants he follows the German armies. I do not know how many he has killed, but it is he who cut the cross upon the foreheads, for it is the badge of his house."

It was true. The murdered sentries had each had a saltire cross slashed across their brows, as by a hunting-knife. The colonel bent his stiff back and ran his forefinger over the map which lay upon the table.

"The Chateau Noir is not more than four leagues," he said.

"Three and a kilometre, colonel."

"You know the place?"

"I used to work there."

Colonel von Gramm rang the bell.

"Give this man food and detain him," said he to the sergeant.

"Why detain me, colonel? I can tell you no more."

"We shall need you as guide."

"As guide? But the count? If I were to fall into his hands? Ah, colonel—"

The Prussian commander waved him away. "Send Captain Baumgarten to me at once," said he.

The officer who answered the summons was a man of middle-age, heavy-jawed, blue-eyed, with a curving yellow moustache, and a brick-red face which turned to an ivory white where his helmet had sheltered it. He was bald, with a shining, tightly stretched scalp, at the back of which, as in a mirror, it was a favourite mess-joke of the subalterns to trim their moustaches. As a soldier he was slow, but reliable and brave. The colonel could trust him where a more dashing officer might be in danger.

"You will proceed to Chateau Noir tonight, captain," said he. "A guide has been provided. You will arrest the count and bring him back. If there is an attempt at rescue, shoot him at once."

"How many men shall I take, colonel?"

"Well, we are surrounded by spies, and our only chance is to pounce upon him before he knows that we are on the way. A large force will attract attention. On the other hand, you must not risk being cut off."

"I might march north, colonel, as if to join General Goeben. Then I could turn down this road which I see upon your map, and get to Chateau Noir before they could hear of us. In that case, with twenty men—"

"Very good, captain. I hope to see you with your prisoner tomorrow morning."

It was a cold December night when Captain Baumgarten marched out of Les Andelys with his twenty Poseners, and took the main road to the north west. Two miles out he turned suddenly down a narrow, deeply rutted track, and made swiftly for his man. A thin, cold rain was falling, swishing among the tall poplar trees and rustling in the fields on either side. The captain walked first with Moser, a veteran sergeant, beside him. The sergeant's wrist was fastened to that of the French peasant, and it had been whispered in his ear that in case of an ambush the first bullet fired would be through his head. Behind them the twenty infantrymen plodded along through the darkness with their faces sunk to the rain, and their boots squeaking in the soft, wet clay. They knew where they were going, and why, and the thought upheld them, for they were bitter at the loss of their comrades. It was a cavalry job, they knew, but the cavalry were all on with the advance, and, besides, it was more fitting that the regiment should avenge its own dead men.

It was nearly eight when they left Les Andelys. At half-past eleven their guide stopped at a place where two high pillars, crowned with some heraldic stonework, flanked a huge iron gate. The wall in which it had been the opening had crumbled away, but the great gate still towered above the brambles and weeds which had overgrown its base. The Prussians made their way round it and advanced stealthily, under the shadow of a tunnel of oak branches, up the long avenue, which was still cumbered by the leaves of last autumn. At the top they halted and reconnoitred.

The black chateau lay in front of them. The moon had shone out between two rain-clouds, and threw the old house into silver and shadow. It was shaped like an L, with a low arched door in front, and lines of small windows like the open ports of a man-of-war. Above was a dark roof, breaking at the corners into little round overhanging turrets, the whole lying silent in the moonshine, with a drift of ragged clouds blackening the heavens behind it. A single light gleamed in one of the lower windows.

The captain whispered his orders to his men. Some were to creep to the front door, some to the back. Some were to watch the east, and some the west. He and the sergeant stole on tiptoe to the lighted window.

It was a small room into which they looked, very meanly furnished. An elderly man, in the dress of a menial, was reading a tattered paper by the light of a guttering candle. He leaned back in his wooden chair with his feet upon a box, while a bottle of white wine stood with a half-filled tumbler upon a stool beside him. The sergeant thrust his needle-gun through the glass, and the man sprang to his feet with a shriek.

"Silence, for your life! The house is surrounded, and you cannot escape. Come round and open the door, or we will show you no mercy when we come in."

"For God's sake, don't shoot! I will open it! I will open it!" He rushed from the room with his paper still crumpled up in his hand. An instant later, with a groaning of old locks and a rasping of bars, the low door swung open, and the Prussians poured into the stone-flagged passage.

"Where is Count Eustace de Chateau Noir?"

"My master! He is out, sir."

"Out at this time of night? Your life for a lie!"

"It is true, sir. He is out!"

"Where?"

"I do not know."

"Doing what?"

"I cannot tell. No, it is no use your cocking your pistol, sir.

You may kill me, but you cannot make me tell you that which I do not know."

"Is he often out at this hour?"

"Frequently."

"And when does he come home?"

"Before daybreak."

Captain Baumgarten rasped out a German oath. He had had his journey for nothing, then. The man's answers were only too likely to be true. It was what he might have expected. But at least he would search the house and make sure. Leaving a picket at the front door and another at the back, the sergeant and he drove the trembling butler in front of them—his shaking candle sending strange, flickering shadows over the old tapestries and the low, oak-raftered ceilings. They searched the whole house, from the huge stone-flagged kitchen below to the dining-hall on the second floor, with its gallery for musicians, and its panelling black with age, but nowhere was there a living creature. Up above, in an attic, they found Marie, the elderly wife of the butler; but the owner kept no other servants, and of his own presence there was no trace.

It was long, however, before Captain Baumgarten had satisfied himself upon the point. It was a difficult house to search. Thin stairs, which only one man could ascend at a time, connected lines of tortuous corridors. The walls were so thick that each room was cut off from its neighbour. Huge fireplaces yawned in each, while the windows were six feet deep in the wall. Captain Baumgarten stamped with his feet, tore down curtains, and struck with the pommel of his sword. If there were secret hiding-places, he was not fortunate enough to find them.

"I have an idea," said he, at last, speaking in German to the sergeant. "You will place a guard over this fellow, and make sure that he communicates with no one."

"Yes, captain."

"And you will place four men in ambush at the front and at the back. It is likely enough that about daybreak our bird may return to the nest."

"And the others, captain?"

"Let them have their suppers in the kitchen. The fellow will serve you with meat and wine. It is a wild night, and we shall be better here than on the country road."

"And yourself, captain?"

"I will take my supper up here in the dining-hall. The logs are laid and we can light the fire. You will call me if there is any alarm. What can you give me for supper—you?"

"Alas, monsieur, there was a time when I might have answered, 'What you wish!' but now it is all that we can do to find a bottle of new claret and a cold pullet."

"That will do very well. Let a guard go about with him, sergeant, and let him feel the end of a bayonet if he plays us any tricks."

Captain Baumgarten was an old campaigner. In the Eastern provinces, and before that in Bohemia, he had learned the art of quartering himself upon the enemy. While the butler brought his supper he occupied himself in making his preparations for a comfortable night. He lit the candelabrum of ten candles upon the centre table. The fire was already burning up, crackling merrily, and sending spurts of blue, pungent smoke into the room. The captain walked to the window and looked out. The moon had gone in again, and it was raining heavily. He could hear the deep sough of the wind, and see the dark loom of the trees, all swaying in the one direction. It was a sight which gave a zest to his comfortable quarters, and to the cold fowl and the bottle of wine which the butler had brought up for him. He was tired and hungry after his long tramp, so he threw his sword, his helmet, and his revolver-belt down upon a chair, and fell to eagerly upon his supper. Then, with his glass of wine before him and his cigar between his lips, he tilted his chair back and looked about him.

He sat within a small circle of brilliant light which gleamed upon his silver shoulder-straps, and threw out his terra-cotta face, his heavy eyebrows, and his yellow moustache. But outside that circle things were vague and shadowy in the old dining-hall. Two sides were oak-panelled and two were hung with faded tapestry, across which huntsmen and dogs and stags were still dimly streaming. Above the fireplace were rows of heraldic shields with the blazonings of the family and of its alliances, the fatal saltire cross breaking out on each of them.

Four paintings of old seigneurs of Chateau Noir faced the fireplace, all men with hawk noses and bold, high features, so like each other that only the dress could distinguish the Crusader from the Cavalier of the Fronde. Captain Baumgarten, heavy with his repast, lay back in his chair looking up at them through the clouds of his tobacco smoke, and pondering over the strange chance which had sent him, a man from the Baltic coast, to eat his supper in the ancestral hall of these proud Norman chieftains. But the fire was hot, and the captain's eyes were heavy. His chin sank slowly upon his chest, and the ten candles gleamed upon the broad, white scalp.

Suddenly a slight noise brought him to his feet. For an instant it seemed to his dazed senses that one of the pictures opposite had walked from its frame. There, beside the table, and almost within arm's length of him, was standing a huge man, silent, motionless, with no sign of life save his fierce-glinting eyes. He was black-haired, olive-skinned, with a pointed tuft of black beard, and a great, fierce nose, towards which all his features seemed to run. His cheeks were wrinkled like a last year's apple, but his sweep of shoulder, and bony, corded hands, told of a strength which was unsapped by age. His arms were folded across his arching chest, and his mouth was set in a fixed smile.

"Pray do not trouble yourself to look for your weapons," he said, as the Prussian cast a swift glance at the empty chair in which they had been laid. "You have been, if you will allow me to say so, a little indiscreet to make yourself so much at home in a house every wall of which is honeycombed with secret passages. You will be amused to hear that forty men were watching you at your supper. Ah! what then?"

Captain Baumgarten had taken a step forward with clenched fists. The Frenchman held up tho revolver which he grasped in his right hand, while with the left he hurled the German back into his chair.

"Pray keep your seat," said he. "You have no cause to trouble about your men. They have already been provided for. It is astonishing with these stone floors how little one can hear what goes on beneath. You have been relieved of your command, and have now only to think of yourself. May I ask what your name is?"

"I am Captain Baumgarten of the 24th Posen Regiment."

"Your French is excellent, though you incline, like most of your countrymen, to turn the 'p' into a 'b.' I have been amused to hear them cry '*Avez bitie sur moi!*' You know, doubtless, who it is who addresses you."

"The Count of Chateau Noir."

"Precisely. It would have been a misfortune if you had visited my chateau and I had been unable to have a word with you. I have had to do with many German soldiers, but never with an officer before. I have much to talk to you about."

Captain Baumgarten sat still in his chair. Brave as he was, there was something in this man's manner which made his skin creep with apprehension. His eyes glanced to right and to left, but his weapons were gone, and in a struggle he saw that he was but a child to this gigantic adversary. The count had picked up the claret bottle and held it to the light.

"Tut! tut!" said he. "And was this the best that Pierre could do for you? I am ashamed to look you in the face, Captain Baumgarten. We must improve upon this."

He blew a call upon a whistle which hung from his shooting-jacket. The old manservant was in the room in an instant.

"Chambertin from bin 15!" he cried, and a minute later a grey bottle, streaked with cobwebs, was carried in as a nurse bears an infant. The count filled two glasses to the brim.

"Drink!" said he. "It is the very best in my cellars, and not to be matched between Rouen and Paris. Drink, sir, and be happy! There are cold joints below. There are two lobsters, fresh from Honfleur. Will you not venture upon a second and more savoury supper?"

The German officer shook his head. He drained the glass, however, and his host filled it once more, pressing him to give an order for this or that dainty.

"There is nothing in my house which is not at your disposal. You have but to say the word. Well, then, you will allow me to tell you a story while you drink your wine. I have so longed to tell it to some German officer. It is about my son, my only child, Eustace, who was taken and died in escaping. It is a curious little story, and I think that I can promise you that you will never forget it.

"You must know, then, that my boy was in the artillery—a fine young fellow, Captain Baumgarten, and the pride of his mother. She died within a week of the news of his death reaching us. It was brought by a brother officer who was at his side throughout, and who escaped while my lad died. I want to tell you all that he told me.

"Eustace was taken at Weissenburg on the 4th of August. The prisoners were broken up into parties, and sent back into Germany by different routes. Eustace was taken upon the 5th to a village called Lauterburg, where he met with kindness from the German officer in command. This good colonel had the hungry lad to supper, offered him the best he had, opened a bottle of good wine, as I have tried to do for you, and gave him a cigar from his own case. Might I entreat you to take one from mine?"

The German again shook his head. His horror of his companion had increased as he sat watching the lips that smiled and the eyes that glared.

"The colonel, as I say, was good to my boy. But, unluckily, the prisoners were moved next day across the Rhine into Ettlingen. They were not equally fortunate there. The officer who guarded them was a ruffian and a villain, Captain Baumgarten. He took a pleasure in humiliating and ill-treating the brave men who had fallen into his power. That night upon my son answering fiercely back to some taunt of his, he struck him in the eye, like this!"

The crash of the blow rang through the hall. The German's face fell forward, his hand up, and blood oozing through his fingers. The count settled down in his chair once more.

"My boy was disfigured by the blow, and this villain made his appearance the object of his jeers. By the way, you look a little comical yourself at the present moment, captain, and your colonel would certainly say that you had been getting into mischief. To continue, however, my boy's youth and his destitution—for his pockets were empty—moved the pity of a kind-hearted major, and he advanced him ten Napoleons from his own pocket without security of any kind. Into your hands, Captain Baumgarten, I return these ten gold pieces, since I cannot learn the name of the lender. I am grateful from my heart for this kindness shown to my boy.

"The vile tyrant who commanded the escort accompanied the prisoners to Durlack, and from there to Carlsruhe. He heaped every outrage upon my lad, because the spirit of the Chateau Noirs would not stoop to turn away his wrath by a feigned submission. Ay, this cowardly villain, whose heart's blood shall yet clot upon this hand, dared to strike my son with his open hand, to kick him, to tear hairs from his moustache—to use him thus—and thus—and thus!"

The German writhed and struggled. He was helpless in the hands of this huge giant whose blows were raining upon him. When at last, blinded and half-senseless, he staggered to his feet, it was only to be hurled back again into the great oaken chair. He sobbed in his impotent anger and shame.

"My boy was frequently moved to tears by the humiliation of his position," continued the count. "You will understand me when I say that it is a bitter thing to be helpless in the hands of an insolent and remorseless enemy. On arriving at Carlsruhe, however, his face, which had been wounded by the brutality of his guard, was bound up by a young Bavarian subaltern who was touched by his appearance. I regret to see that your eye is bleeding so. Will you permit me to bind it with my silk handkerchief?"

He leaned forward, but the German dashed his hand aside.

"I am in your power, you monster!" he cried; "I can endure your brutalities, but not your hypocrisy."

The count shrugged his shoulders.

"I am taking things in their order, just as they occurred," said he. "I was under vow to tell it to the first German officer with whom I could talk *tete-a-tete.* Let me see, I had got as far as the young Bavarian at Carlsruhe. I regret extremely that you will not permit me to use such slight skill in surgery as I possess. At Carlsruhe, my lad was shut up in the old caserne, where he remained for a fortnight. The worst pang of his captivity was that some unmannerly curs in the garrison would taunt him with his position as he sat by his window in the evening. That reminds me, captain, that you are not quite situated upon a bed of roses yourself, are you now? You came to trap a wolf, my man, and now the beast has you down with his fangs in your throat. A family man, too, I should judge, by that well-filled tunic. Well, a widow the more will make little matter, and they do not usually remain widows long. Get back into the chair, you dog!

"Well, to continue my story—at the end of a fortnight my son and his friend escaped. I need not trouble you with the dangers which they ran, or with the privations which they endured. Suffice it that to disguise themselves they had to take the clothes of two peasants, whom they waylaid in a wood. Hiding by day and travelling by night, they had got as far into France as Remilly, and were within a mile—a single mile, captain—of crossing the German lines when a patrol of Uhlans came right upon them. Ah! it was hard, was it not, when they had come so far and were so near to safety?" The count blew a double call upon his whistle, and three hard-faced peasants entered the room.

"These must represent my Uhlans," said he. "Well, then, the captain in command, finding that these men were French soldiers in civilian dress within the German lines, proceeded to hang them without trial or ceremony. I think, Jean, that the centre beam is the strongest."

The unfortunate soldier was dragged from his chair to where a noosed rope had been flung over one of the huge oaken rafters which spanned the room. The cord was slipped over his head, and he felt its harsh grip round his throat. The three peasants seized the other end, and looked to the count for his orders. The officer, pale, but firm, folded his arms and stared defiantly at the man who tortured him.

"You are now face to face with death, and I perceive from your lips that you are praying. My son was also face to face with death, and he prayed, also. It happened that a general officer came up, and he heard the lad praying for his mother, and it moved him so—he being himself a father—that he ordered his Uhlans away, and he remained with his aide-de-camp only, beside the condemned men. And when he heard all the lad had to tell—that he was the only child of an old family, and that his mother was in failing health—he threw off the rope as I throw off this, and he kissed him on either cheek, as I kiss you, and he bade him go, as I bid you go, and may every kind wish of that noble general, though it could not stave off the fever which slew my son, descend now upon your head."

And so it was that Captain Baumgarten, disfigured, blinded, and bleeding, staggered out into the wind and the rain of that wild December dawn.

9

The Los Amigos Fiasco

I used to be the leading practitioner of Los Amigos. Of course, every one has heard of the great electrical generating gear there. The town is wide spread, and there are dozens of little townlets and villages all around, which receive their supply from the same centre, so that the works are on a very large scale. The Los Amigos folk say that they are the largest upon earth, but then we claim that for everything in Los Amigos except the gaol and the death-rate. Those are said to be the smallest.

Now, with so fine an electrical supply, it seemed to be a sinful waste of hemp that the Los Amigos criminals should perish in the old-fashioned manner. And then came the news of the electrocutions in the East, and how the results had not after all been so instantaneous as had been hoped. The Western engineers raised their eyebrows when they read of the puny shocks by which these men had perished, and they vowed in Los Amigos that when an irreclaimable came their way he should be dealt handsomely by, and have the run of all the big dynamos. There should be no reserve, said the engineers, but he should have all that they had got. And what the result of that would be none could predict, save that it must be absolutely blasting and deadly. Never before had a man been so charged with electricity as they would charge him. He was to be smitten by the essence of ten thunderbolts. Some prophesied combustion, and some disintegration and disappearance. They were waiting eagerly to settle the question by actual demonstration, and it was just at that moment that Duncan Warner came that way.

Warner had been wanted by the law, and by nobody else, for many years. Desperado, murderer, train robber, and road agent, he was a man beyond the pale of human pity. He had deserved a dozen deaths, and the Los Amigos folk grudged him so gaudy a one as that. He seemed to feel himself to be unworthy of it, for he made two frenzied attempts at escape. He was a powerful, muscular man, with a lion heart, tangled black locks, and a sweeping beard which covered his broad chest. When he was tried, there was no finer head in all the crowded court. It's no new thing to find the best face looking from the dock. But his good looks could not balance his bad deeds. His advocate did all he knew, but the cards lay against him, and Duncan Warner was handed over to the mercy of the big Los Amigos dynamos.

I was there at the committee meeting when the matter was discussed. The town council had chosen four experts to look after the arrangements. Three of them were admirable. There was Joseph M'Connor, the very man who had designed the dynamos, and there was Joshua Westmacott, the chairman of the Los Amigos Electrical Supply Company, Limited. Then there was myself as the chief medical man, and lastly an old German of the name of Peter Stulpnagel. The Germans were a strong body at Los Amigos, and they all voted for their man. That was how he got on the committee. It was said that he had been a wonderful electrician at home, and he was eternally working with wires and insulators and Leyden jars; but, as he never seemed to get any further, or to have any results worth publishing, he came at last to be regarded as a harmless crank, who had made science his hobby. We three practical men smiled when we heard that he had been elected as our colleague, and at the meeting we fixed it all up very nicely among ourselves without much thought of the old fellow who sat with his ears scooped forward in his hands, for he was a trifle hard of hearing, taking no more part in the proceedings than the gentlemen of the press who scribbled their notes on the back benches.

We did not take long to settle it all. In New York a strength of some two thousand volts had been used, and death had not been instantaneous. Evidently their shock had been too weak. Los Amigos should not fall into that error. The charge should be six times greater, and therefore, of course, it would be six times more effective. Nothing could possibly be more logical. The whole concentrated force of the great dynamos should be employed on Duncan Warner.

So we three settled it, and had already risen to break up the meeting, when our silent companion opened his mouth for the first time.

"Gentlemen," said he, "you appear to me to show an extraordinary ignorance upon the subject of electricity. You have not mastered the first principles of its actions upon a human being."

The committee was about to break into an angry reply to this brusque comment, but the chairman of the Electrical Company tapped his forehead to claim its indulgence for the crankiness of the speaker.

"Pray tell us, sir," said he, with an ironical smile, "what is there in our conclusions with which you find fault?"

"With your assumption that a large dose of electricity will merely increase the effect of a small dose. Do you not think it possible that it might have an entirely different result? Do you know anything, by actual experiment, of the effect of such powerful shocks?"

"We know it by analogy," said the chairman pompously. "All drugs increase their effect when they increase their dose; for example—for example—"

"Whisky," said Joseph M'Connor.

"Quite so. Whisky. You see it there."

Peter Stulpnagel smiled and shook his head.

"Your argument is not very good," said he. "When I used to take whisky, I used to find that one glass would excite me, but that six would send me to sleep, which is just the opposite. Now, suppose that electricity were to act in just the opposite way also, what then?"

We three practical men burst out laughing. We had known that our colleague was queer, but we never had thought that he would be as queer as this.

"What then?" repeated Peter Stulpnagel.

"We'll take our chances," said the chairman.

"Pray consider," said Peter, "that workmen who have touched the wires, and who have received shocks of only a few hundred volts, have died instantly. The fact is well known. And yet when a much greater force was used upon a criminal at New York, the man struggled for some little time. Do you not clearly see that the smaller dose is the more deadly?"

"I think, gentlemen, that this discussion has been carried on quite long enough," said the chairman, rising again. "The point, I take it, has already been decided by the majority of the committee, and Duncan Warner shall be electrocuted on Tuesday by the full strength of the Los Amigos dynamos. Is it not so?"

"I agree," said Joseph M'Connor.

"I agree," said I.

"And I protest," said Peter Stulpnagel.

"Then the motion is carried, and your protest will be duly entered in the minutes," said the chairman, and so the sitting was dissolved.

The attendance at the electrocution was a very small one. We four members of the committee were, of course, present with the executioner, who was to act under their orders. The others were the United States Marshal, the governor of the gaol, the chaplain, and three members of the press. The room was a small brick chamber, forming an out-house to the Central Electrical station. It had been used as a laundry, and had an oven and copper at one side, but no other furniture save a single chair for the condemned man. A metal plate for his feet was placed in front of it, to which ran a thick insulated wire. Above, another wire depended from the ceiling, which could be connected with a small metallic rod projecting from a cap which was to be placed upon his head. When this connection was established Duncan Warner's hour was come.

There was a solemn hush as we waited for the coming of the prisoner. The practical engineers looked a little pale, and fidgeted nervously with the wires. Even the hardened Marshal was ill at ease, for a mere hanging was one thing, and this blasting of flesh and blood a very different one. As to the pressmen, their faces were whiter than the sheets which lay before them. The only man who appeared to feel none of the influence of these preparations was the little German crank, who strolled from one to the other with a smile on his lips and mischief in his eyes. More than once he even went so far as to burst into a shout of laughter, until the chaplain sternly rebuked him for his ill-timed levity.

"How can you so far forget yourself, Mr. Stulpnagel," said he, "as to jest in the presence of death?"

But the German was quite unabashed.

"If I were in the presence of death I should not jest," said he, "but since I am not I may do what I choose."

This flippant reply was about to draw another and a sterner reproof from the chaplain, when the door was swung open and two warders entered leading Duncan Warner between them. He glanced round him with a set face, stepped resolutely forward, and seated himself upon the chair.

"Touch her off!" said he.

It was barbarous to keep him in suspense. The chaplain murmured a few words in his ear, the attendant placed the cap upon his head, and then, while we all held our breath, the wire and the metal were brought in contact.

"Great Scott!" shouted Duncan Warner.

He had bounded in his chair as the frightful shock crashed through his system. But he was not dead. On the contrary, his eyes gleamed far more brightly than they had done before. There was only one change, but it was a singular one. The black had passed from his hair and beard as the shadow passes from a landscape. They were both as white as snow. And yet there was no other sign of decay. His skin was smooth and plump and lustrous as a child's.

The Marshal looked at the committee with a reproachful eye.

"There seems to be some hitch here, gentlemen," said he.

We three practical men looked at each other.

Peter Stulpnagel smiled pensively.

"I think that another one should do it," said I.

Again the connection was made, and again Duncan Warner sprang in his chair and shouted, but, indeed, were it not that he still remained in the chair none of us would have recognised him. His hair and his beard had shredded off in an instant, and the room looked like a barber's shop on a Saturday night. There he sat, his eyes still shining, his skin radiant with the glow of perfect health, but with a scalp as bald as a Dutch cheese, and a chin without so much as a trace of down. He began to revolve one of his arms, slowly and doubtfully at first, but with more confidence as he went on.

"That joint," said he, "has puzzled half the doctors on the Pacific slope. It's as good as new, and as limber as a hickory twig."

"You are feeling pretty well?" asked the old German.

"Never better in my life," said Duncan Warner cheerily.

The situation was a painful one. The Marshal glared at the committee. Peter Stulpnagel grinned and rubbed his hands. The engineers scratched their heads. The bald-headed prisoner revolved his arm and looked pleased.

"I think that one more shock—" began the chairman.

"No, sir," said the Marshal; "we've had foolery enough for one morning. We are here for an execution, and an execution we'll have."

"What do you propose?"

"There's a hook handy upon the ceiling. Fetch a rope, and we'll soon set this matter straight."

There was another awkward delay while the warders departed for the cord. Peter Stulpnagel bent over Duncan Warner, and whispered something in his ear. The desperado stared in surprise.

"You don't say?" he asked.

The German nodded.

"What! No ways?"

Peter shook his head, and the two began to laugh as though they shared some huge joke between them.

The rope was brought, and the Marshal himself slipped the

noose over the criminal's neck. Then the two warders, the assistant and he swung their victim into the air. For half an hour he hung—a dreadful sight—from the ceiling. Then in solemn silence they lowered him down, and one of the warders went out to order the shell to be brought round. But as he touched ground again what was our amazement when Duncan Warner put his hands up to his neck, loosened the noose, and took a long, deep breath.

"Paul Jefferson's sale is goin' well," he remarked, "I could see the crowd from up yonder," and he nodded at the hook in the ceiling.

"Up with him again!" shouted the Marshal, "We'll get the life out of him somehow."

In an instant the victim was up at the hook once more.

They kept him there for an hour, but when he came down he was perfectly garrulous.

"Old man Plunket goes too much to the Arcady Saloon," said he. "Three times he's been there in an hour; and him with a family. Old man Plunket would do well to swear off."

It was monstrous and incredible, but there it was. There was no getting round it. The man was there talking when he ought to have been dead. We all sat staring in amazement, but United States Marshal Carpenter was not a man to be euchred so easily. He motioned the others to one side, so that the prisoner was left standing alone.

"Duncan Warner," said he slowly, "you are here to play your part, and I am here to play mine. Your game is to live if you can, and my game is to carry out the sentence of the law. You've beat us on electricity, I'll give you one there. And you've beat us on hanging, for you seem to thrive on it. But it's my turn to beat you now, for my duty has to be done."

He pulled a six-shooter from his coat as he spoke, and fired all the shots through the body of the prisoner. The room was so filled with smoke that we could see nothing, but when it cleared the prisoner was still standing there, looking down in disgust at the front of his coat.

"Coats must be cheap where you come from," said he. "Thirty dollars it cost me, and look at it now. The six holes in front are bad enough, but four of the balls have passed out, and a pretty fine state the back must be in."

The Marshal's revolver fell from his hand, and he dropped his arms to his sides, a beaten man.

"Maybe some of you gentlemen can tell me what this means," said he, looking helplessly at the committee.

Peter Stulpnagel took a step forward.

"I'll tell you all about it," said he.

"You seem to be the only person who knows anything."

"I *am* the only person who knows anything. I should have warned these gentlemen; but, as they would not listen to me, I have allowed them to learn by experience. What you have done with your electricity is that you have increased the man's vitality until he can deny death for centuries."

"Centuries!"

"Yes, it will take the wear of hundreds of years to exhaust the enormous nervous energy with which you have drenched him. Electricity is life, and you have charged him with it to the utmost. Perhaps in fifty years you might execute him, but I am not sanguine about it."

"Great Scott! What shall I do with him?" cried the unhappy Marshal.

Peter Stulpnagel shrugged his shoulders.

"It seems to me that it does not much matter what you do with him now," said he.

"Maybe we could drain the electricity out of him again. Suppose we hang him up by the heels?"

"No, no, it's out of the question."

"Well, well, he shall do no more mischief in Los Amigos, anyhow," said the Marshal, with decision. "He shall go into the new gaol. The prison will wear him out."

"On the contrary," said Peter Stulpnagel, "I think that it is much more probable that he will wear out the prison."

It was rather a fiasco, and for years we didn't talk more about it than we could help, but it's no secret now, and I thought you might like to jot down the facts in your case-book.

10

How It Happened

She was a writing medium. This is what she wrote:—

I can remember some things upon that evening most distinctly, and others are like some vague, broken dreams. That is what makes it so difficult to tell a connected story. I have no idea now what it was that had taken me to London and brought me back so late. It just merges into all my other visits to London. But from the time that I got out at the little country station everything is extraordinarily clear. I can live it again—every instant of it.

I remember so well walking down the platform and looking at the illuminated clock at the end which told me that it was half-past eleven. I remember also my wondering whether I could get home before midnight. Then I remember the big motor, with its glaring head-lights and glitter of polished brass, waiting for me outside. It was my new thirty-horse-power Robur, which had only been delivered that day. I remember also asking Perkins, my chauffeur, how she had gone, and his saying that he thought she was excellent.

"I'll try her myself," said I, and I climbed into the driver's seat.

"The gears are not the same," said he. "Perhaps, sir, I had better drive."

"No; I should like to try her," said I.

And so we started on the five-mile drive for home.

My old car had the gears as they used always to be in notches on a bar. In this car you passed the gear-lever through a gate to get on the higher ones. It was not difficult to master, and soon I thought that I understood it. It was foolish, no doubt, to begin to learn a new system in the dark, but one often does foolish things, and one has not always to pay the full price for them. I got along very well until I came to Claystall Hill. It is one of the worst hills in England, a mile and a half long and one in six in places, with three fairly sharp curves. My park gates stand at the very foot of it upon the main London road.

We were just over the brow of this hill, where the grade is steepest, when the trouble began. I had been on the top speed, and wanted to get her on the free; but she stuck between gears, and I had to get her back on the top again. By this time she was going at a great rate, so I clapped on both brakes, and one after the other they gave way. I didn't mind so much when I felt my footbrake snap, but when I put all my weight on my side-brake, and the lever clanged to its full limit without a catch, it brought a cold sweat out of me. By this time we were fairly tearing down the slope. The lights were brilliant, and I brought her round the first curve all right. Then we did the second one, though it was a close shave for the ditch. There was a mile of straight then with the third curve beneath it, and after that the gate of the park. If I could shoot into that harbour all would be well, for the slope up to the house would bring her to a stand.

Perkins behaved splendidly. I should like that to be known. He was perfectly cool and alert. I had thought at the very beginning of taking the bank, and he read my intention.

"I wouldn't do it, sir," said he. "At this pace it must go over and we should have it on the top of us."

Of course he was right. He got to the electric switch and had it off, so we were in the free; but we were still running at a fearful pace. He laid his hands on the wheel.

"I'll keep her steady," said he, "if you care to jump and chance it. We can never get round that curve. Better jump, sir."

"No," said I; "I'll stick it out. You can jump if you like."

"I'll stick it with you, sir," said he.

If it had been the old car I should have jammed the gear-lever into the reverse, and seen what would happen. I expect she would have stripped her gears or smashed up somehow, but it would have been a chance. As it was, I was helpless. Perkins tried to climb across, but you couldn't do it going at that pace. The wheels were whirring like a high wind and the big body creaking and groaning with the strain. But the lights were brilliant, and one could steer to an inch. I remember thinking what an awful and yet majestic sight we should appear to any one who met us. It was a narrow road, and we were just a great, roaring, golden death to any one who came in our path.

We got round the corner with one wheel three feet high upon the bank. I thought we were surely over, but after staggering for a moment she righted and darted onwards. That was the third corner and the last one. There was only the park gate now. It was facing us, but, as luck would have it, not facing us directly. It was about twenty yards to the left up the main road into which we ran. Perhaps I could have done it, but I expect that the steering-gear had been jarred when we ran on the bank. The wheel did not turn easily. We shot out of the lane. I saw the open gate on the left. I whirled round my wheel with all the strength of my wrists. Perkins and I threw our bodies across, and then the next instant, going at fifty miles an hour, my right front wheel struck full on the right-hand pillar of my own gate. I heard the crash. I was conscious of flying through the air, and then—and then—!

When I became aware of my own existence once more I was among some brushwood in the shadow of the oaks upon the lodge side of the drive. A man was standing beside me. I imagined at first that it was Perkins, but when I looked again I saw that it was Stanley, a man whom I had known at college some years before, and for whom I had a really genuine affection. There was always something peculiarly sympathetic to me in Stanley's personality;

and I was proud to think that I had some similar influence upon him. At the present moment I was surprised to see him, but I was like a man in a dream, giddy and shaken and quite prepared to take things as I found them without questioning them.

"What a smash!" I said. "Good Lord, what an awful smash!"

He nodded his head, and even in the gloom I could see that he was smiling the gentle, wistful smile which I connected with him.

I was quite unable to move. Indeed, I had not any desire to try to move. But my senses were exceedingly alert. I saw the wreck of the motor lit up by the moving lanterns. I saw the little group of people and heard the hushed voices. There were the lodge-keeper and his wife, and one or two more. They were taking no notice of me, but were very busy round the car. Then suddenly I heard a cry of pain.

"The weight is on him. Lift it easy," cried a voice.

"It's only my leg!" said another one, which I recognized as Perkins's. "Where's master?" he cried.

"Here I am," I answered, but they did not seem to hear me. They were all bending over something which lay in front of the car.

Stanley laid his hand upon my shoulder, and his touch was inexpressibly soothing. I felt light and happy, in spite of all.

"No pain, of course?" said he.

"None," said I.

"There never is," said he.

And then suddenly a wave of amazement passed over me. Stanley! Stanley! Why, Stanley had surely died of enteric at Bloemfontein in the Boer War!

"Stanley!" I cried, and the words seemed to choke my throat—"Stanley, you are dead."

He looked at me with the same old gentle, wistful smile.

"So are you," he answered.

BRAM STOKER

(1847-1912)

11

Dracula's Guest

When we started for our drive the sun was shining brightly on Munich, and the air was full of the joyousness of early summer. Just as we were about to depart, Herr Delbrück (the maître d'hôtel of the Quatre Saisons, where I was staying) came down, bareheaded, to the carriage and, after wishing me a pleasant drive, said to the coachman, still holding his hand on the handle of the carriage door:

"Remember you are back by nightfall. The sky looks bright but there is a shiver in the north wind that says there may be a sudden storm. But I am sure you will not be late." Here he smiled, and added, "for you know what night it is."

Johann answered with an emphatic, "Ja, mein Herr," and, touching his hat, drove off quickly. When we had cleared the town, I said, after signalling to him to stop:

"Tell me, Johann, what is tonight?"

He crossed himself, as he answered laconically: "Walpurgis nacht." Then he took out his watch, a great, old-fashioned German silver thing as big as a turnip, and looked at it, with his eyebrows gathered together and a little impatient shrug of his shoulders. I realised that this was his way of respectfully protesting against the unnecessary delay, and sank back in the carriage, merely motioning him to proceed. He started off rapidly, as if to make up for lost time. Every now and then the horses seemed to throw up their heads and sniffed the air suspiciously. On such occasions I often looked round in alarm. The road was pretty bleak, for we were traversing a sort of high, wind-swept plateau. As we drove, I saw a road that looked but little used, and which seemed to dip through a little, winding valley. It looked so inviting that, even at the risk of offending him, I called Johann to stop—and when he had pulled up, I told him I would like to drive down that road. He made all sorts of excuses, and frequently crossed himself as he spoke. This somewhat piqued my curiosity, so I asked him various questions. He answered fencingly, and repeatedly looked at his watch in protest. Finally I said:

"Well, Johann, I want to go down this road. I shall not ask you to come unless you like; but tell me why you do not like to go, that is all I ask." For answer he seemed to throw himself off the box, so quickly did he reach the ground. Then he stretched out his hands appealingly to me, and implored me not to go. There was just enough of English mixed with the German for me to understand the drift of his talk. He seemed always just about to tell me something—the very idea of which evidently frightened him; but each time he pulled himself up, saying, as he crossed himself: "Walpurgis Nacht!"

I tried to argue with him, but it was difficult to argue with a man when I did not know his language. The advantage certainly rested with him, for although he began to speak in English, of a very crude and broken kind, he always got excited and broke into his native tongue—and every time he did so, he looked at his watch. Then the horses became restless and sniffed the air. At this he grew very pale, and, looking around in a frightened way, he suddenly jumped forward, took them by the bridles and led them on some twenty feet. I followed, and asked why he had done this. For answer he crossed himself, pointed to the spot we had left and drew his carriage in the direction of the other road, indicating a cross, and said, first in German, then in English: "Buried him—him what killed themselves."

I remembered the old custom of burying suicides at crossroads: "Ah! I see, a suicide. How interesting!" But for the life of me I could not make out why the horses were frightened.

Whilst we were talking, we heard a sort of sound between a yelp and a bark. It was far away; but the horses got very restless, and it took Johann all his time to quiet them. He was pale, and said, "It sounds like a wolf—but yet there are no wolves here now."

"No?" I said, questioning him; "isn't it long since the wolves were so near the city?"

"Long, long," he answered, "in the spring and summer; but with the snow the wolves have been here not so long."

Whilst he was petting the horses and trying to quiet them, dark clouds drifted rapidly across the sky. The sunshine passed away, and a breath of cold wind seemed to drift past us. It was only a breath, however, and more in the nature of a warning than a fact, for the sun came out brightly again. Johann looked under his lifted hand at the horizon and said:

"The storm of snow, he comes before long time." Then he looked at his watch again, and, straightway holding his reins firmly—for the horses were still pawing the ground restlessly and shaking their heads—he climbed to his box as though the time had come for proceeding on our journey.

I felt a little obstinate and did not at once get into the carriage.

"Tell me," I said, "about this place where the road leads," and I pointed down.

Again he crossed himself and mumbled a prayer, before he answered, "It is unholy."

"What is unholy?" I enquired.

"The village."

"Then there is a village?"

"No, no. No one lives there hundreds of years." My curiosity was piqued, "But you said there was a village."

"There was."

"Where is it now?"

Whereupon he burst out into a long story in German and English, so mixed up that I could not quite understand exactly what he said, but roughly I gathered that long ago, hundreds of years, men had died there and been buried in their graves; and sounds were heard under the clay, and when the graves were opened, men and women were found rosy with life, and their mouths red with blood. And so, in haste to save their lives (aye, and their souls!—and here he crossed himself) those who were left fled away to other places, where the living lived, and the dead were dead and not—not something. He was evidently afraid to speak the last words. As he proceeded with his narration, he grew more and more excited. It seemed as if his imagination had got hold of him, and he ended in a perfect paroxysm of fear—white-faced, perspiring, trembling and looking round him, as if expecting that some dreadful presence would manifest itself there in the bright sunshine on the open plain. Finally, in an agony of desperation, he cried:

"Walpurgis nacht!" and pointed to the carriage for me to get in. All my English blood rose at this, and, standing back, I said:

"You are afraid, Johann—you are afraid. Go home; I shall return alone; the walk will do me good." The carriage door was open. I took from the seat my oak walking-stick—which I always carry on my holiday excursions—and closed the door, pointing back to Munich, and said, "Go home, Johann—Walpurgis nacht doesn't concern Englishmen."

The horses were now more restive than ever, and Johann was trying to hold them in, while excitedly imploring me not to do anything so foolish. I pitied the poor fellow, he was deeply in earnest; but all the same I could not help laughing. His English was quite gone now. In his anxiety he had forgotten that his only means of making me understand was to talk my language, so he jabbered away in his native German. It began to be a little tedious. After giving the direction, 'Home!' I turned to go down the cross-road into the valley.

With a despairing gesture, Johann turned his horses towards Munich. I leaned on my stick and looked after him. He went slowly along the road for a while: then there came over the crest of the hill a man tall and thin. I could see so much in the distance. When he drew near the horses, they began to jump and kick about, then to scream with terror. Johann could not hold them in; they bolted down the road, running away madly. I watched them out of sight, then looked for the stranger, but I found that he, too, was gone.

With a light heart I turned down the side road through the deepening valley to which Johann had objected. There was not the slightest reason, that I could see, for his objection; and I daresay I tramped for a couple of hours without thinking of time or distance, and certainly without seeing a person or a house. So far as the place was concerned, it was desolation itself. But I did not notice this particularly till, on turning a bend in the road, I came upon a scattered fringe of wood; then I recognised that I had been impressed unconsciously by the desolation of the region through which I had passed.

I sat down to rest myself, and began to look around. It struck me that it was considerably colder than it had been at the commencement of my walk—a sort of sighing sound seemed to be around me, with, now and then, high overhead, a sort of muffled roar. Looking upwards I noticed that great thick clouds were drifting rapidly across the sky from North to South at a great height. There were signs of coming storm in some lofty stratum of the air. I was a little chilly, and, thinking that it was the sitting still after the exercise of walking, I resumed my journey.

The ground I passed over was now much more picturesque. There were no striking objects that the eye might single out; but in all there was a charm of beauty. I took little heed of time and it was only when the deepening twilight forced itself upon me that I began to think of how I should find my way home. The brightness of the day had gone. The air was cold, and the drifting of clouds high overhead was more marked. They were accompanied by a sort of far-away rushing sound, through which seemed to come at intervals that mysterious cry which the driver had said came from a wolf. For a while I hesitated. I had said I would see the deserted village, so on I went, and presently came on a wide stretch of open country, shut in by hills all around. Their sides were covered with trees which spread down to the plain, dotting, in clumps, the gentler slopes and hollows which showed here and there. I followed with my eye the winding of the road, and saw that it curved close to one of the densest of these clumps and was lost behind it.

As I looked there came a cold shiver in the air, and the snow began to fall. I thought of the miles and miles of bleak country I had passed, and then hurried on to seek the shelter of the wood in front. Darker and darker grew the sky, and faster and heavier fell the snow, till the earth before and around me was a glistening white carpet the further edge of which was lost in misty vagueness. The road was here but crude, and when on the level its boundaries were not so marked, as when it passed through the cuttings; and in a little while I found that I must have strayed from it, for I missed underfoot the hard surface, and my feet sank deeper in the grass and moss. Then the wind grew stronger and blew with ever increasing force, till I was fain to run before it. The air became icy-cold, and in spite of my exercise I began to suffer. The snow was now falling so thickly and whirling around me in such rapid eddies that I could hardly keep my eyes open. Every now and then the heavens were torn asunder by vivid lightning, and in the flashes I could see ahead of me a great mass of trees, chiefly yew and cypress all heavily coated with snow.

I was soon amongst the shelter of the trees, and there, in comparative silence, I could hear the rush of the wind high overhead. Presently the blackness of the storm had become merged in the darkness of the night. By and by the storm seemed to be passing away: it now only came in fierce puffs or blasts. At such moments the weird sound of the wolf appeared to be echoed by many similar sounds around me.

Now and again, through the black mass of drifting cloud, came a straggling ray of moonlight, which lit up the expanse, and showed me that I was at the edge of a dense mass of cypress and yew trees. As the snow had ceased to fall, I walked out from the shelter and began to investigate more closely. It appeared to me that, amongst so many old foundations as I had passed, there might be still standing a house in which, though in ruins, I could find some sort of shelter for a while. As I skirted the edge of the copse, I found that a low wall encircled it, and following this I presently found an opening. Here the cypresses formed an alley leading up to a square mass of some kind of building. Just as I caught sight of this, however, the drifting clouds obscured the moon, and I passed up the path in darkness. The wind must have grown colder, for I felt myself shiver as I walked; but there was hope of shelter, and I groped my way blindly on.

I stopped, for there was a sudden stillness. The storm had passed; and, perhaps in sympathy with nature's silence, my heart seemed to cease to beat. But this was only momentarily; for suddenly the moonlight broke through the clouds, showing me that I was in a graveyard, and that the square object before me was a great massive tomb of marble, as white as the snow that lay on and all around it. With the moonlight there came a fierce sigh of the storm, which appeared to resume its course with a long, low howl, as of many dogs or wolves. I was awed and shocked, and felt the cold perceptibly grow upon me till it seemed to grip me by the heart. Then while the flood of moonlight still fell on the marble tomb, the storm gave further evidence of renewing, as though it was returning on its track. Impelled by some sort of fascination, I approached the sepulchre to see what it was, and why such a thing stood alone in such a place. I walked around it, and read, over the Doric door, in German:

COUNTESS DOLINGEN OF GRATZ
IN STYRIA
SOUGHT AND FOUND DEATH
1801

On the top of the tomb, seemingly driven through the solid marble—for the structure was composed of a few vast blocks of stone—was a great iron spike or stake. On going to the back I saw, graven in great Russian letters:

'The dead travel fast.'

There was something so weird and uncanny about the whole thing that it gave me a turn and made me feel quite faint. I began to wish, for the first time, that I had taken Johann's advice. Here a thought struck me, which came under almost mysterious circumstances and with a terrible shock. This was Walpurgis Night!

Walpurgis Night, when, according to the belief of millions of people, the devil was abroad—when the graves were opened and the dead came forth and walked. When all evil things of earth and air and water held revel. This very place the driver had specially shunned. This was the depopulated village of centuries ago. This was where the suicide lay; and this was the place where I was alone—unmanned, shivering with cold in a shroud of snow with a wild storm gathering again upon me! It took all my philosophy, all the religion I had been taught, all my courage, not to collapse in a paroxysm of fright.

And now a perfect tornado burst upon me. The ground shook as though thousands of horses thundered across it; and this time the storm bore on its icy wings, not snow, but great hailstones which drove with such violence that they might have come from the thongs of Balearic slingers—hailstones that beat down leaf and branch and made the shelter of the cypresses of no more avail than though their stems were standing-corn. At the first I had rushed to the nearest tree; but I was soon fain to leave it and seek the only spot that seemed to afford refuge, the deep Doric doorway of the marble tomb. There, crouching against the massive bronze door, I gained a certain amount of protection from the beating of the hailstones, for now they only drove against me as they ricocheted from the ground and the side of the marble.

As I leaned against the door, it moved slightly and opened inwards. The shelter of even a tomb was welcome in that pitiless tempest, and I was about to enter it when there came a flash of forked-lightning that lit up the whole expanse of the heavens. In the instant, as I am a living man, I saw, as my eyes were turned into the darkness of the tomb, a beautiful woman, with rounded cheeks and red lips, seemingly sleeping on a bier. As the thunder broke overhead, I was grasped as by the hand of a giant and hurled out into the storm. The whole thing was so sudden that, before I could realise the shock, moral as well as physical, I found the hailstones beating me down. At the same time I had a strange, dominating feeling that I was not alone. I looked towards the tomb. Just then there came another blinding flash, which seemed to strike the iron stake that surmounted the tomb and to pour through to the earth, blasting and crumbling the marble, as in a burst of flame. The dead woman rose for a moment of agony, while she was lapped in the flame, and her bitter scream of pain was drowned in the thundercrash. The last thing I heard was this mingling of dreadful sound, as again I was seized in the giant-grasp and dragged away, while the hailstones beat on me, and the air around seemed reverberant with the howling of wolves. The last sight that I remembered was a vague, white, moving mass, as if all the graves around me had sent out the phantoms of their sheeted-dead, and that they were closing in on me through the white cloudiness of the driving hail.

Gradually there came a sort of vague beginning of consciousness; then a sense of weariness that was dreadful. For a time I remembered nothing; but slowly my senses returned. My feet seemed positively racked with pain, yet I could not move them. They seemed to be numbed. There was an icy feeling at the back of my neck and all down my spine, and my ears, like my feet, were dead, yet in torment; but there was in my breast a sense of warmth which was, by comparison, delicious. It was as a nightmare—a physical nightmare, if one may use such an expression; for some heavy weight on my chest made it difficult for me to breathe.

This period of semi-lethargy seemed to remain a long time, and as it faded away I must have slept or swooned. Then came a sort of loathing, like the first stage of sea-sickness, and a wild desire to be free from something—I knew not what. A vast stillness enveloped me, as though all the world were asleep or dead—only broken by the low panting as of some animal close to me. I felt a warm rasping at my throat, then came a consciousness of the awful truth, which chilled me to the heart and sent the blood surging up through my brain. Some great animal was lying on me and now licking my throat. I feared to stir, for some instinct of prudence bade me lie still; but the brute seemed to realise that there was now some change in me, for it raised its head. Through my eyelashes I saw above me the two great flaming eyes of a gigantic wolf. Its sharp white teeth gleamed in the gaping red mouth, and I could feel its hot breath fierce and acrid upon me.

For another spell of time I remembered no more. Then I became conscious of a low growl, followed by a yelp, renewed again and again. Then, seemingly very far away, I heard a 'Holloa! holloa!' as of many voices calling in unison. Cautiously I raised my head and looked in the direction whence the sound came; but the cemetery blocked my view. The wolf still continued to yelp in a strange way, and a red glare began to move round the grove of cypresses, as though following the sound. As the voices drew closer, the wolf yelped faster and louder. I feared to make either sound or motion. Nearer came the red glow, over the white pall which stretched into the darkness around me. Then all at once from beyond the trees there came at a trot a troop of horsemen bearing torches. The wolf rose from my breast and made for the cemetery. I saw one of the horsemen (soldiers by their caps and their long military cloaks) raise his carbine and take aim. A companion knocked up his arm, and I heard the ball whizz over my head. He had evidently taken my body for that of the wolf. Another sighted the animal as it slunk away, and a shot followed. Then, at a gallop, the troop rode forward—some towards me, others following the wolf as it disappeared amongst the snow-clad cypresses.

As they drew nearer I tried to move, but was powerless, although I could see and hear all that went on around me. Two or three of the soldiers jumped from their horses and knelt beside me. One of them raised my head, and placed his hand over my heart.

"Good news, comrades!" he cried. "His heart still beats!"

Then some brandy was poured down my throat; it put vigour into me, and I was able to open my eyes fully and look around. Lights and shadows were moving among the trees, and I heard men call to one another. They drew together, uttering frightened exclamations; and the lights flashed as the others came pouring out of the cemetery pell-mell, like men possessed. When the further ones came close to us, those who were around me asked them eagerly:

"Well, have you found him?"

The reply rang out hurriedly:

"No! No! Come away quick—quick! This is no place to stay, and on this of all nights!"

"What was it?" was the question, asked in all manner of keys. The answer came variously and all indefinitely as though the men were moved by some common impulse to speak, yet were restrained by some common fear from giving their thoughts.

"It—it—indeed!" gibbered one, whose wits had plainly given out for the moment.

"A wolf—and yet not a wolf!" another put in shudderingly.

"No use trying for him without the sacred bullet," a third remarked in a more ordinary manner.

"Serve us right for coming out on this night! Truly we have earned our thousand marks!" were the ejaculations of a fourth.

"There was blood on the broken marble," another said after a pause—"the lightning never brought that there. And for him—is he safe? Look at his throat! See, comrades, the wolf has been lying on him and keeping his blood warm."

The officer looked at my throat and replied:

"He is all right; the skin is not pierced. What does it all mean? We should never have found him but for the yelping of the wolf."

"What became of it?" asked the man who was holding up my head, and who seemed the least panic-stricken of the party, for his hands were steady and without tremor. On his sleeve was the chevron of a petty officer.

"It went to its home," answered the man, whose long face was pallid, and who actually shook with terror as he glanced around him fearfully. "There are graves enough there in which it may lie. Come, comrades—come quickly! Let us leave this cursed spot."

The officer raised me to a sitting posture, as he uttered a word of command; then several men placed me upon a horse. He sprang to the saddle behind me, took me in his arms, gave the word to advance; and, turning our faces away from the cypresses, we rode away in swift, military order.

As yet my tongue refused its office, and I was perforce silent. I must have fallen asleep; for the next thing I remembered was finding myself standing up, supported by a soldier on each side of me. It was almost broad daylight, and to the north a red streak of sunlight was reflected, like a path of blood, over the waste of snow. The officer was telling the men to say nothing of what they had seen, except that they found an English stranger, guarded by a large dog.

"Dog! That was no dog," cut in the man who had exhibited such fear. "I think I know a wolf when I see one."

The young officer answered calmly: "I said a dog."

"Dog!" reiterated the other ironically. It was evident that his courage was rising with the sun; and, pointing to me, he said, "Look at his throat. Is that the work of a dog, master?"

Instinctively I raised my hand to my throat, and as I touched it I cried out in pain. The men crowded round to look, some stooping down from their saddles; and again there came the calm voice of the young officer:

"A dog, as I said. If aught else were said we should only be laughed at."

I was then mounted behind a trooper, and we rode on into the suburbs of Munich. Here we came across a stray carriage, into which I was lifted, and it was driven off to the Quatre Saisons—the young officer accompanying me, whilst a trooper followed with his horse, and the others rode off to their barracks.

When we arrived, Herr Delbrück rushed so quickly down the steps to meet me, that it was apparent he had been watching within. Taking me by both hands he solicitously led me in. The officer saluted me and was turning to withdraw, when I recognised his purpose, and insisted that he should come to my rooms. Over a glass of wine I warmly thanked him and his brave comrades for saving me. He replied simply that he was more than glad, and that Herr Delbrück had at the first taken steps to make all the searching party pleased; at which ambiguous utterance the maître d'hôtel smiled, while the officer pleaded duty and withdrew.

"But Herr Delbrück," I enquired, "how and why was it that the soldiers searched for me?"

He shrugged his shoulders, as if in depreciation of his own deed, as he replied:

"I was so fortunate as to obtain leave from the commander of the regiment in which I served, to ask for volunteers."

"But how did you know I was lost?" I asked.

"The driver came hither with the remains of his carriage, which had been upset when the horses ran away."

"But surely you would not send a search-party of soldiers merely on this account?"

"Oh, no!" he answered; "but even before the coachman arrived, I had this telegram from the Boyar whose guest you are," and he took from his pocket a telegram which he handed to me, and I read:

> *Bistritz*
>
> Be careful of my guest—his safety is most precious to me. Should aught happen to him, or if he be missed, spare nothing to find him and ensure his safety. He is English and therefore adventurous. There are often dangers from snow and wolves and night. Lose not a moment if you suspect harm to him. I answer your zeal with my fortune.—*Dracula.*

As I held the telegram in my hand, the room seemed to whirl around me; and, if the attentive maître d'hôtel had not caught me, I think I should have fallen. There was something so strange in all this, something so weird and impossible to imagine, that there grew on me a sense of my being in some way the sport of opposite forces—the mere vague idea of which seemed in a way to paralyse me. I was certainly under some form of mysterious protection. From a distant country had come, in the very nick of time, a message that took me out of the danger of the snow-sleep and the jaws of the wolf.

E G SWAIN

(1861-1938)

12

Bone to His Bone

William Whitehead, Fellow of Emmanuel College, in the University of Cambridge, became Vicar of Stoneground in the year 1731. The annals of his incumbency were doubtless short and simple: they have not survived. In his day were no newspapers to collect gossip, no Parish Magazines to record the simple events of parochial life. One event, however, of greater moment then than now, is recorded in two places. Vicar Whitehead failed in health after 23 years of work, and journeyed to Bath in what his monument calls 'the vain hope of being restored.' The duration of his visit is unknown; it is reasonable to suppose that he made his journey in the summer, it is certain that by the month of November his physician told him to lay aside all hope of recovery.

Then it was that the thoughts of the patient turned to the comfortable straggling vicarage he had left at Stoneground, in which he had hoped to end his days. He prayed that his successor might be as happy there as he had been himself. Setting his affairs in order, as became one who had but a short time to live, he executed a will, bequeathing to the Vicars of Stoneground, for ever, the close of ground he had recently purchased because it lay next the vicarage garden.

And by a codicil, he added to the bequest his library of books. Within a few days, William Whitehead was gathered to his fathers.

A mural tablet in the north aisle of the church, records, in Latin, his services and his bequests, his two marriages, and his fruitless journey to Bath. The house he loved, but never again saw, was taken down 40 years later, and re-built by Vicar James Devie. The garden, with Vicar Whitehead's 'close of ground' and other adjacent lands, was opened out and planted, somewhat before 1850, by Vicar Robert Towerson. The aspect of everything has changed. But in a convenient chamber on the first floor of the present vicarage the library of Vicar Whitehead stands very much as he used it and loved it, and as he bequeathed it to his successors 'for ever.'

The books there are arranged as he arranged and ticketed them. Little slips of paper, sometimes bearing interesting fragments of writing, still mark his places. His marginal comments still give life to pages from which all other interest has faded, and he would have but a dull imagination who could sit in the chamber amidst these books without ever being carried back 180 years into the past, to the time when the newest of them left the printer's hands.

Of those into whose possession the books have come, some have doubtless loved them more, and some less; some, perhaps, have left them severely alone. But neither those who loved them, nor those who loved them not, have lost them, and they passed, some century and a half after William Whitehead's death, into the hands of Mr. Batchel, who loved them as a father loves his children. He lived alone, and had few domestic cares to distract his mind. He was able, therefore, to enjoy to the full what Vicar Whitehead had enjoyed so long before him. During many a long summer evening would he sit poring over long-forgotten books; and since the chamber, otherwise called the library, faced the south, he could also spend sunny winter mornings there without discomfort. Writing at a small table, or reading as he stood at a tall desk, he would browse amongst the books like an ox in a pleasant pasture.

There were other times also, at which Mr. Batchel would use the books. Not being a sound sleeper (for book-loving men seldom are), he elected to use as a bedroom one of the two chambers which opened at either side into the library. The arrangement enabled him to beguile many a sleepless hour amongst the books, and in view of these nocturnal visits he kept a candle standing in a sconce above the desk, and matches always ready to his hand.

There was one disadvantage in this close proximity of his bed to the library. Owing, apparently, to some defect in the fittings of the room, which, having no mechanical tastes, Mr. Batchel had never investigated, there could be heard, in the stillness of the night, exactly such sounds as might arise from a person moving about amongst the books. Visitors using the other adjacent room would often remark at breakfast, that they had heard their host in the library at one or two o'clock in the morning, when, in fact, he had not left his bed. Invariably Mr. Batchel allowed them to suppose that he had been where they thought him. He disliked idle controversy, and was unwilling to afford an opening for supernatural talk. Knowing well enough the sounds by which his guests had been deceived, he wanted no other explanation of them than his own, though it was of too vague a character to count as an explanation. He conjectured that the window-sashes, or the doors, or 'something,' were defective, and was too phlegmatic and too unpractical to make any investigation. The matter gave him no concern.

Persons whose sleep is uncertain are apt to have their worst nights when they would like their best. The consciousness of a special need for rest seems to bring enough mental disturbance to forbid it. So on Christmas Eve, in the year 1907, Mr. Batchel, who would have liked to sleep well, in view of the labours of Christmas Day, lay hopelessly wide awake. He exhausted all the known devices for courting sleep, and, at the end, found himself wider awake than ever. A brilliant moon shone into his room, for he hated window-blinds. There was a light wind blowing, and the sounds in the library were more than usually suggestive of a person moving about. He almost determined to have the sashes 'seen to,' although he could seldom be induced to have anything 'seen to.' He disliked changes, even for the better, and would submit to great inconvenience rather than have things altered with which he had become familiar.

As he revolved these matters in his mind, he heard the clocks strike the hour of midnight, and having now lost all hope of falling asleep, he rose from his bed, got into a large dressing gown which hung in readiness for such occasions, and passed into the library, with the intention of reading himself sleepy, if he could.

The moon, by this time, had passed out of the south, and the library seemed all the darker by contrast with the moonlit chamber he had left. He could see nothing but two blue-grey rectangles formed by the windows against the sky, the furniture of the room being altogether invisible. Groping along to where the table stood, Mr. Batchel felt over its surface for the matches which usually lay there; he found, however, that the table was cleared of everything. He raised his right hand, therefore, in order to feel his way to a shelf where the matches were sometimes mislaid, and at that moment, whilst his hand was in mid-air, the matchbox was gently put into it!

Such an incident could hardly fail to disturb even a phlegmatic person, and Mr. Batchel cried "Who's this?" somewhat nervously. There was no answer. He struck a match, looked hastily round the room, and found it empty, as usual. There was everything, that is to say, that he was accustomed to see, but no other person than himself.

It is not quite accurate, however, to say that everything was in its usual state. Upon the tall desk lay a quarto volume that he had certainly not placed there. It was his quite invariable practice to replace his books upon the shelves after using them, and what we may call his library habits were precise and methodical. A book out of place like this, was not only an offence against good order, but a sign that his privacy had been intruded upon. With some surprise, therefore, he lit the candle standing ready in the sconce, and proceeded to examine the book, not sorry, in the disturbed condition in which he was, to have an occupation found for him.

The book proved to be one with which he was unfamiliar, and this made it certain that some other hand than his had removed it from its place. Its title was 'The Compleat Gard'ner' of M. de la

Quintinye made English by John Evelyn Esquire. It was not a work in which Mr. Batchel felt any great interest. It consisted of divers reflections on various parts of husbandry, doubtless entertaining enough, but too deliberate and discursive for practical purposes. He had certainly never used the book, and growing restless now in mind, said to himself that some boy having the freedom of the house, had taken it down from its place in the hope of finding pictures.

But even whilst he made this explanation he felt its weakness. To begin with, the desk was too high for a boy. The improbability that any boy would place a book there was equalled by the improbability that he would leave it there. To discover its uninviting character would be the work only of a moment, and no boy would have brought it so far from its shelf.

Mr. Batchel had, however, come to read, and habit was too strong with him to be wholly set aside. Leaving 'The Compleat Gard'ner' on the desk, he turned round to the shelves to find some more congenial reading.

Hardly had he done this when he was startled by a sharp rap upon the desk behind him, followed by a rustling of paper. He turned quickly about and saw the quarto lying open. In obedience to the instinct of the moment, he at once sought a natural cause for what he saw. Only a wind, and that of the strongest, could have opened the book, and laid back its heavy cover; and though he accepted, for a brief moment, that explanation, he was too candid to retain it longer. The wind out of doors was very light. The window sash was closed and latched, and, to decide the matter finally, the book had its back, and not its edges, turned towards the only quarter from which a wind could strike.

Mr. Batchel approached the desk again and stood over the book. With increasing perturbation of mind (for he still thought of the matchbox) he looked upon the open page. Without much reason beyond that he felt constrained to do something, he read the words of the half completed sentence at the turn of the page—

'at dead of night he left the house and passed into the solitude of the garden.'

But he read no more, nor did he give himself the trouble of discovering whose midnight wandering was being described, although the habit was singularly like one of his own. He was in no condition for reading, and turning his back upon the volume he slowly paced the length of the chamber, 'wondering at that which had come to pass.'

He reached the opposite end of the chamber and was in the act of turning, when again he heard the rustling of paper, and by the time he had faced round, saw the leaves of the book again turning over. In a moment the volume lay at rest, open in another place, and there was no further movement as he approached it. To make sure that he had not been deceived, he read again the words as they entered the page. The author was following a not uncommon practise of the time, and throwing common speech into forms suggested by Holy Writ: "So dig," it said, "that ye may obtain."

This passage, which to Mr. Batchel seemed reprehensible in its levity, excited at once his interest and his disapproval. He was prepared to read more, but this time was not allowed. Before his eye could pass beyond the passage already cited, the leaves of the book slowly turned again, and presented but a termination of five words and a colophon.

The words were, 'to the North, an Ilex.' These three passages, in which he saw no meaning and no connection, began to entangle themselves together in Mr. Batchel's mind. He found himself repeating them in different orders, now beginning with one, and now with another. Any further attempt at reading he felt to be impossible, and he was in no mind for any more experiences of the unaccountable. Sleep was, of course, further from him than ever, if that were conceivable. What he did, therefore, was to blow out the candle, to return to his moonlit bedroom, and put on more clothing, and then to pass downstairs with the object of going out of doors.

It was not unusual with Mr. Batchel to walk about his garden at night-time. This form of exercise had often, after a wakeful hour, sent him back to his bed refreshed and ready for sleep. The convenient access to the garden at such times lay through his study, whose French windows opened on to a short flight of steps, and upon these he now paused for a moment to admire the snow-like appearance of the lawns, bathed as they were in the moonlight. As he paused, he heard the city clocks strike the half-hour after midnight, and he could not forbear repeating aloud,

"At dead of night he left the house, and passed into the solitude of the garden."

It was solitary enough. At intervals the screech of an owl, and now and then the noise of a train, seemed to emphasise the solitude by drawing attention to it and then leaving it in possession of the night. Mr. Batchel found himself wondering and conjecturing what Vicar Whitehead, who had acquired the close of land to secure quiet and privacy for garden, would have thought of the railways to the west and north. He turned his face northwards, whence a whistle had just sounded, and saw a tree beautifully outlined against the sky. His breath caught at the sight. Not because the tree was unfamiliar. Mr. Batchel knew all his trees. But what he had seen was 'to the north, an Ilex.'

Mr. Batchel knew not what to make of it all. He had walked into the garden hundreds of times and as often seen the Ilex, but the words out of the 'Compleat Gard'ner' seemed to be pursuing him in a way that made him almost afraid. His temperament, however, as has been said already, was phlegmatic. It was commonly said, and Mr. Batchel approved the verdict, whilst he condemned its inexactness, that 'his nerves were made of fiddle-string,' so he braced himself afresh and set upon his walk round the silent garden, which he was accustomed to begin in a northerly direction, and was now too proud to change. He usually passed the Ilex at the beginning of his perambulation, and so would pass it now.

He did not pass it. A small discovery, as he reached it, annoyed and disturbed him. His gardener, as careful and punctilious as himself, never failed to house all his tools at the end of a day's work. Yet there, under the Ilex, standing upright in moonlight brilliant enough to cast a shadow of it, was a spade.

Mr. Batchel's second thought was one of relief. After his extraordinary experiences in the library (he hardly knew now whether they had been real or not) something quite commonplace would act sedatively, and he determined to carry the spade to the tool-house.

The soil was quite dry, and the surface even a little frozen, so Mr. Batchel left the path, walked up to the spade, and would have drawn it towards him. But it was as if he had made the attempt upon the trunk of the Ilex itself. The spade would not be moved. Then, first with one hand, and then with both, he tried to raise it, and still it stood firm. Mr. Batchel, of course, attributed this to the frost, slight as it was. Wondering at the spade's being there, and annoyed at its being frozen, he was about to leave it and continue his walk, when the remaining words of the 'Compleat Gard'ner' seemed rather to utter themselves, than to await his will—

"So dig, that ye may obtain."

Mr. Batchel's power of independent action now deserted him. He took the spade, which no longer resisted, and began to dig. "Five spadefuls and no more," he said aloud. "This is all foolishness."

Four spadefuls of earth he then raised and spread out before him in the moonlight. There was nothing unusual to be seen. Nor did Mr. Batchel decide what he would look for, whether coins, jewels, documents in canisters, or weapons. In point of fact, he dug against what he deemed his better judgment, and expected nothing. He spread before him the fifth and last spadeful of earth, not quite without result, but with no result that was at all sensational. The earth contained a bone. Mr. Batchel's knowledge of anatomy was sufficient to show him that it was a human bone. He identified it, even by moonlight, as the *radius*, a bone of the forearm, as he removed the earth from it, with his thumb.

Such a discovery might be thought worthy of more than the very ordinary interest Mr. Batchel showed. As a matter of fact, the presence of a human bone was easily to be accounted for. Recent excavations within the church had caused the upturning of numberless bones, which had been collected and reverently buried. But an earth-stained bone is also easily overlooked, and this *radius* had obviously found its way into the garden with some of the earth brought out of the church.

Mr. Batchel was glad, rather than regretful at this termination to his adventure. He was once more provided with something to do. The re-interment of such bones as this had been his constant care, and he decided at once to restore the bone to consecrated earth. The time seemed opportune. The eyes of the curious were closed in sleep, he himself was still alert and wakeful. The spade remained by his side and the bone in his hand. So he betook himself, there and then, to the churchyard. By the still generous light of the moon, he found a place where the earth yielded to his spade, and within a few minutes the bone was laid decently to earth, some 18 inches deep.

The city clocks struck one as he finished. The whole world seemed asleep, and Mr. Batchel slowly returned to the garden with his spade. As he hung it in its accustomed place he felt stealing over him the welcome desire to sleep. He walked quietly on to the house and ascended to his room. It was now dark: the moon had passed on and left the room in shadow. He lit a candle, and before undressing passed into the library. He had an irresistible curiosity to see the passages in John Evelyn's book which had so strangely adapted themselves to the events of the past hour.

In the library a last surprise awaited him. The desk upon which the book had lain was empty. 'The Compleat Gard'ner' stood in its place on the shelf. And then Mr. Batchel knew that he had handled a bone of William Whitehead, and that in response to his own entreaty.

EDGAR ALLAN POE

(1809-1849)

13

The Facts in the Case of M. Valdemar

Of course I shall not pretend to consider it any matter for wonder, that the extraordinary case of M. Valdemar has excited discussion. It would have been a miracle had it not—especially under the circumstances. Through the desire of all parties concerned, to keep the affair from the public, at least for the present, or until we had farther opportunities for investigation—through our endeavours to effect this—a garbled or exaggerated account made its way into society, and became the source of many unpleasant misrepresentations; and, very naturally, of a great deal of disbelief.

It is now rendered necessary that I give the facts—as far as I comprehend them myself. They are, succinctly, these:

My attention, for the last three years, had been repeatedly drawn to the subject of Mesmerism; and, about nine months ago, it occurred to me, quite suddenly, that in the series of experiments made hitherto, there had been a very remarkable and most unaccountable omission: no person had as yet been mesmerized in articulo mortis. It remained to be seen, first, whether, in such condition, there existed in the patient any susceptibility to the magnetic influence; secondly, whether, if any existed, it was impaired or increased by the condition; thirdly, to what extent, or for how long a period, the encroachments of Death might be arrested by the process. There were other points to be ascertained, but these most excited my curiosity—the last in especial, from the immensely important character of its consequences.

In looking around me for some subject by whose means I might test these particulars, I was brought to think of my friend, M. Ernest Valdemar, the well-known compiler of the 'Bibliotheca Forensica,' and author (under the nom de plume of Issachar Marx) of the Polish versions of 'Wallenstein' and 'Gargantua.' M. Valdemar, who has resided principally at Harlem, N. Y., since the year 1839, is (or was) particularly noticeable for the extreme spareness of his person—his lower limbs much resembling those of John Randolph; and, also, for the whiteness of his whiskers, in violent contrast to the blackness of his hair—the latter, in consequence, being very generally mistaken for a wig. His temperament was markedly nervous, and rendered him a good subject for mesmeric experiment. On two or three occasions I had put him to sleep with little difficulty, but was disappointed in other results which his peculiar constitution had naturally led me to anticipate. His will was at no period positively, or thoroughly, under my control, and in regard to clairvoyance, I could accomplish with him nothing to be relied upon. I always attributed my failure at these points to the disordered state of his health. For some months previous to my becoming acquainted with him, his physicians had declared him in a confirmed phthisis. It was his custom, indeed, to speak calmly of his approaching dissolution, as of a matter neither to be avoided nor regretted.

When the ideas to which I have alluded first occurred to me, it was of course very natural that I should think of M. Valdemar. I knew the steady philosophy of the man too well to apprehend any scruples from him; and he had no relatives in America who would be likely to interfere. I spoke to him frankly upon the subject; and, to my surprise, his interest seemed vividly excited. I say to my surprise; for, although he had always yielded his person freely to my experiments, he had never before given me any tokens of sympathy with what I did. His disease was of that character which would admit of exact calculation in respect to the epoch of its termination in death; and it was finally arranged between us that he would send for me about twenty-four hours before the period announced by his physicians as that of his decease.

It is now rather more than seven months since I received, from M. Valdemar himself, the subjoined note:

MY DEAR P___,

You may as well come now. D___ and F___ are agreed that I cannot hold out beyond tomorrow midnight; and I think they have hit the time very nearly.

VALDEMAR.

I received this note within half an hour after it was written, and in fifteen minutes more I was in the dying man's chamber. I had not seen him for ten days, and was appalled by the fearful alteration which the brief interval had wrought in him. His face wore a leaden hue; the eyes were utterly lustreless; and the emaciation was so extreme, that the skin had been broken through by the cheek-bones. His expectoration was excessive. The pulse was barely perceptible. He retained, nevertheless, in a very remarkable manner, both his mental power and a certain degree of physical strength. He spoke with distinctness—took some palliative medicines without aid—and, when I entered the room, was occupied in penciling memoranda in a pocket-book. He was propped up in the bed by pillows. Doctors D___ and F___ were in attendance.

After pressing Valdemar's hand, I took these gentlemen aside, and obtained from them a minute account of the patient's condition. The left lung had been for eighteen months in a semi-osseous or cartilaginous state, and was, of course, entirely useless for all purposes of vitality. The right, in its upper portion, was also partially, if not thoroughly, ossified, while the lower region was merely a mass of purulent tubercles, running one into another.

Several extensive perforations existed; and, at one point, permanent adhesion to the ribs had taken place. These appearances in the right lobe were of comparatively recent date. The ossification had proceeded with very unusual rapidity; no sign of it had discovered a month before, and the adhesion had only been observed during the three previous days. Independently of the phthisis, the patient was suspected of aneurism of the aorta; but on this point the osseous symptoms rendered an exact diagnosis impossible. It was the opinion of both physicians that M. Valdemar would die about midnight on the morrow (Sunday). It was then seven o'clock on Saturday evening.

On quitting the invalid's bed-side to hold conversation with myself, Doctors D___ and F___ had bidden him a final farewell. It had not been their intention to return; but, at my request, they agreed to look in upon the patient about ten the next night.

When they had gone, I spoke freely with M. Valdemar on the subject of his approaching dissolution, as well as, more particularly, of the experiment proposed. He still professed himself quite willing and even anxious to have it made, and urged me to commence it at once. A male and a female nurse were in attendance; but I did not feel myself altogether at liberty to engage in a task of this character with no more reliable witnesses than these people, in case of sudden accident, might prove. I therefore postponed operations until about eight the next night, when the arrival of a medical student, with whom I had some acquaintance, (Mr. Theodore L___l,) relieved me from farther embarrassment. It had been my design, originally, to wait for the physicians; but I was induced to proceed, first, by the urgent entreaties of M. Valdemar, and secondly, by my conviction that I had not a moment to lose, as he was evidently sinking fast.

Mr. L___l was so kind as to accede to my desire that he would take notes of all that occurred; and it is from his memoranda that what I now have to relate is, for the most part, either condensed or copied verbatim.

It wanted about five minutes of eight when, taking the patient's hand, I begged him to state, as distinctly as he could, to Mr. L___l, whether he (M. Valdemar) was entirely willing that I should make the experiment of mesmerizing him in his then condition.

He replied feebly, yet quite audibly, "Yes, I wish to be mesmerized"—adding immediately afterwards, "I fear you have deferred it too long."

While he spoke thus, I commenced the passes which I had already found most effectual in subduing him. He was evidently influenced with the first lateral stroke of my hand across his forehead; but although I exerted all my powers, no farther perceptible effect was induced until some minutes after ten o'clock, when Doctors D___ and F___ called, according to appointment. I explained to them, in a few words, what I designed, and as they opposed no objection, saying that the patient was already in the death agony, I proceeded without hesitation—exchanging, however, the lateral passes for downward ones, and directing my gaze entirely into the right eye of the sufferer.

By this time his pulse was imperceptible and his breathing was stertorous, and at intervals of half a minute.

This condition was nearly unaltered for a quarter of an hour. At the expiration of this period, however, a natural although a very deep sigh escaped the bosom of the dying man, and the stertorous breathing ceased—that is to say, its stertorousness was no longer apparent; the intervals were undiminished. The patient's extremities were of an icy coldness.

At five minutes before eleven, I perceived unequivocal signs of the mesmeric influence. The glassy roll of the eye was changed for that expression of uneasy inward examination which is never seen except in cases of sleep-waking, and which it is quite impossible to mistake. With a few rapid lateral passes I made the lids quiver, as in incipient sleep, and with a few more I closed them altogether. I was not satisfied, however, with this, but continued the manipulations vigorously, and with the fullest exertion of the will, until I had completely stiffened the limbs of the slumberer, after placing them in a seemingly easy position. The legs were at full length; the arms were nearly so, and reposed on the bed at a moderate distance from the loins. The head was very slightly elevated.

When I had accomplished this, it was fully midnight, and I requested the gentlemen present to examine M. Valdemar's condition. After a few experiments, they admitted him to be in an unusually perfect state of mesmeric trance. The curiosity of both the physicians was greatly excited. Dr. D___ resolved at once to remain with the patient all night, while Dr. F___ took leave with a promise to return at daybreak. Mr. L___l and the nurses remained.

We left M. Valdemar entirely undisturbed until about three o'clock in the morning, when I approached him and found him in precisely the same condition as when Dr. F___ went away—that is to say, he lay in the same position; the pulse was imperceptible; the breathing was gentle (scarcely noticeable, unless through the application of a mirror to the lips;) the eyes were closed naturally; and the limbs were as rigid and as cold as marble. Still, the general appearance was certainly not that of death.

As I approached M. Valdemar I made a kind of half effort to influence his right arm into pursuit of my own, as I passed the latter gently to and fro above his person. In such experiments with this patient, I had never perfectly succeeded before, and assuredly I had little thought of succeeding now; but to my astonishment, his arm very readily, although feebly, followed every direction I assigned it with mine. I determined to hazard a few words of conversation.

"M. Valdemar," I said, "are you asleep?" He made no answer, but I perceived a tremor about the lips, and was thus induced to repeat the question, again and again. At its third repetition, his whole frame was agitated by a very slight shivering; the eyelids unclosed themselves so far as to display a white line of a ball; the lips moved sluggishly, and from between them, in a barely audible whisper, issued the words:

"Yes; asleep now. Do not wake me!—let me die so!"

I here felt the limbs and found them as rigid as ever. The right arm, as before, obeyed the direction of my hand. I questioned the sleep-waker again:

"Do you still feel pain in the breast, M. Valdemar?"

The answer now was immediate, but even less audible than before:

"No pain—I am dying."

I did not think it advisable to disturb him farther just then, and nothing more was said or done until the arrival of Dr. F___, who came a little before sunrise, and expressed unbounded astonishment at finding the patient still alive. After feeling the pulse and applying a mirror to the lips, he requested me to speak to the sleep-waker again. I did so, saying:

"M. Valdemar, do you still sleep?"

As before, some minutes elapsed ere a reply was made; and during the interval the dying man seemed to be collecting his energies to speak. At my fourth repetition of the question, he said very faintly, almost inaudibly:

"Yes; still asleep—dying."

It was now the opinion, or rather the wish, of the physicians, that M. Valdemar should be suffered to remain undisturbed in his present apparently tranquil condition, until death should supervene—and this, it was generally agreed, must now take place within a few minutes. I concluded, however, to speak to him once more, and merely repeated my previous question.

While I spoke, there came a marked change over the countenance of the sleep-waker. The eyes rolled themselves slowly open, the pupils disappearing upwardly; the skin generally assumed a cadaverous hue, resembling not so much parchment as white paper; and the circular hectic spots which, hitherto, had been strongly defined in the centre of each cheek, went out at once. I use this expression, because the suddenness of their departure put me in mind of nothing so much as the extinguishment of a candle by a puff of the breath. The upper lip, at the same time, writhed itself away from the teeth, which it had previously covered completely; while the lower jaw fell with an audible jerk, leaving the mouth widely extended, and disclosing in full view the swollen and blackened tongue. I presume that no member of the party then present had been unaccustomed to death-bed horrors; but so hideous beyond conception was the appearance of M. Valdemar at this moment, that there was a general shrinking back from the region of the bed.

I now feel that I have reached a point of this narrative at which every reader will be startled into positive disbelief. It is my business, however, simply to proceed.

There was no longer the faintest sign of vitality in M. Valdemar; and concluding him to be dead, we were consigning him to the charge of the nurses, when a strong vibratory motion was observable in the tongue. This continued for perhaps a minute. At the expiration of this period, there issued from the distended and motionless jaws a voice—such as it would be madness in me to attempt describing. There are, indeed, two or three epithets which might be considered as applicable to it in part; I might say, for example, that the sound was harsh, and broken and hollow; but the hideous whole is indescribable, for the simple reason that no similar sounds have ever jarred upon the ear of humanity. There were two particulars, nevertheless, which I thought then, and still think, might fairly be stated as characteristic of the intonation—as well adapted to convey some idea of its unearthly peculiarity. In the first place, the voice seemed to reach our ears—at least mine—from a vast distance, or from some deep cavern within the earth. In the second place, it impressed me (I fear, indeed, that it will be impossible to make myself comprehended) as gelatinous or glutinous matters impress the sense of touch.

I have spoken both of "sound" and of "voice." I mean to say that the sound was one of distinct—of even wonderfully, thrillingly distinct—syllabification. M. Valdemar spoke—obviously in reply to the question I had propounded to him a few minutes before. I had asked him, it will be remembered, if he still slept. He now said:

"Yes;—no;—I have been sleeping—and now—now—I am dead.

No person present even affected to deny, or attempted to repress, the unutterable, shuddering horror which these few words, thus uttered, were so well calculated to convey. Mr. L___l (the student) swooned. The nurses immediately left the chamber, and could not be induced to return. My own impressions I would not pretend to render intelligible to the reader. For nearly an hour, we busied ourselves, silently—without the utterance of a word—in endeavours to revive Mr. L___l. When he came to himself, we addressed ourselves again to an investigation of M. Valdemar's condition.

It remained in all respects as I have last described it, with the exception that the mirror no longer afforded evidence of respiration. An attempt to draw blood from the arm failed. I should mention, too, that this limb was no farther subject to my will. I endeavoured in vain to make it follow the direction of my hand. The only real indication, indeed, of the mesmeric influence, was now found in the vibratory movement of the tongue, whenever I addressed M. Valdemar a question. He seemed to be making an effort to reply, but had no longer sufficient volition. To queries put to him by any other person than myself he seemed utterly insensible—although I endeavoured to place each member of the company in mesmeric rapport with him. I believe that I have now related all that is necessary to an understanding of the sleep-waker's state at this epoch. Other nurses were procured; and at ten o'clock I left the house in company with the two physicians and Mr. L___l.

In the afternoon we all called again to see the patient. His condition remained precisely the same. We had now some discussion as to the propriety and feasibility of awakening him; but we had little difficulty in agreeing that no good purpose would be served by so doing. It was evident that, so far, death (or what is usually termed death) had been arrested by the mesmeric process. It seemed clear to us all that to awaken M. Valdemar would be merely to insure his instant, or at least his speedy dissolution.

From this period until the close of last week—an interval of nearly seven months—we continued to make daily calls at M. Valdemar's house, accompanied, now and then, by medical and other friends. All this time the sleeper-waker remained exactly as I have last described him. The nurses' attentions were continual.

It was on Friday last that we finally resolved to make the experiment of awakening, or attempting to awaken him; and it is the (perhaps) unfortunate result of this latter experiment which has given rise to so much discussion in private circles—to so much of what I cannot help thinking unwarranted popular feeling.

For the purpose of relieving M. Valdemar from the mesmeric trance, I made use of the customary passes. These, for a time, were unsuccessful. The first indication of revival was afforded by a partial descent of the iris. It was observed, as especially remarkable, that this lowering of the pupil was accompanied by the profuse outflowing of a yellowish ichor (from beneath the lids) of a pungent and highly offensive odour.

It was now suggested that I should attempt to influence the patient's arm, as heretofore. I made the attempt and failed. Dr. F___ then intimated a desire to have me put a question. I did so, as follows:

"M. Valdemar, can you explain to us what are your feelings or wishes now?"

There was an instant return of the hectic circles on the cheeks; the tongue quivered, or rather rolled violently in the mouth (although the jaws and lips remained rigid as before;) and at length the same hideous voice which I have already described, broke forth:

"For God's sake!—quick!—quick!—put me to sleep—or, quick!—waken me!—quick!—I say to you that I am dead!"

I was thoroughly unnerved, and for an instant remained undecided what to do. At first I made an endeavour to re-compose the patient; but, failing in this through total abeyance of the will, I retraced my steps and as earnestly struggled to awaken him. In this attempt I soon saw that I should be successful—or at least I soon fancied that my success would be complete—and I am sure that all in the room were prepared to see the patient awaken.

For what really occurred, however, it is quite impossible that any human being could have been prepared.

As I rapidly made the mesmeric passes, amid ejaculations of "dead! dead!" absolutely bursting from the tongue and not from the lips of the sufferer, his whole frame at once—within the space of a single minute, or even less, shrunk—crumbled—absolutely rotted away beneath my hands. Upon the bed, before that whole company, there lay a nearly liquid mass of loathsome—of detestable putridity.

14

The Masque of the Red Death

The 'Red Death' had long devastated the country. No pestilence had ever been so fatal, or so hideous. Blood was its Avatar and its seal—the redness and the horror of blood. There were sharp pains, and sudden dizziness, and then profuse bleeding at the pores, with dissolution. The scarlet stains upon the body and especially upon the face of the victim, were the pest ban which shut him out from the aid and from the sympathy of his fellow-men. And the whole seizure, progress and termination of the disease, were the incidents of half an hour.

But the Prince Prospero was happy and dauntless and sagacious. When his dominions were half depopulated, he summoned to his presence a thousand hale and light-hearted friends from among the knights and dames of his court, and with these retired to the deep seclusion of one of his castellated abbeys. This was an extensive and magnificent structure, the creation of the prince's own eccentric yet august taste. A strong and lofty wall girdled it in. This wall had gates of iron. The courtiers, having entered, brought furnaces and massy hammers and welded the bolts. They resolved to leave means neither of ingress nor egress to the sudden impulses of despair or of frenzy from within. The abbey was amply provisioned. With such precautions the courtiers might bid defiance to contagion. The external world could take care of itself. In the meantime it was folly to grieve, or to think. The prince had provided all the appliances of pleasure. There were buffoons, there were improvisatori, there were ballet-dancers, there were musicians, there was Beauty, there was wine. All these and security were within. Without was the 'Red Death.'

It was toward the close of the fifth or sixth month of his seclusion, and while the pestilence raged most furiously abroad, that the Prince Prospero entertained his thousand friends at a masked ball of the most unusual magnificence.

It was a voluptuous scene, that masquerade. But first let me tell of the rooms in which it was held. These were seven—an imperial suite. In many palaces, however, such suites form a long and straight vista, while the folding doors slide back nearly to the walls on either hand, so that the view of the whole extent is scarcely impeded. Here the case was very different, as might have been expected from the duke's love of the *bizarre*. The apartments were so irregularly disposed that the vision embraced but little more than one at a time. There was a sharp turn at every twenty or thirty yards, and at each turn a novel effect. To the right and left, in the middle of each wall, a tall and narrow Gothic window looked out upon a closed corridor which pursued the windings of the suite. These windows were of stained glass whose colour varied in accordance with the prevailing hue of the decorations of the chamber into which it opened. That at the eastern extremity was hung, for example in blue—and vividly blue were its windows. The second chamber was purple in its ornaments and tapestries, and here the panes were purple. The third was green throughout, and so were the casements. The fourth was furnished and lighted with orange—the fifth with white—the sixth with violet. The seventh apartment was closely shrouded in black velvet tapestries that hung all over the ceiling and down the walls, falling in heavy folds upon a carpet of the same material and hue. But in this chamber only, the colour of the windows failed to correspond with the decorations. The panes here were scarlet—a deep blood colour. Now in no one of the seven apartments was there any lamp or candelabrum, amid the profusion of golden ornaments that lay scattered to and fro or depended from the roof. There was no light of any kind emanating from lamp or candle within the suite of chambers. But in the corridors that followed the suite, there stood, opposite to each window, a heavy tripod, bearing a brazier of fire, that projected its rays through the tinted glass and so glaringly illumined the room. And thus were produced a multitude of gaudy and fantastic appearances. But in the western or black chamber the effect of the fire-light that streamed upon the dark hangings through the blood-tinted panes, was ghastly in the extreme, and produced so wild a look upon the countenances of those who entered, that there were few of the company bold enough to set foot within its precincts at all.

It was in this apartment, also, that there stood against the western wall, a gigantic clock of ebony. Its pendulum swung to and fro with a dull, heavy, monotonous clang; and when the minute-hand made the circuit of the face, and the hour was to be stricken, there came from the brazen lungs of the clock a sound which was clear and loud and deep and exceedingly musical, but of so peculiar a note and emphasis that, at each lapse of an hour, the musicians of the orchestra were constrained to pause, momentarily, in their performance, to harken to the sound; and thus the waltzers perforce ceased their evolutions; and there was a brief disconcert of the whole gay company; and, while the chimes of the clock yet rang, it was observed that the giddiest grew pale, and the more aged and sedate passed their hands over their brows as if in confused revery or meditation. But when the echoes had fully ceased, a light laughter at once pervaded the assembly; the musicians looked at each other and smiled as if at their own nervousness and folly, and made whispering vows, each to the other, that the next chiming of the clock should produce in them no similar emotion; and then, after the lapse of sixty minutes, (which embrace three thousand and six hundred seconds of the Time that flies,) there came yet another chiming of the clock, and then were the same disconcert and tremulousness and meditation as before.

But, in spite of these things, it was a gay and magnificent revel. The tastes of the duke were peculiar. He had a fine eye for colours and effects. He disregarded the *decora* of mere fashion. His plans were bold and fiery, and his conceptions glowed with barbaric lustre. There are some who would have thought him mad. His followers felt that he was not. It was necessary to hear and see and touch him to be *sure* that he was not.

He had directed, in great part, the movable embellishments of the seven chambers, upon occasion of this great *fête*; and it was his own guiding taste which had given character to the masqueraders. Be sure they were grotesque. There were much glare and glitter and piquancy and phantasm—much of what has been since seen in 'Hernani.' There were arabesque figures with unsuited limbs and appointments. There were delirious fancies such as the madman fashions. There were much of the beautiful, much of the wanton, much of the *bizarre*, something of the terrible, and not a little of that which might have excited disgust. To and fro in the seven chambers there stalked, in fact, a multitude of dreams. And these—the dreams—writhed in and about taking hue from the rooms, and causing the wild music of the orchestra to seem as the echo of their steps. And, anon, there strikes the ebony clock which stands in the hall of the velvet. And then, for a moment, all is still, and all is silent save the voice of the clock. The dreams are stiff-frozen as they stand. But the echoes of the chime die away—they have endured but an instant—and a light, half-subdued laughter floats after them as they depart. And now again the music swells, and the dreams live, and writhe to and fro more merrily than ever, taking hue from the many tinted windows through which stream the rays from the tripods. But to the chamber which lies most westwardly of the seven, there are now none of the maskers who venture; for the night is waning away; and there flows a ruddier light through the blood-coloured panes; and the blackness of the sable drapery appals; and to him whose foot falls upon the sable carpet, there comes from the near clock of ebony a muffled peal more solemnly emphatic than any which reaches *their* ears who indulged in the more remote gaieties of the other apartments.

But these other apartments were densely crowded, and in them beat feverishly the heart of life. And the revel went whirlingly on, until at length there commenced the sounding of midnight upon the clock. And then the music ceased, as I have told; and the evolutions of the waltzers were quieted; and there was an uneasy cessation of all things as before. But now there were twelve strokes to be sounded by the bell of the clock; and thus it happened, perhaps, that more of thought crept, with more of time, into the meditations of the thoughtful among those who revelled. And thus too, it happened, perhaps, that before the last echoes of the last chime had utterly sunk into silence, there were many individuals in the crowd who had found leisure to become aware of the presence of a masked figure which had arrested the attention of no single individual before. And the rumour of this new presence having spread itself whisperingly around, there arose at length from the whole company a buzz, or murmur, expressive of disapprobation and surprise—then, finally, of terror, of horror, and of disgust.

In an assembly of phantasms such as I have painted, it may well be supposed that no ordinary appearance could have excited such sensation. In truth the masquerade licence of the night was nearly unlimited; but the figure in question had out-Heroded Herod, and gone beyond the bounds of even the prince's indefinite decorum. There are chords in the hearts of the most reckless which cannot be touched without emotion. Even with the utterly lost, to whom life and death are equally jests, there are matters of which no jest can be made. The whole company, indeed, seemed now deeply to feel that in the costume and bearing of the stranger neither wit nor propriety existed. The figure was tall and gaunt, and shrouded from head to foot in the habiliments of the grave. The mask which concealed the visage was made so nearly to resemble the countenance of a stiffened corpse that the closest scrutiny must have had difficulty in detecting the cheat. And yet all this might have been endured, if not approved, by the mad revellers around. But the mummer had gone so far as to assume the type of the Red Death. His vesture was dabbled in *blood*—and his broad brow, with all the features of the face, was besprinkled with the scarlet horror.

When the eyes of the Prince Prospero fell upon this spectral image (which, with a slow and solemn movement, as if more fully to sustain its role, stalked to and fro among the waltzers) he was seen to be convulsed, in the first moment with a strong shudder either of terror or distaste; but, in the next, his brow reddened with rage.

"Who dares,"—he demanded hoarsely of the courtiers who stood near him—"who dares insult us with this blasphemous mockery? Seize him and unmask him—that we may know whom we have to hang, at sunrise, from the battlements!"

It was in the eastern or blue chamber in which stood the Prince Prospero as he uttered these words. They rang throughout the seven rooms loudly and clearly, for the prince was a bold and robust man, and the music had become hushed at the waving of his hand.

It was in the blue room where stood the prince, with a group of pale courtiers by his side. At first, as he spoke, there was a slight rushing movement of this group in the direction of the intruder, who at the moment was also near at hand, and now, with deliberate and stately step, made closer approach to the speaker. But from a certain nameless awe with which the mad assumptions of the mummer had inspired the whole party, there were found none who put forth hand to seize him; so that, unimpeded, he passed within a yard of the prince's person; and, while the vast assembly, as if with one impulse, shrank from the centres of the rooms to the walls, he made his way uninterruptedly, but with the same solemn and measured step which had distinguished him from the first, through the blue chamber to the purple—through the purple to the green—through the green to the orange—through this again to the white—and even thence to the violet, ere a decided movement had been made to arrest him. It was then, however, that the Prince Prospero, maddening with rage and the shame of his own momentary cowardice, rushed hurriedly through the six chambers, while none followed him on account of a deadly terror that had seized upon all. He bore aloft a drawn dagger, and had approached, in rapid impetuosity, to within three or four feet of the retreating figure, when the latter, having attained the extremity of the velvet apartment, turned suddenly and confronted his pursuer. There was a sharp cry—and the dagger dropped gleaming upon the sable carpet, upon which, instantly afterwards, fell prostrate in death the Prince Prospero. Then, summoning the wild courage of despair, a throng of the revellers at once threw themselves into the black apartment, and, seizing the mummer, whose tall figure stood erect and motionless within the shadow of the ebony clock, gasped in unutterable horror at finding the grave cerements and corpse-like mask, which they handled with so violent a rudeness, untenanted by any tangible form.

And now was acknowledged the presence of the Red Death. He had come like a thief in the night. And one by one dropped the revellers in the blood-bedewed halls of their revel, and died each in the despairing posture of his fall. And the life of the ebony clock went out with that of the last of the gay. And the flames of the tripods expired. And Darkness and Decay and the Red Death held illimitable dominion over all.

15

The Tell-Tale Heart

TRUE!—nervous—very, very dreadfully nervous I had been and am; but why will you say that I am mad? The disease had sharpened my senses—not destroyed—not dulled them. Above all was the sense of hearing acute. I heard all things in the heaven and in the earth. I heard many things in hell. How, then, am I mad? Hearken! and observe how healthily—how calmly I can tell you the whole story.

It is impossible to say how first the idea entered my brain; but once conceived, it haunted me day and night. Object there was none. Passion there was none. I loved the old man. He had never wronged me. He had never given me insult. For his gold I had no desire. I think it was his eye! yes, it was this! He had the eye of a vulture—a pale blue eye, with a film over it. Whenever it fell upon me, my blood ran cold; and so by degrees—very gradually—I made up my mind to take the life of the old man, and thus rid myself of the eye forever.

Now this is the point. You fancy me mad. Madmen know nothing. But you should have seen me. You should have seen how wisely I proceeded—with what caution—with what foresight—with what dissimulation I went to work! I was never kinder to the old man than during the whole week before I killed him. And every night, about midnight, I turned the latch of his door and opened it—oh so gently! And then, when I had made an opening sufficient for my head, I put in a dark lantern, all closed, closed, that no light shone out, and then I thrust in my head. Oh, you would have laughed to see how cunningly I thrust it in! I moved it slowly—very, very slowly, so that I might not disturb the old man's sleep. It took me an hour to place my whole head within the opening so far that I could see him as he lay upon his bed. Ha! would a madman have been so wise as this? And then, when my head was well in the room, I undid the lantern cautiously—oh, so cautiously—cautiously (for the hinges creaked)—I undid it just so much that a single thin ray fell upon the vulture eye. And this I did for seven long nights—every night just at midnight—but I found the eye always closed; and so it was impossible to do the work; for it was not the old man who vexed me, but his Evil Eye. And every morning, when the day broke, I went boldly into the chamber, and spoke courageously to him, calling him by name in a hearty tone, and inquiring how he has passed the night. So you see he would have been a very profound old man, indeed, to suspect that every night, just at twelve, I looked in upon him while he slept.

Upon the eighth night I was more than usually cautious in opening the door. A watch's minute hand moves more quickly than did mine. Never before that night had I felt the extent of my own powers—of my sagacity. I could scarcely contain my feelings of triumph. To think that there I was, opening the door, little by little, and he not even to dream of my secret deeds or thoughts. I fairly chuckled at the idea; and perhaps he heard me; for he moved on the bed suddenly, as if startled. Now you may think that I drew back—but no. His room was as black as pitch with the thick darkness, (for the shutters were close fastened, through fear of robbers,) and so I knew that he could not see the opening of the door, and I kept pushing it on steadily, steadily.

I had my head in, and was about to open the lantern, when my thumb slipped upon the tin fastening, and the old man sprang up in bed, crying out—"Who's there?"

I kept quite still and said nothing. For a whole hour I did not move a muscle, and in the meantime I did not hear him lie down. He was still sitting up in the bed listening;—just as I have done, night after night, hearkening to the death watches in the wall.

Presently I heard a slight groan, and I knew it was the groan of mortal terror. It was not a groan of pain or of grief—oh, no!—it was the low stifled sound that arises from the bottom of the soul when overcharged with awe. I knew the sound well. Many a night, just at midnight, when all the world slept, it has welled up from my own bosom, deepening, with its dreadful echo, the terrors that distracted me. I say I knew it well. I knew what the old man felt, and pitied him, although I chuckled at heart. I knew that he had been lying awake ever since the first slight noise, when he had turned in the bed. His fears had been ever since growing upon him. He had been trying to fancy them causeless, but could not. He had been saying to himself—"It is nothing but the wind in the chimney—it is only a mouse crossing the floor," or "It is merely a cricket which has made a single chirp." Yes, he had been trying to comfort himself with these suppositions: but he had found all in vain. All in vain; because Death, in approaching him had stalked with his black shadow before him, and enveloped the victim. And it was the mournful influence of the unperceived shadow that caused him to feel—although he neither saw nor heard—to feel the presence of my head within the room.

When I had waited a long time, very patiently, without hearing him lie down, I resolved to open a little—a very, very little crevice in the lantern. So I opened it—you cannot imagine how stealthily, stealthily—until, at length a simple dim ray, like the thread of the spider, shot from out the crevice and fell full upon the vulture eye.

It was open—wide, wide open—and I grew furious as I gazed upon it. I saw it with perfect distinctness—all a dull blue, with a hideous veil over it that chilled the very marrow in my bones; but I could see nothing else of the old man's face or person: for I had directed the ray as if by instinct, precisely upon the damned spot.

And have I not told you that what you mistake for madness

is but over-acuteness of the sense?—now, I say, there came to my ears a low, dull, quick sound, such as a watch makes when enveloped in cotton. I knew that sound well, too. It was the beating of the old man's heart. It increased my fury, as the beating of a drum stimulates the soldier into courage.

But even yet I refrained and kept still. I scarcely breathed. I held the lantern motionless. I tried how steadily I could maintain the ray upon the eve. Meantime the hellish tattoo of the heart increased. It grew quicker and quicker, and louder and louder every instant. The old man's terror must have been extreme! It grew louder, I say, louder every moment!—do you mark me well I have told you that I am nervous: so I am. And now at the dead hour of the night, amid the dreadful silence of that old house, so strange a noise as this excited me to uncontrollable terror. Yet, for some minutes longer I refrained and stood still. But the beating grew louder, louder! I thought the heart must burst. And now a new anxiety seized me—the sound would be heard by a neighbour! The old man's hour had come! With a loud yell, I threw open the lantern and leaped into the room. He shrieked once—once only. In an instant I dragged him to the floor, and pulled the heavy bed over him. I then smiled gaily, to find the deed so far done. But, for many minutes, the heart beat on with a muffled sound. This, however, did not vex me; it would not be heard through the wall. At length it ceased. The old man was dead. I removed the bed and examined the corpse. Yes, he was stone, stone dead. I placed my hand upon the heart and held it there many minutes. There was no pulsation. He was stone dead. His eye would trouble me no more.

If still you think me mad, you will think so no longer when I describe the wise precautions I took for the concealment of the body. The night waned, and I worked hastily, but in silence. First of all I dismembered the corpse. I cut off the head and the arms and the legs.

I then took up three planks from the flooring of the chamber, and deposited all between the scantlings. I then replaced the boards so cleverly, so cunningly, that no human eye—not even his—could have detected any thing wrong. There was nothing to wash out—

no stain of any kind—no blood-spot whatever. I had been too wary for that. A tub had caught all—ha! ha!

When I had made an end of these labors, it was four o'clock—still dark as midnight. As the bell sounded the hour, there came a knocking at the street door. I went down to open it with a light heart,—for what had I now to fear? There entered three men, who introduced themselves, with perfect suavity, as officers of the police. A shriek had been heard by a neighbour during the night; suspicion of foul play had been aroused; information had been lodged at the police office, and they (the officers) had been deputed to search the premises.

I smiled,—for what had I to fear? I bade the gentlemen welcome. The shriek, I said, was my own in a dream. The old man, I mentioned, was absent in the country. I took my visitors all over the house. I bade them search—search well. I led them, at length, to his chamber. I showed them his treasures, secure, undisturbed. In the enthusiasm of my confidence, I brought chairs into the room, and desired them here to rest from their fatigues, while I myself, in the wild audacity of my perfect triumph, placed my own seat upon the very spot beneath which reposed the corpse of the victim.

The officers were satisfied. My manner had convinced them. I was singularly at ease. They sat, and while I answered cheerily, they chatted of familiar things. But, ere long, I felt myself getting pale and wished them gone. My head ached, and I fancied a ringing in my ears: but still they sat and still chatted. The ringing became more distinct:—It continued and became more distinct: I talked more freely to get rid of the feeling: but it continued and gained definiteness—until, at length, I found that the noise was not within my ears.

No doubt I now grew *very* pale;—but I talked more fluently, and with a heightened voice. Yet the sound increased—and what could I do? It was a low, dull, quick sound—much such a sound as a watch makes when enveloped in cotton. I gasped for breath—and yet the officers heard it not. I talked more quickly—more vehemently; but the noise steadily increased. I arose and argued about trifles, in a high key and with violent gesticulations; but the noise steadily increased. Why would they not be gone? I paced the floor to and fro with heavy strides, as if excited to fury by the observations of the men—but the noise steadily increased. Oh God! what could I do? I foamed—I raved—I swore! I swung the chair upon which I had been sitting, and grated it upon the boards, but the noise arose over all and continually increased. It grew louder—louder—louder! And still the men chatted pleasantly, and smiled. Was it possible they heard not? Almighty God!—no, no! They heard!—they suspected!—they knew!—they were making a mockery of my horror!-this I thought, and this I think. But anything was better than this agony! Anything was more tolerable than this derision! I could bear those hypocritical smiles no longer! I felt that I must scream or die! and now—again!—hark! louder! louder! louder! louder!

"Villains!" I shrieked, "dissemble no more! I admit the deed!—tear up the planks! here, here!—It is the beating of his hideous heart!"

16
The Black Cat

For the most wild, yet most homely narrative which I am about to pen, I neither expect nor solicit belief. Mad indeed would I be to expect it, in a case where my very senses reject their own evidence. Yet, mad am I not—and very surely do I not dream. But to-morrow I die, and today I would unburthen my soul. My immediate purpose is to place before the world, plainly, succinctly, and without comment, a series of mere household events. In their consequences, these events have terrified—have tortured—have destroyed me. Yet I will not attempt to expound them. To me, they have presented little but Horror—to many they will seem less terrible than *barroques*. Hereafter, perhaps, some intellect may be found which will reduce my phantasm to the common-place—some intellect more calm, more logical, and far less excitable than my own, which will perceive, in the circumstances I detail with awe, nothing more than an ordinary succession of very natural causes and effects.

From my infancy I was noted for the docility and humanity of my disposition. My tenderness of heart was even so conspicuous as to make me the jest of my companions. I was especially fond of animals, and was indulged by my parents with a great variety of pets. With these I spent most of my time, and never was so happy as when feeding and caressing them. This peculiarity of character grew with my growth, and in my manhood, I derived from it one of my principal sources of pleasure. To those who have cherished an affection for a faithful and sagacious dog, I need hardly be at the trouble of explaining the nature or the intensity of the gratification thus derivable. There is something in the unselfish and self-sacrificing love of a brute, which goes directly to the heart of him who has had frequent occasion to test the paltry friendship and gossamer fidelity of mere *Man*.

I married early, and was happy to find in my wife a disposition not uncongenial with my own. Observing my partiality for domestic pets, she lost no opportunity of procuring those of the most agreeable kind. We had birds, gold-fish, a fine dog, rabbits, a small monkey, and *a cat*.

This latter was a remarkably large and beautiful animal, entirely black, and sagacious to an astonishing degree. In speaking of his intelligence, my wife, who at heart was not a little tinctured with superstition, made frequent allusion to the ancient popular notion, which regarded all black cats as witches in disguise. Not that she was ever *serious* upon this point—and I mention the matter at all for no better reason than that it happens, just now, to be remembered.

Pluto—this was the cat's name—was my favorite pet and playmate. I alone fed him, and he attended me wherever I went about the house. It was even with difficulty that I could prevent him from following me through the streets.

Our friendship lasted, in this manner, for several years, during which my general temperament and character—through the instrumentality of the Fiend Intemperance—had (I blush to confess it) experienced a radical alteration for the worse. I grew, day by day, more moody, more irritable, more regardless of the feelings of others. I suffered myself to use intemperate language to my wife. At length, I even offered her personal violence. My pets, of course, were made to feel the change in my disposition. I not only neglected, but ill-used them. For Pluto, however, I still retained sufficient regard to restrain me from maltreating him, as I made no scruple of maltreating the rabbits, the monkey, or even the dog, when by accident, or through affection, they came in my way. But my disease grew upon me—for what disease is like Alcohol!—and at length even Pluto, who was now becoming old, and consequently somewhat peevish—even Pluto began to experience the effects of my ill temper.

One night, returning home, much intoxicated, from one of my haunts about town, I fancied that the cat avoided my presence. I seized him; when, in his fright at my violence, he inflicted a slight wound upon my hand with his teeth. The fury of a demon instantly possessed me. I knew myself no longer. My original soul seemed, at once, to take its flight from my body and a more than fiendish malevolence, gin-nurtured, thrilled every fibre of my frame. I took from my waistcoat-pocket a pen-knife, opened it, grasped the poor beast by the throat, and deliberately cut one of its eyes from the socket! I blush, I burn, I shudder, while I pen the damnable atrocity.

When reason returned with the morning—when I had slept off the fumes of the night's debauch—I experienced a sentiment half of horror, half of remorse, for the crime of which I had been guilty; but it was, at best, a feeble and equivocal feeling, and the soul remained untouched. I again plunged into excess, and soon drowned in wine all memory of the deed.

In the meantime the cat slowly recovered. The socket of the lost eye presented, it is true, a frightful appearance, but he no longer appeared to suffer any pain. He went about the house as usual, but, as might be expected, fled in extreme terror at my approach. I had so much of my old heart left, as to be at first grieved by this evident dislike on the part of a creature which had once so loved me. But this feeling soon gave place to irritation. And then came, as if to my final and irrevocable overthrow, the spirit of PERVERSENESS. Of this spirit philosophy takes no account. Yet I am not more sure that my soul lives, than I am that perverseness is one of the primitive impulses of the human heart—one of the indivisible primary faculties, or sentiments, which give direction to the character of Man. Who has not, a hundred times, found himself committing a vile or a silly action, for no other reason than because he knows he should not? Have we not a perpetual inclination, in the teeth of our best judgment, to violate that which is *Law*, merely because we understand it to be such? This spirit of perverseness, I say, came to my final overthrow. It was this unfathomable longing of the soul *to vex itself*—to offer violence to its own nature—to do wrong for the wrong's sake only—that urged me to continue and finally to consummate the injury I had inflicted upon the unoffending brute. One morning, in cool blood, I slipped a noose about its neck and hung it to the limb of a tree;—hung it with the tears streaming from my eyes, and with the bitterest remorse at my heart;—hung it *because* I knew that it had loved me, and *because* I felt it had given me no reason of offence;—hung it *because* I knew that in so doing I was committing a sin—a deadly sin that would so jeopardize my immortal soul as to place it—if such a thing wore possible—even beyond the reach of the infinite mercy of the Most Merciful and Most Terrible God.

On the night of the day on which this cruel deed was done, I was aroused from sleep by the cry of fire. The curtains of my bed were in flames. The whole house was blazing. It was with great difficulty that my wife, a servant, and myself, made our escape from the conflagration. The destruction was complete. My entire worldly wealth was swallowed up, and I resigned myself thenceforward to despair.

I am above the weakness of seeking to establish a sequence of cause and effect, between the disaster and the atrocity. But I am detailing a chain of facts—and wish not to leave even a possible link imperfect. On the day succeeding the fire, I visited the ruins. The walls, with one exception, had fallen in. This exception was found in a compartment wall, not very thick, which stood about the middle of the house, and against which had rested the head of my bed. The plastering had here, in great measure, resisted the action of the fire—a fact which I attributed to its having been recently spread. About this wall a dense crowd were collected, and many persons seemed to be examining a particular portion of it with very minute and eager attention. The words "strange!" "singular!" and other similar expressions, excited my curiosity. I approached and saw, as if graven in *bas relief* upon the white surface, the figure of a gigantic *cat.* The impression was given with an accuracy truly marvellous. There was a rope about the animal's neck.

When I first beheld this apparition—for I could scarcely regard it as less—my wonder and my terror were extreme. But at length reflection came to my aid. The cat, I remembered, had been hung in a garden adjacent to the house. Upon the alarm of fire, this garden had been immediately filled by the crowd—by some one of whom the animal must have been cut from the tree and thrown, through an open window, into my chamber. This had probably been done with the view of arousing me from sleep. The falling of other walls had compressed the victim of my cruelty into the substance of the freshly-spread plaster; the lime of which, with the flames, and the *ammonia* from the carcass, had then accomplished the portraiture as I saw it.

Although I thus readily accounted to my reason, if not altogether to my conscience, for the startling fact just detailed, it did not the less fail to make a deep impression upon my fancy. For months I could not rid myself of the phantasm of the cat; and, during this period, there came back into my spirit a half-sentiment that seemed, but was not, remorse. I went so far as to regret the loss of the animal, and to look about me, among the vile haunts which I now habitually frequented, for another pet of the same species, and of somewhat similar appearance, with which to supply its place.

One night as I sat, half stupified, in a den of more than infamy, my attention was suddenly drawn to some black object, reposing upon the head of one of the immense hogsheads of Gin, or of Rum, which constituted the chief furniture of the apartment. I had been looking steadily at the top of this hogshead for some minutes, and what now caused me surprise was the fact that I had not sooner perceived the object thereupon. I approached it, and touched it with my hand. It was a black cat—a very large one—fully as large as Pluto, and closely resembling him in every respect but one. Pluto had not a white hair upon any portion of his body; but this cat had a large, although indefinite splotch of white, covering nearly the whole region of the breast. Upon my touching him, he immediately arose, purred loudly, rubbed against my hand, and appeared delighted with my notice. This, then, was the very creature of which I was in search. I at once offered to purchase it of the landlord; but this person made no claim to it—knew nothing of it—had never seen it before.

I continued my caresses, and, when I prepared to go home, the animal evinced a disposition to accompany me. I permitted it to do so; occasionally stooping and patting it as I proceeded. When it reached the house it domesticated itself at once, and became immediately a great favorite with my wife.

For my own part, I soon found a dislike to it arising within me. This was just the reverse of what I had anticipated; but—I know not how or why it was—its evident fondness for myself rather disgusted and annoyed. By slow degrees, these feelings of disgust and annoyance rose into the bitterness of hatred. I avoided the creature; a certain sense of shame, and the remembrance of my former deed of cruelty, preventing me from physically abusing it. I did not, for some weeks, strike, or otherwise violently ill use it; but gradually—very gradually—I came to look upon it with unutterable loathing, and to flee silently from its odious presence, as from the breath of a pestilence.

What added, no doubt, to my hatred of the beast, was the discovery, on the morning after I brought it home, that, like Pluto, it also had been deprived of one of its eyes. This circumstance, however, only endeared it to my wife, who, as I have already said, possessed, in a high degree, that humanity of feeling which had once been my distinguishing trait, and the source of many of my simplest and purest pleasures.

With my aversion to this cat, however, its partiality for myself seemed to increase. It followed my footsteps with a pertinacity which it would be difficult to make the reader comprehend. Whenever I sat, it would crouch beneath my chair, or spring upon my knees, covering me with its loathsome caresses. If I arose to walk it would get between my feet and thus nearly throw me down, or, fastening its long and sharp claws in my dress, clamber, in this manner, to my breast. At such times, although I longed to destroy it with a blow, I was yet withheld from so doing, partly by a memory of my former crime, but chiefly—let me confess it at once—by absolute dread of the beast.

This dread was not exactly a dread of physical evil—and yet I should be at a loss how otherwise to define it. I am almost ashamed to own—yes, even in this felon's cell, I am almost ashamed to own—that the terror and horror with which the animal inspired me, had been heightened by one of the merest chimaeras it would be possible to conceive. My wife had called my attention, more than once, to the character of the mark of white hair, of which I have spoken, and which constituted the sole visible difference between the strange beast and the one I had destroyed. The reader will remember that this mark, although large, had been originally very indefinite; but, by slow degrees—degrees nearly imperceptible, and which for a long time my Reason struggled to reject as fanciful—it had, at length, assumed a rigorous distinctness of outline. It was now the representation of an object that I shudder to name—and for this, above all, I loathed, and dreaded, and would have rid myself of the monster *had I dared*—it was now, I say, the image of a hideous—of a ghastly thing—of the GALLOWS!—oh, mournful and terrible engine of Horror and of Crime—of Agony and of Death!

And now was I indeed wretched beyond the wretchedness of mere Humanity. And *a brute beast*—whose fellow I had contemptuously destroyed—*a brute beast* to work out for *me*—for me a man, fashioned in the image of the High God—so much of insufferable wo! Alas! neither by day nor by night knew I the blessing of Rest any more! During the former the creature left me no moment alone; and, in the latter, I started, hourly, from dreams of unutterable fear, to find the hot breath of *the thing* upon my face, and its vast weight—an incarnate Night-Mare that I had no power to shake off—incumbent eternally upon my *heart!*

Beneath the pressure of torments such as these, the feeble remnant of the good within me succumbed. Evil thoughts became my sole intimates—the darkest and most evil of thoughts. The moodiness of my usual temper increased to hatred of all things and of all mankind; while, from the sudden, frequent, and ungovernable outbursts of a fury to which I now blindly abandoned myself, my uncomplaining wife, alas! was the most usual and the most patient of sufferers.

One day she accompanied me, upon some household errand, into the cellar of the old building which our poverty compelled us to inhabit. The cat followed me down the steep stairs, and, nearly throwing me headlong, exasperated me to madness. Uplifting an axe, and forgetting, in my wrath, the childish dread which had hitherto stayed my hand, I aimed a blow at the animal which, of course, would have proved instantly fatal had it descended as I wished. But this blow was arrested by the hand of my wife. Goaded, by the interference, into a rage more than demoniacal, I withdrew my arm from her grasp and buried the axe in her brain. She fell dead upon the spot, without a groan.

This hideous murder accomplished, I set myself forthwith, and with entire deliberation, to the task of concealing the body. I knew that I could not remove it from the house, either by day or by night, without the risk of being observed by the neighbors. Many projects entered my mind. At one period I thought of cutting the corpse into minute fragments, and destroying them by fire. At another, I resolved to dig a grave for it in the floor of the cellar. Again, I deliberated about casting it in the well in the yard—about packing it in a box, as if merchandize, with the usual arrangements, and so getting a porter to take it from the house. Finally I hit upon what I considered a far better expedient than either of these. I determined to wall it up in the cellar—as the monks of the middle ages are recorded to have walled up their victims.

For a purpose such as this the cellar was well adapted. Its walls were loosely constructed, and had lately been plastered throughout with a rough plaster, which the dampness of the atmosphere had prevented from hardening. Moreover, in one of the walls was a projection, caused by a false chimney, or fireplace, that had been filled up, and made to resemble the red of the cellar. I made no doubt that I could readily displace the bricks at this point, insert the corpse, and wall the whole up as before, so that no eye could detect any thing suspicious. And in this calculation I was not deceived. By means of a crow-bar I easily dislodged the bricks, and, having carefully deposited the body against the inner wall, I propped it in that position, while, with little trouble, I re-laid the whole structure as it originally stood. Having procured mortar, sand, and hair, with every possible precaution, I prepared a plaster which could not be distinguished from the old, and with this I very carefully went over the new brickwork. When I had finished, I felt satisfied that all was right. The wall did not present the slightest appearance of having been disturbed. The rubbish on the floor was picked up with the minutest care. I looked around triumphantly, and said to myself—"Here at least, then, my labor has not been in vain."

My next step was to look for the beast which had been the cause of so much wretchedness; for I had, at length, firmly resolved to put it to death. Had I been able to meet with it, at the moment, there could have been no doubt of its fate; but it appeared that the crafty animal had been alarmed at the violence of my previous anger, and forebore to present itself in my present mood. It is impossible to describe, or to imagine, the deep, the blissful sense of relief which the absence of the detested creature occasioned in my bosom. It did not make its appearance during the night—and thus for one night at least, since its introduction into the house, I soundly and tranquilly slept; aye, slept even with the burden of murder upon my soul!

The second and the third day passed, and still my tormentor came not. Once again I breathed as a freeman. The monster, in terror, had fled the premises forever! I should behold it no more! My happiness was supreme! The guilt of my dark deed disturbed me but little. Some few inquiries had been made, but these had been readily answered. Even a search had been instituted—but of course nothing was to be discovered. I looked upon my future felicity as secured.

Upon the fourth day of the assassination, a party of the police came, very unexpectedly, into the house, and proceeded again to make rigorous investigation of the premises. Secure, however, in the inscrutability of my place of concealment, I felt no embarrassment whatever. The officers bade me accompany them in their search. They left no nook or corner unexplored. At length, for the third or fourth time, they descended into the cellar. I quivered not in a muscle. My heart beat calmly as that of one who slumbers in innocence. I walked the cellar from end to end. I folded my arms upon my bosom, and roamed easily to and fro. The police were thoroughly satisfied and prepared to depart. The glee at my heart was too strong to be restrained. I burned to say if but one word, by way of triumph, and to render doubly sure their assurance of my guiltlessness.

"Gentlemen," I said at last, as the party ascended the steps, "I delight to have allayed your suspicions. I wish you all health, and a little more courtesy. By the bye, gentlemen, this—this is a very well constructed house." [In the rabid desire to say something easily, I scarcely knew what I uttered at all.]—"I may say an *excellently* well constructed house. These walls—are you going, gentlemen?—these walls are solidly put together;" and here, through the mere phrenzy of bravado, I rapped heavily, with a cane which I held in my hand, upon that very portion of the brick-work behind which stood the corpse of the wife of my bosom.

But may God shield and deliver me from the fangs of the Arch-Fiend! No sooner had the reverberation of my blows sunk into silence, than I was answered by a voice from within the tomb!—by a cry, at first muffled and broken, like the sobbing of a child, and then quickly swelling into one long, loud, and continuous scream, utterly anomalous and inhuman—a howl—a wailing shriek, half of horror and half of triumph, such as might have arisen only out of hell, conjointly from the throats of the dammed in their agony and of the demons that exult in the damnation.

Of my own thoughts it is folly to speak. Swooning, I staggered to the opposite wall. For one instant the party upon the stairs remained motionless, through extremity of terror and of awe. In the next, a dozen stout arms were toiling at the wall. It fell bodily. The corpse, already greatly decayed and clotted with gore, stood erect before the eyes of the spectators. Upon its head, with red extended mouth and solitary eye of fire, sat the hideous beast whose craft had seduced me into murder, and whose informing voice had consigned me to the hangman. I had walled the monster up within the tomb!

EDITH NESBIT

(1858-1924)

17

John Charrington's Wedding

No one ever thought that May Forster would marry John Charrington; but he thought differently, and things which John Charrington intended had a queer way of coming to pass. He asked her to marry him before he went up to Oxford. She laughed and refused him. He asked her again next time he came home. Again she laughed, tossed her dainty blonde head and again refused. A third time he asked her; she said it was becoming a confirmed bad habit, and laughed at him more than ever.

John was not the only man who wanted to marry her: she was the belle of our village coterie, and we were all in love with her more or less; it was a sort of fashion, like heliotrope ties or Inverness capes. Therefore we were as much annoyed as surprised when John Charrington walked into our little local Club—we held it in a loft over the saddler's, I remember—and invited us all to his wedding.

"Your wedding?"

"You don't mean it?"

"Who's the happy pair? When's it to be?"

John Charrington filled his pipe and lighted it before he replied. Then he said:

"I'm sorry to deprive you fellows of your only joke—but Miss Forster and I are to be married in September."

"You don't mean it?"

"He's got the mitten again, and it's turned his head."

"No," I said, rising, "I see it's true. Lend me a pistol someone—or a first-class fare to the other end of Nowhere. Charrington has bewitched the only pretty girl in our twenty-mile radius. Was it mesmerism, or a love-potion, Jack?"

"Neither, sir, but a gift you'll never have—perseverance—and the best luck a man ever had in this world."

There was something in his voice that silenced me, and all chaff of the other fellows failed to draw him further.

The queer thing about it was that when we congratulated Miss Forster, she blushed and smiled and dimpled, for all the world as though she were in love with him, and had been in love with him all the time. Upon my word, I think she had. Women are strange creatures.

We were all asked to the wedding. In Brixham everyone who was anybody knew everybody else who was anyone. My sisters were, I truly believe, more interested in the trousseau than the bride herself, and I was to be best man. The coming marriage was much canvassed at afternoon tea-tables, and at our little Club over the saddler's, and the question was always asked, "Does she care for him?"

I used to ask that question myself in the early days of their engagement, but after a certain evening in August I never asked it again. I was coming home from the Club through the churchyard. Our church is on a thyme-grown hill, and the turf about it is so thick and soft that one's footsteps are noiseless.

I made no sound as I vaulted the low lichened wall, and threaded my way between the tombstones. It was at the same instant that I heard John Charrington's voice, and saw her. May was sitting on a low flat gravestone, her face turned towards the full splendour of the western sun. Its expression ended, at once and for ever, any question of love for him; it was transfigured to a beauty I should not have believed possible, even to that beautiful little face.

John lay at her feet, and it was his voice that broke the stillness of the golden August evening.

"My dear, my dear, I believe I should come back from the dead if you wanted me!"

I coughed at once to indicate my presence, and passed on into the shadow fully enlightened.

The wedding was to be early in September. Two days before I had to run up to town on business. The train was late, of course, for we are on the South-Eastern, and as I stood grumbling with my watch in my hand, whom should I see but John Charrington and May Forster. They were walking up and down the unfrequented end of the platform, arm in arm, looking into each other's eyes, careless of the sympathetic interest of the porters.

Of course I knew better than to hesitate a moment before burying myself in the booking—office, and it was not till the train drew up at the platform, that I obtrusively passed the pair with my Gladstone, and took the corner in a first-class smoking-carriage. I did this with as good an air of not seeing them as I could assume. I pride myself on my discretion, but if John were travelling alone I wanted his company. I had it.

"Hullo, old man," came his cheery voice as he swung his bag into my carriage; "here's luck; I was expecting a dull journey!"

"Where are you off to?" I asked, discretion still bidding me turn my eyes away, though I saw, without looking, that hers were red-rimmed.

"To old Branbridge's," he answered, shutting the door and leaning out for a last word with his sweetheart.

"Oh, I wish you wouldn't go, John," she was saying in a low, earnest voice. "I feel certain something will happen."

"Do you think I should let anything happen to keep me, and the day after tomorrow our wedding day?"

"Don't go," she answered, with a pleading intensity which would have sent my Gladstone onto the platform and me after it. But she wasn't speaking to me. John Charrington was made differently: he rarely changed his opinions, never his resolutions.

He only stroked the little ungloved hands that lay on the carriage door.

"I must, May. The old boy's been awfully good to me, and now he's dying I must go and see him, but I shall come home in time for—" the rest of the parting was lost in a whisper and in the rattling lurch of the starting train.

"You're sure to come?" she spoke as the train moved.

"Nothing shall keep me," he answered; and we steamed out. After he had seen the last of the little figure on the platform he leaned back in his corner and kept silence for a minute.

When he spoke it was to explain to me that his godfather, whose heir he was, lay dying at Peasmarsh Place, some fifty miles away, and had sent for John, and John had felt bound to go.

"I shall be surely back tomorrow," he said, "or, if not, the day after, in heaps of time. Thank heaven, one hasn't to get up in the middle of the night to get married nowadays!"

"And suppose Mr. Branbridge dies?"

"Alive or dead I mean to be married on Thursday!" John answered, lighting a cigar and unfolding *The Times.*

At Peasmarsh station we said 'goodbye', and he got out, and I saw him ride off; I went on to London, where I stayed the night.

When I got home the next afternoon, a very wet one, by the way, my sister greeted me with:

"Where's Mr. Charrington?"

"Goodness knows," I answered testily. Every man, since Cain, has resented that kind of question.

"I thought you might have heard from him," she went on, "as you're to give him away tomorrow."

"Isn't he back?" I asked, for I had confidently expected to find him at home.

"No, Geoffrey," my sister Fanny always had a way of jumping to conclusions, especially such conclusions as were least favourable to her fellow-creatures—"he has not returned, and, what is more, you may depend upon it he won't. You mark my words, there'll be no wedding tomorrow."

My sister Fanny has a power of annoying me which no other human being possesses.

"You mark my words," I retorted with asperity, "you had better give up making such a thundering idiot of yourself. There'll be more wedding tomorrow than ever you'll take the first part in." A prophecy which, by the way, came true.

But though I could snarl confidently to my sister, I did not feel so comfortable when late that night, I, standing on the doorstep of John's house, heard that he had not returned. I went home gloomily through the rain. Next morning brought a brilliant blue sky, gold sun, and all such softness of air and beauty of cloud as go to make up a perfect day. I woke with a vague feeling of having gone to bed anxious, and of being rather averse to facing that anxiety in the light of full wakefulness.

But with my shaving-water came a note from John which relieved my mind and sent me up to the Forsters with a light heart.

May was in the garden. I saw her blue gown through the hollyhocks as the lodge gates swung to behind me. So I did not go up to the house, but turned aside down the turfed path.

"He's written to you too," she said, without preliminary greeting, when I reached her side.

"Yes, I'm to meet him at the station at three, and come straight on to the church."

Her face looked pale, but there was a brightness in her eyes, and a tender quiver about the mouth that spoke of renewed happiness.

"Mr. Branbridge begged him so to stay another night that he had not the heart to refuse," she went on. "He is so kind, but I wish he hadn't stayed."

I was at the station at half past two. I felt rather annoyed with John. It seemed a sort of slight to the beautiful girl who loved him, that he should come as it were out of breath, and with the dust of travel upon him, to take her hand, which some of us would have given the best years of our lives to take.

But when the three o'clock train glided in, and glided out again having brought no passengers to our little station, I was more than annoyed. There was no other train for thirty-five minutes; I calculated that, with much hurry, we might just get to the church in time for the ceremony; but, oh, what a fool to miss that first train! What other man could have done it?

That thirty-five minutes seemed a year, as I wandered round the station reading the advertisements and the timetables, and the company's bye-laws, and getting more and more angry with John Charrington. This confidence in his own power of getting everything he wanted the minute he wanted it was leading him too far. I hate waiting. Everyone does, but I believe I hate it more than anyone else. The three thirty-five was late, of course.

"Drive to the church!" I said, as someone shut the door. "Mr. Charrington hasn't come by this train."

I ground my pipe between my teeth and stamped with impatience as I watched the signals. Click. The signal went down. Five minutes later I flung myself into the carriage that I had brought for John.

Anxiety now replaced anger. What had become of the man? Could he have been taken suddenly ill? I had never known him have a day's illness in his life. And even so he might have telegraphed. Some awful accident must have happened to him. The thought that he had played her false never—no, not for a moment—entered my head. Yes, some thing terrible had happened to him, and on me lay the task of telling his bride. I almost wished the carriage would upset and break my head so that someone else might tell her, not I, who—but that's nothing to do with this story.

It was five minutes to four as we drew up at the churchyard gate. A double row of eager onlookers lined the path from lychgate to porch. I sprang from the carriage and passed up between them. Our gardener had a good front place near the door. I stopped.

"Are they waiting still, Byles?" I asked, simply to gain time, for of course I knew they were by the waiting crowd's attentive attitude.

"Waiting, sir? No, no, sir; why, it must be over by now."

"Over! Then Mr. Charrington's come?"

"To the minute, sir; must have missed you somehow, and I say, sir," lowering his voice, "I never see Mr. John the least bit so afore, but my opinion is he's been drinking pretty free. His clothes was all dusty and his face like a sheet. I tell you I didn't like the looks of him at all, and the folks inside are saying all sorts of things. You'll see, something's gone very wrong with Mr. John, and he's tried liquor. He looked like a ghost, and in he went with his eyes straight before him, with never a look or a word for none of us: him that was always such a gentleman!"

I had never heard Byles make so long a speech. The crowd in the churchyard were talking in whispers and getting ready rice and slippers to throw at the bride and bridegroom. The ringers were ready with their hands on the ropes to ring out the merry peal as the bride and bridegroom should come out.

A murmur from the church announced them; out they came. Byles was right. John Charrington did not look himself. There was dust on his coat, his hair was disarranged. He seemed to have been in some row, for there was a black mark above his eyebrow. He was deathly pale. But his pallor was not greater than that of the bride, who might have been carved in ivory—dress, veil, orange blossoms, face and all.

As they passed out the ringers stooped—there were six of them—and then, on the ears expecting the gay wedding peal, came the slow tolling of the passing bell.

A thrill of horror at so foolish a jest from the ringers passed through us all. But the ringers themselves dropped the ropes and fled like rabbits out into the sunlight. The bride shuddered, and grey shadows came about her mouth, but the bridegroom led her on down the path where the people stood with the handfuls of rice; but the handfuls were never thrown, and the wedding bells never rang. In vain the ringers were urged to remedy their mistake: they protested with many whispered expletives that they would see themselves further first.

In a hush like the hush in the chamber of death the bridal pair passed into their carriage and its door slammed behind them.

Then the tongues were loosed. A babel of anger, wonder, conjecture from the guests and the spectators.

"If I'd seen his condition, sir," said old Forster to me as we drove off, "I would have stretched him on the floor of the church, sir, by heaven I would, before I'd have let him marry my daughter!"

Then he put his head out of the window.

"Drive like hell," he cried to the coachman; "don't spare the horses."

He was obeyed. We passed the bride's carriage. I forbore to look at it, and old Forster turned his head away and swore. We reached home before it.

We stood in the doorway, in the blazing afternoon sun, and in about half a minute we heard wheels crunching the gravel. When the carriage stopped in front of the steps old Forster and I ran down.

"Great heaven, the carriage is empty! And yet—"

I had the door open in a minute, and this is what I saw . . .

No sign of John Charrington; and of May, his wife, only a huddled heap of white satin lying half on the floor of the carriage and half on the seat.

"I drove straight here, sir," said the coachman, as the bride's father lifted her out; "and I'll swear no one got out of the carriage."

We carried her into the house in her bridal dress and drew back her veil. I saw her face. Shall I ever forget it? White, white and drawn with agony and horror, bearing such a look of terror as I have never seen since except in dreams. And her hair, her radiant blonde hair, I tell you it was white like snow.

As we stood, her father and I, half mad with the horror and mystery of it, a boy came up the avenue—a telegraph boy. They brought the orange envelope to me. I tore it open.

Mr. Charrington was thrown from the dogcart on his way to the station at half past one. Killed on the spot!

And he was married to May Forster in our parish church at half past three, in presence of half the parish.

"I shall be married, dead, or alive!"

What had passed in that carriage on the homeward drive? No one knows—no one will ever know. Oh, May! Oh, my dear!

Before a week was over they laid her beside her husband in our little churchyard on the thyme-covered hill—the churchyard where they had kept their love-trysts.

Thus was accomplished John Charrington's wedding.

GERTRUDE ATHERTON

(1857-1948)

18

Death and the Woman

Her husband was dying, and she was alone with him. Nothing could exceed the desolation of her surroundings. She and the man who was going from her were in the third-floor-back of a New York boarding-house. It was summer, and the other boarders were in the country; all the servants except the cook had been dismissed, and she, when not working, slept profoundly on the fifth floor. The landlady also was out of town on a brief holiday.

The window was open to admit the thick unstirring air; no sound rose from the row of long narrow yards, nor from the tall deep houses annexed. The latter deadened the rattle of the streets. At intervals the distant elevated lumbered protestingly along, its grunts and screams muffled by the hot suspended ocean.

She sat there plunged in the profoundest grief that can come to the human soul, for in all other agony hope flickers, however forlornly. She gazed dully at the unconscious breathing form of the man who had been friend, and companion, and lover, during five years of youth too vigorous and hopeful to be warped by uneven fortune. It was wasted by disease; the face was shrunken;

the night-garment hung loosely about a body which had never been disfigured by flesh, but had been muscular with exercise and full-blooded with health. She was glad that the body was changed; glad that its beauty, too, had gone some other-where than into the coffin. She had loved his hands as apart from himself; loved their strong warm magnetism. They lay limp and yellow on the quilt: she knew that they were already cold, and that moisture was gathering on them. For a moment something convulsed within her. They had gone too. She repeated the words twice, and, after them, 'forever.' And the while the sweetness of their pressure came back to her.

She leaned suddenly over him. He was in there still, somewhere. Where? If he had not ceased to breathe, the Ego, the Soul, the Personality was still in the sodden clay which had shaped to give it speech. Why could it not manifest itself to her? Was it still conscious in there, unable to project itself through the disintegrating matter which was the only medium its Creator had vouchsafed it? Did it struggle there, seeing her agony, sharing it, longing for the complete disintegration which should put an end to its torment? She called his name, she even shook him slightly, mad to tear the body apart and find her mate, yet even in that tortured moment realizing that violence would hasten his going.

The dying man took no notice of her, and she opened his gown and put her cheek to his heart, calling him again. There had never been more perfect union; how could the bond still be so strong if he were not at the other end of it? He was there, her other part; until dead he must be living. There was no intermediate state. Why should he be as entombed and unresponding as if the screws were in the lid? But the faintly beating heart did not quicken beneath her lips. She extended her arms suddenly, describing eccentric lines, above, about him, rapidly opening and closing her hands as if to clutch some escaping object; then sprang to her feet, and went to the window. She feared insanity. She had asked to be left alone with her dying husband, and she did not wish to lose her reason and shriek a crowd of people about her.

The green plots in the yards were not apparent, she noticed.

Something heavy, like a pall, rested upon them. Then she understood that the day was over and that night was coming.

She returned swiftly to the bedside, wondering if she had remained away hours or seconds, and if he were dead. His face was still discernible, and Death had not relaxed it. She laid her own against it, then withdrew it with shuddering flesh, her teeth smiting each other as if an icy wind had passed.

She let herself fall back in the chair, clasping her hands against her heart, watching with expanding eyes the white sculptured face which, in the glittering dark, was becoming less defined of outline. Did she light the gas it would draw mosquitoes, and she could not shut from him the little air he must be mechanically grateful for. And she did not want to see the opening eye—the falling jaw.

Her vision became so fixed that at length she saw nothing, and closed her eyes and waited for the moisture to rise and relieve the strain. When she opened them his face had disappeared; the humid waves above the house-tops put out even the light of the stars, and night was come.

Fearfully, she approached her ear to his lips; he still breathed. She made a motion to kiss him, then threw herself back in a quiver of agony—they were not the lips she had known, and she would have nothing less.

His breathing was so faint that in her half-reclining position she could not hear it, could not be aware of the moment of his death. She extended her arm resolutely and laid her hand on his heart. Not only must she feel his going, but, so strong had been the comradeship between them, it was a matter of loving honor to stand by him to the last.

She sat there in the hot heavy night, pressing her hand hard against the ebbing heart of the unseen, and awaited Death. Suddenly an odd fancy possessed her. Where was Death? Why was he tarrying? Who was detaining him? From what quarter would he come? He was taking his leisure, drawing near with footsteps as measured as those of men keeping time to a funeral march. By a wayward deflection she thought of the slow music that was always turned on in the theatre when the heroine was about to appear, or something eventful to happen. She had always thought that sort of thing ridiculous and inartistic. So had He.

She drew her brows together angrily, wondering at her levity, and pressed her relaxed palm against the heart it kept guard over. For a moment the sweat stood on her face; then the pent-up breath burst from her lungs. He still lived.

Once more the fancy wantoned above the stunned heart. Death—where was he? What a curious experience: to be sitting alone in a big house—she knew that the cook had stolen out—waiting for Death to come and snatch her husband from her. No; he would not snatch, he would steal upon his prey as noiselessly as the approach of Sin to Innocence—an invisible, unfair, sneaking enemy, with whom no man's strength could grapple. If he would only come like a man, and take his chances like a man! Women had been known to reach the hearts of giants with the dagger's point. But he would creep upon her.

She gave an exclamation of horror. Something was creeping over the window-sill. Her limbs palsied, but she struggled to her feet and looked back, her eyes dragged about against her own volition. Two small green stars glared menacingly at her just above the sill; then the cat possessing them leaped downward, and the stars disappeared.

She realized that she was horribly frightened. "Is it possible?" she thought. "Am I afraid of Death, and of Death that has not yet come? I have always been rather a brave woman; He used to call me heroic; but then with him it was impossible to fear anything. And I begged them to leave me alone with him as the last of earthly boons. Oh, shame!"

But she was still quaking as she resumed her seat, and laid her hand again on his heart. She wished that she had asked Mary to sit outside the door; there was no bell in the room. To call would be worse than desecrating the house of God, and she would not leave him for one moment. To return and find him dead—gone alone!

Her knees smote each other. It was idle to deny it; she was in a state of unreasoning terror. Her eyes rolled apprehensively about; she wondered if she should see It when It came; wondered how far off It was now. Not very far; the heart was barely pulsing. She had heard of the power of the corpse to drive brave men to frenzy, and had wondered, having no morbid horror of the dead. But this! To wait—and wait—and wait—perhaps for hours—past the midnight—on to the small hours—while that awful, determined, leisurely Something stole nearer and nearer.

She bent to him who had been her protector with a spasm of anger. Where was the indomitable spirit that had held her all these years with such strong and loving clasp? How could he leave her? How could he desert her? Her head fell back and moved restlessly against the cushion; moaning with the agony of loss, she recalled him as he had been. Then fear once more took possession of her, and she sat erect, rigid, breathless, awaiting the approach of Death.

Suddenly, far down in the house, on the first floor, her strained hearing took note of a sound—a wary, muffled sound, as if some one were creeping up the stair, fearful of being heard. Slowly! It seemed to count a hundred between the laying down of each foot. She gave a hysterical gasp. Where was the slow music?

Her face, her body, were wet—as if a wave of death—sweat had broken over them. There was a stiff feeling at the roots of her hair; she wondered if it were really standing erect. But she could not raise her hand to ascertain. Possibly it was only the colouring matter freezing and bleaching. Her muscles were flabby, her nerves twitched helplessly.

She knew that it was Death who was coming to her through the silent deserted house; knew that it was the sensitive ear of her intelligence that heard him, not the dull, coarse-grained ear of the body.

He toiled up the stair painfully, as if he were old and tired with much. work. But how could he afford to loiter, with all the work he had to do? Every minute, every second, he must be in demand to hook his cold, hard finger about a soul struggling to escape from its putrefying tenement. But probably he had his emissaries, his minions: for only those worthy of the honour did he come in person.

He reached the first landing and crept like a cat down the hall to the next stair, then crawled slowly up as before. Light as the footfalls were, they were squarely planted, unfaltering; slow, they never halted.

Mechanically she pressed her jerking hand closer against the heart; its beats were almost done. They would finish, she calculated, just as those footfalls paused beside the bed.

She was no longer a human being; she was an Intelligence and an EAR. Not a sound came from without, even the Elevated appeared to be temporarily off duty; but inside the big quiet house that footfall was waxing louder, louder, until iron feet crashed on iron stairs and echo thundered.

She had counted the steps—one—two—three—irritated beyond endurance at the long deliberate pauses between. As they climbed and clanged with slow precision she continued to count, audibly and with equal precision, noting their hollow reverberation. How many steps had the stair? She wished she knew. No need! The colossal trampling announced the lessening distance in an increasing volume of sound not to be misunderstood. It turned the curve; it reached the landing; it advanced—slowly—down the hall; it paused before her door. Then knuckles of iron shook the frail panels. Her nerveless tongue gave no invitation. The knocking became more imperious; the very walls vibrated. The handle turned, swiftly and firmly. With a wild instinctive movement she flung herself into the arms of her husband.

When Mary opened the door and entered the room she found a dead woman lying across a dead man.

H G WELLS

(1866-1946)

19

The Red Room

"I can assure you," said I, "that it will take a very tangible ghost to frighten me." And I stood up before the fire with my glass in my hand.

"It is your own choosing," said the man with the withered arm, and glanced at me askance.

"Eight-and-twenty years," said I, "I have lived, and never a ghost have I seen as yet."

The old woman sat staring hard into the fire, her pale eyes wide open. "Ay," she broke in; "and eight-and-twenty years you have lived and never seen the likes of this house, I reckon. There's a many things to see, when one's still but eight-and-twenty." She swayed her head slowly from side to side. "A many things to see and sorrow for."

I half suspected the old people were trying to enhance the spiritual terrors of their house by their droning insistence. I put down my empty glass on the table and looked about the room, and caught a glimpse of myself, abbreviated and broadened to an impossible sturdiness, in the queer old mirror at the end of the room. "Well," I said, "if I see anything tonight, I shall be so much the wiser. For I come to the business with an open mind."

"It's your own choosing," said the man with the withered arm once more.

I heard the faint sound of a stick and a shambling step on the flags in the passage outside. The door creaked on its hinges as a second old man entered, more bent, more wrinkled, more aged even than the first. He supported himself by the help of a crutch, his eyes were covered by a shade, and his lower lip, half averted, hung pale and pink from his decaying yellow teeth. He made straight for an armchair on the opposite side of the table, sat down clumsily, and began to cough. The man with the withered hand gave the newcomer a short glance of positive dislike; the old woman took no notice of his arrival, but remained with her eyes fixed steadily on the fire.

"I said—it's your own choosing," said the man with the withered hand, when the coughing had ceased for a while.

"It's my own choosing," I answered.

The man with the shade became aware of my presence for the first time, and threw his head back for a moment, and sidewise, to see me. I caught a momentary glimpse of his eyes, small and bright and inflamed. Then he began to cough and splutter again.

"Why don't you drink?" said the man with the withered arm, pushing the beer toward him. The man with the shade poured out a glassful with a shaking hand, that splashed half as much again on the deal table. A monstrous shadow of him crouched upon the wall, and mocked his action as he poured and drank. I must confess I had scarcely expected these grotesque custodians. There is, to my mind, something inhuman in senility, something crouching and atavistic; the human qualities seem to drop from old people insensibly day by day. The three of them made me feel uncomfortable with their gaunt silences, their bent carriage, their evident unfriendliness to me and to one another. And that night, perhaps, I was in the mood for uncomfortable impressions. I resolved to get away from their vague fore-shadowings of the evil things upstairs.

"If," said I, "you will show me to this haunted room of yours, I will make myself comfortable there."

The old man with the cough jerked his head back so suddenly

that it startled me, and shot another glance of his red eyes at me from out of the darkness under the shade, but no one answered me. I waited a minute, glancing from one to the other. The old woman stared like a dead body, glaring into the fire with lack-lustre eyes.

"If," I said, a little louder, "if you will show me to this haunted room of yours, I will relieve you from the task of entertaining me."

"There's a candle on the slab outside the door," said the man with the withered hand, looking at my feet as he addressed me. "But if you go to the Red Room tonight—"

"This night of all nights!" said the old woman, softly.

"—You go alone."

"Very well," I answered, shortly, "and which way do I go?"

"You go along the passage for a bit," said he, nodding his head on his shoulder at the door, "until you come to a spiral staircase; and on the second landing is a door covered with green baize. Go through that, and down the long corridor to the end, and the Red Room is on your left up the steps."

"Have I got that right?" I said, and repeated his directions.

He corrected me in one particular.

"And you are really going?" said the man with the shade, looking at me again for the third time with that queer, unnatural tilting of the face.

"This night of all nights!" whispered the old woman.

"It is what I came for," I said, and moved toward the door. As I did so, the old man with the shade rose and staggered round the table, so as to be closer to the others and to the fire. At the door I turned and looked at them, and saw they were all close together, dark against the firelight, staring at me over their shoulders, with an intent expression on their ancient faces.

"Good night," I said, setting the door open. "It's your own choosing," said the man with the withered arm.

I left the door wide open until the candle was well alight, and then I shut them in, and walked down the chilly, echoing passage.

I must confess that the oddness of these three old pensioners in whose charge her ladyship had left the castle, and the deep-toned, old-fashioned furniture of the housekeeper's room, in which they foregathered, had affected me curiously in spite of my effort to keep myself at a matter-of-fact phase. They seemed to belong to another age, an older age, an age when things spiritual were indeed to be feared, when common sense was uncommon, an age when omens and witches were credible, and ghosts beyond denying. Their very existence, thought I, is spectral; the cut of their clothing, fashions born in dead brains; the ornaments and conveniences in the room about them even are ghostly—the thoughts of vanished men, which still haunt rather than participate in the world of today. And the passage I was in, long and shadowy, with a film of moisture glistening on the wall, was as gaunt and cold as a thing that is dead and rigid. But with an effort I sent such thoughts to the right-about. The long, drafty subterranean passage was chilly and dusty, and my candle flared and made the shadows cower and quiver. The echoes rang up and down the spiral staircase, and a shadow came sweeping up after me, and another fled before me into the darkness overhead. I came to the wide landing and stopped there for a moment listening to a rustling that I fancied I heard creeping behind me, and then, satisfied of the absolute silence, pushed open the unwilling baize-covered door and stood in the silent corridor.

The effect was scarcely what I expected, for the moonlight, coming in by the great window on the grand staircase, picked out everything in vivid black shadow or reticulated silvery illumination. Everything seemed in its proper position; the house might have been deserted on the yesterday instead of twelve months ago. There were candles in the sockets of the sconces, and whatever dust had gathered on the carpets or upon the polished flooring was distributed so evenly as to be invisible in my candlelight. A waiting stillness was over everything. I was about to advance, and stopped abruptly. A bronze group stood upon the landing hidden from me by a corner of the wall; but its shadow fell with marvelous distinctness upon the white paneling, and gave me the impression of some one crouching to waylay me. The thing jumped upon my attention suddenly. I stood rigid for half a moment, perhaps. Then, with my hand in the pocket that held the revolver, I advanced, only to discover a Ganymede and Eagle, glistening in the moonlight. That incident for a time restored my nerve, and a dim porcelain Chinaman on a buhl table, whose head rocked as I passed, scarcely startled me.

The door of the Red Room and the steps up to it were in a shadowy corner. I moved my candle from side to side in order to see clearly the nature of the recess in which I stood, before opening the door. Here it was, thought I, that my predecessor was found, and the memory of that story gave me a sudden twinge of apprehension. I glanced over my shoulder at the black Ganymede in the moonlight, and opened the door of the Red Room rather hastily, with my face half turned to the pallid silence of the corridor.

I entered, closed the door behind me at once, turned the key I found in the lock within, and stood with the candle held aloft surveying the scene of my vigil, the great Red Room of Lorraine Castle, in which the young Duke had died; or rather in which he had begun his dying, for he had opened the door and fallen headlong down the steps I had just ascended. That had been the end of his vigil, of his gallant attempt to conquer the ghostly tradition of the place, and never, I thought, had apoplexy better served the ends of superstition. There were other and older stories that clung to the room, back to the half-incredible beginning of it all, the tale of a timid wife and the tragic end that came to her husband's jest of frightening her. And looking round that huge shadowy room with its black window bays, its recesses and alcoves, its dusty brown-red hangings and dark gigantic furniture, one could well understand the legends that had sprouted in its black corners, its germinating darknesses. My candle was a little tongue of light in the vastness of the chamber; its rays failed to pierce to the opposite end of the room, and left an ocean of dull red mystery and suggestion, sentinel shadows and watching darknesses beyond its island of light. And the stillness of desolation brooded over it all.

I must confess some impalpable quality of that ancient room disturbed me. I tried to fight the feeling down. I resolved to make a systematic examination of the place, and so, by leaving nothing to the imagination, dispel the fanciful suggestions of the obscurity before they obtained a hold upon me. After satisfying myself of the fastening of the door, I began to walk round the room, peering round each article of furniture, tucking up the valances of the bed and opening its curtains wide. In one place there was a distinct echo to my footsteps, the noises I made seemed so little that they enhanced rather than broke the silence of the place. I pulled up the blinds and examined the fastenings of the several windows. Attracted by the fall of a particle of dust, I leaned forward and looked up the blackness of the wide chimney. Then, trying to preserve my scientific attitude of mind, I walked round and began tapping the oak paneling for any secret opening, but I desisted before reaching the alcove. I saw my face in a mirror—white.

There were two big mirrors in the room, each with a pair of sconces bearing candles, and on the mantelshelf, too, were candles in china candlesticks. All these I lit one after the other. The fire was laid—an unexpected consideration from the old housekeeper—and I lit it, to keep down any disposition to shiver, and when it was burning well I stood round with my back to it and regarded the room again. I had pulled up a chintz-covered armchair and a table to form a kind of barricade before me. On this lay my revolver, ready to hand. My precise examination had done me a little good, but I still found the remoter darkness of the place and its perfect stillness too stimulating for the imagination. The echoing of the stir and crackling of the fire was no sort of comfort to me. The shadow in the alcove at the end of the room began to display that undefinable quality of a presence, that odd suggestion of a lurking living thing that comes so easily in silence and solitude. And to reassure myself, I walked with a candle into it and satisfied myself that there was nothing tangible there. I stood that candle upon the floor of the alcove and left it in that position.

By this time I was in a state of considerable nervous tension, although to my reason there was no adequate cause for my condition. My mind, however, was perfectly clear. I postulated quite unreservedly that nothing supernatural could happen, and to pass the time I began stringing some rhymes together, Ingoldsby fashion, concerning the original legend of the place. A few I spoke aloud, but the echoes were not pleasant. For the same reason I also abandoned, after a time, a conversation with myself upon the impossibility of ghosts and haunting. My mind reverted to the three old and distorted people downstairs, and I tried to keep it upon that topic.

The sombre reds and grays of the room troubled me; even with its seven candles the place was merely dim. The light in the alcove flaring in a draft, and the fire flickering, kept the shadows and penumbra perpetually shifting and stirring in a noiseless flighty dance. Casting about for a remedy, I recalled the wax candles I had seen in the corridor, and, with a slight effort, carrying a candle and leaving the door open, I walked out into the moonlight, and presently returned with as many as ten. These I put in the various knick-knacks of china with which the room was sparsely adorned, and lit and placed them where the shadows had lain deepest, some on the floor, some in the window recesses, arranging and rearranging them until at last my seventeen candles were so placed that not an inch of the room but had the direct light of at least one of them. It occurred to me that when the ghost came I could warn him not to trip over them. The room was now quite brightly illuminated. There was something very cheering and reassuring in these little silent streaming flames, and to notice their steady diminution of length offered me an occupation and gave me a reassuring sense of the passage of time.

Even with that, however, the brooding expectation of the vigil weighed heavily enough upon me. I stood watching the minute hand of my watch creep towards midnight.

Then something happened in the alcove. I did not see the candle go out, I simply turned and saw that the darkness was there, as one might start and see the unexpected presence of a stranger. The black shadow had sprung back to its place. "By Jove," said I aloud, recovering from my surprise, "that draft's a strong one;" and taking the matchbox from the table, I walked across the room in a leisurely manner to relight the corner again. My first match would not strike, and as I succeeded with the second, something seemed to blink on the wall before me. I turned my head involuntarily and saw that the two candles on the little table by the fireplace were extinguished. I rose at once to my feet.

"Odd," I said. "Did I do that myself in a flash of absent-mindedness?"

I walked back, relit one, and as I did so I saw the candle in the right sconce of one of the mirrors wink and go right out, and almost immediately its companion followed it. The flames vanished as if the wick had been suddenly nipped between a finger and thumb, leaving the wick neither glowing nor smoking, but black. While I stood gaping the candle at the foot of the bed went out, and the shadows seemed to take another step toward me.

"This won't do!" said I, and first one and then another candle on the mantelshelf followed.

"What's up?" I cried, with a queer high note getting into my voice somehow. At that the candle on the corner of the wardrobe went out, and the one I had relit in the alcove followed.

"Steady on!" I said, "Those candles are wanted," speaking with a half-hysterical facetiousness, and scratching away at a match the while, "for the mantel candlesticks." My hands trembled so much that twice I missed the rough paper of the matchbox. As the mantel emerged from darkness again, two candles in the remoter end of the room were eclipsed. But with the same match I also relit the larger mirror candles, and those on the floor near the doorway, so that for the moment I seemed to gain on the extinctions. But then in a noiseless volley there vanished four lights at once in different corners of the room, and I struck another match in quivering haste, and stood hesitating whither to take it.

As I stood undecided, an invisible hand seemed to sweep out the two candles on the table. With a cry of terror I dashed at the alcove, then into the corner and then into the window, relighting three as two more vanished by the fireplace, and then, perceiving a better way, I dropped matches on the iron-bound deedbox in the corner, and caught up the bedroom candlestick. With this I avoided the delay of striking matches, but for all that the steady process of extinction went on, and the shadows I feared and fought against returned, and crept in upon me, first a step gained on this side of me, then on that. I was now almost frantic with the horror of the coming darkness, and my self-possession deserted me. I leaped panting from candle to candle in a vain struggle against that remorseless advance.

I bruised myself in the thigh against the table, I sent a chair headlong, I stumbled and fell and whisked the cloth from the table in my fall. My candle rolled away from me and I snatched another as I rose. Abruptly this was blown out as I swung it off the table by the wind of my sudden movement, and immediately the two remaining candles followed. But there was light still in the room, a red light, that streamed across the ceiling and staved off the shadows from me. The fire! Of course I could still thrust my candle between the bars and relight it.

I turned to where the flames were still dancing between the glowing coals and splashing red reflections upon the furniture; made two steps toward the grate, and incontinently the flames dwindled and vanished, the glow vanished, the reflections rushed together and disappeared, and as I thrust the candle between the bars darkness closed upon me like the shutting of an eye, wrapped about me in a stifling embrace, sealed my vision, and crushed the last vestiges of self-possession from my brain. And it was not only palpable darkness, but intolerable terror. The candle fell from my hands. I flung out my arms in a vain effort to thrust that ponderous blackness away from me, and lifting up my voice, screamed with all my might, once, twice, thrice. Then I think I must have staggered to my feet. I know I thought suddenly of the moonlit corridor, and with my head bowed and my arms over my face, made a stumbling run for the door.

But I had forgotten the exact position of the door, and I struck myself heavily against the corner of the bed. I staggered back, turned, and was either struck or struck myself against some other bulky furnishing. I have a vague memory of battering myself thus to and fro in the darkness, of a heavy blow at last upon my forehead, of a horrible sensation of falling that lasted an age, of my last frantic effort to keep my footing, and then I remember no more.

I opened my eyes in daylight. My head was roughly bandaged,

and the man with the withered hand was watching my face. I looked about me trying to remember what had happened, and for a space I could not recollect. I rolled my eyes into the corner and saw the old woman, no longer abstracted, no longer terrible, pouring out some drops of medicine from a little blue phial into a glass. "Where am I?" I said. "I seem to remember you, and yet I can not remember who you are."

They told me then, and I heard of the haunted Red Room as one who hears a tale. "We found you at dawn," said he, "and there was blood on your forehead and lips."

I wondered that I had ever disliked him. The three of them in the daylight seemed commonplace old folk enough. The man with the green shade had his head bent as one who sleeps.

It was very slowly I recovered the memory of my experience. "You believe now," said the old man with the withered hand, "that the room is haunted?" He spoke no longer as one who greets an intruder, but as one who condoles with a friend.

"Yes," said I, "the room is haunted."

"And you have seen it. And we who have been here all our lives have never set eyes upon it. Because we have never dared. Tell us, is it truly the old earl who—"

"No," said I, "it is not."

"I told you so," said the old lady, with the glass in her hand. "It is his poor young countess who was frightened—"

"It is not," I said. "There is neither ghost of earl nor ghost of countess in that room; there is no ghost there at all, but worse, far worse, something impalpable—"

"Well?" they said.

"The worst of all the things that haunt poor mortal men," said I; "and that is, in all its nakedness—'Fear!' Fear that will not have light nor sound, that will not bear with reason, that deafens and darkens and overwhelms. It followed me through the corridor, it fought against me in the room—"

I stopped abruptly. There was an interval of silence. My hand went up to my bandages. "The candles went out one after another, and I fled—"

Then the man with the shade lifted his face sideways to see me and spoke.

"That is it," said he. "I knew that was it. A Power of Darkness. To put such a curse upon a home! It lurks there always. You can feel it even in the daytime, even of a bright summer's day, in the hangings, in the curtains, keeping behind you however you face about. In the dusk it creeps in the corridor and follows you, so that you dare not turn. It is even as you say. Fear itself is in that room. Black Fear . . . And there it will be . . . so long as this house of sin endures."

H H MUNRO
(SAKI)
(1870-1916)

20

Laura

"You are not really dying, are you?" asked Amanda.

"I have the doctor's permission to live till Tuesday," said Laura.

"But today is Saturday; this is serious!" gasped Amanda.

"I don't know about it being serious; it is certainly Saturday," said Laura.

"Death is always serious," said Amanda.

"I never said I was going to die. I am presumably going to leave off being Laura, but I shall go on being something. An animal of some kind, I suppose. You see, when one hasn't been very good in the life one has just lived, one reincarnates in some lower organism. And I haven't been very good, when one comes to think of it. I've been petty and mean and vindictive and all that sort of thing when circumstances have seemed to warrant it."

"Circumstances never warrant that sort of thing," said Amanda hastily.

"If you don't mind my saying so," observed Laura, "Egbert is a circumstance that would warrant any amount of that sort of thing. You're married to him—that's different; you've sworn to love, honour, and endure him: I haven't."

"I don't see what's wrong with Egbert," protested Amanda.

"Oh, I daresay the wrongness has been on my part," admitted Laura dispassionately; "he has merely been the extenuating circumstance. He made a thin, peevish kind of fuss, for instance, when I took the collie puppies from the farm out for a run the other day."

"They chased his young broods of speckled Sussex and drove two sitting hens off their nests, besides running all over the flower beds. You know how devoted he is to his poultry and garden."

"Anyhow, he needn't have gone on about it for the entire evening and then have said, 'Let's say no more about it' just when I was beginning to enjoy the discussion. That's where one of my petty vindictive revenges came in," added Laura with an unrepentant chuckle; "I turned the entire family of speckled Sussex into his seedling shed the day after the puppy episode."

"How could you?" exclaimed Amanda.

"It came quite easy," said Laura; "two of the hens pretended to be laying at the time, but I was firm."

"And we thought it was an accident!"

"You see," resumed Laura, "I really have some grounds for supposing that my next incarnation will be in a lower organism. I shall be an animal of some kind. On the other hand, I haven't been a bad sort in my way, so I think I may count on being a nice animal, something elegant and lively, with a love of fun. An otter, perhaps."

"I can't imagine you as an otter," said Amanda.

"Well, I don't suppose you can imagine me as an angel, if it comes to that," said Laura.

Amanda was silent. She couldn't.

"Personally I think an otter life would be rather enjoyable," continued Laura; "salmon to eat all the year round, and the satisfaction of being able to fetch the trout in their own homes without having to wait for hours till they condescend to rise to the fly you've been dangling before them; and an elegant svelte figure—"

"Think of the otter hounds," interposed Amanda; "how dreadful to be hunted and harried and finally worried to death!"

"Rather fun with half the neighbourhood looking on, and anyhow not worse than this Saturday-to-Tuesday business of dying by inches; and then I should go on into something else. If I had been a moderately good otter I suppose I should get back into human shape of some sort; probably something rather primitive—a little brown, unclothed Nubian boy, I should think."

"I wish you would be serious," sighed Amanda; "you really ought to be if you're only going to live till Tuesday."

As a matter of fact Laura died on Monday.

"So dreadfully upsetting," Amanda complained to her uncle-in-law, Sir Lulworth Quayne. "I've asked quite a lot of people down for golf and fishing, and the rhododendrons are just looking their best."

"Laura always was inconsiderate," said Sir Lulworth; "she was born during Goodwood week, with an Ambassador staying in the house who hated babies."

"She had the maddest kind of ideas," said Amanda; "do you know if there was any insanity in her family?"

"Insanity? No, I never heard of any. Her father lives in West Kensington, but I believe he's sane on all other subjects."

"She had an idea that she was going to be reincarnated as an otter," said Amanda.

"One meets with those ideas of reincarnation so frequently, even in the West," said Sir Lulworth, "that one can hardly set them down as being mad. And Laura was such an unaccountable person in this life that I should not like to lay down definite rules as to what she might be doing in an after state."

"You think she really might have passed into some animal form?" asked Amanda. She was one of those who shape their opinions rather readily from the standpoint of those around them.

Just then Egbert entered the breakfast-room, wearing an air of bereavement that Laura's demise would have been insufficient, in itself, to account for.

"Four of my speckled Sussex have been killed," he exclaimed; "the very four that were to go to the show on Friday. One of them was dragged away and eaten right in the middle of that new carnation bed that I've been to such trouble and expense over. My best flower bed and my best fowls singled out for destruction; it almost seems as if the brute that did the deed had special knowledge how to be as devastating as possible in a short space of time."

"Was it a fox, do you think?" asked Amanda.

"Sounds more like a polecat," said Sir Lulworth.

"No," said Egbert, "there were marks of webbed feet all over the place, and we followed the tracks down to the stream at the bottom of the garden; evidently an otter."

Amanda looked quickly and furtively across at Sir Lulworth.

Egbert was too agitated to eat any breakfast, and went out to superintend the strengthening of the poultry yard defences.

"I think she might at least have waited till the funeral was over," said Amanda in a scandalised voice.

"It's her own funeral, you know," said Sir Lulworth; "it's a nice point in etiquette how far one ought to show respect to one's own mortal remains."

Disregard for mortuary convention was carried to further lengths next day; during the absence of the family at the funeral ceremony the remaining survivors of the speckled Sussex were massacred. The marauder's line of retreat seemed to have embraced most of the flower beds on the lawn, but the strawberry beds in the lower garden had also suffered.

"I shall get the otter hounds to come here at the earliest possible moment," said Egbert savagely.

"On no account! You can't dream of such a thing!" exclaimed Amanda. "I mean, it wouldn't do, so soon after a funeral in the house."

"It's a case of necessity," said Egbert; "once an otter takes to that sort of thing it won't stop."

"Perhaps it will go elsewhere now there are no more fowls left," suggested Amanda.

"One would think you wanted to shield the beast," said Egbert.

"There's been so little water in the stream lately," objected Amanda; "it seems hardly sporting to hunt an animal when it has so little chance of taking refuge anywhere."

"Good gracious!" fumed Egbert, "I'm not thinking about sport. I want to have the animal killed as soon as possible."

Even Amanda's opposition weakened when, during church time on the following Sunday, the otter made its way into the house, raided half a salmon from the larder and worried it into scaly fragments on the Persian rug in Egbert's studio.

"We shall have it hiding under our beds and biting pieces out of our feet before long," said Egbert, and from what Amanda knew of this particular otter she felt that the possibility was not a remote one.

On the evening preceding the day fixed for the hunt Amanda spent a solitary hour walking by the banks of the stream, making what she imagined to be hound noises. It was charitably supposed by those who overheard her performance, that she was practising for farmyard imitations at the forth-coming village entertainment.

It was her friend and neighbour, Aurora Burret, who brought her news of the day's sport.

"Pity you weren't out; we had quite a good day. We found at once, in the pool just below your garden."

"Did you—kill?" asked Amanda.

"Rather. A fine she-otter. Your husband got rather badly bitten in trying to 'tail it.' Poor beast, I felt quite sorry for it, it had such a human look in its eyes when it was killed. You'll call me silly, but do you know who the look reminded me of? My dear woman, what is the matter?"

When Amanda had recovered to a certain extent from her attack of nervous prostration Egbert took her to the Nile Valley to recuperate. Change of scene speedily brought about the desired recovery of health and mental balance. The escapades of an adventurous otter in search of a variation of diet were viewed in their proper light. Amanda's normally placid temperament reasserted itself. Even a hurricane of shouted curses, coming from her husband's dressing-room, in her husband's voice, but hardly in his usual vocabulary, failed to disturb her serenity as she made a leisurely toilet one evening in a Cairo hotel.

"What is the matter? What has happened?" she asked in amused curiosity.

"The little beast has thrown all my clean shirts into the bath! Wait till I catch you, you little—"

"What little beast?" asked Amanda, suppressing a desire to laugh; Egbert's language was so hopelessly inadequate to express his outraged feelings.

"A little beast of a naked brown Nubian boy," spluttered Egbert.

And now Amanda is seriously ill.

21

The Cobweb

The farmhouse kitchen probably stood where it did as a matter of accident or haphazard choice; yet its situation might have been planned by a master-strategist in farmhouse architecture. Dairy and poultry-yard, and herb garden, and all the busy places of the farm seemed to lead by easy access into its wide flagged haven, where there was room for everything and where muddy boots left traces that were easily swept away. And yet, for all that it stood so well in the centre of human bustle, its long, latticed window, with the wide window-seat, built into an embrasure beyond the huge fireplace, looked out on a wild spreading view of hill and heather and wooded combe. The window nook made almost a little room in itself, quite the pleasantest room in the farm as far as situation and capabilities went. Young Mrs. Ladbruk, whose husband had just come into the farm by way of inheritance, cast covetous eyes on this snug corner, and her fingers itched to make it bright and cosy with chintz curtains and bowls of flowers, and a shelf or two of old china. The musty farm parlour, looking out on to a prim, cheerless garden imprisoned within high, blank walls, was not a room that lent itself readily either to comfort or decoration.

"When we are more settled I shall work wonders in the way of making the kitchen habitable," said the young woman to her occasional visitors. There was an unspoken wish in those words, a wish which was unconfessed as well as unspoken. Emma Ladbruk was the mistress of the farm; jointly with her husband she might have her say, and to a certain extent her way, in ordering its affairs. But she was not mistress of the kitchen.

On one of the shelves of an old dresser, in company with chipped sauce-boats, pewter jugs, cheese-graters, and paid bills, rested a worn and ragged Bible, on whose front page was the record, in faded ink, of a baptism dated ninety-four years ago. 'Martha Crale' was the name written on that yellow page. The yellow, wrinkled old dame who hobbled and muttered about the kitchen, looking like a dead autumn leaf which the winter winds still pushed hither and thither, had once been Martha Crale; for seventy odd years she had been Martha Mountjoy. For longer than anyone could remember she had pattered to and fro between oven and wash-house and dairy, and out to chicken-run and garden, grumbling and muttering and scolding, but working unceasingly. Emma Ladbruk, of whose coming she took as little notice as she would of a bee wandering in at a window on a summer's day, used at first to watch her with a kind of frightened curiosity. She was so old and so much a part of the place, it was difficult to think of her exactly as a living thing. Old Shep, the white-nozzled, stiff-limbed collie, waiting for his time to die, seemed almost more human than the withered, dried-up old woman. He had been a riotous, roystering puppy, mad with the joy of life, when she was already a tottering, hobbling dame; now he was just a blind, breathing carcase, nothing more, and she still worked with frail energy, still swept and baked and washed, fetched and carried. If there were something in these wise old dogs that did not perish utterly with death, Emma used to think to herself, what generations of ghost-dogs there must be out on those hills, that Martha had reared and fed and tended and spoken a last goodbye word to in that old kitchen. And what memories she must have of human generations that had passed away in her time. It was difficult for anyone, let alone a stranger like Emma, to get her to talk of the days that had been; her shrill, quavering speech was of doors that had been left unfastened, pails that had got mislaid, calves whose feeding-time was overdue, and the various little faults and lapses that chequer a farmhouse routine. Now and again, when election time came round, she would unstore her recollections of the old names round which the fight had waged in the days gone by. There had been a Palmerston, that had been a name down Tiverton way; Tiverton was not a far journey as the crow flies, but to Martha it was almost a foreign country. Later there had been Northcotes and Aclands, and many other newer names that she had forgotten; the names changed, but it was always Libruls and Toories, Yellows and Blues. And they always quarrelled and shouted as to who was right and who was wrong. The one they quarrelled about most was a fine old gentleman with an angry face—she had seen his picture on the walls. She had seen it on the floor too, with a rotten apple squashed over it, for the farm had changed its politics from time to time. Martha had never been on one side or the other; none of 'they' had ever done the farm a stroke of good. Such was her sweeping verdict, given with all a peasant's distrust of the outside world.

When the half-frightened curiosity had somewhat faded away, Emma Ladbruk was uncomfortably conscious of another feeling towards the old woman. She was a quaint old tradition, lingering about the place, she was part and parcel of the farm itself, she was something at once pathetic and picturesque—but she was dreadfully in the way. Emma had come to the farm full of plans for little reforms and improvements, in part the result of training in the newest ways and methods, in part the outcome of her own ideas and fancies. Reforms in the kitchen region, if those deaf old ears could have been induced to give them even a hearing, would have met with short shrift and scornful rejection, and the kitchen region spread over the zone of dairy and market business and half the work of the household. Emma, with the latest science of dead-poultry dressing at her fingertips, sat by, an unheeded watcher, while old Martha trussed the chickens for the market-stall as she had trussed them for nearly fourscore years—all leg and no breast. And the hundred hints anent effective cleaning and labour-lightening and the things that make for wholesomeness which the young woman was ready to impart or to put into action dropped away into nothingness before that wan, muttering, unheeding presence. Above all, the coveted window corner, that was to be a dainty, cheerful oasis in the gaunt old kitchen, stood now choked and lumbered with a litter of odds and ends that Emma, for all her nominal authority, would not have dared or cared to displace; over them seemed to be spun the protection of something that was like a human cobweb. Decidedly Martha was in the way. It would have been an unworthy meanness to have wished to see the span of that brave old life shortened by a few paltry months, but as the days sped by Emma was conscious that the wish was there, disowned though it might be, lurking at the back of her mind.

She felt the meanness of the wish come over her with a qualm of self-reproach one day when she came into the kitchen and found an unaccustomed state of things in that usually busy quarter. Old Martha was not working. A basket of corn was on the floor by her side, and out in the yard the poultry were beginning to clamour a protest of overdue feeding-time. But Martha sat huddled in a shrunken bunch on the window seat, looking out with her dim old eyes as though she saw something stranger than the autumn landscape.

"Is anything the matter, Martha?" asked the young woman.

"'Tis death, 'tis death a-coming," answered the quavering voice; "I knew 'twere coming. I knew it. 'Tweren't for nothing that old Shep's been howling all morning. An' last night I heard the screech-owl give the death-cry, and there were something white as run across the yard yesterday; 'tweren't a cat nor a stoat, 'twere something. The fowls knew 'twere something; they all drew off to one side. Ay, there's been warnings. I knew it were a-coming."

The young woman's eyes clouded with pity. The old thing sitting there so white and shrunken had once been a merry, noisy child, playing about in lanes and hay-lofts and farmhouse garrets; that had been eighty odd years ago, and now she was just a frail old body cowering under the approaching chill of the death that was coming at last to take her. It was not probable that much could be done for her, but Emma hastened away to get assistance and counsel. Her husband, she knew, was down at a tree-felling some little distance off, but she might find some other intelligent soul who knew the old woman better than she did. The farm, she soon found out, had that faculty common to farmyards of swallowing up and losing its human population. The poultry followed her in interested fashion, and swine grunted interrogations at her from behind the bars of their styes, but barnyard and rickyard, orchard and stables and dairy, gave no reward to her search. Then, as she retraced her steps towards the kitchen, she came suddenly on her cousin, young Mr. Jim, as every one called him, who divided his time between amateur horse-dealing, rabbit-shooting, and flirting with the farm maids.

"I'm afraid old Martha is dying," said Emma. Jim was not the sort of person to whom one had to break news gently.

"Nonsense," he said; "Martha means to live to a hundred. She told me so, and she'll do it."

"She may be actually dying at this moment, or it may just be the beginning of the break-up," persisted Emma, with a feeling of contempt for the slowness and dulness of the young man.

A grin spread over his good-natured features.

"It don't look like it," he said, nodding towards the yard. Emma turned to catch the meaning of his remark. Old Martha stood in the middle of a mob of poultry scattering handfuls of grain around her. The turkey-cock, with the bronzed sheen of his feathers and the purple-red of his wattles, the gamecock, with the glowing metallic lustre of his Eastern plumage, the hens, with their ochres and buffs and umbers and their scarlet combs, and the drakes, with their bottle-green heads, made a medley of rich colour, in the centre of which the old woman looked like a withered stalk standing amid a riotous growth of gaily-hued flowers. But she threw the grain deftly amid the wilderness of beaks, and her quavering voice carried as far as the two people who were watching her. She was still harping on the theme of death coming to the farm.

"I knew 'twere a-coming. There's been signs an' warnings."

"Who's dead, then, old Mother?" called out the young man.

"'Tis young Mister Ladbruk," she shrilled back; "they've just a-carried his body in. Run out of the way of a tree that was coming down an' ran hisself on to an iron post. Dead when they picked un up. Aye, I knew 'twere coming."

And she turned to fling a handful of barley at a belated group of guinea-fowl that came racing toward her.

The farm was a family property, and passed to the rabbit-shooting cousin as the next-of-kin. Emma Ladbruk drifted out of its history as a bee that had wandered in at an open window might flit its way out again. On a cold grey morning she stood waiting, with her boxes already stowed in the farm cart, till the last of the market produce should be ready, for the train she was to catch was of less importance than the chickens and butter and eggs that were to be offered for sale. From where she stood she could see an angle of the long latticed window that was to have been cosy with curtains and gay with bowls of flowers. Into her mind came the thought that for months, perhaps for years, long after she had been utterly forgotten, a white, unheeding face would be seen peering out through those latticed panes, and a weak muttering voice would be heard quavering up and down those flagged passages. She made her way to a narrow barred casement that opened into the farm larder. Old Martha was standing at a table trussing a pair of chickens for the market stall as she had trussed them for nearly fourscore years.

22

Sredni Vashtar

Conradin was ten years old, and the doctor had pronounced his professional opinion that the boy would not live another five years. The doctor was silky and effete, and counted for little, but his opinion was endorsed by Mrs. De Ropp, who counted for nearly everything. Mrs. De Ropp was Conradin's cousin and guardian, and in his eyes she represented those three-fifths of the world that are necessary and disagreeable and real; the other two-fifths, in perpetual antagonism to the foregoing, were summed up in himself and his imagination. One of these days Conradin supposed he would succumb to the mastering pressure of wearisome necessary things—such as illnesses and coddling restrictions and drawn-out dullness. Without his imagination, which was rampant under the spur of loneliness, he would have succumbed long ago.

Mrs. De Ropp would never, in her honestest moments, have confessed to herself that she disliked Conradin, though she might have been dimly aware that thwarting him 'for his good' was a duty which she did not find particularly irksome. Conradin hated her with a desperate sincerity which he was perfectly able to mask. Such few pleasures as he could contrive for himself gained an added relish from the likelihood that they would be displeasing to his guardian, and from the realm of his imagination she was locked out—an unclean thing, which should find no entrance.

In the dull, cheerless garden, overlooked by so many windows that were ready to open with a message not to do this or that, or a reminder that medicines were due, he found little attraction. The few fruit-trees that it contained were set jealously apart from his plucking, as though they were rare specimens of their kind blooming in an arid waste; it would probably have been difficult to find a market-gardener who would have offered ten shillings for their entire yearly produce. In a forgotten corner, however, almost hidden behind a dismal shrubbery, was a disused tool-shed of respectable proportions, and within its walls Conradin found a haven, something that took on the varying aspects of a playroom and a cathedral. He had peopled it with a legion of familiar phantoms, evoked partly from fragments of history and partly from his own brain, but it also boasted two inmates of flesh and blood. In one corner lived a ragged-plumaged Houdan hen, on which the boy lavished an affection that had scarcely another outlet. Further back in the gloom stood a large hutch, divided into two compartments, one of which was fronted with close iron bars. This was the abode of a large polecat-ferret, which a friendly butcher-boy had once smuggled, cage and all, into its present quarters, in exchange for a long-secreted hoard of small silver. Conradin was dreadfully afraid of the lithe, sharp-fanged beast, but it was his most treasured possession. Its very presence in the tool-shed was a secret and fearful joy, to be kept scrupulously from the knowledge of the Woman, as he privately dubbed his cousin. And one day, out of Heaven knows what material, he spun the beast a wonderful name, and from that moment it grew into a god and a religion. The Woman indulged in religion once a week at a church near by, and took Conradin with her, but to him the church service was an alien rite in the House of Rimmon. Every Thursday, in the dim and musty silence of the tool-shed, he worshipped with mystic and elaborate ceremonial before the wooden hutch where dwelt Sredni Vashtar, the great ferret. Red flowers in their season and scarlet berries in the winter-time were offered at his shrine, for he was a god who laid some special stress on the fierce impatient side of things, as opposed to the Woman's religion, which, as far as Conradin could observe, went to great lengths in the contrary direction. And on great festivals powdered nutmeg was strewn in front of his hutch, an important feature of the offering being that the nutmeg had to be stolen. These festivals were of irregular occurrence, and were chiefly appointed to celebrate some passing event. On one occasion, when Mrs. De Ropp suffered from acute toothache for three days, Conradin kept up the festival during the entire three days, and almost succeeded in persuading himself that Sredni Vashtar was personally responsible for the toothache. If the malady had lasted for another day the supply of nutmeg would have given out.

The Houdan hen was never drawn into the cult of Sredni Vashtar. Conradin had long ago settled that she was an Anabaptist. He did not pretend to have the remotest knowledge as to what an Anabaptist was, but he privately hoped that it was dashing and not very respectable. Mrs. De Ropp was the ground plan on which he based and detested all respectability.

After a while Conradin's absorption in the tool-shed began to attract the notice of his guardian. "It is not good for him to be pottering down there in all weathers," she promptly decided, and at breakfast one morning she announced that the Houdan hen had been sold and taken away overnight. With her short-sighted eyes she peered at Conradin, waiting for an outbreak of rage and sorrow, which she was ready to rebuke with a flow of excellent precepts and reasoning. But Conradin said nothing: there was nothing to be said. Something perhaps in his white set face gave her a momentary qualm, for at tea that afternoon there was toast on the table, a delicacy which she usually banned on the ground that it was bad for him; also because the making of it 'gave trouble,' a deadly offence in the middle-class feminine eye.

"I thought you liked toast," she exclaimed, with an injured air, observing that he did not touch it.

"Sometimes," said Conradin.

In the shed that evening there was an innovation in the worship of the hutch-god. Conradin had been wont to chant his praises, tonight be asked a boon.

"Do one thing for me, Sredni Vashtar."

The thing was not specified. As Sredni Vashtar was a god he must be supposed to know. And choking back a sob as he looked at that other empty corner, Conradin went back to the world he so hated.

And every night, in the welcome darkness of his bedroom, and every evening in the dusk of the tool-shed, Conradin's bitter litany went up: "Do one thing for me, Sredni Vashtar."

Mrs. De Ropp noticed that the visits to the shed did not cease, and one day she made a further journey of inspection.

"What are you keeping in that locked hutch?" she asked. "I believe it's guinea-pigs. I'll have them all cleared away."

Conradin shut his lips tight, but the Woman ransacked his bedroom till she found the carefully hidden key, and forthwith marched down to the shed to complete her discovery. It was a cold afternoon, and Conradin had been bidden to keep to the house. From the furthest window of the dining-room the door of the shed could just be seen beyond the corner of the shrubbery, and there Conradin stationed himself. He saw the Woman enter, and then be imagined her opening the door of the sacred hutch and peering down with her short-sighted eyes into the thick straw bed where his god lay hidden. Perhaps she would prod at the straw in her clumsy impatience. And Conradin fervently breathed his prayer for the last time. But he knew as he prayed that he did not believe. He knew that the Woman would come out presently with that pursed smile he loathed so well on her face, and that in an hour or two the gardener would carry away his wonderful god, a god no longer, but a simple brown ferret in a hutch. And he knew that the Woman would triumph always as she triumphed now, and that he would grow ever more sickly under her pestering and domineering and superior wisdom, till one day nothing would matter much more with him, and the doctor would be proved right. And in the sting and misery of his defeat, he began to chant loudly and defiantly the hymn of his threatened idol:

Sredni Vashtar went forth.
His thoughts were red thoughts and his teeth were white.
His enemies called for peace, but he brought them death.
Sredni Vashtar the Beautiful.

And then of a sudden he stopped his chanting and drew closer to the window-pane. The door of the shed still stood ajar as it had been left, and the minutes were slipping by. They were long minutes, but they slipped by nevertheless. He watched the starlings running and flying in little parties across the lawn; he counted them over and over again, with one eye always on that swinging door. A sour-faced maid came in to lay the table for tea, and still Conradin stood and waited and watched. Hope had crept by inches into his heart, and now a look of triumph began to blaze in his eyes that had only known the wistful patience of defeat. Under his breath, with a furtive exultation, he began once again the pæan of victory and devastation. And presently his eyes were rewarded: out through that doorway came a long, low, yellow-and-brown beast, with eyes a-blink at the waning daylight, and dark wet stains around the fur of jaws and throat. Conradin dropped on his knees. The great polecat-ferret made its way down to a small brook at the foot of the garden, drank for a moment, then crossed a little plank bridge and was lost to sight in the bushes. Such was the passing of Sredni Vashtar.

"Tea is ready," said the sour-faced maid; "where is the mistress?"

"She went down to the shed some time ago," said Conradin. And while the maid went to summon her mistress to tea, Conradin fished a toasting-fork out of the sideboard drawer and proceeded to toast himself a piece of bread. And during the toasting of it and the buttering of it with much butter and the slow enjoyment of eating it, Conradin listened to the noises and silences which fell in quick spasms beyond the dining-room door. The loud foolish screaming of the maid, the answering chorus of wondering ejaculations from the kitchen region, the scuttering footsteps and hurried embassies for outside help, and then, after a lull, the scared sobbings and the shuffling tread of those who bore a heavy burden into the house.

"Whoever will break it to the poor child? I couldn't for the life of me!" exclaimed a shrill voice. And while they debated the matter among themselves, Conradin made himself another piece of toast.

H P LOVECRAFT

(1890-1937)

23

Ex Oblivione

When the last days were upon me, and the ugly trifles of existence began to drive me to madness like the small drops of water that torturers let fall ceaselessly upon one spot of their victim's body, I loved the irradiate refuge of sleep. In my dreams I found a little of the beauty I had vainly sought in life, and wandered through old gardens and enchanted woods.

Once when the wind was soft and scented I heard the south calling, and sailed endlessly and languorously under strange stars.

Once when the gentle rain fell I glided in a barge down a sunless stream under the earth till I reached another world of purple twilight, iridescent arbours, and undying roses.

And once I walked through a golden valley that led to shadowy groves and ruins, and ended in a mighty wall green with antique vines, and pierced by a little gate of bronze.

Many times I walked through that valley, and longer and longer would I pause in the spectral half-light where the giant trees squirmed and twisted grotesquely, and the grey ground stretched damply from trunk to trunk, sometimes disclosing the mould-stained stones of buried temples. And always the goal of my fancies was the mighty vine-grown wall with the little gate of bronze therein.

After a while, as the days of waking became less and less bearable from their greyness and sameness, I would often drift in opiate peace through the valley and the shadowy groves, and wonder how I might seize them for my eternal dwelling-place, so that I need no more crawl back to a dull world stript of interest and new colours. And as I looked upon the little gate in the mighty wall, I felt that beyond it lay a dream-country from which, once it was entered, there would be no return.

So each night in sleep I strove to find the hidden latch of the gate in the ivied antique wall, though it was exceedingly well hidden. And I would tell myself that the realm beyond the wall was not more lasting merely, but more lovely and radiant as well.

Then one night in the dream-city of Zakarion I found a yellowed papyrus filled with the thoughts of dream-sages who dwelt of old in that city, and who were too wise ever to be born in the waking world. Therein were written many things concerning the world of dream, and among them was lore of a golden valley and a sacred grove with temples, and a high wall pierced by a little bronze gate. When I saw this lore, I knew that it touched on the scenes I had haunted, and I therefore read long in the yellowed papyrus.

Some of the dream-sages wrote gorgeously of the wonders beyond the irrepassable gate, but others told of horror and disappointment. I knew not which to believe, yet longed more and more to cross forever into the unknown land; for doubt and secrecy are the lure of lures, and no new horror can be more terrible than the daily torture of the commonplace. So when I learned of the drug which would unlock the gate and drive me through, I resolved to take it when next I awaked.

Last night I swallowed the drug and floated dreamily into the golden valley and the shadowy groves; and when I came this time to the antique wall, I saw that the small gate of bronze was ajar. From beyond came a glow that weirdly lit the giant twisted trees and the tops of the buried temples, and I drifted on songfully, expectant of the glories of the land from whence I should never return.

But as the gate swung wider and the sorcery of drug and dream pushed me through, I knew that all sights and glories were at an end; for in that new realm was neither land nor sea, but only the white void of unpeopled and illimitable space. So, happier than I had ever dared hoped to be, I dissolved again into that native infinity of crystal oblivion from which the daemon Life had called me for one brief and desolate hour.

24

The Terrible Old Man

It was the design of Angelo Ricci and Joe Czanek and Manuel Silva to call on the Terrible Old Man. This old man dwells all alone in a very ancient house on Water Street near the sea, and is reputed to be both exceedingly rich and exceedingly feeble; which forms a situation very attractive to men of the profession of Messrs. Ricci, Czanek, and Silva, for that profession was nothing less dignified than robbery.

The inhabitants of Kingsport say and think many things about the Terrible Old Man which generally keep him safe from the attention of gentlemen like Mr. Ricci and his colleagues, despite the almost certain fact that he hides a fortune of indefinite magnitude somewhere about his musty and venerable abode. He is, in truth, a very strange person, believed to have been a captain of East India clipper ships in his day; so old that no one can remember when he was young, and so taciturn that few know his real name. Among the gnarled trees in the front yard of his aged and neglected place he maintains a strange collection of large stones, oddly grouped and painted so that they resemble the idols in some obscure Eastern temple. This collection frightens away most of the small boys who love to taunt the Terrible Old

Man about his long white hair and beard, or to break the small-paned windows of his dwelling with wicked missiles; but there are other things which frighten the older and more curious folk who sometimes steal up to the house to peer in through the dusty panes. These folk say that on a table in a bare room on the ground floor are many peculiar bottles, in each a small piece of lead suspended pendulum-wise from a string. And they say that the Terrible Old Man talks to these bottles, addressing them by such names as Jack, Scar-Face, Long Tom, Spanish Joe, Peters, and Mate Ellis, and that whenever he speaks to a bottle the little lead pendulum within makes certain definite vibrations as if in answer.

Those who have watched the tall, lean, Terrible Old Man in these peculiar conversations, do not watch him again. But Angelo Ricci and Joe Czanek and Manuel Silva were not of Kingsport blood; they were of that new and heterogeneous alien stock which lies outside the charmed circle of New England life and traditions, and they saw in the Terrible Old Man merely a tottering, almost helpless grey-beard, who could not walk without the aid of his knotted cane, and whose thin, weak hands shook pitifully. They were really quite sorry in their way for the lonely, unpopular old fellow, whom everybody shunned, and at whom all the dogs barked singularly. But business is business, and to a robber whose soul is in his profession, there is a lure and a challenge about a very old and very feeble man who has no account at the bank, and who pays for his few necessities at the village store with Spanish gold and silver minted two centuries ago.

Messrs. Ricci, Czanek, and Silva selected the night of April 11th for their call. Mr. Ricci and Mr. Silva were to interview the poor old gentleman, whilst Mr. Czanek waited for them and their presumable metallic burden with a covered motor-car in Ship Street, by the gate in the tall rear wall of their host's grounds. Desire to avoid needless explanations in case of unexpected police intrusions prompted these plans for a quiet and unostentatious departure.

As prearranged, the three adventurers started out separately in order to prevent any evil-minded suspicions afterward. Messrs. Ricci and Silva met in Water Street by the old man's front gate, and although they did not like the way the moon shone down upon the painted stones through the budding branches of the gnarled trees, they had more important things to think about than mere idle superstition. They feared it might be unpleasant work making the Terrible Old Man loquacious concerning his hoarded gold and silver, for aged sea-captains are notably stubborn and perverse. Still, he was very old and very feeble, and there were two visitors. Messrs. Ricci and Silva were experienced in the art of making unwilling persons voluble, and the screams of a weak and exceptionally venerable man can be easily muffled. So they moved up to the one lighted window and heard the Terrible Old Man talking childishly to his bottles with pendulums. Then they donned masks and knocked politely at the weather-stained oaken door.

Waiting seemed very long to Mr. Czanek as he fidgeted restlessly in the covered motor-car by the Terrible Old Man's back gate in Ship Street. He was more than ordinarily tender-hearted, and he did not like the hideous screams he had heard in the ancient house just after the hour appointed for the deed. Had he not told his colleagues to be as gentle as possible with the pathetic old sea-captain? Very nervously he watched that narrow oaken gate in the high and ivy-clad stone wall. Frequently he consulted his watch, and wondered at the delay. Had the old man died before revealing where his treasure was hidden, and had a thorough search become necessary? Mr. Czanek did not like to wait so long in the dark in such a place. Then he sensed a soft tread or tapping on the walk inside the gate, heard a gentle fumbling at the rusty latch, and saw the narrow, heavy door swing inward. And in the pallid glow of the single dim street-lamp he strained his eyes to see what his colleagues had brought out of that sinister house which loomed so close behind. But when he looked, he did not see what he had expected; for his colleagues were not there at all, but only the Terrible Old Man leaning quietly on his knotted cane and smiling hideously. Mr. Czanek had never before noticed the colour of that man's eyes; now he saw that they were yellow.

Little things make considerable excitement in little towns, which is the reason that Kingsport people talked all that spring and summer about the three unidentifiable bodies, horribly slashed as with many cutlasses, and horribly mangled as by the tread of many cruel boot-heels, which the tide washed in. And some people even spoke of things as trivial as the deserted motor-car found in Ship Street, or certain especially inhuman cries, probably of a stray animal or migratory bird, heard in the night by wakeful citizens. But in this idle village gossip the Terrible Old Man took no interest at all. He was by nature reserved, and when one is aged and feeble, one's reserve is doubly strong. Besides, so ancient a sea-captain must have witnessed scores of things much more stirring in the far-off days of his unremembered youth.

25

The Picture in the House

Searchers after horror haunt strange, far places. For them are the catacombs of Ptolemais, and the carven mausolea of the nightmare countries. They climb to the moonlit towers of ruined Rhine castles, and falter down black cobwebbed steps beneath the scattered stones of forgotten cities in Asia. The haunted wood and the desolate mountain are their shrines, and they linger around the sinister monoliths on uninhabited islands. But the true epicure in the terrible, to whom a new thrill of unutterable ghastliness is the chief end and justification of existence, esteems most of all the ancient, lonely farmhouses of backwoods New England; for there the dark elements of strength, solitude, grotesqueness and ignorance combine to form the perfection of the hideous.

Most horrible of all sights are the little unpainted wooden houses remote from travelled ways, usually squatted upon some damp grassy slope or leaning against some gigantic outcropping of rock. Two hundred years and more they have leaned or squatted there, while the vines have crawled and the trees have swelled and spread. They are almost hidden now in lawless luxuriances of green and guardian shrouds of shadow; but the small-paned windows still stare shockingly, as if blinking through a lethal stupor which wards off madness by dulling the memory of unutterable things.

In such houses have dwelt generations of strange people, whose like the world has never seen. Seized with a gloomy and fanatical belief which exiled them from their kind, their ancestors sought the wilderness for freedom. There the scions of a conquering race indeed flourished free from the restrictions of their fellows, but cowered in an appalling slavery to the dismal phantasms of their own minds. Divorced from the enlightenment of civilization, the strength of these Puritans turned into singular channels; and in their isolation, morbid self-repression, and struggle for life with relentless Nature, there came to them dark furtive traits from the prehistoric depths of their cold Northern heritage. By necessity practical and by philosophy stern, these folks were not beautiful in their sins. Erring as all mortals must, they were forced by their rigid code to seek concealment above all else; so that they came to use less and less taste in what they concealed. Only the silent, sleepy, staring houses in the backwoods can tell all that has lain hidden since the early days, and they are not communicative, being loath to shake off the drowsiness which helps them forget. Sometimes one feels that it would be merciful to tear down these houses, for they must often dream.

It was to a time-battered edifice of this description that I was driven one afternoon in November, 1896, by a rain of such chilling copiousness that any shelter was preferable to exposure. I had been travelling for some time amongst the people of the Miskatonic Valley in quest of certain genealogical data; and from the remote, devious, and problematical nature of my course, had deemed it convenient to employ a bicycle despite the lateness of the season. Now I found myself upon an apparently abandoned road which I had chosen as the shortest cut to Arkham, overtaken by the storm at a point far from any town, and confronted with no refuge save the antique and repellent wooden building which blinked with bleared windows from between two huge leafless elms near the foot of a rocky hill. Distant though it is from the remnant of a road, this house none the less impressed me unfavorably the very moment I espied it. Honest, wholesome structures do not stare at travellers so slyly and hauntingly, and in my genealogical researches I had encountered legends of a century before which biased me against places of this kind. Yet the force of the elements was such as to overcome my scruples, and I did not hesitate to wheel my machine up the weedy rise to the closed door which seemed at once so suggestive and secretive.

I had somehow taken it for granted that the house was abandoned, yet as I approached it I was not so sure, for though the walks were indeed overgrown with weeds, they seemed to retain their nature a little too well to argue complete desertion. Therefore instead of trying the door I knocked, feeling as I did so a trepidation I could scarcely explain. As I waited on the rough, mossy rock which served as a door-step, I glanced at the neighbouring windows and the panes of the transom above me, and noticed that although old, rattling, and almost opaque with dirt, they were not broken. The building, then, must still be inhabited, despite its isolation and general neglect. However, my rapping evoked no response, so after repeating the summons I tried the rusty latch and found the door unfastened. Inside was a little vestibule with walls from which the plaster was falling, and through the doorway came a faint but peculiarly hateful odour. I entered, carrying my bicycle, and closed the door behind me. Ahead rose a narrow staircase, flanked by a small door probably leading to the cellar, while to the left and right were closed doors leading to rooms on the ground floor.

Leaning my cycle against the wall I opened the door at the left, and crossed into a small low-ceiled chamber but dimly lighted by its two dusty windows and furnished in the barest and most primitive possible way. It appeared to be a kind of sitting-room, for it had a table and several chairs, and an immense fireplace above which ticked an antique clock on a mantel. Books and papers were very few, and in the prevailing gloom I could not readily discern the titles. What interested me was the uniform air of archaism as displayed in every visible detail. Most of the houses in this region I had found rich in relics of the past, but here the antiquity was curiously complete; for in all the room I could not discover a single article of definitely post-revolutionary date. Had the furnishings been less humble, the place would have been a collector's paradise.

As I surveyed this quaint apartment, I felt an increase in that aversion first excited by the bleak exterior of the house. Just what it was that I feared or loathed, I could by no means define; but something in the whole atmosphere seemed redolent of unhallowed age, of unpleasant crudeness, and of secrets which should be forgotten. I felt disinclined to sit down, and wandered about examining the various articles which I had noticed. The first object of my curiosity was a book of medium size lying upon the table and presenting such an antediluvian aspect that I marvelled at beholding it outside a museum or library. It was bound in leather with metal fittings, and was in an excellent state of preservation; being altogether an unusual sort of volume to encounter in an abode so lowly. When I opened it to the title page my wonder grew even greater, for it proved to be nothing less rare than Pigafetta's account of the Congo region, written in Latin from the notes of the sailor Lopex and printed at Frankfurt in 1598. I had often heard of this work, with its curious illustrations by the brothers De Bry, hence for a moment forgot my uneasiness in my desire to turn the pages before me. The engravings were indeed interesting, drawn wholly from imagination and careless descriptions, and represented negroes with white skins and Caucasian features; nor would I soon have closed the book had not an exceedingly trivial circumstance upset my tired nerves and revived my sensation of disquiet. What annoyed me was merely the persistent way in which the volume tended to fall open of itself at Plate XII, which represented in gruesome detail a butcher's shop of the cannibal Anziques. I experienced some shame at my susceptibility to so slight a thing, but the drawing nevertheless disturbed me, especially in connection with some adjacent passages descriptive of Anzique gastronomy.

I had turned to a neighbouring shelf and was examining its meagre literary contents—an eighteenth century Bible, a 'Pilgrim's Progress' of like period, illustrated with grotesque woodcuts and printed by the almanack-maker Isaiah Thomas, the rotting bulk of Cotton Mather's 'Magnalia Christi Americana,' and a few other books of evidently equal age—when my attention was aroused by the unmistakable sound of walking in the room overhead. At first astonished and startled, considering the lack of response to my recent knocking at the door, I immediately afterward concluded that the walker had just awakened from a sound sleep, and listened with less surprise as the footsteps sounded on the creaking stairs. The tread was heavy, yet seemed to contain a curious quality of cautiousness; a quality which I disliked the more because the tread was heavy. When I had entered the room I had shut the door behind me. Now, after a moment of silence during which the walker may have been inspecting my bicycle in the hall, I heard a fumbling at the latch and saw the panelled portal swing open again.

In the doorway stood a person of such singular appearance that I should have exclaimed aloud but for the restraints of good breeding. Old, white-bearded, and ragged, my host possessed a countenance and physique which inspired equal wonder and respect. His height could not have been less than six feet, and despite a general air of age and poverty he was stout and powerful in proportion. His face, almost hidden by a long beard which grew high on the cheeks, seemed abnormally ruddy and less wrinkled than one might expect; while over a high forehead fell a shock of white hair little thinned by the years. His blue eyes, though a trifle bloodshot, seemed inexplicably keen and burning. But for his horrible unkemptness the man would have been as distinguished-looking as he was impressive. This unkemptness, however, made him offensive despite his face and figure. Of what his clothing consisted I could hardly tell, for it seemed to me no more than a mass of tatters surmounting a pair of high, heavy boots; and his lack of cleanliness surpassed description.

The appearance of this man, and the instinctive fear he inspired, prepared me for something like enmity; so that I almost shuddered through surprise and a sense of uncanny incongruity when he motioned me to a chair and addressed me in a thin, weak voice full of fawning respect and ingratiating hospitality. His speech was very curious, an extreme form of Yankee dialect I had thought long extinct; and I studied it closely as he sat down opposite me for conversation.

"Ketched in the rain, be ye?" he greeted. "Glad ye was nigh the haouse en' hed the sense ta come right in. I calc'late I was asleep, else I'd a heerd ye—I ain't as young as I uster be, an' I need a paowerful sight o' naps naowadays. Trav'lin fur? I hain't seed many folks 'long this rud sence they tuk off the Arkham stage."

I replied that I was going to Arkham, and apologized for my rude entry into his domicile, whereupon he continued.

"Glad ta see ye, young Sir—new faces is scurce arount here, an' I hain't got much ta cheer me up these days. Guess yew hail from Bosting, don't ye? I never ben thar, but I kin tell a taown man when I see 'im—we hed one fer deestrick schoolmaster in '84, but he quit suddent an' no one never heerd on 'im sence—" here the old man lapsed into a kind of chuckle, and made no explanation when I questioned him. He seemed to be in an aboundingly good humour, yet to possess those eccentricities which one might guess from his grooming. For some time he rambled on with an almost feverish geniality, when it struck me to ask him how he came by so rare a book as Pigafetta's 'Regnum Congo.' The effect of this volume had not left me, and I felt a certain hesitancy in speaking of it, but curiosity overmastered all the vague fears which had steadily accumulated since my first glimpse of the house. To my relief, the question did not seem an awkward one, for the old man answered freely and volubly.

"Oh, that Afriky book? Cap'n Ebenezer Holt traded me thet in '68—him as was kilt in the war." Something about the name of Ebenezer Holt caused me to look up sharply. I had encountered it in my genealogical work, but not in any record since the Revolution. I wondered if my host could help me in the task at which I was laboring, and resolved to ask him about it later on. He continued.

"Ebenezer was on a Salem merchantman for years, an' picked up a sight o' queer stuff in every port. He got this in London, I guess—he uster like ter buy things at the shops. I was up ta his haouse onct, on the hill, tradin' hosses, when I see this book. I relished the picters, so he give it in on a swap. 'Tis a queer book—here, leave me git on my spectacles—" The old man fumbled among his rags, producing a pair of dirty and amazingly antique glasses with small octagonal lenses and steel bows. Donning these, he reached for the volume on the table and turned the pages lovingly.

"Ebenezer cud read a leetle o' this—'tis Latin—but I can't. I had two er three schoolmasters read me a bit, and Passon Clark, him they say got draownded in the pond—kin yew make anything outen it?" I told him that I could, and translated for his benefit a paragraph near the beginning. If I erred, he was not scholar enough to correct me; for he seemed childishly pleased at my English version. His proximity was becoming rather obnoxious, yet I saw no way to escape without offending him. I was amused at the childish fondness of this ignorant old man for the pictures in a book he could not read, and wondered how much better he could read the few books in English which adorned the room. This revelation of simplicity removed much of the ill-defined apprehension I had felt, and I smiled as my host rambled on:

"Queer haow picters kin set a body thinkin'. Take this un here near the front. Hey yew ever seed trees like thet, with big leaves a floppin' over an' daown? And them men—them can't be niggers—they dew beat all. Kinder like Injuns, I guess, even ef they be in Afriky. Some o' these here critters looks like monkeys, or half monkeys an' half men, but I never heerd o' nothin' like this un." Here he pointed to a fabulous creature of the artist, which one might describe as a sort of dragon with the head of an alligator.

"But naow I'll show ye the best un—over here nigh the middle—" The old man's speech grew a trifle thicker and his eyes assumed a brighter glow; but his fumbling hands, though seemingly clumsier than before, were entirely adequate to their mission. The book fell open, almost of its own accord and as if from frequent consultation at this place, to the repellent twelfth plate showing a butcher's shop amongst the Anzique cannibals. My sense of restlessness returned, though I did not exhibit it. The especially bizarre thing was that the artist had made his Africans look like white men—the limbs and quarters hanging about the walls of the shop were ghastly, while the butcher with his axe was hideously incongruous. But my host seemed to relish the view as much as I disliked it.

"What d'ye think o' this—ain't never see the like hereabouts, eh? When I see this I telled Eb Holt, 'That's suthin' ta stir ye up an' make yer blood tickle.' When I read in Scripter about slayin'—like them Midianites was slew—I kinder think things, but I ain't got no picter of it. Here a body kin see all they is to it—I s'pose 'tis sinful, but ain't we all born an' livin' in sin?—Thet feller bein' chopped up gives me a tickle every time I look at 'im—I hey ta keep lookin' at 'im—see whar the butcher cut off his feet? Thar's his head on thet bench, with one arm side of it, an' t'other arm's on the other side o' the meat block."

As the man mumbled on in his shocking ecstasy the expression on his hairy, spectacled face became indescribable, but his voice sank rather than mounted. My own sensations can scarcely be recorded. All the terror I had dimly felt before rushed upon me actively and vividly, and I knew that I loathed the ancient and abhorrent creature so near me with an infinite intensity. His madness, or at least his partial perversion, seemed beyond dispute. He was almost whispering now, with a huskiness more terrible than a scream, and I trembled as I listened.

"As I says, 'tis queer haow picters sets ye thinkin'. D'ye know, young Sir, I'm right sot on this un here. Arter I got the book off Eb I uster look at it a lot, especial when I'd heerd Passon Clark rant o' Sundays in his big wig. Onct I tried suthin' funny—here, young Sir, don't git skeert—all I done was ter look at the picter afore I kilt the sheep for market—killin' sheep was kinder more fun arter lookin' at it—" The tone of the old man now sank very low, sometimes becoming so faint that his words were hardly audible. I listened to the rain, and to the rattling of the bleared, small-paned windows, and marked a rumbling of approaching thunder quite unusual for the season. Once a terrific flash and peal shook the frail house to its foundations, but the whisperer seemed not to notice it.

"Killin' sheep was kinder more fun—but d'ye know, 'twan't quite satisfyin'. Queer haow a cravin' gits a holt on ye—As ye love the Almighty, young man, don't tell nobody, but I swar ter Gawd thet picter begun to make me hungry fer victuals I couldn't raise nor buy—here, set still, what's ailin' ye?—I didn't do nothin', only

I wondered haow 'twud be ef I did—They say meat makes blood an' flesh, an' gives ye new life, so I wondered ef 'twudn't make a man live longer an' longer ef 'twas more the same—" But the whisperer never continued. The interruption was not produced by my fright, nor by the rapidly increasing storm amidst whose fury I was presently to open my eyes on a smoky solitude of blackened ruins. It was produced by a very simple though somewhat unusual happening.

The open book lay flat between us, with the picture staring repulsively upward. As the old man whispered the words 'more the same' a tiny splattering impact was heard, and something showed on the yellowed paper of the upturned volume. I thought of the rain and of a leaky roof, but rain is not red. On the butcher's shop of the Anzique cannibals a small red spattering glistened picturesquely, lending vividness to the horror of the engraving. The old man saw it, and stopped whispering even before my expression of horror made it necessary; saw it and glanced quickly toward the floor of the room he had left an hour before. I followed his glance, and beheld just above us on the loose plaster of the ancient ceiling a large irregular spot of wet crimson which seemed to spread even as I viewed it. I did not shriek or move, but merely shut my eyes. A moment later came the titanic thunderbolt of thunderbolts; blasting that accursed house of unutterable secrets and bringing the oblivion which alone saved my mind.

26

The Cats of Ulthar

It is said that in Ulthar, which lies beyond the river Skai, no man may kill a cat; and this I can verily believe as I gaze upon him who sitteth purring before the fire. For the cat is cryptic, and close to strange things which men cannot see. He is the soul of antique Aegyptus, and bearer of tales from forgotten cities in Meroë and Ophir. He is the kin of the jungle's lords, and heir to the secrets of hoary and sinister Africa. The Sphinx is his cousin, and he speaks her language; but he is more ancient than the Sphinx, and remembers that which she hath forgotten.

In Ulthar, before ever the burgesses forbade the killing of cats, there dwelt an old cotter and his wife who delighted to trap and slay the cats of their neighbours. Why they did this I know not; save that many hate the voice of the cat in the night, and take it ill that cats should run stealthily about yards and gardens at twilight. But whatever the reason, this old man and woman took pleasure in trapping and slaying every cat which came near to their hovel; and from some of the sounds heard after dark, many villagers fancied that the manner of slaying was exceedingly peculiar. But the villagers did not discuss such things with the old man and his wife;

because of the habitual expression on the withered faces of the two, and because their cottage was so small and so darkly hidden under spreading oaks at the back of a neglected yard. In truth, much as the owners of cats hated these odd folk, they feared them more; and instead of berating them as brutal assassins, merely took care that no cherished pet or mouser should stray toward the remote hovel under the dark trees. When through some unavoidable oversight a cat was missed, and sounds heard after dark, the loser would lament impotently; or console himself by thanking Fate that it was not one of his children who had thus vanished. For the people of Ulthar were simple, and knew not whence it is all cats first came.

One day a caravan of strange wanderers from the South entered the narrow cobbled streets of Ulthar. Dark wanderers they were, and unlike the other roving folk who passed through the village twice every year. In the market-place they told fortunes for silver, and bought gay beads from the merchants. What was the land of these wanderers none could tell; but it was seen that they were given to strange prayers, and that they had painted on the sides of their wagons strange figures with human bodies and the heads of cats, hawks, rams, and lions. And the leader of the caravan wore a head-dress with two horns and a curious disc betwixt the horns.

There was in this singular caravan a little boy with no father or mother, but only a tiny black kitten to cherish. The plague had not been kind to him, yet had left him this small furry thing to mitigate his sorrow; and when one is very young, one can find great relief in the lively antics of a black kitten. So the boy whom the dark people called Menes smiled more often than he wept as he sate playing with his graceful kitten on the steps of an oddly painted wagon.

On the third morning of the wanderers' stay in Ulthar, Menes could not find his kitten; and as he sobbed aloud in the market-place certain villagers told him of the old man and his wife, and of sounds heard in the night. And when he heard these things his sobbing gave place to meditation, and finally to prayer. He stretched out his arms toward the sun and prayed in a tongue no villager could understand; though indeed the villagers did not try very hard to understand, since their attention was mostly taken up by the sky and the odd shapes the clouds were assuming. It was very peculiar, but as the little boy uttered his petition there seemed to form overhead the shadowy, nebulous figures of exotic things; of hybrid creatures crowned with horn-flanked discs. Nature is full of such illusions to impress the imaginative.

That night the wanderers left Ulthar, and were never seen again. And the householders were troubled when they noticed that in all the village there was not a cat to be found. From each hearth the familiar cat had vanished; cats large and small, black, grey, striped, yellow, and white. Old Kranon, the burgomaster, swore that the dark folk had taken the cats away in revenge for the killing of Menes' kitten; and cursed the caravan and the little boy. But Nith, the lean notary, declared that the old cotter and his wife were more likely persons to suspect; for their hatred of cats was notorious and increasingly bold. Still, no one durst complain to the sinister couple; even when little Atal, the innkeeper's son, vowed that he had at twilight seen all the cats of Ulthar in that accursed yard under the trees, pacing very slowly and solemnly in a circle around the cottage, two abreast, as if in performance of some unheard-of rite of beasts. The villagers did not know how much to believe from so small a boy; and though they feared that the evil pair had charmed the cats to their death, they preferred not to chide the old cotter till they met him outside his dark and repellent yard.

So Ulthar went to sleep in vain anger; and when the people awaked at dawn—behold! every cat was back at his accustomed hearth! Large and small, black, grey, striped, yellow, and white, none was missing. Very sleek and fat did the cats appear, and sonorous with purring content. The citizens talked with one another of the affair, and marvelled not a little. Old Kranon again insisted that it was the dark folk who had taken them, since cats did not return alive from the cottage of the ancient man and his wife. But all agreed on one thing: that the refusal of all the cats to eat their portions of meat or drink their saucers of milk was exceedingly curious. And for two whole days the sleek, lazy cats of Ulthar would touch no food, but only doze by the fire or in the sun.

It was fully a week before the villagers noticed that no lights were appearing at dusk in the windows of the cottage under the trees. Then the lean Nith remarked that no one had seen the old man or his wife since the night the cats were away. In another week the burgomaster decided to overcome his fears and call at the strangely silent dwelling as a matter of duty, though in so doing he was careful to take with him Shang the blacksmith and Thul the cutter of stone as witnesses. And when they had broken down the frail door they found only this: two cleanly picked human skeletons on the earthen floor, and a number of singular beetles crawling in the shadowy corners.

There was subsequently much talk among the burgesses of Ulthar. Zath, the coroner, disputed at length with Nith, the lean notary; and Kranon and Shang and Thul were overwhelmed with questions. Even little Atal, the innkeeper's son, was closely questioned and given a sweetmeat as reward. They talked of the old cotter and his wife, of the caravan of dark wanderers, of small Menes and his black kitten, of the prayer of Menes and of the sky during that prayer, of the doings of the cats on the night the caravan left, and of what was later found in the cottage under the dark trees in the repellent yard.

And in the end the burgesses passed that remarkable law which is told of by traders in Hatheg and discussed by travellers in Nir; namely, that in Ulthar no man may kill a cat.

HARRIET BEECHER STOWE

(1811-1896)

27

The Ghost in the Cap'n Brown House

"Now, Sam, tell us certain true, is there any such things as ghosts?"

"Be there ghosts?" said Sam, immediately translating into his vernacular grammar: "wal, now that are's jest the question, ye see."

"Well, grandma thinks there are, and Aunt Lois thinks it's all nonsense. Why, Aunt Lois don't even believe the stories in Cotton Mather's 'Magnalia.'"

"Wanter know?" said Sam, with a tone of slow, languid meditation.

We were sitting on a bank of the Charles River, fishing. The soft melancholy red of evening was fading off in streaks on the glassy water, and the houses of Oldtown were beginning to loom through the gloom, solemn and ghostly. There are times and tones and moods of nature that make all the vulgar, daily real seem shadowy, vague, and supernatural, as if the outlines of this hard material present were fading into the invisible and unknown. So Oldtown, with its elmtrees, its great square white houses, its meeting-house and tavern and blacksmith's shop and mill, which at high noon seem as real and as commonplace as possible, at this hour of the evening were dreamy and solemn. They rose up blurred, indistinct, dark; here and there winking candles sent long lines of light through the shadows, and little drops of unforeseen rain rippled the sheeny dankness of the water.

"Wal, you see, boys, in them things it's jest as well to mind your granny. There's a consid'able sight o' gumption in grandmas. You look at the folks that's allus tellin' you what they don't believe,—they don't believe this, and they don't believe that,—and what sort o' folks is they? Why, like yer Aunt Lois, sort o' stringy and dry. There ain't no 'sorption got out o' not bet ievin' nothin'."

"Lord a massy! we don't know nothin' 'bout them things. We hain't ben there, and can't say that there ain't no ghosts and sich; can we, now?'

We agreed to that fact, and sat a little closer to Sam in the gathering gloom.

"Tell us about the Cap'n Brown house, Sam."

"Ye didn't never go over the Cap'n Brown house?"

No, we had not that advantage.

"Wal, yer see, Cap'n Brown he made all his money to sea, in furrin parts, and then come here to Oldtown to settle down.

"Now, there ain't now knowin' 'bout these 'ere old shipmasters, where they's ben, or what they's ben a doin', or how they got their money. Ask me no questions, and I'll tell ye no lies, is 'bout the best philosophy for them. Wal, it didn't do no good to ask Cap'n Brown questions too close, 'cause you didn't git no satisfaction. Nobody rightly knew 'bout who his folks was, or where they come from, and, ef a body asked him, he used to say that the very fust he know'd 'bout himself he was a young man walkin' the streets in London.

"But, yer see, boys, he hed money, and that is about all folks wanter know when a man comes to settle down. And he bought that 'are place, and built that 'are house. He built it all sea-cap'n fashion, so's to feel as much at home as he could. The parlor was like a ship's cabin. The table and chairs was fastened down to the floor, and the closets was made with holes to set the casters and the decanters and bottles in, jest's they be at sea; and there was stanchions to hold on by; and they say that blowy nights the cap'n used to fire up pretty well with his grog, till he hed about all he could carry, and then he'd set and hold on, and hear the wind blow, and kind o' feel out to sea right there to hum. There wasn't no Mis' Cap'n Brown, and there didn't seem likely to be none. And whether there ever hed been one, nobody know'd. He hed an old black Guinea niggerwoman, named Quassia, that did his work. She was shaped pretty much like one o' these 'ere great crooknecked-squashes. She wa'n't no gret beauty, I can tell you; and she used to wear a gret red turban and a yaller short gown and red petticoat, and a gret string o' gold beads round her neck, and gret big gold hoops in her ears, made right in the middle o' Africa among the heathen there. For all she was black, she thought a heap o' herself, and was consid'able sort o predominative over the cap'n. Lord massy! boys, it's allus so. Get a man and a woman together,—any sort woman you're a mind to, don't care who 'tis,—and one way or another she gets the rule over him, and he jest has to train to her fife. Some does it one way, and some does it another; some does it by jawin', and some does it by kissin', and some does it by faculty and contrivance; but one way or another they alters does it. Old Cap'n Brown was a good stout, stocky kind o' John Bull sort o' fellow, and a good judge o' sperits, and alters kep' the best in them are cupboards o' his'n; but, fust and last, things in his house went pretty much as old Quassia said.

"Folks got to kind o' respectin' Quassia. She come to meetin' Sunday regular, and sot all fixed up in red and yaller and green, with glass beads and what not, lookin' for all the world like one o' them ugly Indian idols; but she was well-behaved as any Christian. She was a master hand at cookin'. Her bread and biscuits couldn't be beat, and no couldn't her pies, and there wa'n't no such pound-cake as she made nowhere. Wal, this 'ere story I'm a goin' to tell you was told me by Cinthy Pendleton. There ain't a more respectable gal, old or young, than Cinthy nowheres. She lives over to Sherburne now, and I hear tell she's sot up a manty-makin' business; but then she used to do tailorin' in Oldtown. She was a member o' the church, and a good Christian as ever was. Wal, ye see, Quassia she got Cinthy to come up and spend a week to the Cap'n Brown house, a doin' taitorin' and a fixin' over his close: 'twas along toward the fust o' March. Cinthy she sot by the fire in the front parlor with her goose and her press-board and her work: for there wa'n't no company callin', and the snow was drifted four feet deep right across the front door; so there wa'n't much danger o' any body comin' in. And the cap'n he was a perlite man to wimmen; and Cinthy she liked it jest as well not to have company, 'cause the cap'n he'd make himself entertainin' teltin' on her sea-stories, and all about this adventures among the Ammonites, and Perresites, and Jebusites, and all sorts o' heathen people he'd been among. 'Wal, that 'are week there come on the master snow-storm. Of all the snow-storms that bed ben, that 'are was the beater; and I tell you the wind blew as if 'twas the last chance it was ever goin' to hey. Wal, it's kind o' scary like to be shet up in a lone house with all natur' a kind o' breakin' out, and goin' on so, and the snow a comin' down so thick ye can't see 'cross the street, and the wind a pipin' and a squeelin' and a rumblin' and a tumblin' fust down this chimney and then down that. I tell you, it sort o' sets a feller thinkin' o' the three great things,—death, judgment, and etarnaty; and I don't care who the folks is, nor how good they be, there's times when they must be feelin' putty consid'able solemn.

"Wal, Cinthy she said she kind o' felt so along, and she bed a sort o' queer feelin' come over her as if there was somebody or somethin' round the house more'n appeared. She said she sort o' felt it in the air; but it seemed to her silly, and she tried to get over it. But two or three times, she said, when it got to be dusk, she felt somebody go by her up the stairs. The front entry wa'n't very light in the day time, and in the storm, come five o'clock, it was so dark that all you could see was jest a gleam o' somethin', and two or three times when she started to go up stairs she see a soft white suthin' that seemed goin' up before her, and she stopped with her heart a beatin' like a trip-hammer, and she sort o' saw it go up and along the entry to the cap'n's door, and then it seemed to go right through, 'cause the door didn't open.

"Wal, Cinthy says she to old Quassia, says she, 'Is there anybody lives in this house but us?'

"'Anybody lives here?' says Quassia: 'What you mean?' says she.

"Says Cinthy, 'I thought somebody went past me on the stairs last night and tonight.'

"Lord massy! how old Quassia did screech and laugh. 'Good Lord!' says she, 'how foolish white folks is! Somebody went past you? Was't the capt'in?'

"'No, it wa'n't the cap'n,' says she: 'it was somethin' soft and white, and moved very still; it was like somethin' in the air,' says she.

"Then Quassia she haw-hawed louder. Says she, 'It's hysterikes, Miss Cinthy; that's all it is.'

"Wal, Cinthy she was kind o' 'shamed, but for all that she couldn't help herself. Sometimes evenin's she'd be a settin' with the cap'n, and she'd think she'd hear somebody a movin' in his room overhead; and she knowed it wa'n't Quassia, 'cause Quassia was ironin' in the kitchen.

She took pains once or twice to find out that 'are. "Wal, ye see, the cap'n's room was the gret front upper chamber over the parlor, and then right opposite to it was the gret spae chamber where Cinthy slept. It was jest as grand as could be, with a gret four-post mahogany bedstead and damask curtains brought over from England; but it was cold enough to freeze a white bear solid,—the way spare chambers alters is. Then there was the entry between, run straight through the house: one side was old Quassia's room, and the other was a sort o' storeroom, where the old cap'n kep' all sorts o' traps.

"Wal, Cinthy she kep' a hevin' things happen and a seem' thins, till she didn't railly know what was in it. Once when she come into the parlor jest at sundown, she was sure she see a white figure a vanishin' out o' the door that went towards the side entry. She said it was so dusk, that all she could see was jest this white figure, and it jest went out still as a cat as she come in. Wal, Cinthy didn't like to speak to the cap'n about it. She was a close woman, putty prudent,

Cinthy was. But one night, 'bout the middle o' the week, this 'ere thing kind o' come to a crisis. Cinthy said she'd ben up putty late a sewin' and a finishin' off down in the parlour; and the cap'n he sot up with her, and was consid'able cheerful and entertainin', tellin' her all about things over the Bermudys, and off to Chiny and Japan, and round the world ginerally. The storm that bed been a blowin' all the week was about as furious as ever; and the cap'n he stirred up a mess o' flip, and bed it for her hot to go to bed on. He was a good-natured critter, and alters had feelin's for lone women; and I s'pose he knew 'twas sort o' desolate for Cinthy.

"Wal, takin' the flip so right the last think afore goin' to bed, she went right off to sleep as sound as a nut, and slep' on till somehwere about mornin', when she said somethin' waked her broad awake in a minute. Her eyes flew wide open like a spring, and the storm hed gone down and the moon come out: and there, standin' right in the moonlight by her bed, was a woman jest as white as a sheet, with black hair hangin' down to her waist, and the brightest, mourn-fullest black eyes you ever see. She stood there bookin' right at Cinthy; and Cinthy thinks that was what waked her up; 'cause, you know, ef anybody stands and looks steady at folks asleep it's apt to wake 'em.

"Any way, Cinthy said she felt jest as ef she was turnin' to stone. She couldn't move nor speak. She lay a minute, and then she shut her eyes, and begun to say her prayers; and a minute after she opened 'em, and it was gone.

JACOB GRIMM

(1785-1863)

WILHELM GRIMM

(1786-1859)

28

The Children of Hamelin

In the year 1284 a mysterious man appeared in Hameln. He was wearing a coat of many coloured, bright cloth, for which reason he was called the Pied Piper. He claimed to be a ratcatcher, and he promised that for a certain sum that he would rid the city of all mice and rats. The citizens struck a deal, promising him a certain price. The ratcatcher then took a small fife from his pocket and began to blow on it. Rats and mice immediately came from every house and gathered around him. We he thought that he had them all he led them to the River Weser where he pulled up his clothes and walked into the water. The animals all followed him, fell in, and drowned.

Now that the citizens had been freed of their plague, they regretted having promised so much money, and, using all kinds of excuses, they refused to pay him. Finally he went away, bitter and angry. He returned on June 26, Saint John's and Saint Paul's Day, early in the morning at seven o'clock (others say it was at noon), now dressed in a hunter's costume, with a dreadful look on his face and wearing a strange red hat. He sounded his fife in the streets, but this time it wasn't rats and mice that came to him, but rather children: a great number of boys and girls from their fourth year on. Among them was the mayor's grown daughter. The swarm followed him, and he led them to a mountain, where he disappeared with them.

All this was seen by a babysitter who, carrying a child in her arms, had followed them from a distance, but had then turned around and carried the news back to the town. The anxious parents ran in droves to the town gates seeking their children. The mothers cried out and sobbed pitifully. Within the hour messengers were sent everywhere by water and by land inquiring if the children—or any of them—had been seen, but it was all for naught.

In total, one hundred thirty were lost. Two, as some say, had lagged behind and came back. One of them was blind and the other mute. The blind one was not able to point out the place, but was able to tell how they had followed the piper. The mute one was able to point out the place, although he (or she) had heard nothing. One little boy in shirtsleeves had gone along with the others, but had turned back to fetch his jacket and thus escaped the tragedy, for when he returned, the others had already disappeared into a cave within a hill. This cave is still shown.

Until the middle of the eighteenth century, and probably still today, the street through which the children were led out to the town gate was called the *bungelose* (drumless, soundless, quiet) street, because no dancing or music was allowed there. Indeed, when a bridal procession on its way to church crossed this street, the musicians would have to stop playing. The mountain near Hamelin where the children disappeared is called Poppenberg. Two stone monuments in the form of crosses have been erected there, one on the left side, and one on the right. Some say that the children were led into a cave, and that they came out again in Transylvania.

The citizens of Hamelin recorded this event in their town register, and they came to date all their proclamations according to the years and days since the loss of their children.

According to Seyfried the 22nd rather than the 26th of June was entered into the town register.

The following lines were described on the town hall:

In the year 1284 after the birth of Christ
From Hamelin were led away
One hundred thirty children, born at this place
Led away by a piper into a mountain.

And on the new gate was inscribed: Centum ter denos cum magus ab urbe puellos duxerat ante annos CCLXXII condita porta fuit. (This gate was built 272 years after the magician led one hundred thirty children from the city)

In the year 1572 the mayor had the story portrayed in the church windows. The accompanying inscription has become largely illegible. In addition, a coin was minted in memory of the event.

29

The Singing Bone

In a certain country there was once great lamentation over a wild boar that laid waste the farmers' fields, killed the cattle, and ripped up people's bodies with his tusks. The King promised a large reward to any one who would free the land from this plague; but the beast was so big and strong that no one dared to go near the forest in which it lived. At last the King gave notice that whosoever should capture or kill the wild boar should have his only daughter to wife.

Now there lived in the country two brothers, sons of a poor man, who declared themselves willing to undertake the hazardous enterprise; the elder, who was crafty and shrewd, out of pride; the younger, who was innocent and simple, from a kind heart. The King said, "In order that you may be the more sure of finding the beast, you must go into the forest from opposite sides." So the elder went in on the west side, and the younger on the east.

When the younger had gone a short way, a little man stepped up to him. He held in his hand a black spear and said, "I give you this spear because your heart is pure and good; with this you can boldly attack the wild boar, and it will do you no harm."

He thanked the little man, shouldered the spear, and went on fearlessly.

Before long he saw the beast, which rushed at him; but he held the spear towards it, and in its blind fury it ran so swiftly against it that its heart was cloven in twain. Then he took the monster on his back and went homewards with it to the King.

As he came out at the other side of the wood, there stood at the entrance a house where people were making merry with wine and dancing. His elder brother had gone in here, and thinking that after all the boar would not run away from him, was going to drink until he felt brave. But when he saw his young brother coming out of the wood laden with his booty, his envious, evil heart gave him no peace. He called out to him, "Come in, dear brother, rest and refresh yourself with a cup of wine."

The youth, who suspected no evil, went in and told him about the good little man who had given him the spear wherewith he had slain the boar.

The elder brother kept him there until the evening, and then they went away together, and when in the darkness they came to a bridge over a brook, the elder brother let the other go first; and when he was half-way across he gave him such a blow from behind that he fell down dead. He buried him beneath the bridge, took the boar, and carried it to the King, pretending that he had killed it; whereupon he obtained the King's daughter in marriage. And when his younger brother did not comeback he said, "The boar must have killed him," and every one believed it.

But as nothing remains hidden from God, so this black deed also was to come to light.

Years afterwards a shepherd was driving his herd across the bridge, and saw lying in the sand beneath, a snow-white little bone. He thought that it would make a good mouth-piece, so he clambered down, picked it up, and cut out of it a mouth-piece for his horn. But when he blew through it for the first time, to his great astonishment, the bone began of its own accord to sing:

"Ah, friend, thou blowest upon my bone!
    Long have I lain beside the water;
My brother slew me for the boar,
    And took for his wife the King's young daughter."

"What a wonderful horn!" said the shepherd; "it sings by itself; I must take it to my lord the King." And when he came with it to the King the horn again began to sing its little song. The King understood it all, and caused the ground below the bridge to be dug up, and then the whole skeleton of the murdered man came to light. The wicked brother could not deny the deed, and was sewn up in a sack and drowned. But the bones of the murdered man were laid to rest in a beautiful tomb in the churchyard.

JEROME K JEROME

(1859-1927)

30

The Dancing Partner

"This story," commenced MacShaugnassy, "comes from Furtwangen, a small town in the Black Forest. There lived there a very wonderful old fellow named Nicholau Geibel. His business was the making of mechanical toys, at which work he had acquired an almost European reputation. He made rabbits that would emerge from the heart of a cabbage, flop their ears, smooth their whiskers, and disappear again; cats that would wash their faces, and mew so naturally that dogs would mistake them for real cats, and fly at them; dolls, with phonographs concealed within them, that would raise their hats and say, 'Good morning; how do you do?' and some that would even sing a song.

"But he was something more than a mere mechanic; he was an artist. His work was with him a hobby, almost a passion. His shop was filled with all manner of strange things that never would, or could, be sold—things he had made for the pure love of making them. He had contrived a mechanical donkey that would trot for two hours by means of stored electricity, and trot, too, much faster than the live article, and with less need for exertion on the part of the driver; a bird that would shoot up into the air, fly around and around in a circle, and drop to earth at the exact spot from where it started; a skeleton that, supported by an upright iron bar, would dance a hornpipe; a life-size lady doll that could play the fiddle; and a gentleman with a hollow inside who could smoke a pipe and drink more lager beer than any three average German students put together, which is saying much.

"Indeed, it was the belief of the town that old Geibel could make a man capable of doing everything that a respectable man need want to do. One day he made a man who did too much, and it came about in this way:

"Young Doctor Follen had a baby, and the baby had a birthday. Its first birthday put Doctor Follen's household into somewhat of a flurry, but on the occasion of its second birthday, Mrs. Doctor Follen gave a ball in honor of the event. Old Geibel and his daughter Olga were among the guests.

"During the afternoon of the next day some three or four of Olga's bosom friends, who had also been present at the ball, dropped in to have a chat about it. They naturally fell to discussing the men, and to criticizing their dancing. Old Geibel was in the room, but he appeared to be absorbed in his newspaper, and the girls took no notice of him.

"'There seem to be fewer men who can dance at every ball you go to,' said one of the girls.

"'Yes, and don't the ones who can, give themselves airs,' said another; 'they make quite a favour of asking you.'

"'And how stupidly they talk,' added a third. 'They always say exactly the same things: "How charming you are looking tonight." "Do you often go to Vienna? Oh, you should, it's delightful." "What a charming dress you have on." "What a warm day it has been." "Do you like Wagner?" I do wish they'd think of something new.'

"'Oh, I never mind how they talk,' said a fourth. 'If a man dances well he may be a fool for all I care.'

"'He generally is,' slipped in a thin girl, rather spitefully.

"'I go to a ball to dance,' continued the previous speaker, not noticing the interruption. 'All I ask of a partner is that he shall hold me firmly, take me round steadily, and not get tired before I do.'

"'A clockwork figure would be the thing for you,' said the girl who had interrupted.

"'Bravo!' cried one of the others, clapping her hands, 'what a capital idea!'

"'What's a capital idea?' they asked.

"'Why, a clockwork dancer, or, better still, one that would go by electricity and never run down.'

"The girls took up the idea with enthusiasm.

"'Oh, what a lovely partner he would make,' said one; 'he would never kick you, or tread on your toes.'

"'Or tear your dress,' said another.

"'Or get out of step.'

"'Or get giddy and lean on you.'

"'And he would never want to mop his face with his handkerchief. I do hate to see a man do that after every dance.'

"'And wouldn't want to spend the whole evening in the supper room.'

"'Why, with a phonograph inside him to grind out all the stock remarks, you would not be able to tell him from a real man,' said the girl who had first suggested the idea.

"'Oh, yes, you would,' said the thin girl, 'he would be so much nicer.'

"Old Geibel had laid down his paper, and was listening with both his ears. On one of the girls glancing in his direction, however, he hurriedly hid himself again behind it.

"After the girls were gone, he went into his workshop, where Olga heard him walking up and down, and every now and them chuckling to himself; and that night he talked to her a good deal about dancing and dancing men—asked what they usually said and did—what dances were most popular—what steps were gone through, with many other questions bearing on the subject.

"Then for a couple of weeks he kept much to his factory, and was very thoughtful and busy, though prone at unexpected moments to break into a quiet low laugh, as if enjoying a joke that nobody else knew of.

"A month later another ball took in place in Furtwangen.

On this occasion it was given by old Wetzel, the wealthy timber merchant, to celebrate his niece's betrothal, and Geibel and his daughter were again among the invited.

"When the hour arrived to set out, Olga sought her father. Not finding him in the house, she tapped at the door of his workshop. He appeared in his shirt-sleeves, looking hot but radiant.

"'Don't wait for me,' he said, 'you go on, I'll follow you. I've got something to finish.'

"As she turned to obey he called after her, 'Tell them I'm going to bring a young man with me—such a nice young man, and an excellent dancer. All the girls will like him.' Then he laughed and closed the door.

"Her father generally kept his doings secret from everybody, but she had a pretty shrewd suspicion of what he had been planning, and so, to a certain extent, was able to prepare the guests for what was coming. Anticipation ran high, and the arrival of the famous mechanist was eagerly awaited.

"At length the sound of wheels was heard outside, followed by a great commotion in the passage, and old Wenzel himself, his jolly face red with excitement and suppressed laughter, burst into the room and announced in stentorian tones:

"'Herr Geibel—and a friend.'

"Herr Geibel and his 'friend' entered, greeted with shouts of laughter and applause, and advanced to the centre of the room.

"'Allow me, ladies and gentlemen,' said Herr Geibel, 'to introduce you to my friend, Lieutenant Fritz. Fritz, my dear fellow, bow to the ladies and gentlemen.'

"Geibel placed his hand encouragingly on Fritz's shoulder, and the Lieutenant bowed low, accompanying the action with a harsh clicking noise in his throat, unpleasantly suggestive of a death-rattle. But that was only a detail.

"'He walks a little stiffly' (old Geibel took his arm and walked him forward a few steps. He certainly did walk stiffly), 'but then, walking is not his forte. He is essentially a dancing man. I have only been able to teach him the waltz as yet, but at that he is faultless. Come, which of you ladies may I introduce him to as a partner?

He keeps perfect time; he never gets tired; he won't kick you or trad on your dress; he will hold you as firmly as you like, and go as quickly or a slowly as you please; he never gets giddy; and he is full of conversation. Come, speak up for yourself, my boy.'

"The old gentleman twisted one of the buttons at the back of his coat, and immediately Fritz opened his mouth, and in thin tones that appeared to proceed from the back of his head, remarked suddenly, 'May I have the pleasure?' and then shut his mouth again with a snap.

"That Lieutenant Fritz had made a strong impression on the company was undoubted, yet none of the girls seemed inclined to dance with him. They looked askance at his waxen face, with its staring eyes and fixed smile, and shuddered. At last old Geibel came to the girl who had conceived the idea.

"'It is your own suggestion, carried out to the letter,' said Geibel, 'an electric dancer. You owe it to the gentleman to give him a trial.'

"She was a bright, saucy little girl, fond of a frolic. Her host added his entreaties, and she consented.

"Her Geibel fixed the figure to her. Its right arm was screwed round her waist, and held her firmly; its delicately jointed left hand was made to fasten upon her right. The old toymaker showed her how to regulate its speed, and how to stop it, and release herself.

"'It will take you round in a complete circle,' he explained; 'be careful that no one knocks against you, and alters its course.'

"The music struck up. Old Geibel put the current in motion, and Annette and her strange partner began to dance.

"For a while everyone stood watching them. The figure performed its purpose admirably. Keeping perfect time and step, and holding its little partner tight clasped in an unyielding embrace, it revolved steadily, pouring forth at the same time a constant flow of squeaky conversation, broken by brief intervals of grinding silence.

"'How charming you are looking tonight,' it remarked in its thin, far-away voice. 'What a lovely day it has been. Do you like dancing? How well our steps agree. You will give me another, won't you? Oh, don't be so cruel. What a charming gown you have on. Isn't waltzing delightful? I could go on dancing for ever—with you. Have you had supper?'

"As she grew more familiar with the uncanny creature, the girl's nervousness wore off, and she entered into the fun of the thing.

"'Oh, he's just lovely,' she cried, laughing; 'I could go on dancing with him all my life.'

"Couple after couple now joined them, and soon all the dancers in the room were whirling round behind them. Nicholaus Geibel stood looking on, beaming with childish delight at his success.

"Old Wenzel approached him, and whispered something in his ear. Geibel laughed and nodded, and the two worked their way quietly towards the door.

"'This is the young people's house tonight,' said Wenzel, as soon as they were outside; 'you and I will have a quiet pipe and glass of hock, over in the counting-house.'

"Meanwhile the dancing grew more fast and furious. Little Annette loosened the screw regulating her partner's rate of progress, and the figure flew round with her swifter and swifter. Couple after couple dropped out exhausted, but they only went the faster, till at length they remained dancing alone.

"Madder and madder became the waltz. The music lagged behind: the musicians, unable to keep pace, ceased, and sat staring. The younger guests applauded, but the older faces began to grow anxious.

"'Hadn't you better stop, dear,' said one of the women, 'you'll make yourself so tired.'

"But Annette did not answer.

"'I believe she's fainted,' cried out a girl who had caught sight of her face as it was swept by.

"One of the men sprang forward and clutched at the figure, but its impetus threw him down on to the floor, where its steel-cased feet laid bare his cheek. The thing evidently did not intend to part with its prize so easily.

"Had any one retained a cool head, the figure, one cannot help thinking, might easily have been stopped. Two or three men acting in concert might have lifted it bodily off the floor, or have jammed it into a corner. But few human heads are capable of remaining cool under excitement. Those who are not present think how stupid must have been those wh were; those who are reflect afterwards how simple it would have been to do this, that, or the other, if only they had thought of it at the time.

"The women grew hysterical. The men shouted contradictory directions to one another. Tow of them made a bungling rush at the figure, which had the end result of forcing it out of its orbit at the centre of the room, and sending it crashing against the walls and furniture. A stream of blood showed itself down the girl's white frock, and followed her along the floor. The affair was becoming horrible. The women rushed screaming from the room. The men followed them.

"One sensible suggestion was made: 'Find Geibel—fetch Geibel.'

"No one had noticed him leave the room, no one knew where he was. A party went in search of him. The others, too unnerved to go back into the ballroom, crowded outside the door and listened. They could hear the steady whir of the wheels upon the polished floor as the thing spun round and round; the dull thud as every now and again it dashed itself and its burden against some opposing object and ricocheted off in a new direction.

"And everlastingly it talked in that thin ghostly voice, repeating over and over the same formula: 'How charming you look tonight. What a lovely day it has been. Oh, don't be so cruel. I could go on dancing for ever—with you. Have you had supper?'

"Of course they sought Geibel everywhere but where he was. They looked in every room in the house, then they rushed off in a body to his own place, and spent precious minutes waking up his deaf old housekeeper. At last it occurred to one of the party that Wenzel was missing also, and then the idea of the counting-house across the yard presented itself to them, and there they found him.

"He rose up, very pale, and followed them; and he and old Wenzel forced their way through the crowd of guests gathered outside, and entered the room, and locked the door behind them.

"From within there came the muffled sound of low voices and quick steps, followed by a confused scuffling noise, then silence, then the low voices again.

"After a time the door opened, and those near it pressed forward to enter, but old Wenzel's broad head and shoulders barred the way.

"'I want you—and you, Bekler,' he said, addressing a couple of the elder men. His voice was calm, but his face was deadly white. 'The rest of you, please go—get the women away as quickly as you can.'

"From that day old Nicholaus Geibel confined himself to the making of mechanical rabbits, and cats that mewed and washed their faces."

JOHN LANG

(1816-1864)

31

Fisher's Ghost

In the colony of New South Wales, at a place called Penrith, distant from Sydney about thirty-seven miles, lived a farmer named Fisher. He had been, originally, transported, but had become free by servitude. Unceasing toil, and great steadiness of character, had acquired for him a considerable property, for a person in his station of life. His lands and stock were not worth less than four thousand pounds. He was unmarried and was about forty-five years old.

Suddenly Fisher disappeared; and one of his neighbours—a man named Smith—gave out that he had gone to England, but would return in two or three years. Smith produced a document, purporting to be executed by Fisher; and, according to this document, Fisher had appointed Smith to act as his agent during his absence. Fisher was a man of very singular habits and eccentric character and his silence about his departure, instead of creating surprise, was declared to be 'exactly like him'.

About six months after Fisher's disappearance, an old man called Ben Weir, who had a small farm near Penrith and who always drove his own cart to market, was returning from Sydney one night when he beheld, seated on a rail which bounded the road—Fisher. The night was very dark and the distance of the fence from the middle of the road was, at least, twelve yards. Weir, nevertheless, saw Fisher's figure seated on the rail. He pulled his old mare up, and called out, "Fisher, is that you?" No answer was returned; but there, still on the rail, sat the form of the man with whom he had been on the most intimate terms. Weir—who was not drunk, though he had taken several glasses of strong liquor on the road—jumped off his cart and approached the rail. To his surprise, the form vanished.

"Well," exclaimed old Weir, "this is very curious, anyhow;" and, breaking several branches of a sapling so as to mark the exact spot, he remounted his cart, put his old mare into a jog-trot and soon reached his home.

Ben was not likely to keep this vision a secret from his old woman. All that he had seen he faithfully related to her.

"Hold our nonsense, Ben!" was old Betty's reply. "You know you have been a drinking and disturbing of your imagination. Ain't Fisher agone to England? And if he had a come back, do you think we shouldn't a heard on it?"

"Ay, Betty!" said old Ben, "But he'd a cruel gash in his forehead and the blood was all fresh like. Faith, it makes me shudder to think on't. It were his ghost."

"How can you talk so foolish, Ben?" said the old woman. "You must be drunk sure-ly to get on about ghosteses."

"I tell thee I am not drunk," rejoined old Ben, angrily. "There's been foul play, Betty; I'm sure on't. There sat Fisher on the rail—not more than a matter of two mile from this. Egad, it were on his own fence that he sat. There he was, in his shirt-sleeves, with his arms a folded; just as he used to sit when he was a waiting for anybody coming up the road. Bless you, Betty, I seed 'im till I was as close as I am to thee; when, all on a sudden, he vanished, like smoke."

"Nonsense, Ben: don't talk of it," said old Betty, "or the neighbours will only laugh at you. Come to bed and you'll forget all about it before tomorrow morning."

Old Ben went to bed; but he did not next morning forget all

about what he had seen on the previous night: on the contrary, he was more positive than before. However, at the earnest and often repeated request of the old woman, he promised not to mention having seen Fisher's ghost, for fear that it might expose him to ridicule.

On the following Thursday night, when old Ben was returning from market—again in his cart—he saw, seated upon the same rail, the identical apparition. He had purposely abstained from drinking that day and was in the full possession of all his senses. On this occasion old Ben was too much alarmed to stop. He urged the old mare on and got home as speedily as possible. As soon as he had unharnessed and fed the mare and taken his purchases out of the cart, he entered his cottage, lighted his pipe, sat over the fire with his better half and gave her an account of how he had disposed of his produce and what he had brought back from Sydney in return. After this he said to her, "Well, Betty, I'm not drunk tonight, anyhow, am I?"

"No," said Betty. "You are quite sober, sensible like, tonight, Ben; and therefore you have come home without any ghost in your head. Ghosts! Don't believe there is such things."

"Well, you are satisfied I am not drunk; but perfectly sober," said the old man.

"Yes, Ben," said Betty.

"Well, then," said Ben, "I tell thee what, Betty. I saw Fisher tonight agin!"

"Stuff!" cried old Betty.

"You may say stuff," said the old farmer; "but I tell you what—I saw him as plainly as I did last Thursday night. Smith is a bad 'un! Do you think Fisher would ever have left this country without coming to bid you and me goodbye?"

"It's all fancy!" said old Betty. "Now drink your grog and smoke your pipe and think no more about the ghost. I won't hear on't."

"I'm as fond of my grog and my pipe as most men," said old Ben; "but I'm not going to drink anything tonight. It may be all fancy, as you call it, but I am now going to tell Mr. Grafton all I saw, and what I think;" and with these words he got up and left the house.

Mr. Grafton was a gentleman who lived about a mile from old Weir's farm. He had been formerly a lieutenant in the navy, but was now on half-pay and was a settler in the new colony; he was, moreover, in the commission of the peace.

When old Ben arrived at Mr. Grafton's house, Mr. Grafton was about to retire to bed; but he requested old Ben might be shown in. He desired the farmer to take a seat by the fire and then enquired what was the latest news in Sydney.

"The news in Sydney, sir, is very small," said old Ben; "wheat is falling, but maize still keeps its price—seven and sixpence a bushel: but I want to tell you, sir, something that will astonish you."

"What is it, Ben?" asked Mr. Grafton.

"Why, sir," resumed old Ben, "you know I am not a weak-minded man, nor a fool, exactly; for I was born and bred in Yorkshire."

"No, Ben, I don't believe you to be weak-minded, nor do I think you a fool," said Mr. Grafton; "but what can you have to say that you come at this late hour and that you require such a preface?"

"That I have seen the ghost of Fisher, sir," said the old man; and he detailed the particulars of which the reader is already in possession.

Mr. Grafton was at first disposed to think with old Betty, that Ben had seen Fisher's Ghost through an extra glass or two of rum on the first night; and that on the second night, when perfectly sober, he was unable to divest himself of the idea previously entertained. But after a little consideration the words "How very singular!" involuntarily escaped him.

"Go home, Ben," said Mr. Grafton, "and let me see you tomorrow at sunrise. We will go together to the place where you say you saw the ghost."

Mr. Grafton used to encourage the aboriginal natives of New South Wales (that race which has been very aptly described 'the last link in the human chain') to remain about his premises. At the head of a little tribe then encamped on Mr. Grafton's estate, was a sharp young man named Johnny Crook. The peculiar faculty of the aboriginal natives of New South Wales, of tracking the human foot not only over grass but over the hardest rock; and of tracking the whereabouts of runaways by signs imperceptible to civilised eyes, is well known; and this man, Johnny Crook, was famous for his skill in this particular art of tracking. He had recently been instrumental in the apprehension of several desperate bushrangers whom he had tracked over twenty-seven miles of rocky country and fields, which they had crossed bare-footed, in the hope of checking the black fellow in the progress of his keen pursuit with the horse police.

When old Ben Weir made his appearance in the morning at Mr. Grafton's house, the black chief, Johnny Crook, was summoned to attend. He came and brought with him several of his subjects. The party set out, old Weir showing the way. The leaves on the branches of the saplings which he had broken on the first night of seeing the ghost were withered and sufficiently pointed out the exact rail on which the phantom was represented to have sat. There were stains upon the rail. Johnny Crook, who had then no idea of what he was required for, pronounced these stains to be 'White man's blood;' and, after searching about for some time, he pointed to a spot whereon he said a human body had been laid.

In New South Wales long droughts are not very uncommon; and not a single shower of rain had fallen for seven months previously—not sufficient even to lay the dust upon the roads.

In consequence of the time that had elapsed, Crook had no small difficulty to contend with; but in about two hours he succeeded in tracking the footsteps of one man to the unfrequented side of a pond at some distance. He gave it as his opinion that another man had been dragged thither. The savage walked round and round the pond, eagerly examining its borders and the sedges and weeds springing up around it. At first he seemed baffled. No clue had been washed ashore to show that anything unusual had been sunk in the pond; but, having finished this examination, he laid himself down on his face and looked keenly along the surface of the smooth and stagnant water. Presently he jumped up, uttered a cry peculiar to the natives when gratified by finding some long-sought object, clapped his hands and, pointing to the middle of the pond to where the decomposition of some sunken substance had produced a slimy coating streaked with prismatic colours, he exclaimed, "White man's fat!" The pond was immediately searched; and, below the spot indicated, the remains of a body were discovered. A large stone and a rotted silk handkerchief were found near the body; these had been used to sink it.

That it was the body of Fisher there could be no question. It might have been identified by the teeth; but on the waistcoat there were some large brass buttons which were immediately recognised, both by Mr. Grafton and by old Ben Weir, as Fisher's property. He had worn those buttons on his waistcoat for several years.

Leaving the body by the side of the pond and old Ben and the blacks to guard it, Mr. Grafton cantered up to Fisher's house. Smith was not only in possession of all the missing man's property, but had removed to Fisher's house. It was about a mile and a half distant. He enquired for Mr. Smith. Mr. Smith, who was at breakfast, came out and invited Mr. Grafton to alight; Mr. Grafton accepted the invitation and after a few desultory observations said, "Mr. Smith, I am anxious to purchase a piece of land on the other side of the road, belonging to this estate, and I would give a fair price for it. Have you the power to sell?"

"Oh yes, sir," replied Smith. "The power which I hold from Fisher is a general power;" and he forthwith produced a document purporting to be signed by Fisher, but which was not witnessed.

"If you are not very busy, I should like to show you the piece of land I allude to," said Mr. Grafton.

"Oh certainly, sir. I am quite at your service," said Smith; and he then ordered his horse to be saddled.

It was necessary to pass the pond where the remains of Fisher's body were then exposed. When they came near to the spot, Mr. Grafton, looking Smith full in the face, said, "Mr. Smith, I wish to show you something. Look here!" He pointed to the decomposed body and narrowly watching Mr. Smith's countenance, remarked:

"These are the remains of Fisher. How do you account for their being found in this pond?"

Smith, with the greatest coolness, got off his horse, minutely examined the remains and then admitted that there was no doubt they were Fisher's. He confessed himself at a loss to account for their discovery, unless it could be (he said) that somebody had waylaid him on the road when he left his home for Sydney; had murdered him for the gold and banknotes which he had about his person and had then thrown him into the pond. "My hands, thank heaven!" he concluded, "are clean. If my old friend could come to life again, he would tell you that I had no hand in his horrible murder."

Mr. Grafton knew not what to think. He was not a believer in ghosts. Could it be possible, he began to ask himself, that old Weir had committed this crime and—finding it weigh heavily on his conscience and fearing that he might be detected—had trumped up the story about the ghost—had pretended that he was led to the spot by supernatural agency—and thus by bringing the murder voluntarily to light, hoped to stifle all suspicion? But then, he considered Weir's excellent character, his kind disposition and good-nature. These at once put to flight his suspicion of Weir; but still he was by no means satisfied of Smith's guilt, much as appearances were against him.

Fisher's servants were examined and stated that their master had often talked of going to England on a visit to his friends and of leaving Mr. Smith to manage his farm; and that though they were surprised when Mr. Smith came and said he had 'gone at last', they did not think it at all unlikely that he had done so. An inquest was held and a verdict of wilful murder found against Thomas Smith. He was thereupon transmitted to Sydney for trial, at the ensuing sessions, in the supreme court. The case naturally excited great interest in the colony; and public opinion respecting Smith's guilt was evenly balanced.

The day of trial came; and the court was crowded almost to suffocation. The Attorney-General very truly remarked that there were circumstances connected with the case which were without any precedent in the annals of jurisprudence. The only witnesses were old Weir and Mr. Grafton. Smith, who defended himself with great composure and ability, cross-examined them at considerable length and with consummate skill. The prosecution having closed, Smith addressed the jury (which consisted of military officers) in his defence. He admitted that the circumstances were strong against him; but he most ingeniously proceeded to explain them. The power of attorney, which he produced, he contended had been regularly granted by Fisher and he called several witnesses who swore that they believed the signature to be that of the deceased. He, further, produced a will, which had been drawn up by Fisher's attorney, and by that will Fisher had appointed Smith his sole executor, in the event of his death. He declined, he said, to throw any suspicion on Weir; but he would appeal to the common sense of the jury whether the ghost story was entitled to any credit; and, if it were not, to ask themselves why it had been invented? He alluded to the fact—which in cross-examination Mr. Grafton swore to—that when the remains were first shown to him, he did not conduct himself as a guilty man would have been likely to do, although he was horror-stricken on beholding the hideous spectacle. He concluded by invoking the Almighty to bear witness that he was innocent of the diabolical crime for which he had been arranged. The judge (the late Sir Francis Forbes) recapitulated the evidence. It was not an easy matter to deal with that part of it which had reference to the apparition: and if the charge of the judge had any leaning one way or the other, it was decidedly in favour of an acquittal. The jury retired; but, after deliberating for seven hours, they returned to the court, with a verdict of guilty.

The judge then sentenced the prisoner to be hanged on the following Monday. It was on a Thursday night that he was convicted. On the Sunday, Smith expressed a wish to see a clergyman. His wish was instantly attended to, when he confessed that he, and he alone, committed the murder; and that it was upon the very rail where Weir swore that he had seen Fisher's ghost sitting, that he had knocked out Fisher's brains with a tomahawk. The power of attorney he likewise confessed was a forgery, but declared that the will was genuine.

This is very extraordinary, but is, nevertheless, true in substance, if not in every particular. Most persons who have visited Sydney for any length of time will no doubt have had it narrated to them.

JONAS LIE
(1833-1908)

32

The Fisherman and the Draug

On Kvalholm, down in Helgeland, dwelt a poor fisherman, Elias by name, with his wife Karen, who had been in service at the parson's over at Alstad. They had built them a hut here, and he used to go out fishing by the day about the Lofotens.

There could be very little doubt that the lonely Kvalholm was haunted. Whenever her husband was away, Karen heard all manner of uncanny shrieks and noises, which could mean no good. One day, when she was up on the hillside, mowing grass to serve as winter fodder for their couple of sheep, she heard, quite plainly, a chattering on the strand beneath the hill, but look over she durst not.

They had a child every year, but that was no burden, for they were both thrifty, hard-working folks. When seven years had gone by, there were six children in the house; but that same autumn Elias had scraped together so much that he thought he might now venture to buy a *Sexæring*, and henceforward go fishing in his own boat.

One day, as he was walking along with a *Kvejtepig* in his hand, and thinking the matter over, he unexpectedly came upon a monstrous seal, which lay sunning itself right behind a rock on the strand, and was as much surprised to see the man as the man was to see the seal. But Elias was not slack; from the top of the rock on which he stood, he hurled the long heavy Kvejtepig right into the monster's back, just below the neck.

The seal immediately rose up on its tail right into the air as high as a boat's mast, and looked so evilly and viciously at him with its bloodshot eyes, at the same time showing its grinning teeth, that Elias thought he should have died on the spot for sheer fright. Then it plunged into the sea, and lashed the water into bloody foam behind it. Elias didn't stop to see more, but that same evening there drifted into the boat place on Kvalcreek, on which his house stood, a Kvejtepole, with the hooked iron head snapped off.

Elias thought no more about it, but in the course of the autumn he bought his *Sexæring*, for which he had been building a little boat-shed the whole summer.

One night as he lay awake, thinking of his new *Sexæring*, it occurred to him that his boat would balance better, perhaps, if he stuck an extra log of wood on each side of it. He was so absurdly fond of the boat that it was a mere pastime for him to light a lantern and go down to have a look at it.

Now as he stood looking at it there by the light of the lantern, he suddenly caught a glimpse in the corner opposite, on a coil of nets, of a face which exactly resembled the seal's. For an instant it grinned savagely at him and the light, its mouth all the time growing larger and larger; and then a big man whisked out of the door, not so quickly, however, but that Elias could catch a glimpse, by the light of the lantern, of a long iron hooked spike sticking out of his back. And now he began to put one and two together. Still he was less anxious about his life than about his boat; so he there and then sat him down in it with the lantern, and kept watch. When his wife came in the morning, she found him sleeping there, with the burnt-out lantern by his side.

One morning in January, while he was out fishing in his boat with two other men, he heard, in the dark, a voice from a skerry at the very entrance of the creek. It laughed scornfully, and said, "When it *comes to a Femböring*, Elias, look to thyself!"

But there was many a long year yet before it *did* come to that; but one autumn, when his son Bernt was sixteen, Elias knew he could manage it, so he took his whole family with him in his boat to Ranen, to exchange his *Sexæring* for a *Femböring*. The only person left at home was a little Finn girl, whom they had taken into service some few years before, and who had only lately been confirmed.

Now there was a boat, a little *Femböring*, for four men and a boy, that Elias just then had his eye upon—a boat which the best boat-builder in the place had finished and tarred over that very autumn. Elias had a very good notion of what a boat should be, and it seemed to him that he had never seen a *Femböring* so well built *below* the water-line. *Above* the water-line, indeed, it looked only middling, so that, to one of less experience than himself, the boat would have seemed rather a heavy goer than otherwise, and anything but a smart craft.

Now the boat-master knew all this just as well as Elias. He said he thought it would be the swiftest sailer in Ranen, but that Elias should have it cheap, all the same, if only he would promise one thing, and that was, to make no alteration whatever in the boat, nay, not so much as adding a fresh coat of tar. Only when Elias had expressly given his word upon it did he get the boat.

But 'yon laddie' who had taught the boat-master how to build his boats so cunningly *below* the water-line—*above* the water-line he had had to use his native wits, and they were scant enough—must surely have been there beforehand, and bidden him both sell it cheaply, so that Elias might get it, and stipulate besides that the boat should not be looked at too closely. In this way it escaped the usual tarring fore and aft.

Elias now thought about sailing home, but went first into the town, provided himself and family with provisions against Christmas, and indulged in a little nip of brandy besides. Glad as he was over the day's bargain, he, and his wife too, took an extra drop in their e'en, and their son Bernt had a taste of it too.

After that they sailed off homewards in their new boat. There was no other ballast in the boat but himself, his old woman, the children, and the Christmas provisions. His son Bernt sat by the main-sheet; his wife, helped by her next eldest son, held the sail-ropes; Elias himself sat at the rudder, while the two younger brothers of twelve and fourteen were to take it in turns to bail out.

They had eight miles of sea to sail over, and when they got into the open, it was plain that the boat would be tested pretty stiffly on its first voyage. A gale was gradually blowing up, and crests of foam began to break upon the heavy sea.

And now Elias saw what sort of a boat he really had. She skipped over the waves like a sea-mew; not so much as a splash came into the boat, and he therefore calculated that he would have no need to take in all his clews against the wind, which an ordinary *Femböring* would have been forced to do in such weather.

Out on the sea, not very far away from him, he saw another *Femböring*, with a full crew, and four clews in the sail, just like his own. It lay on the same course, and he thought it rather odd that he had not noticed it before. It made as if it would race him, and when Elias perceived that, he could not for the life of him help letting out a clew again.

And now he went racing along like a dart, past capes and islands and rocks, till it seemed to Elias as if he had never had such a splendid sail before. Now, too, the boat showed itself what it really was, the best boat in Ranen.

The weather, meantime, had become worse, and they had already got a couple of dangerous seas right upon them. They broke in over the main-sheet in the forepart of the boat where Bernt sat, and sailed out again to leeward near the stern.

Since the gloom had deepened, the other boat had kept almost alongside, and they were now so close together that they could easily have pitched the baling-can from one to the other.

So they raced on, side by side, in constantly stiffer seas, till night-fall, and beyond it. The fourth clew ought now to have been taken in again, but Elias didn't want to give in, and thought he might bide a bit till they took it in in the other boat also, which they needs *must* do soon. Ever and anon the brandy-flask was brought out and passed round, for they had now both cold and wet to hold out against.

The sea-fire, which played on the dark billows near Elias's own boat, shone with an odd vividness in the foam round the other boat, just as if a fire-shovel was ploughing up and turning over the water. In the bright phosphorescence he could plainly make out the rope-ends on board her. He could also see distinctly the folks on board, with their sou'westers on their heads; but as their larboard side lay nearest, of course they all had their backs towards him, and were well-nigh hidden by the high heeling hull.

Suddenly a tremendous roller burst upon them. Elias had long caught a glimpse of its white crest through the darkness, right over the prow where Bernt sat. It filled the whole boat for a moment, the planks shook and trembled beneath the weight of it, and then, as the boat, which had lain half on her beam-ends, righted herself and sped on again, it streamed off behind to leeward.

While it was still upon him, he fancied he heard a hideous yell from the other boat; but when it was over, his wife, who sat by the shrouds, said, with a voice which pierced his very soul: "Good God, Elias! the sea has carried off Martha and Nils!"—their two youngest children, the first nine, the second seven years old, who had been sitting in the hold near Bernt. Elias merely answered: "Don't let go the lines, Karen, or you'll lose yet more!"

They had now to take in the fourth clew, and, when this was done, Elias found that it would be well to take in the fifth and last clew too, for the gale was ever on the increase; but, on the other hand, in order to keep the boat free of the constantly heavier seas, he dare not lessen the sail a bit more than he was absolutely obliged to do; but they found that the scrap of sail they could carry gradually grew less and less. The sea seethed so that it drove right into their faces, and Bernt and his next eldest brother Anthony, who had hitherto helped his mother with the sail-lines, had, at last, to hold in the yards, an expedient one only resorts to when the boat cannot bear even the last clew—here the fifth.

The companion boat, which had disappeared in the meantime, now suddenly ducked up alongside again, with precisely the same amount of sail as Elias's boat; but he now began to feel that he didn't quite like the look of the crew on board there. The two who stood and held in the yards (he caught a glimpse of their pale faces beneath their sou'westers) seemed to him, by the odd light of the shining foam, more like corpses than men, nor did they speak a single word.

A little way off to larboard he again caught sight of the high white back of a fresh roller coming through the dark, and he got ready betimes to receive it. The boat was laid to with its prow turned aslant towards the on-rushing wave, while the sail was made as large as possible, so as to get up speed enough to cleave the heavy sea and sail out of it again. In rushed the roller with a roar like a foss; again, for an instant, they lay on their beam ends; but, when it was over, the wife no longer sat by the sail ropes, nor did Anthony stand there any longer holding the yards—they had both gone overboard.

This time also Elias fancied he heard the same hideous yell in the air; but in the midst of it he plainly heard his wife anxiously calling him by name. All that he said when he grasped the fact that she was washed overboard, was, "In Jesus' Name!" His first and dearest wish was to follow after her, but he felt at the same time that it became him to save the rest of the freight he had on board, that is to say, Bernt and his other two sons, one twelve, the other fourteen years old, who had been baling out for a time, but had afterwards taken their places in the stern behind him.

Bernt had now to look to the yards all alone, and the other two helped as best they could. The rudder Elias durst not let slip, and he held it fast with a hand of iron, which continuous exertion had long since made insensible to feeling.

A moment afterwards the comrade boat ducked up again: it had vanished for an instant as before. Now, too, he saw more of the heavy man who sat in the stern there in the same place as himself. Out of his back, just below his sou'wester (as he turned round it showed quite plainly), projected an iron spike six inches long, which Elias had no difficulty in recognising again. And now, as he calmly thought it all over, he was quite clear about two things: one was that it was the *Draug* itself which was steering its half-boat close beside him, and leading him to destruction; the other was that it was written in heaven that he was to sail his last course that night. For he who sees the Draug on the sea is a doomed man. He said nothing to the others, lest they should lose heart, but in secret he commended his soul to God.

During the last hour or so he had been forced out of his proper course by the storm; the air also had become dense with snow; and Elias knew that he must wait till dawn before land could be sighted. Meanwhile he sailed along much the same as before. Now and then the boys in the stern complained that they were freezing; but, in the plight they were now in, that couldn't be helped, and, besides, Elias had something else to think about. A terrible longing for vengeance had come over him, and, but for the necessity of saving the lives of his three lads, he would have tried by a sudden turn to sink the accursed boat which kept alongside of him the whole time as if to mock him; he now understood its evil errand only too well. If the *Kvejtepig* could reach the Draug before, a knife or a gaff might surely do the same thing now, and he felt that he would gladly have given his life for one good grip of the being who had so mercilessly torn from him his dearest in this world and would fain have still more.

At three or four o'clock in the morning they saw coming upon them through the darkness a breaker of such a height that at first Elias thought they must be quite close ashore near the surf swell. Nevertheless, he soon recognised it for what it really was—a huge billow. Then it seemed to him as if there was a laugh over in the other boat, and something said, "There goes thy boat, Elias!" He, foreseeing the calamity, now cried aloud: "In Jesus' Name!" and then bade his sons hold on with all their might to the withy-bands by the rowlocks when the boat went under, and not let go till it was above the water again. He made the elder of them go forward to Bernt; and himself held the youngest close by his side, stroked him once or twice furtively down the cheeks, and made sure that he had a good grip. The boat, literally buried beneath the foaming roller, was lifted gradually up by the bows and then went under. When it rose again out of the water, with the keel in the air, Elias, Bernt, and the twelve-year-old Martin lay alongside, holding on by the withy-bands; but the third of the brothers was gone.

They had now first of all to get the shrouds on one side cut through, so that the mast might come to the surface alongside instead of disturbing the balance of the boat below; and then they must climb up on the swaying bottom of the boat and stave in the key-holes, to let out the air which kept the boat too high in the water, and so ease her. After great exertions they succeeded, and Elias, who had got up on the top first, now helped the other two up after him.

There they sat through the long dark winter night, clinging convulsively on by their hands and knees to the boat's bottom, which was drenched by the billows again and again.

After the lapse of a couple of hours died Martin, whom his father had held up the whole time as far as he was able, of sheer exhaustion, and glided down into the sea. They had tried to cry for help several times, but gave it up at last as a bad job.

Whilst they two thus sat all alone on the bottom of the boat, Elias said to Bernt he must now needs believe that he too was about to be "along o' mother!" but that he had a strong hope that Bernt, at any rate, would be saved, if he only held out like a man. Then he told him all about the *Draug*, whom he had struck below the neck with the *Kvejtepig*, and how it had now revenged itself upon him, and certainly would not forbear till it was 'quits with him.'

It was towards nine o'clock in the morning when the grey dawn began to appear. Then Elias gave to Bernt, who sat alongside him, his silver watch with the brass chain, which he had snapped in two in order to drag it from beneath his closely buttoned jacket. He held on for a little time longer, but, as it got lighter, Bernt saw that his father's face was deadly pale, his hair too had parted here and there, as often happens when death is at hand, and his skin was chafed off his hands from holding on to the keel. The son understood now that his father was nearly at the last gasp, and tried, so far as the pitching and tossing would allow it, to hold him up; but when Elias marked it, he said, "Nay, look to thyself, Bernt, and hold on fast. I go to mother—in Jesus' Name!" and with that he cast himself down headlong from the top of the boat.

Every one who has sat on the keel of a boat long enough knows that when the sea has got its own it grows much calmer, though not immediately. Bernt now found it easier to hold on, and still more of hope came to him with the brightening day. The storm abated, and, when it got quite light, it seemed to him that he knew where he was, and that it was outside his own homestead, Kvalholm, that he lay driving.

He now began again to cry for help, but his chief hope was in a current which he knew bore landwards at a place where a headland broke in upon the surge, and there the water was calmer. And he did, in fact, drive closer and closer in, and came at last so near to one of the rocks that the mast, which was floating by the side of the boat all the time, surged up and down in the swell against the sloping cliff. Stiff as he now was in all his limbs from sitting and holding on, he nevertheless succeeded, after a great effort, in clambering up the cliff, where he hauled the mast ashore, and made the *Femböring* fast.

The Finn girl, who was alone in the house, had been thinking, for the last two hours, that she had heard cries for help from time to time, and as they kept on she mounted the hill to see what it was. There she saw Bernt up on the cliff, and the overturned *Femböring* bobbing up and down against it. She immediately dashed down to the boat-place, got out the old rowing-boat, and rowed along the shore and round the island right out to him.

Bernt lay sick under her care the whole winter through, and didn't go a fishing all that year. Ever after this, too, it seemed to folks as if the lad were a little bit daft.

On the open sea he never would go again, for he had got the sea-scare. He wedded the Finn girl, and moved over to Malang, where he got him a clearing in the forest, and he lives there now, and is doing well, they say.

JOSEPH SHERIDAN LE FANU

(1814-1873)

33

The Child That Went With the Fairies

Eastward of the old city of Limerick, about ten Irish miles under the range of mountains known as the Slieveelim hills, famous as having afforded Sarsfield a shelter among their rocks and hollows, when he crossed them in his gallant descent upon the cannon and ammunition of King William, on its way to the beleaguering army, there runs a very old and narrow road. It connects the Limerick road to Tipperary with the old road from Limerick to Dublin, and runs by bog and pasture, hill and hollow, straw-thatched village, and roofless castle, not far from twenty miles.

Skirting the healthy mountains of which I have spoken, at one part it becomes singularly lonely. For more than three Irish miles it traverses a deserted country. A wide, black bog, level as a lake, skirted with copse, spreads at the left, as you journey northward, and the long and irregular line of mountain rises at the right, clothed in heath, broken with lines of grey rock that resemble the bold and irregular outlines of fortifications, and riven with many a gully, expanding here and there into rocky and wooded glens, which open as they approach the road.

A scanty pasturage, on which browsed a few scattered sheep or kine, skirts this solitary road for some miles, and under shelter of a hillock, and of two or three great ash-trees, stood, not many years ago, the little thatched cabin of a widow named Mary Ryan.

Poor was this widow in a land of poverty. The thatch had acquired the grey tint and sunken outlines, that show how the alternations of rain and sun have told upon that perishable shelter.

But whatever other dangers threatened, there was one well provided against by the care of other times. Round the cabin stood half a dozen mountain ashes, as the rowans, inimical to witches, are there called. On the worn planks of the door were nailed two horse-shoes, and over the lintel and spreading along the thatch, grew, luxuriant, patches of that ancient cure for many maladies, and prophylactic against the machinations of the evil one, the house-leek. Descending into the doorway, in the *chiaroscuro* of the interior, when your eye grew sufficiently accustomed to that dim light, you might discover, hanging at the head of the widow's wooden-roofed bed, her beads and a phial of holy water.

Here certainly were defences and bulwarks against the intrusion of that unearthly and evil power, of whose vicinity this solitary family were constantly reminded by the outline of Lisnavoura, that lonely hillhaunt of the 'Good people,' as the fairies are called euphemistically, whose strangely dome-like summit rose not half a mile away, looking like an outwork of the long line of mountain that sweeps by it.

It was at the fall of the leaf, and an autumnal sunset threw the lengthening shadow of haunted Lisnavoura, close in front of the solitary little cabin, over the undulating slopes and sides of Slieveelim. The birds were singing among the branches in the thinning leaves of the melancholy ash-trees that grew at the roadside in front of the door. The widow's three younger children were playing on the road, and their voices mingled with the evening song of the birds. Their elder sister, Nell, was 'within in the house,' as their phrase is, seeing after the boiling of the potatoes for supper.

Their mother had gone down to the bog, to carry up a hamper of turf on her back. It is, or was at least, a charitable custom—

and if not disused, long may it continue—for the wealthier people when cutting their turf and stacking it in the bog, to make a smaller stack for the behoof of the poor, who were welcome to take from it so long as it lasted, and thus the potato pot was kept boiling, and hearth warm that would have been cold enough but for that good-natured bounty, through wintry months.

Moll Ryan trudged up the steep 'bohereen' whose banks were overgrown with thorn and brambles, and stooping under her burden, re-entered her door, where her dark-haired daughter Nell met her with a welcome, and relieved her of her hamper.

Moll Ryan looked round with a sigh of relief, and drying her forehead, uttered the Munster ejaculation:

"Eiah, wisha! It's tired I am with it, God bless it. And where's the craythurs, Nell?"

"Playin' out on the road, mother; didn't ye see them and you comin' up?"

"No; there was no one before me on the road," she said, uneasily; "not a soul, Nell; and why didn't ye keep an eye on them?"

"Well, they're in the haggard, playin' there, or round by the back o' the house. Will I call them in?"

"Do so, good girl, in the name o' God. The hens is comin' home, see, and the sun was just down over Knockdoulah, an' I comin' up."

So out ran tall, dark-haired Nell, and standing on the road, looked up and down it; but not a sign of her two little brothers, Con and Bill, or her little sister, Peg, could she see. She called them; but no answer came from the little haggard, fenced with straggling bushes. She listened, but the sound of their voices was missing. Over the stile, and behind the house she ran—but there all was silent and deserted.

She looked down toward the bog, as far as she could see; but they did not appear. Again she listened—but in vain. At first she had felt angry, but now a different feeling overcame her, and she grew pale. With an undefined boding she looked toward the heathy boss of Lisnavoura, now darkening into the deepest purple against the flaming sky of sunset.

Again she listened with a sinking heart, and heard nothing but the farewell twitter and whistle of the birds in the bushes around. How many stories had she listened to by the winter hearth, of children stolen by the fairies, at nightfall, in lonely places! With this fear she knew her mother was haunted.

No one in the country round gathered her little flock about her so early as this frightened widow, and no door 'in the seven parishes' was barred so early.

Sufficiently fearful, as all young people in that part of the world are of such dreaded and subtle agents, Nell was even more than usually afraid of them, for her terrors were infected and redoubled by her mother's. She was looking towards Lisnavoura in a trance of fear, and crossed herself again and again, and whispered prayer after prayer. She was interrupted by her mother's voice on the road calling her loudly. She answered, and ran round to the front of the cabin, where she found her standing.

"And where in the world's the craythurs—did ye see sight o' them anywhere?" cried Mrs. Ryan, as the girl came over the stile.

"Arrah! mother, 'tis only what they're run down the road a bit. We'll see them this minute coming back. It's like goats they are, climbin' here and runnin' there; an' if I had them here, in my hand, maybe I wouldn't give them a hiding all round."

"May the Lord forgive you, Nell! the childhers gone. They're took, and not a soul near us, and Father Tom three miles away! And what'll I do, or who's to help us this night? Oh, wirristhru, wirristhru! The craythurs is gone!"

"Whisht, mother, be aisy: don't ye see them comin' up?"

And then she shouted in menacing accents, waving her arm, and beckoning the children, who were seen approaching on the road, which some little way off made a slight dip, which had concealed them. They were approaching from the westward, and from the direction of the dreaded hill of Lisnavoura.

But there were only two of the children, and one of them, the little girl, was crying. Their mother and sister hurried forward to meet them, more alarmed than ever.

"Where is Billy—where is he?" cried the mother, nearly breathless, so soon as she was within hearing.

"He's gone—they took him away; but they said he'll come back again," answered little Con, with the dark brown hair.

"He's gone away with the grand ladies," blubbered the little girl.

"What ladies—where? Oh, Leum, asthora! My darlin', are you gone away at last? Where is he? Who took him? What ladies are you talkin' about? What way did he go?" she cried in distraction.

"I couldn't see where he went, mother; 'twas like as if he was going to Lisnavoura."

With a wild exclamation the distracted woman ran on towards the hill alone, clapping her hands, and crying aloud the name of her lost child.

Scared and horrified, Nell, not daring to follow, gazed after her, and burst into tears; and the other children raised high their lamentations in shrill rivalry.

Twilight was deepening. It was long past the time when they were usually barred securely within their habitation. Nell led the younger children into the cabin, and made them sit down by the turf fire, while she stood in the open door, watching in great fear for the return of her mother.

After a long while they did see their mother return. She came in and sat down by the fire, and cried as if her heart would break.

"Will I bar the doore, mother?" asked Nell.

"Ay, do—didn't I lose enough, this night, without lavin' the doore open, for more o' yez to go; but first take an' sprinkle a dust o' the holy waters over ye, acuishla, and bring it here till I throw a taste iv it over myself and the craythurs; an' I wondher, Nell, you'd forget to do the like yourself, lettin' the craythurs out so near nightfall. Come here and sit on my knees, asthora, come to me, mavourneen, and hould me fast, in the name o' God, and I'll hould you fast that none can take yez from me, and tell me all about it, and what it was—the Lord between us and harm—an' how it happened, and who was in it."

And the door being barred, the two children, sometimes

speaking together, often interrupting one another, often interrupted by their mother, managed to tell this strange story, which I had better relate connectedly and in my own language.

The Widow Ryan's three children were playing, as I have said, upon the narrow old road in front of her door. Little Bill or Leum, about five years old, with golden hair and large blue eyes, was a very pretty boy, with all the clear tints of healthy childhood, and that gaze of earnest simplicity which belongs not to town children of the same age. His little sister Peg, about a year older, and his brother Con, a little more than a year elder than she, made up the little group.

Under the great old ash-trees, whose last leaves were falling at their feet, in the light of an October sunset, they were playing with the hilarity and eagerness of rustic children, clamouring together, and their faces were turned toward the west and storied hill of Lisnavoura.

Suddenly a startling voice with a screech called to them from behind, ordering them to get out of the way, and turning, they saw a sight, such as they never beheld before. It was a carriage drawn by four horses that were pawing and snorting, in impatience, as it just pulled up. The children were almost under their feet, and scrambled to the side of the road next their own door.

This carriage and all its appointments were old-fashioned and gorgeous, and presented to the children, who had never seen anything finer than a turf car, and once, an old chaise that passed that way from Killaloe, a spectacle perfectly dazzling.

Here was antique splendour. The harness and trappings were scarlet, and blazing with gold. The horses were huge, and snow white, with great manes, that as they tossed and shook them in the air, seemed to stream and float sometimes longer and sometimes shorter, like so much smoke—their tails were long, and tied up in bows of broad scarlet and gold ribbon. The coach itself was glowing with colours, gilded and emblazoned. There were footmen in gay liveries, and three-cocked hats, like the coachman's; but he had a great wig, like a judge's, and their hair was frizzed out and powdered, and a long thick 'pigtail,' with a bow to it, hung down the back of each.

All these servants were diminutive, and ludicrously out of proportion with the enormous horses of the equipage, and had sharp, sallow features, and small, restless fiery eyes, and faces of cunning and malice that chilled the children. The little coachman was scowling and showing his white fangs under his cocked hat, and his little blazing beads of eyes were quivering with fury in their sockets as he whirled his whip round and round over their heads, till the lash of it looked like a streak of fire in the evening sun, and sounded like the cry of a legion of 'fillapoueeks' in the air.

"Stop the princess on the highway!" cried the coachman, in a piercing treble.

"Stop the princess on the highway!" piped each footman in turn, scowling over his shoulder down on the children, and grinding his keen teeth.

The children were so frightened they could only gape and turn white in their panic. But a very sweet voice from the open window of the carriage reassured them, and arrested the attack of the lackeys.

A beautiful and 'very grand-looking' lady was smiling from it on them, and they all felt pleased in the strange light of that smile.

"The boy with the golden hair, I think," said the lady, bending her large and wonderfully clear eyes on little Leum.

The upper sides of the carriage were chiefly of glass, so that the children could see another woman inside, whom they did not like so well.

This was a black woman, with a wonderfully long neck, hung round with many strings of large variously-coloured beads, and on her head was a sort of turban of silk striped with all the colours of the rainbow, and fixed in it was a golden star.

This black woman had a face as thin almost as a death's-head, with high cheekbones, and great goggle eyes, the whites of which, as well as her wide range of teeth, showed in brilliant contrast with her skin, as she looked over the beautiful lady's shoulder, and whispered something in her ear.

"Yes; the boy with the golden hair, I think," repeated the lady.

And her voice sounded sweet as a silver bell in the children's ears, and her smile beguiled them like the light of an enchanted lamp, as she leaned from the window with a look of ineffable fondness on the golden-haired boy, with the large blue eyes; insomuch that little Billy, looking up, smiled in return with a wondering fondness, and when she stooped down, and stretched her jewelled arms towards him, he stretched his little hands up, and how they touched the other children did not know; but, saying, "Come and give me a kiss, my darling," she raised him, and he seemed to ascend in her small fingers as lightly as a feather, and she held him in her lap and covered him with kisses.

Nothing daunted, the other children would have been only too happy to change places with their favoured little brother. There was only one thing that was unpleasant, and a little frightened them, and that was the black woman, who stood and stretched forward, in the carriage as before. She gathered a rich silk and gold handkerchief that was in her fingers up to her lips, and seemed to thrust ever so much of it, fold after fold, into her capacious mouth, as they thought to smother her laughter, with which she seemed convulsed, for she was shaking and quivering, as it seemed, with suppressed merriment; but her eyes, which remained uncovered, looked angrier than they had ever seen eyes look before.

But the lady was so beautiful they looked on her instead, and she continued to caress and kiss the little boy on her knee; and smiling at the other children she held up a large russet apple in her fingers, and the carriage began to move slowly on, and with a nod inviting them to take the fruit, she dropped it on the road from the window; it rolled some way beside the wheels, they following, and then she dropped another, and then another, and so on. And the same thing happened to all; for just as either of the children who ran beside had caught the rolling apple, somehow it slipt into a hole or ran into a ditch, and looking up they saw the lady drop another from the window, and so the chase was taken up and continued till they got, hardly knowing how far they had gone, to the old cross-road that leads to Owney. It seemed that there the horses' hoofs and carriage wheels rolled up a wonderful dust, which being caught in one of those eddies that whirl the dust up into a column, on the calmest day, enveloped the children for a moment, and passed whirling on towards Lisnavoura, the carriage, as they fancied, driving in the centre of it; but suddenly it subsided, the straws and leaves floated to the ground, the dust dissipated itself, but the white horses and the lackeys, the gilded carriage, the lady and their little golden-haired brother were gone.

At the same moment suddenly the upper rim of the clear setting sun disappeared behind the hill of Knockdoula, and it was twilight. Each child felt the transition like a shock—and the sight of the rounded summit of Lisnavoura, now closely overhanging them, struck them with a new fear.

They screamed their brother's name after him, but their cries were lost in the vacant air. At the same time they thought they heard a hollow voice say, close to them, "Go home."

Looking round and seeing no one, they were scared, and hand in hand—the little girl crying wildly, and the boy white as ashes, from fear, they trotted homeward, at their best speed, to tell, as we have seen, their strange story.

Molly Ryan never more saw her darling. But something of the lost little boy was seen by his former playmates.

Sometimes when their mother was away earning a trifle at haymaking, and Nelly washing the potatoes for their dinner, or 'beatling' clothes in the little stream that flows in the hollow close by, they saw the pretty face of little Billy peeping in archly at the door, and smiling silently at them, and as they ran to embrace him, with cries of delight, he drew back, still smiling archly, and when they got out into the open day, he was gone, and they could see no trace of him anywhere.

This happened often, with slight variations in the circumstances of the visit. Sometimes he would peep for a longer time, sometimes for a shorter time, sometimes his little hand would come in, and, with bended finger, beckon them to follow; but always he was smiling with the same arch look and wary silence—and always he was gone when they reached the door. Gradually these visits grew less and less frequent, and in about eight months they ceased altogether, and little Billy, irretrievably lost, took rank in their memories with the dead.

One wintry morning, nearly a year and a half after his disappearance, their mother having set out for Limerick soon after cockcrow, to sell some fowls at the market, the little girl, lying by the side of her elder sister, who was fast asleep, just at the grey of the morning heard the latch lifted softly, and saw little Billy enter and close the door gently after him. There was light enough to see that he was barefoot and ragged, and looked pale and famished. He went straight to the fire, and cowered over the turf embers, and rubbed his hands slowly, and seemed to shiver as he gathered the smouldering turf together.

The little girl clutched her sister in terror and whispered, "Waken, Nelly, waken; here's Billy come back!"

Nelly slept soundly on, but the little boy, whose hands were extended close over the coals, turned and looked toward the bed, it seemed to her, in fear, and she saw the glare of the embers reflected on his thin cheek as he turned toward her. He rose and went, on tiptoe, quickly to the door, in silence, and let himself out as softly as he had come in.

After that, the little boy was never seen any more by any one of his kindred.

"Fairy doctors," as the dealers in the preternatural, who in such cases were called in, are termed, did all that in them lay—but in vain. Father Tom came down, and tried what holier rites could do, but equally without result. So little Billy was dead to mother, brother, and sisters; but no grave received him. Others whom affection cherished, lay in holy ground, in the old churchyard of Abington, with headstone to mark the spot over which the survivor might kneel and say a kind prayer for the peace of the departed soul. But there was no landmark to show where little Billy was hidden from their loving eyes, unless it was in the old hill of Lisnavoura, that cast its long shadow at sunset before the cabin-door; or that, white and filmy in the moonlight, in later years, would occupy his brother's gaze as he returned from fair or market, and draw from him a sigh and a prayer for the little brother he had lost so long ago, and was never to see again.

M R JAMES

(1862-1936)

34

Two Doctors

It is a very common thing, in my experience, to find papers shut up in old books; but one of the rarest things to come across any such that are at all interesting. Still it does happen, and one should never destroy them unlooked at. Now it was a practice of mine before the war occasionally to buy old ledgers of which the paper was good, and which possessed a good many blank leaves, and to extract these and use them for my own notes and writings. One such I purchased for a small sum in 1911. It was tightly clasped, and its boards were warped by having for years been obliged to embrace a number of extraneous sheets. Three-quarters of this inserted matter had lost all vestige of importance for any living human being: one bundle had not. That it belonged to a lawyer is certain, for it is endorsed: *The strangest case I have yet met*, and bears initials, and an address in Gray's Inn. It is only materials for a case, and consists of statements by possible witnesses. The man who would have been the defendant or prisoner seems never to have appeared. The *dossier* is not complete, but, such as it is, it furnishes a riddle in which the supernatural appears to play a part. You must see what you can make of it.

The following is the setting and the tale as I elicit it.

Dr. Abell was walking in his garden one afternoon waiting for his horse to be brought round that he might set out on his visits for the day. As the place was Islington, the month June, and the year 1718, we conceive the surroundings as being countrified and pleasant. To him entered his confidential servant, Luke Jennett, who had been with him twenty years.

"I said I wished to speak to him, and what I had to say might take some quarter of an hour. He accordingly bade me go into his study, which was a room opening on the terrace path where he was walking, and came in himself and sat down. I told him that, much against my will, I must look out for another place. He inquired what was my reason, in consideration I had been so long with him. I said if he would excuse me he would do me a great kindness, because (this appears to have been common form even in 1718) I was one that always liked to have everything pleasant about me. As well as I can remember, he said that was his case likewise, but he would wish to know why I should change my mind after so many years, and, says he, 'you know there can be no talk of a remembrance of you in my will if you leave my service now.' I said I had made my reckoning of that.

"'Then,' says he, 'you must have some complaint to make, and if I could I would willingly set it right.' And at that I told him, not seeing how I could keep it back, the matter of my former affidavit and of the bedstaff in the dispensing-room, and said that a house where such things happened was no place for me. At which he, looking very black upon me, said no more, but called me fool, and said he would pay what was owing me in the morning; and so, his horse being waiting, went out. So for that night I lodged with my sister's husband near Battle Bridge and came early next morning to my late master, who then made a great matter that I had not lain in his house and stopped a crown out of my wages owing.

"After that I took service here and there, not for long at a time, and saw no more of him till I came to be Dr. Quinn's man at Dodds Hall in Islington."

There is one very obscure part in this statement, namely, the reference to the former affidavit and the matter of the bedstaff. The former affidavit is not in the bundle of papers. It is to be feared that it was taken out to be read because of its special oddity, and not put back. Of what nature the story was may be guessed later, but as yet no clue has been put into our hands.

The Rector of Islington, Jonathan Pratt, is the next to step forward. He furnishes particulars of the standing and reputation of Dr. Abell and Dr. Quinn, both of whom lived and practised in his parish.

"It is not to be supposed," he says, "that a physician should be a regular attendant at morning and evening prayers, or at the Wednesday lectures, but within the measure of their ability I would say that both these persons fulfilled their obligations as loyal members of the Church of England. At the same time (as you desire my private mind) I must say, in the language of the schools, *distinguo*. Dr. A. was to me a source of perplexity, Dr. Q. to my eye a plain, honest believer, not inquiring over closely into points of belief, but squaring his practice to what lights he had. The other interested himself in questions to which Providence, as I hold, designs no answer to be given us in this state: he would ask me, for example, what place I believed those beings now to hold in the scheme of creation which by some are thought neither to have stood fast when the rebel angels fell, nor to have joined with them to the full pitch of their transgression.

"As was suitable, my first answer to him was a question, what warrant he had for supposing any such beings to exist? For that there was none in Scripture I took it he was aware. It appeared—for as I am on the subject, the whole tale may be given—that he grounded himself on such passages as that of the satyr which Jerome tells us conversed with Antony; but thought too that some parts of Scripture might be cited in support. 'And besides,' said he, 'you know 'tis the universal belief among those that spend their days and nights abroad, and I would add that if your calling took you so continuously as it does me about the country lanes by night, you might not be so surprised as I see you to be by my suggestion.' 'You are then of John Milton's mind,' I said, 'and hold that

Millions of spiritual creatures walk the earth Unseen, both when we wake and when we sleep.'

"'I do not know,' he said, 'why Milton should take upon himself to say "unseen"; though to be sure he was blind when he wrote that. But for the rest, why, yes, I think he was in the right.' 'Well,' I said, 'though not so often as you, I am not seldom called abroad pretty late; but I have no mind of meeting a satyr in our Islington lanes in all the years I have been here; and if you have had the better luck, I am sure the Royal Society would be glad to know of it.'

"I am reminded of these trifling expressions because Dr. A. took them so ill, stamping out of the room in a huff with some such word as that these high and dry parsons had no eyes but for a prayerbook or a pint of wine.

"But this was not the only time that our conversation took a remarkable turn. There was an evening when he came in, at first seeming gay and in good spirits, but afterwards as he sat and smoked by the fire falling into a musing way; out of which to rouse him I said pleasantly that I supposed he had had no meetings of late with his odd friends. A question which did effectually arouse him, for he looked most wildly, and as if scared, upon me, and said, '*You* were never there? I did not see you. Who brought you?' And then in a more collected tone, 'What was this about a meeting? I believe I must have been in a doze.' To which I answered that I was thinking of fauns and centaurs in the dark lane, and not of a witches' Sabbath; but it seemed he took it differently.

"'Well,' said he, 'I can plead guilty to neither; but I find you very much more of a sceptic than becomes your cloth. If you care to know about the dark lane you might do worse than ask my housekeeper that lived at the other end of it when she was a child.' 'Yes,' said I, 'and the old women in the almshouse and the children in the kennel. If I were you, I would send to your brother Quinn for a bolus to clear your brain.' 'Damn Quinn,' says he; 'talk no more of him: he has embezzled four of my best patients this month; I believe it is that cursed man of his, Jennett, that used to be with me, his tongue is never still; it should be nailed to the pillory if he had his deserts.' This, I may say, was the only time of his showing me that he had any grudge against either Dr. Quinn or Jennett, and as was my business, I did my best to persuade him he was mistaken in them. Yet it could not be denied that some respectable families in the parish had given him the cold shoulder, and for no reason that they were willing to allege. The end was that he said he had not done so ill at Islington but that he could afford to live at ease elsewhere when he chose, and anyhow he bore Dr. Quinn no malice. I think I now remember what observation of mine drew him into the train of thought which he next pursued. It was, I believe, my mentioning some juggling tricks which my brother in the East Indies had seen at the court of the Rajah of Mysore. 'A convenient thing enough,' said Dr. Abell to me, 'if by some arrangement a man could get the power of communicating motion and energy to inanimate objects.' 'As if the axe should move itself against him that lifts it; something of that kind?' 'Well, I don't know that that was in my mind so much; but if you could summon such a volume from your shelf or even order it to open at the right page.'

"He was sitting by the fire—it was a cold evening—and stretched out his hand that way, and just then the fire-irons, or at least the poker, fell over towards him with a great clatter, and I did not hear what else he said. But I told him that I could not easily conceive of an arrangement, as he called it, of such a kind that would not include as one of its conditions a heavier payment than any Christian would care to make; to which he assented. 'But,' he said, 'I have no doubt these bargains can be made very tempting, very persuasive. Still, you would not favour them, eh, Doctor? No, I suppose not.'

"This is as much as I know of Dr. Abell's mind, and the feeling between these men. Dr. Quinn, as I said, was a plain, honest creature, and a man to whom I would have gone—indeed I have before now gone to him for advice on matters of business. He was, however, every now and again, and particularly of late, not exempt from troublesome fancies. There was certainly a time when he was so much harassed by his dreams that he could not keep them to himself, but would tell them to his acquaintances and among them to me. I was at supper at his house, and he was not inclined to let me leave him at my usual time. 'If you go,' he said, 'there will be nothing for it but I must go to bed and dream of the chrysalis.' 'You might be worse off,' said I. 'I do not think it,' he said, and he shook himself like a man who is displeased with the complexion of his thoughts. 'I only meant,' said I, 'that a chrysalis is an innocent thing.' 'This one is not,' he said, 'and I do not care to think of it.'

"However, sooner than lose my company he was fain to tell me (for I pressed him) that this was a dream which had come to him several times of late, and even more than once in a night. It was to this effect, that he seemed to himself to wake under an extreme compulsion to rise and go out of doors. So he would dress himself and go down to his garden door. By the door there stood a spade which he must take, and go out into the garden, and at a particular place in the shrubbery somewhat clear and upon which the moon shone, for there was always in his dream a full moon, he would feel himself forced to dig. And after some time the spade would uncover something light-coloured, which he would perceive to be a stuff, linen or woollen, and this he must clear with his hands. It was always the same: of the size of a man and shaped like the chrysalis of a moth, with the folds showing a promise of an opening at one end.

"He could not describe how gladly he would have left all at this stage and run to the house, but he must not escape so easily. So with many groans, and knowing only too well what to expect, he parted these folds of stuff, or, as it sometimes seemed to be, membrane, and disclosed a head covered with a smooth pink skin, which breaking as the creature stirred, showed him his own face in a state of death. The telling of this so much disturbed him that I was forced out of mere compassion to sit with him the greater part of the night and talk with him upon indifferent subjects. He said that upon every recurrence of this dream he woke and found himself, as it were, fighting for his breath."

Another extract from Luke Jennett's long continuous statement comes in at this point.

"I never told tales of my master, Dr. Abell, to anybody in the neighbourhood. When I was in another service I remember to have spoken to my fellow-servants about the matter of the bedstaff, but I am sure I never said either I or he were the persons concerned, and it met with so little credit that I was affronted and thought best to keep it to myself. And when I came back to Islington and found Dr. Abell still there, who I was told had left the parish, I was clear that it behoved me to use great discretion, for indeed I was afraid of the man, and it is certain I was no party to spreading any ill report of him. My master, Dr. Quinn, was a very just, honest man, and no maker of mischief. I am sure he never stirred a finger nor said a word by way of inducement to a soul to make them leave going to Dr. Abell and come to him; nay, he would hardly be persuaded to attend them that came, until he was convinced that if he did not they would send into the town for a physician rather than do as they had hitherto done.

"I believe it may be proved that Dr. Abell came into my master's house more than once. We had a new chambermaid out of Hertfordshire, and she asked me who was the gentleman that was looking after the master, that is Dr. Quinn, when he was out, and seemed so disappointed that he was out. She said whoever he was he knew the way of the house well, running at once into the study and then into the dispensing-room, and last into the bed-chamber. I made her tell me what he was like, and what she said was suitable enough to Dr. Abell; but besides she told me she saw the same man at church and some one told her that was the Doctor.

"It was just after this that my master began to have his bad nights, and complained to me and other persons, and in particular what discomfort he suffered from his pillow and bedclothes. He said he must buy some to suit him, and should do his own marketing. And accordingly brought home a parcel which he said was of the right quality, but where he bought it we had then no knowledge, only they were marked in thread with a coronet and a bird. The women said they were of a sort not commonly met with and very fine, and my master said they were the comfortablest he ever used, and he slept now both soft and deep. Also the feather pillows were the best sorted and his head would sink into them as if they were a cloud: which I have myself remarked several times when I came to wake him of a morning, his face being almost hid by the pillow closing over it.

"I had never any communication with Dr. Abell after I came back to Islington, but one day when he passed me in the street and asked me whether I was not looking for another service, to which I answered I was very well suited where I was, but he said I was a tickle-minded fellow and he doubted not he should soon hear I was on the world again, which indeed proved true."

Dr. Pratt is next taken up where he left off.

"On the 16th I was called up out of my bed soon after it was light—that is about five—with a message that Dr. Quinn was dead or dying. Making my way to his house I found there was no doubt which was the truth. All the persons in the house except the one that let me in were already in his chamber and standing about his bed, but none touching him. He was stretched in the midst of the bed, on his back, without any disorder, and indeed had the appearance of one ready laid out for burial. His hands, I think, were even crossed on his breast. The only thing not usual was that nothing was to be seen of his face, the two ends of the pillow or bolster appearing to be closed quite over it. These I immediately pulled apart, at the same time rebuking those present, and especially the man, for not at once coming to the assistance of his master. He, however, only looked at me and shook his head, having evidently no more hope than myself that there was anything but a corpse before us.

"Indeed it was plain to any one possessed of the least experience that he was not only dead, but had died of suffocation. Nor could it be conceived that his death was accidentally caused by the mere folding of the pillow over his face. How should he not, feeling the oppression, have lifted his hands to put it away? whereas not a fold of the sheet which was closely gathered about him, as I now observed, was disordered. The next thing was to procure a physician. I had bethought me of this on leaving my house, and sent on the messenger who had come to me to Dr. Abell; but I now heard that he was away from home, and the nearest surgeon was got, who however could tell no more, at least without opening the body, than we already knew.

"As to any person entering the room with evil purpose (which was the next point to be cleared), it was visible that the bolts of the door were burst from their stanchions, and the stanchions broken away from the door-post by main force; and there was a sufficient body of witness, the smith among them, to testify that this had been done but a few minutes before I came. The chamber being moreover at the top of the house, the window was neither easy of access nor did it show any sign of an exit made that way, either by marks upon the sill or footprints below upon soft mould."

The surgeon's evidence forms of course part of the report of the inquest, but since it has nothing but remarks upon the healthy state of the larger organs and the coagulation of blood in various parts of the body, it need not be reproduced. The verdict was "Death by the visitation of God."

Annexed to the other papers is one which I was at first inclined to suppose had made its way among them by mistake. Upon further consideration I think I can divine a reason for its presence.

It relates to the rifling of a mausoleum in Middlesex which stood in a park (now broken up), the property of a noble family which I will not name. The outrage was not that of an ordinary resurrection man. The object, it seemed likely, was theft. The account is blunt and terrible. I shall not quote it. A dealer in the North of London suffered heavy penalties as a receiver of stolen goods in connexion with the affair.

35

A School Story

Two men in a smoking-room were talking of their private-school days. "At *our* school," said A., "we had a ghost's footmark on the staircase. What was it like? Oh, very unconvincing. Just the shape of a shoe, with a square toe, if I remember right. The staircase was a stone one. I never heard any story about the thing. That seems odd, when you come to think of it. Why didn't somebody invent one, I wonder?"

"You never can tell with little boys. They have a mythology of their own. There's a subject for you, by the way—'The Folklore of Private Schools.'"

"Yes; the crop is rather scanty, though. I imagine, if you were to investigate the cycle of ghost stories, for instance, which the boys at private schools tell each other, they would all turn out to be highly-compressed versions of stories out of books."

"Nowadays the *Strand* and *Pearson's*, and so on, would be extensively drawn upon."

"No doubt: they weren't born or thought of in my time. Let's see. I wonder if I can remember the staple ones that I was told. First, there was the house with a room in which a series of people insisted on passing a night; and each of them in the morning was found kneeling in a corner, and had just time to say, 'I've seen it,' and died."

"Wasn't that the house in Berkeley Square?"

"I dare say it was. Then there was the man who heard a noise in the passage at night, opened his door, and saw someone crawling towards him on all fours with his eye hanging out on his cheek. There was besides, let me think—Yes! the room where a man was found dead in bed with a horseshoe mark on his forehead, and the floor under the bed was covered with marks of horseshoes also; I don't know why. Also there was the lady who, on locking her bedroom door in a strange house, heard a thin voice among the bed-curtains say, 'Now we're shut in for the night.' None of those had any explanation or sequel. I wonder if they go on still, those stories."

"Oh, likely enough—with additions from the magazines, as I said. You never heard, did you, of a real ghost at a private school? I thought not; nobody has that ever I came across."

"From the way in which you said that, I gather that *you* have."

"I really don't know; but this is what was in my mind. It happened at my private school thirty odd years ago, and I haven't any explanation of it.

"The school I mean was near London. It was established in a large and fairly old house—a great white building with very fine grounds about it; there were large cedars in the garden, as there are in so many of the older gardens in the Thames valley, and ancient elms in the three or four fields which we used for our games. I think probably it was quite an attractive place, but boys seldom allow that their schools possess any tolerable features.

"I came to the school in a September, soon after the year 1870; and among the boys who arrived on the same day was one whom I took to: a Highland boy, whom I will call McLeod. I needn't spend time in describing him: the main thing is that I got to know him very well. He was not an exceptional boy in any way—not particularly good at books or games—but he suited me.

"The school was a large one: there must have been from 120 to 130 boys there as a rule, and so a considerable staff of masters was required, and there were rather frequent changes among them.

"One term—perhaps it was my third or fourth—a new master made his appearance. His name was Sampson. He was a tallish, stoutish, pale, black-bearded man. I think we liked him: he had travelled a good deal, and had stories which amused us on our school walks, so that there was some competition among us to get within earshot of him. I remember too—dear me, I have hardly thought of it since then!—that he had a charm on his watch-chain that attracted my attention one day, and he let me examine it. It was, I now suppose, a gold Byzantine coin; there was an effigy of some absurd emperor on one side; the other side had been worn practically smooth, and he had had cut on it—rather barbarously—his own initials, G.W.S., and a date, 24 July, 1865. Yes, I can see it now: he told me he had picked it up in Constantinople: it was about the size of a florin, perhaps rather smaller.

"Well, the first odd thing that happened was this. Sampson was doing Latin grammar with us. One of his favourite methods—perhaps it is rather a good one—was to make us construct sentences out of our own heads to illustrate the rules he was trying to make us learn. Of course that is a thing which gives a silly boy a chance of being impertinent: there are lots of school stories in which that happens—or anyhow there might be. But Sampson was too good a disciplinarian for us to think of trying that on with him. Now, on this occasion he was telling us how to express remembering in Latin: and he ordered us each to make a sentence bringing in the verb memini, 'I remember.' Well, most of us made up some ordinary sentence such as 'I remember my father,' or 'He remembers his book,' or something equally uninteresting: and I dare say a good many put down *memino librum meum*, and so forth: but the boy I mentioned—McLeod—was evidently thinking of something more elaborate than that. The rest of us wanted to have our sentences passed, and get on to something else, so some kicked him under the desk, and I, who was next to him, poked him and whispered to him to look sharp. But he didn't seem to attend. I looked at his paper and saw he had put down nothing at all. So I jogged him again harder than before and upbraided him sharply for keeping us all waiting. That did have some effect. He started and seemed to wake up, and then very quickly he scribbled about a couple of lines on his paper, and showed it up with the rest. As it was the last, or nearly the last, to come in, and as Sampson had a good deal to say to the boys who had written *meminiscimus patri meo* and the rest of it, it turned out that the clock struck twelve before he had got to McLeod, and McLeod had to wait afterwards to have his sentence corrected. There was nothing much going on outside when I got out, so I waited for him to come. He came very slowly when he did arrive, and I guessed there had been some sort of trouble.

"Well," I said, "what did you get?" "Oh, I don't know," said McLeod, "nothing much: but I think Sampson's rather sick with me." "Why, did you show him up some rot?" "No fear," he said. "It was all right as far as I could see: it was like this: *Memento*—that's right enough for remember, and it takes a genitive,—*memento putei inter quatuor taxos.*" "What silly rot!" I said. "What made you shove that down? What does it mean?" "That's the funny part," said McLeod. "I'm not quite sure what it does mean. All I know is, it just came into my head and I corked it down. I know what I *think* it means, because just before I wrote it down I had a sort of picture of it in my head: I believe it means 'Remember the well among the four'—what are those dark sort of trees that have red berries on them?" "Mountain ashes, I s'pose you mean." "I never heard of them," said McLeod; "no, I'll tell you—yews." "Well, and what did Sampson say?" "Why, he was jolly odd about it. When he read it he got up and went to the mantelpiece and stopped quite a long time without saying anything, with his back to me. And then he said, without turning round, and rather quiet, 'What do you suppose that means?' I told him what I thought; only I couldn't remember the name of the silly tree: and then he wanted to know why I put it down, and I had to say something or other. And after that he left off talking about it, and asked me how long I'd been here, and where my people lived, and things like that: and then I came away: but he wasn't looking a bit well."

"I don't remember any more that was said by either of us about this. Next day McLeod took to his bed with a chill or something of the kind, and it was a week or more before he was in school again.

And as much as a month went by without anything happening that was noticeable. Whether or not Mr. Sampson was really startled, as McLeod had thought, he didn't show it. I am pretty sure, of course, now, that there was something very curious in his past history, but I'm not going to pretend that we boys were sharp enough to guess any such thing.

"There was one other incident of the same kind as the last which I told you. Several times since that day we had had to make up examples in school to illustrate different rules, but there had never been any row except when we did them wrong. At last there came a day when we were going through those dismal things which people call Conditional Sentences, and we were told to make a conditional sentence, expressing a future consequence. We did it, right or wrong, and showed up our bits of paper, and Sampson began looking through them. All at once he got up, made some odd sort of noise in his throat, and rushed out by a door that was just by his desk. We sat there for a minute or two, and then—I suppose it was incorrect—but we went up, I and one or two others, to look at the papers on his desk. Of course I thought someone must have put down some nonsense or other, and Sampson had gone off to report him. All the same, I noticed that he hadn't taken any of the papers with him when he ran out. Well, the top paper on the desk was written in red ink—which no one used—and it wasn't in anyone's hand who was in the class. They all looked at it—McLeod and all—and took their dying oaths that it wasn't theirs. Then I thought of counting the bits of paper. And of this I made quite certain: that there were seventeen bits of paper on the desk, and sixteen boys in the form. Well, I bagged the extra paper, and kept it, and I believe I have it now. And now you will want to know what was written on it. It was simple enough, and harmless enough, I should have said.

"*Si tu non veneris ad me, ego veniam ad te*," which means, I suppose, "If you don't come to me, I'll come to you."

"Could you show me the paper?" interrupted the listener.

"Yes, I could: but there's another odd thing about it. That same afternoon I took it out of my locker—I know for certain it was the same bit, for I made a finger-mark on it—and no single trace of writing of any kind was there on it. I kept it, as I said, and since that time I have tried various experiments to see whether sympathetic ink had been used, but absolutely without result.

"So much for that. After about half an hour Sampson looked in again: said he had felt very unwell, and told us we might go. He came rather gingerly to his desk and gave just one look at the uppermost paper: and I suppose he thought he must have been dreaming: anyhow, he asked no questions.

"That day was a half-holiday, and next day Sampson was in school again, much as usual. That night the third and last incident in my story happened.

"We—McLeod and I—slept in a dormitory at right angles to the main building. Sampson slept in the main building on the first floor. There was a very bright full moon. At an hour which I can't tell exactly, but some time between one and two, I was woken up by somebody shaking me. It was McLeod; and a nice state of mind he seemed to be in. 'Come,' he said,—'come! there's a burglar getting in through Sampson's window.' As soon as I could speak, I said, 'Well, why not call out and wake everybody up?' 'No, no,' he said, 'I'm not sure who it is: don't make a row: come and look.' Naturally I came and looked, and naturally there was no one there. I was cross enough, and should have called McLeod plenty of names: only—I couldn't tell why—it seemed to me that there was something wrong—something that made me very glad I wasn't alone to face it. We were still at the window looking out, and as soon as I could, I asked him what he had heard or seen. 'I didn't *hear* anything at all,' he said, 'but about five minutes before I woke you, I found myself looking out of this window here, and there was a man sitting or kneeling on Sampson's window-sill, and looking in, and I thought he was beckoning.' 'What sort of man?' McLeod wriggled. 'I don't know,' he said, 'but I can tell you one thing—he was beastly thin: and he looked as if he was wet all over: and,' he said, looking round and whispering as if he hardly liked to hear himself, 'I'm not at all sure that he was alive.'

"We went on talking in whispers some time longer, and eventually crept back to bed. No one else in the room woke or stirred the whole time. I believe we did sleep a bit afterwards, but we were very cheap next day.

"And next day Mr. Sampson was gone: not to be found: and I believe no trace of him has ever come to light since. In thinking it over, one of the oddest things about it all has seemed to me to be the fact that neither McLeod nor I ever mentioned what we had seen to any third person whatever. Of course no questions were asked on the subject, and if they had been, I am inclined to believe that we could not have made any answer: we seemed unable to speak about it.

"That is my story," said the narrator. "The only approach to a ghost story connected with a school that I know, but still, I think, an approach to such a thing."

The sequel to this may perhaps be reckoned highly conventional; but a sequel there is, and so it must be produced. There had been more than one listener to the story, and, in the latter part of that same year, or of the next, one such listener was staying at a country house in Ireland. One evening his host was turning over a drawer full of odds and ends in the smoking-room. Suddenly he put his hand upon a little box. "Now," he said, "you know about old things; tell me what that is." My friend opened the little box, and found in it a thin gold chain with an object attached to it. He glanced at the object and then took off his spectacles to examine it more narrowly. "What's the history of this?" he asked. "Odd enough," was the answer. "You know the yew thicket in the shrubbery: well, a year or two back we were cleaning out the old well that used to be in the clearing here, and what do you suppose we found?" "Is it possible that you found a body?" said the visitor, with an odd feeling of nervousness. "We did that: but what's more, in every sense of the word, we found two." "Good Heavens! Two? Was there anything to show how they got there? Was this thing found with them?" "It was. Amongst the rags of the clothes that were on one of the bodies. A bad business, whatever the story of it may have been. One body had the arms tight round the other. They must have been there thirty years or more—long enough before we came to this place. You may judge we filled the well up fast enough. Do you make anything of what's cut on that gold coin you have there?" "I think I can," said my friend, holding it to the light (but he read it without much difficulty); "it seems to be G.W.S., 24 July, 1865."

36

The Diary of Mr. Poynter

The sale-room of an old and famous firm of book auctioneers in London is, of course, a great meeting-place for collectors, librarians, dealers: not only when an auction is in progress, but perhaps even more notably when books that are coming on for sale are upon view. It was in such a sale-room that the remarkable series of events began which were detailed to me not many months ago by the person whom they principally affected, namely, Mr. James Denton, M.A., F.S.A., etc., etc., some time of Trinity Hall, now, or lately, of Rendcomb Manor in the county of Warwick.

He, on a certain spring day not many years since, was in London for a few days upon business connected principally with the furnishing of the house which he had just finished building at Rendcomb. It may be a disappointment to you to learn that Rendcomb Manor was new; that I cannot help. There had, no doubt, been an old house; but it was not remarkable for beauty or interest. Even had it been, neither beauty nor interest would have enabled it to resist the disastrous fire which about a couple of years before the date of my story had razed it to the ground. I am glad to say that all that was most valuable in it had been saved, and that it was fully insured. So that it was with a comparatively light heart that Mr. Denton was able to face the task of building a new and considerably more convenient dwelling for himself and his aunt who constituted his whole ménage.

Being in London, with time on his hands, and not far from the sale-room at which I have obscurely hinted, Mr. Denton thought that he would spend an hour there upon the chance of finding, among that portion of the famous Thomas collection of MSS., which he knew to be then on view, something bearing upon the history or topography of his part of Warwickshire.

He turned in accordingly, purchased a catalogue and ascended to the sale-room, where, as usual, the books were disposed in cases and some laid out upon the long tables. At the shelves, or sitting about at the tables, were figures, many of whom were familiar to him. He exchanged nods and greetings with several, and then settled down to examine his catalogue and note likely items. He had made good progress through about two hundred of the five hundred lots—every now and then rising to take a volume from the shelf and give it a cursory glance—when a hand was laid on his shoulder, and he looked up. His interrupter was one of those intelligent men with a pointed beard and a flannel shirt, of whom the last quarter of the nineteenth century was, it seems to me, very prolific.

It is no part of my plan to repeat the whole conversation which ensued between the two. I must content myself with stating that it largely referred to common acquaintances, e.g., to the nephew of Mr. Denton's friend who had recently married and settled in Chelsea, to the sister-inlaw of Mr. Denton's friend who had been seriously indisposed, but was now better, and to a piece of china which Mr. Denton's friend had purchased some months before at a price much below its true value. From which you will rightly infer that the conversation was rather in the nature of a monologue. In due time, however, the friend bethought himself that Mr. Denton was there for a purpose, and said he, "What are you looking out for in particular? I don't think there's much in this lot." "Why, I thought there might be some Warwickshire collections, but I don't see anything under Warwick in the catalogue." "No, apparently not," said the friend. "All the same, I believe I noticed something like a Warwickshire diary. What was the name again? Drayton? Potter? Painter—either a P or a D, I feel sure." He turned over the leaves quickly. "Yes, here it is. Poynter. Lot 486. That might interest you. There are the books, I think: out on the table. Some one has been looking at them. Well, I must be getting on. Goodbye, you'll look us up, won't you? Couldn't you come this afternoon? We've got a little music about four. Well, then, when you're next in town." He went off. Mr. Denton looked at his watch and found to his confusion that he could spare no more than a moment before retrieving his luggage and going for the train. The moment was just enough to show him that there were four largish volumes of the diary—that it concerned the years about 1710, and that there seemed to be a good many insertions in it of various kinds. It seemed quite worth while to leave a commission of five and twenty pounds for it, and this he was able to do, for his usual agent entered the room as he was on the point of leaving it.

That evening he rejoined his aunt at their temporary abode, which was a small dower-house not many hundred yards from the Manor. On the following morning the two resumed a discussion that had now lasted for some weeks as to the equipment of the new house. Mr. Denton laid before his relative a statement of the results of his visit to town—particulars of carpets, of chairs, of wardrobes, and of bedroom china. "Yes, dear," said his aunt, "but I don't see any chintzes here. Did you go to——?" Mr. Denton stamped on the floor (where else, indeed, could he have stamped?). "Oh dear, oh dear," he said, "the one thing I missed. I am sorry. The fact is I was on my way there and I happened to be passing Robins's." His aunt threw up her hands. "Robins's! Then the next thing will be another parcel of horrible old books at some outrageous price. I do think, James, when I am taking all this trouble for you, you might contrive to remember the one or two things which I specially begged you to see after. It's not as if I was asking it for myself. I don't know whether you think I get any pleasure out of it, but if so I can assure you it's very much the reverse. The thought and worry and trouble I have over it you have no idea of, and you have simply to go to the shops and order the things." Mr. Denton interposed a moan of penitence. "Oh, aunt——" "Yes, that's all very well, dear, and I don't want to speak sharply, but you must know how very annoying it is: particularly as it delays the whole of our business for I can't tell how long: here is Wednesday—the Simpsons come tomorrow, and you can't leave them. Then on Saturday we have friends, as you know, coming for tennis. Yes, indeed, you spoke of asking them yourself, but, of course, I had to write the notes, and it is ridiculous, James, to look like that. We must occasionally be civil to our neighbours: you wouldn't like to have it said we were perfect bears. What was I saying? Well, anyhow it comes to this, that it must be Thursday in next week at least, before you can go to town again, and until we have decided upon the chintzes it is impossible to settle upon one single other thing."

Mr. Denton ventured to suggest that as the paint and wallpapers had been dealt with, this was too severe a view: but this his aunt was not prepared to admit at the moment. Nor, indeed, was there any proposition he could have advanced which she would have found herself able to accept. However, as the day went on, she receded a little from this position: examined with lessening disfavour the samples and price lists submitted by her nephew, and even in some cases gave a qualified approval to his choice.

As for him, he was naturally somewhat dashed by the consciousness of duty unfulfilled, but more so by the prospect of a lawn-tennis party, which, though an inevitable evil in August, he had thought there was no occasion to fear in May. But he was to some extent cheered by the arrival on the Friday morning of an intimation that he had secured at the price of £12 10s. the four volumes of Poynter's manuscript diary, and still more by the arrival on the next morning of the diary itself.

The necessity of taking Mr. and Mrs. Simpson for a drive in the car on Saturday morning and of attending to his neighbours and guests that afternoon prevented him from doing more than open the parcel until the party had retired to bed on the Saturday night. It was then that he made certain of the fact, which he had before only suspected, that he had indeed acquired the diary of Mr. William Poynter, Squire of Acrington (about four miles from his own parish)—that same Poynter who was for a time a member of the circle of Oxford antiquaries, the centre of which was Thomas Hearne, and with whom Hearne seems ultimately to have quarrelled—a not uncommon episode in the career of that excellent man. As is the case with Hearne's own collections, the diary of Poynter contained a good many notes from printed books, descriptions of coins and other antiquities that had been brought to his notice, and drafts of letters on these subjects, besides the chronicle of everyday events. The description in the sale-catalogue had given Mr. Denton no idea of the amount of interest which seemed to lie in the book, and he sat up reading in the first of the four volumes until a reprehensibly late hour.

On the Sunday morning, after church, his aunt came into the study and was diverted from what she had been going to say to him by the sight of the four brown leather quartos on the table. "What are these?" she said suspiciously. "New, aren't they? Oh! are these the things that made you forget my chintzes? I thought so. Disgusting. What did you give for them, I should like to know? Over Ten Pounds? James, it is really sinful. Well, if you have money to throw away on this kind of thing, there can be no reason why you should not subscribe—and subscribe handsomely—to my anti-Vivisection League. There is not, indeed, James, and I shall be very seriously annoyed if——. Who did you say wrote them? Old Mr. Poynter, of Acrington? Well, of course, there is some interest in getting together old papers about this neighbourhood. But Ten Pounds!" She picked up one of the volumes—not that which her nephew had been reading—and opened it at random, dashing it to the floor the next instant with a cry of disgust as a earwig fell from between the pages. Mr. Denton picked it up with a smothered expletive and said, "Poor book! I think you're rather hard on Mr. Poynter." "Was I, my dear? I beg his pardon, but you know I cannot abide those horrid creatures. Let me see if I've done any mischief." "No, I think all's well: but look here what you've opened him on." "Dear me, yes, to be sure! how very interesting. Do unpin it, James, and let me look at it."

It was a piece of patterned stuff about the size of the quarto page, to which it was fastened by an old-fashioned pin. James detached it and handed it to his aunt, carefully replacing the pin in the paper.

Now, I do not know exactly what the fabric was; but it had a design printed upon it, which completely fascinated Miss Denton. She went into raptures over it, held it against the wall, made James do the same, that she might retire to contemplate it from a distance: then pored over it at close quarters, and ended her examination by expressing in the warmest terms her appreciation of the taste of the ancient Mr. Poynter who had had the happy idea of preserving this sample in his diary. "It is a most charming pattern," she said, "and remarkable too. Look, James, how delightfully the lines ripple. It reminds one of hair, very much, doesn't it. And then these knots of ribbon at intervals. They give just the relief of colour that is wanted. I wonder—" "I was going to say," said James with deference, "I wonder if it would cost much to have it copied for our curtains." "Copied? how could you have it copied, James?" "Well, I don't know the details, but I suppose that is a printed pattern, and that you could have a block cut from it in wood or metal." "Now, really, that is a capital idea, James. I am almost inclined to be glad that you were so—that you forgot the chintzes on Monday. At any rate, I'll promise to forgive and forget if you get this lovely old thing copied. No one will have anything in the least like it, and mind, James, we won't allow it to be sold. Now I must go, and I've totally forgotten what it was I came in to say: never mind, it'll keep."

After his aunt had gone James Denton devoted a few minutes to examining the pattern more closely than he had yet had a chance of doing. He was puzzled to think why it should have struck Miss Benton so forcibly. It seemed to him not specially remarkable or pretty. No doubt it was suitable enough for a curtain pattern: it ran in vertical bands, and there was some indication that these were intended to converge at the top. She was right, too, in thinking that these main bands resembled rippling—almost curling—

tresses of hair. Well, the main thing was to find out by means of trade directories, or otherwise, what firm would undertake the reproduction of an old pattern of this kind. Not to delay the reader over this portion of the story, a list of likely names was made out, and Mr. Denton fixed a day for calling on them, or some of them, with his sample.

The first two visits which he paid were unsuccessful: but there is luck in odd numbers. The firm in Bermondsey which was third on his list was accustomed to handling this line. The evidence they were able to produce justified their being entrusted with the job. "Our Mr. Cattell" took a fervent personal interest in it. "It's 'eartrending, isn't it, sir," he said, "to picture the quantity of reelly lovely medeevial stuff of this kind that lays well-nigh unnoticed in many of our residential country 'ouses: much of it in peril, I take it, of being cast aside as so much rubbish. What is it Shakespeare says—unconsidered trifles. Ah, I often say he 'as a word for us all, sir. I say Shakespeare, but I'm well aware all don't 'old with me there—I 'ad something of an upset the other day when a gentleman came in a titled man, too, he was, and I think he told me he'd wrote on the topic, and I 'appened to cite out something about 'Ercules and the painted cloth. Dear me, you never see such a pother. But as to this, what you've kindly confided to us, it's a piece of work we shall take a reel enthusiasm in achieving it out to the very best of our ability. What man 'as done, as I was observing only a few weeks back to another esteemed client, man can do, and in three to four weeks' time, all being well, we shall 'ope to lay before you evidence to that effect, sir. Take the address, Mr. 'Iggins, if you please."

Such was the general drift of Mr. Cattell's observations on the occasion of his first interview with Mr. Denton. About a month later, being advised that some samples were ready for his inspection, Mr. Denton met him again, and had, it seems, reason to be satisfied with the faithfulness of the reproduction of the design. It had been finished off at the top in accordance with the indication I mentioned, so that the vertical bands joined. But something still needed to be done in the way of matching the colour of the original. Mr. Cattell had suggestions of a technical kind to offer, with which I need not trouble you. He had also views as to the general desirability of the pattern which were vaguely adverse. "You say you don't wish this to be supplied excepting to personal friends equipped with a authorization from yourself, sir. It shall be done. I quite understand your wish to keep it exclusive: lends it a catchit, does it not, to the suite? What's every man's, it's been said, is no man's."

"Do you think it would be popular if it were generally obtainable?" asked Mr. Denton.

"I 'ardly think it, sir," said Cattell, pensively clasping his beard. "I 'ardly think it. Not popular: it wasn't popular with the man that cut the block, was it, Mr. 'Iggins?"

"Did he find it a difficult job?"

"He'd no call to do so, sir; but the fact is that the artistic temperament—and our men are artists, sir, every man of them—true artists as much as many that the world styles by that term—it's apt to take some strange 'ardly accountable likes or dislikes, and here was an example. The twice or thrice that I went to inspect his progress: language I could understand, for that's 'abitual to him, but reel distaste for what I should call a dainty enough thing, I did not, nor am I now able to fathom. It seemed," said Mr. Cattell, looking narrowly upon Mr. Denton, "as if the man scented something almost Hevil in the design."

"Indeed? did he tell you so? I can't say I see anything sinister in it myself."

"Neether can I, sir. In fact I said as much. 'Come, Gatwick,' I said, 'what's to do here? What's the reason of your prejudice—for I can call it no more than that?' But, no! No explanation was forthcoming. And I was merely reduced, as I am now, to a shrug of the shoulders, and a cui bono. However, here it is," and with that the technical side of the question came to the front again.

The matching of the colours for the background, the hem, and the knots of ribbon was by far the longest part of the business, and necessitated many sendings to and fro of the original pattern and of new samples. During part of August and September, too, the Dentons were away from the Manor. So that it was not until

October was well in that a sufficient quantity of the stuff had been manufactured to furnish curtains for the three or four bedrooms which were to be fitted up with it.

On the feast of Simon and Jude the aunt and nephew returned from a short visit to find all completed, and their satisfaction at the general effect was great. The new curtains, in particular, agreed to admiration with their surroundings. When Mr. Denton was dressing for dinner, and took stock of his room, in which there was a large amount of the chintz displayed, he congratulated himself over and over again on the luck which had first made him forget his aunt's commission and had then put into his hands this extremely effective means of remedying his mistake. The pattern was, as he said at dinner, so restful and yet so far from being dull. And Miss Denton—who, by the way, had none of the stuff in her own room—was much disposed to agree with him.

At breakfast next morning he was induced to qualify his satisfaction to some extent—but very slightly. "There is one thing I rather regret," he said, "that we allowed them to join up the vertical bands of the pattern at the top. I think it would have been better to leave that alone."

"Oh?" said his aunt interrogatively.

"Yes: as I was reading in bed last night they kept catching my eye rather. That is, I found myself looking across at them every now and then. There was an effect as if some one kept peeping out between the curtains in one place or another, where there was no edge, and I think that was due to the joining up of the bands at the top. The only other thing that troubled me was the wind."

"Why, I thought it was a perfectly still night."

"Perhaps it was only on my side of the house, but there was enough to sway my curtains and rustle them more than I wanted."

That night a bachelor friend of James Denton's came to stay, and was lodged in a room on the same floor as his host, but at the end of a long passage, halfway down which was a red baize door, put there to cut off the draught and intercept noise.

The party of three had separated. Miss Denton a good first, the two men at about eleven. James Denton, not yet inclined for bed, sat him down in an arm-chair and read for a time. Then he dozed, and then he woke, and bethought himself that his brown spaniel, which ordinarily slept in his room, had not come upstairs with him. Then he thought he was mistaken: for happening to move his hand which hung down over the arm of the chair within a few inches of the floor, he felt on the back of it just the slightest touch of a surface of hair, and stretching it out in that direction he stroked and patted a rounded something. But the feel of it, and still more the fact that instead of a responsive movement, absolute stillness greeted his touch, made him look over the arm. What he had been touching rose to meet him. It was in the attitude of one that had crept along the floor on its belly, and it was, so far as could be collected, a human figure. But of the face which was now rising to within a few inches of his own no feature was discernible, only hair. Shapeless as it was, there was about it so horrible an air of menace that as he bounded from his chair and rushed from the room he heard himself moaning with fear: and doubtless he did right to fly. As he dashed into the baize door that cut the passage in two, and—forgetting that it opened towards him—beat against it with all the force in him, he felt a soft ineffectual tearing at his back which, all the same, seemed to be growing in power, as if the hand, or whatever worse than a hand was there, were becoming more material as the pursuer's rage was more concentrated. Then he remembered the trick of the door—he got it open—he shut it behind him—he gained his friend's room, and that is all we need know.

It seems curious that, during all the time that had elapsed since the purchase of Poynter's diary, James Denton should not have sought an explanation of the presence of the pattern that had been pinned into it. Well, he had read the diary through without finding it mentioned, and had concluded that there was nothing to be said. But, on leaving Rendcomb Manor (he did not know whether for good), as he naturally insisted upon doing on the day after experiencing the horror I have tried to put into words, he took the diary with him. And at his seaside lodgings he examined more narrowly the portion whence the pattern had been taken. What he remembered having suspected about it turned out to be correct. Two or three leaves were pasted together, but written upon, as was patent when they were held up to the light. They yielded easily to steaming, for the paste had lost much of its strength, and they contained something relevant to the pattern.

The entry was made in 1707.

"Old Mr. Casbury, of Acrington, told me this day much of young Sir Everard Charlett, whom he remember'd Commoner of University College, and thought was of the same Family as Dr. Arthur Charlett, now master of ye Coll. This Charlett was a personable young gent., but a loose atheistical companion, and a great Lifter, as they then call'd the hard drinkers, and for what I know do so now. He was noted, and subject to severall censures at different times for his extravagancies: and if the full history of his debaucheries had bin known, no doubt would have been expell'd ye Coll., supposing that no interest had been imploy'd on his behalf, of which Mr. Casbury had some suspicion. He was a very beautiful person, and constantly wore his own Hair, which was very abundant, from which, and his loose way of living, the cant name for him was Absalom, and he was accustom'd to say that indeed he believ'd he had shortened old David's days, meaning his father, Sir Job Charlett, an old worthy cavalier.

"Note that Mr. Casbury said that he remembers not the year of Sir Everard Charlett's death, but it was 1692 or 3. He died suddenly in October. (Several lines describing his unpleasant habits and reputed delinquencies are omitted.) Having seen him in such topping spirits the night before, Mr. Casbury was amaz'd when he learn'd the death. He was found in the town ditch, the hair as was said pluck'd clean off his head. Most bells in Oxford rung out for him, being a nobleman, and he was buried next night in St. Peter's in the East. But two years after, being to be moved to his country estate by his successor, it was said the coffin, breaking by mischance, proved quite full of Hair: which sounds fabulous, but yet I believe precedents are upon record, as in Dr. Plot's History of Staffordshire.

"His chambers being afterwards stripp'd, Mr. Casbury came

by part of the hangings of it, which 'twas said this Charlett had design'd expressly for a memorial of his Hair, giving the Fellow that drew it a lock to work by, and the piece which I have fasten'd in here was parcel of the same, which Mr. Casbury gave to me. He said he believ'd there was a subtlety in the drawing, but had never discover'd it himself, nor much liked to pore upon it."

The money spent upon the curtains might as well have been thrown into the fire, as they were. Mr. Cattell's comment upon what he heard of the story took the form of a quotation from Shakespeare. You may guess it without difficulty. It began with the words "There are more things."

MARK TWAIN

(1835-1910)

37

A Ghost Story

I took a large room, far up Broadway, in a huge old building whose upper stories had been wholly unoccupied for years until I came. The place had long been given up to dust and cobwebs, to solitude and silence. I seemed groping among the tombs and invading the privacy of the dead, that first night I climbed up to my quarters. For the first time in my life a superstitious dread came over me; and as I turned a dark angle of the stairway and an invisible cobweb swung its slazy woof in my face and clung there, I shuddered as one who had encountered a phantom.

I was glad enough when I reached my room and locked out the mold and the darkness. A cheery fire was burning in the grate, and I sat down before it with a comforting sense of relief. For two hours I sat there, thinking of bygone times; recalling old scenes, and summoning half-forgotten faces out of the mists of the past; listening, in fancy, to voices that long ago grew silent for all time, and to once familiar songs that nobody sings now. And as my reverie softened down to a sadder and sadder pathos, the shrieking of the winds outside softened to a wail, the angry beating of the rain against the panes diminished to a tranquil patter, and one by one the noises in the street subsided, until the hurrying footsteps of the last belated straggler died away in the distance and left no sound behind.

The fire had burned low. A sense of loneliness crept over me. I arose and undressed, moving on tiptoe about the room, doing stealthily what I had to do, as if I were environed by sleeping enemies whose slumbers it would be fatal to break. I covered up in bed, and lay listening to the rain and wind and the faint creaking of distant shutters, till they lulled me to sleep.

I slept profoundly, but how long I do not know. All at once I found myself awake, and filled with a shuddering expectancy. All was still. All but my own heart—I could hear it beat. Presently the bedclothes began to slip away slowly toward the foot of the bed, as if some one were pulling them! I could not stir; I could not speak. Still the blankets slipped deliberately away, till my breast was uncovered. Then with a great effort I seized them and drew them over my head. I waited, listened, waited. Once more that steady pull began, and once more I lay torpid a century of dragging seconds till my breast was naked again. At last I roused my energies and snatched the covers back to their place and held them with a strong grip. I waited. By and by I felt a faint tug, and took a fresh grip. The tug strengthened to a steady strain—it grew stronger and stronger. My hold parted, and for the third time the blankets slid away. I groaned. An answering groan came from the foot of the bed! Beaded drops of sweat stood upon my forehead. I was more dead than alive. Presently I heard a heavy footstep in my room—the step of an elephant, it seemed to me—it was not like anything human. But it was moving from me—there was relief in that. I heard it approach the door—pass out without moving bolt or lock—and wander away among the dismal corridors, straining the floors and joists till they creaked again as it passed—and then silence reigned once more.

When my excitement had calmed, I said to myself, "This is a dream—simply a hideous dream." And so I lay thinking it over until I convinced myself that it was a dream, and then a comforting laugh relaxed my lips and I was happy again. I got up and struck a light; and when I found that the locks and bolts were just as I had left them, another soothing laugh welled in my heart and rippled from my lips. I took my pipe and lit it, and was just sitting down before the fire, when—down went the pipe out of my nerveless fingers, the blood forsook my cheeks, and my placid breathing was cut short with a gasp! In the ashes on the hearth, side by side with my own bare footprint, was another, so vast that in comparison mine was but an infant's! Then I had had a visitor, and the elephant tread was explained.

I put out the light and returned to bed, palsied with fear. I lay a long time, peering into the darkness, and listening. Then I heard a grating noise overhead, like the dragging of a heavy body across the floor; then the throwing down of the body, and the shaking of my windows in response to the concussion. In distant parts of the building I heard the muffled slamming of doors. I heard, at intervals, stealthy footsteps creeping in and out among the corridors, and up and down the stairs. Sometimes these noises approached my door, hesitated, and went away again. I heard the clanking of chains faintly, in remote passages, and listened while the clanking grew nearer—while it wearily climbed the stairways, marking each move by the loose surplus of chain that fell with an accented rattle upon each succeeding step as the goblin that bore it advanced. I heard muttered sentences; half-uttered screams that seemed smothered violently; and the swish of invisible garments, the rush of invisible wings. Then I became conscious that my chamber was invaded—that I was not alone. I heard sighs and breathings about my bed, and mysterious whisperings. Three little spheres of soft phosphorescent light appeared on the ceiling directly over my head, clung and glowed there a moment, and then dropped—two of them upon my face and one upon the pillow. They spattered, liquidly, and felt warm. Intuition told me they had turned to gouts of blood as they fell—I needed no light to satisfy myself of that. Then I saw pallid faces, dimly luminous, and white uplifted hands, floating bodiless in the air—floating a moment and then disappearing. The whispering ceased, and the voices and the sounds, and a solemn stillness followed. I waited and listened. I felt that I must have light or die. I was weak with fear. I slowly raised myself toward a sitting posture, and my face came in contact with a clammy hand! All strength went from me apparently, and I fell back like a stricken invalid. Then I heard the rustle of a garment—it seemed to pass to the door and go out.

When everything was still once more, I crept out of bed, sick and feeble, and lit the gas with a hand that trembled as if it were aged with a hundred years. The light brought some little cheer to my spirits. I sat down and fell into a dreamy contemplation of that great footprint in the ashes. By and by its outlines began to waver and grow dim. I glanced up and the broad gas-flame was slowly wilting away. In the same moment I heard that elephantine tread again. I noted its approach, nearer and nearer, along the musty halls, and dimmer and dimmer the light waned. The tread reached my very door and paused—the light had dwindled to a sickly blue, and all things about me lay in a spectral twilight. The door did not open, and yet I felt a faint gust of air fan my cheek, and presently was conscious of a huge, cloudy presence before me. I watched it with fascinated eyes. A pale glow stole over the Thing; gradually its cloudy folds took shape—an arm appeared, then legs, then a body, and last a great sad face looked out of the vapor. Stripped of its filmy housings, naked, muscular and comely, the majestic Cardiff Giant loomed above me!

All my misery vanished—for a child might know that no harm could come with that benignant countenance. My cheerful spirits returned at once, and in sympathy with them the gas flamed up brightly again. Never a lonely outcast was so glad to welcome company as I was to greet the friendly giant. I said:

"Why, is it nobody but you? Do you know, I have been scared to death for the last two or three hours? I am most honestly glad to see you. I wish I had a chair—Here, here, don't try to sit down in that thing—"

But it was too late. He was in it before I could stop him and down he went—I never saw a chair shivered so in my life.

"Stop, stop, you'll ruin ev—"

Too late again. There was another crash, and another chair was resolved into its original elements.

"Confound it, haven't you got any judgment at all? Do you want to ruin all the furniture on the place? Here, here, you petrified fool—"

But it was no use. Before I could arrest him he had sat down on the bed, and it was a melancholy ruin.

"Now what sort of a way is that to do? First you come lumbering about the place bringing a legion of vagabond goblins along with you to worry me to death, and then when I overlook an indelicacy of costume which would not be tolerated anywhere by cultivated people except in a respectable theater, and not even there if the nudity were of your sex, you repay me by wrecking all the furniture you can find to sit down on. And why will you? You damage yourself as much as you do me. You have broken off the end of your spinal column, and littered up the floor with chips of your hams till the place looks like a marble yard. You ought to be ashamed of yourself—you are big enough to know better."

"Well, I will not break any more furniture. But what am I to do? I have not had a chance to sit down for a century." And the tears came into his eyes.

"Poor devil," I said, "I should not have been so harsh with you. And you are an orphan, too, no doubt. But sit down on the floor here—nothing else can stand your weight—and besides, we cannot be sociable with you away up there above me; I want you down where I can perch on this high counting-house stool and gossip with you face to face."

So he sat down on the floor, and lit a pipe which I gave him, threw one of my red blankets over his shoulders, inverted my sitz-bath on his head, helmet fashion, and made himself picturesque and comfortable. Then he crossed his ankles, while I renewed the fire, and exposed the flat, honeycombed bottoms of his prodigious feet to the grateful warmth.

"What is the matter with the bottom of your feet and the back of your legs, that they are gouged up so?"

"Infernal chilblains—I caught them clear up to the back of my head, roosting out there under Newell's farm. But I love the place; I love it as one loves his old home. There is no peace for me like the peace I feel when I am there."

We talked along for half an hour, and then I noticed that he looked tired, and spoke of it.

"Tired?" he said. "Well, I should think so. And now I will tell you all about it, since you have treated me so well. I am the spirit of the Petrified Man that lies across the street there in the museum. I am the ghost of the Cardiff Giant. I can have no rest, no peace, till they have given that poor body burial again. Now what was the most natural thing for me to do, to make men satisfy this wish? Terrify them into it!—haunt the place where the body lay! So I haunted the museum night after night. I even got other spirits to help me. But it did no good, for nobody ever came to the museum at midnight. Then it occurred to me to come over the way and haunt this place a little. I felt that if I ever got a hearing I must succeed, for I had the most efficient company that perdition could furnish. Night after night we have shivered around through these mildewed halls, dragging chains, groaning, whispering, tramping up and down stairs, till, to tell you the truth, I am almost worn out. But when I saw a light in your room tonight I roused my energies again and went at it with a deal of the old freshness. But I am tired out—entirely fagged out. Give me, I beseech you, give me some hope!"

I lit off my perch in a burst of excitement, and exclaimed:

"This transcends everything! Everything that ever did occur! Why you poor blundering old fossil, you have had all your trouble for nothing—you have been haunting a plaster cast of yourself—the real Cardiff Giant is in Albany!—[A fact. The original fraud was ingeniously and fraudfully duplicated, and exhibited in New York as the "only genuine" Cardiff Giant (to the unspeakable disgust of the owners of the real colossus) at the very same time that the latter was drawing crowds at a museum in Albany,]—Confound it, don't you know your own remains?"

I never saw such an eloquent look of shame, of pitiable humiliation, overspread a countenance before.

The Petrified Man rose slowly to his feet, and said:

"Honestly, is that true?"

"As true as I am sitting here."

He took the pipe from his mouth and laid it on the mantel, then stood irresolute a moment (unconsciously, from old habit, thrusting his hands where his pantaloons pockets should have been, and meditatively dropping his chin on his breast) and finally said:

"Well—I never felt so absurd before. The Petrified Man has sold everybody else, and now the mean fraud has ended by selling its own ghost! My son, if there is any charity left in your heart for a poor friendless phantom like me, don't let this get out. Think how you would feel if you had made such an ass of yourself."

I heard his stately tramp die away, step by step down the stairs and out into the deserted street, and felt sorry that he was gone, poor fellow—and sorrier still that he had carried off my red blanket and my bathtub.

38

Cannibalism in the Cars

I visited St. Louis lately, and on my way West, after changing cars at Terre Haute, Indiana, a mild, benevolent-looking gentleman of about forty-five, or maybe fifty, came in at one of the way-stations and sat down beside me. We talked together pleasantly on various subjects for an hour, perhaps, and I found him exceedingly intelligent and entertaining. When he learned that I was from Washington, he immediately began to ask questions about various public men, and about Congressional affairs; and I saw very shortly that I was conversing with a man who was perfectly familiar with the ins and outs of political life at the Capital, even to the ways and manners, and customs of procedure of Senators and Representatives in the Chambers of the national Legislature. Presently two men halted near us for a single moment, and one said to the other:

"Harris, if you'll do that for me, I'll never forget you, my boy."

My new comrade's eye lighted pleasantly. The words had touched upon a happy memory, I thought. Then his face settled into thoughtfulness—almost into gloom. He turned to me and said,

"Let me tell you a story; let me give you a secret chapter of my life—a chapter that has never been referred to by me since its events transpired. Listen patiently, and promise that you will not interrupt me."

I said I would not, and he related the following strange adventure, speaking sometimes with animation, sometimes with melancholy, but always with feeling and earnestness.

The stranger's narrative:

"On the 19th of December, 1853, I started from St. Louis on the evening train bound for Chicago. There were only twenty-four passengers, all told. There were no ladies and no children. We were in excellent spirits, and pleasant acquaintanceships were soon formed. The journey bade fair to be a happy one; and no individual in the party, I think, had even the vaguest presentiment of the horrors we were soon to undergo.

"At 11 p.m. it began to snow hard. Shortly after leaving the small village of Welden, we entered upon that tremendous prairie solitude that stretches its leagues on leagues of houseless dreariness far away toward the jubilee Settlements. The winds, unobstructed by trees or hills, or even vagrant rocks, whistled fiercely across the level desert, driving the falling snow before it like spray from the crested waves of a stormy sea. The snow was deepening fast; and we knew, by the diminished speed of the train, that the engine was plowing through it with steadily increasing difficulty. Indeed, it almost came to a dead halt sometimes, in the midst of great drifts that piled themselves like colossal graves across the track. Conversation began to flag. Cheerfulness gave place to grave concern. The possibility of being imprisoned in the snow, on the bleak prairie, fifty miles from any house, presented itself to every mind, and extended its depressing influence over every spirit.

"At two o'clock in the morning I was aroused out of an uneasy slumber by the ceasing of all motion about me. The appalling truth flashed upon me instantly—we were captives in a snow-drift! 'All hands to the rescue!' Every man sprang to obey. Out into the wild night, the pitchy darkness, the billowy snow, the driving storm, every soul leaped, with the consciousness that a moment lost now might bring destruction to us all. Shovels, hands, boards—anything, everything that could displace snow, was brought into instant requisition. It was a weird picture, that small company of frantic men fighting the banking snows, half in the blackest shadow and half in the angry light of the locomotive's reflector.

"One short hour sufficed to prove the utter uselessness of our efforts. The storm barricaded the track with a dozen drifts while we dug one away. And worse than this, it was discovered that the last grand charge the engine had made upon the enemy had broken the fore-and-aft shaft of the driving-wheel! With a free track before us we should still have been helpless. We entered the car wearied with labor, and very sorrowful. We gathered about the stoves, and gravely canvassed our situation. We had no provisions whatever—in this lay our chief distress. We could not freeze, for there was a good supply of wood in the tender. This was our only comfort. The discussion ended at last in accepting the disheartening decision of the conductor, viz., that it would be death for any man to attempt to travel fifty miles on foot through snow like that. We could not send for help, and even if we could it would not come. We must submit, and await, as patiently as we might, succor or starvation! I think the stoutest heart there felt a momentary chill when those words were uttered.

"Within the hour conversation subsided to a low murmur here and there about the car, caught fitfully between the rising and falling of the blast; the lamps grew dim; and the majority of the castaways settled themselves among the flickering shadows to think—to forget the present, if they could—to sleep, if they might.

"The eternal night—it surely seemed eternal to us—wore its lagging hours away at last, and the cold gray dawn broke in the east. As the light grew stronger the passengers began to stir and give signs of life, one after another, and each in turn pushed his slouched hat up from his forehead, stretched his stiffened limbs, and glanced out of the windows upon the cheerless prospect. It was cheer less, indeed!—not a living thing visible anywhere, not a human habitation; nothing but a vast white desert; uplifted sheets of snow drifting hither and thither before the wind—a world of eddying flakes shutting out the firmament above.

"All day we moped about the cars, saying little, thinking much. Another lingering dreary night—and hunger.

"Another dawning—another day of silence, sadness, wasting hunger, hopeless watching for succor that could not come. A night of restless slumber, filled with dreams of feasting—wakings distressed with the gnawings of hunger.

"The fourth day came and went—and the fifth! Five days of dreadful imprisonment! A savage hunger looked out at every eye. There was in it a sign of awful import—the foreshadowing of a something that was vaguely shaping itself in every heart—a something which no tongue dared yet to frame into words.

"The sixth day passed—the seventh dawned upon as gaunt and haggard and hopeless a company of men as ever stood in the shadow of death. It must out now! That thing which had been growing up in every heart was ready to leap from every lip at last! Nature had been taxed to the utmost—she must yield. RICHARD H. GASTON of Minnesota, tall, cadaverous, and pale, rose up. All knew what was coming. All prepared—every emotion, every semblance of excitement—was smothered—only a calm, thoughtful seriousness appeared in the eyes that were lately so wild.

"'Gentlemen: It cannot be delayed longer! The time is at hand! We must determine which of us shall die to furnish food for the rest!'

"MR. JOHN J. WILLIAMS of Illinois rose and said: 'Gentlemen—I nominate the Rev. James Sawyer of Tennessee.'

"MR. Wm. R. ADAMS of Indiana said: 'I nominate Mr. Daniel Slote of New York.'

"MR. CHARLES J. LANGDON: 'I nominate Mr. Samuel A. Bowen of St. Louis.'

"MR. SLOTE: 'Gentlemen—I desire to decline in favor of Mr. John A. Van Nostrand, Jun., of New Jersey.'

"MR. GASTON: 'If there be no objection, the gentleman's desire will be acceded to.'

"MR. VAN NOSTRAND objecting, the resignation of Mr.

Slote was rejected. The resignations of Messrs. Sawyer and Bowen were also offered, and refused upon the same grounds.

"MR. A. L. BASCOM of Ohio: 'I move that the nominations now close, and that the House proceed to an election by ballot.'

"MR. SAWYER: 'Gentlemen—I protest earnestly against these proceedings. They are, in every way, irregular and unbecoming. I must beg to move that they be dropped at once, and that we elect a chairman of the meeting and proper officers to assist him, and then we can go on with the business before us understandingly.'

"MR. BELL of Iowa: 'Gentlemen—I object. This is no time to stand upon forms and ceremonious observances. For more than seven days we have been without food. Every moment we lose in idle discussion increases our distress. I am satisfied with the nominations that have been made—every gentleman present is, I believe—and I, for one, do not see why we should not proceed at once to elect one or more of them. I wish to offer a resolution—'

"MR. GASTON: 'It would be objected to, and have to lie over one day under the rules, thus bringing about the very delay you wish to avoid. The gentleman from New Jersey—'

"MR. VAN NOSTRAND: 'Gentlemen—I am a stranger among you; I have not sought the distinction that has been conferred upon me, and I feel a delicacy—'

"MR. MORGAN of Alabama (interrupting): 'I move the previous question.'

"The motion was carried, and further debate shut off, of course. The motion to elect officers was passed, and under it Mr. Gaston was chosen chairman, Mr. Blake, secretary, Messrs. Holcomb, Dyer, and Baldwin a committee on nominations, and Mr. R. M. Howland, purveyor, to assist the committee in making selections.

"A recess of half an hour was then taken, and some little caucusing followed. At the sound of the gavel the meeting reassembled, and the committee reported in favor of Messrs. George Ferguson of Kentucky, Lucien Herrman of Louisiana, and W. Messick of Colorado as candidates. The report was accepted.

"MR. ROGERS of Missouri: 'Mr. President, the report being properly before the House now, I move to amend it by substituting for the name of Mr. Herrman that of Mr. Lucius Harris of St. Louis, who is well and honourably known to us all. I do not wish to be understood as casting the least reflection upon the high character and standing of the gentleman from Louisiana far from it. I respect and esteem him as much as any gentleman here present possibly can; but none of us can be blind to the fact that he has lost more flesh during the week that we have lain here than any among us—none of us can be blind to the fact that the committee has been derelict in its duty, either through negligence or a graver fault, in thus offering for our suffrages a gentleman who, however pure his own motives may be, has really less nutriment in him—'

"THE CHAIR: 'The gentleman from Missouri will take his seat. The Chair cannot allow the integrity of the committee to be questioned save by the regular course, under the rules. What action will the House take upon the gentleman's motion?'

"MR. HALLIDAY of Virginia: 'I move to further amend the report by substituting Mr. Harvey Davis of Oregon for Mr. Messick. It may be urged by gentlemen that the hardships and privations of a frontier life have rendered Mr. Davis tough; but, gentlemen, is this a time to cavil at toughness? Is this a time to be fastidious concerning trifles? Is this a time to dispute about matters of paltry significance? No, gentlemen, bulk is what we desire—substance, weight, bulk—these are the supreme requisites now—not talent, not genius, not education. I insist upon my motion.'

"MR. MORGAN (excitedly): 'Mr. Chairman—I do most strenuously object to this amendment. The gentleman from Oregon is old, and furthermore is bulky only in bone—not in flesh. I ask the gentleman from Virginia if it is soup we want instead of solid sustenance? If he would delude us with shadows? If he would mock our suffering with an Oregonian specter? I ask him if he can look upon the anxious faces around him, if he can gaze into our sad eyes, if he can listen to the beating of our expectant hearts, and still thrust this famine-stricken fraud upon us? I ask him if he can think of our desolate state, of our past sorrows, of our dark future, and still unpityingly foist upon us this wreck, this ruin, this tottering swindle, this gnarled and blighted and sapless vagabond from Oregon's hospitable shores? Never!' (Applause.)

"The amendment was put to vote, after a fiery debate, and lost. Mr. Harris was substituted on the first amendment. The balloting then began. Five ballots were held without a choice. On the sixth, Mr. Harris was elected, all voting for him but himself. It was then moved that his election should be ratified by acclamation, which was lost, in consequence of his again voting against himself.

"MR. RADWAY moved that the House now take up the remaining candidates, and go into an election for breakfast. This was carried.

"On the first ballot—there was a tie, half the members favoring one candidate on account of his youth, and half favoring the other on account of his superior size. The President gave the casting vote for the latter, Mr. Messick. This decision created considerable dissatisfaction among the friends of Mr. Ferguson, the defeated candidate, and there was some talk of demanding a new ballot; but in the midst of it a motion to adjourn was carried, and the meeting broke up at once.

"The preparations for supper diverted the attention of the Ferguson faction from the discussion of their grievance for a long time, and then, when they would have taken it up again, the happy announcement that Mr. Harris was ready drove all thought of it to the winds.

"We improvised tables by propping up the backs of car-seats, and sat down with hearts full of gratitude to the finest supper that had blessed our vision for seven torturing days. How changed we were from what we had been a few short hours before! Hopeless, sad-eyed misery, hunger, feverish anxiety, desperation, then; thankfulness, serenity, joy too deep for utterance now. That I know was the cheeriest hour of my eventful life. The winds howled, and blew the snow wildly about our prison house, but they were powerless to distress us any more. I liked Harris. He might have been better done, perhaps, but I am free to say that no man ever agreed with me better than Harris, or afforded me so large a degree of satisfaction. Messick was very well, though rather high-flavored, but for genuine nutritiousness and delicacy of fiber, give me Harris.

Messick had his good points—I will not attempt to deny it, nor do I wish to do it but he was no more fitted for breakfast than a mummy would be, sir—not a bit. Lean?—why, bless me!—and tough? Ah, he was very tough! You could not imagine it—you could never imagine anything like it."

"Do you mean to tell me that—"

"Do not interrupt me, please. After breakfast we elected a man by the name of Walker, from Detroit, for supper. He was very good. I wrote his wife so afterward. He was worthy of all praise. I shall always remember Walker. He was a little rare, but very good. And then the next morning we had Morgan of Alabama for breakfast. He was one of the finest men I ever sat down to handsome, educated, refined, spoke several languages fluently a perfect gentleman he was a perfect gentleman, and singularly juicy. For supper we had that Oregon patriarch, and he was a fraud, there is no question about it—old, scraggy, tough, nobody can picture the reality. I finally said, gentlemen, you can do as you like, but I will wait for another election. And Grimes of Illinois said, 'Gentlemen, I will wait also. When you elect a man that has something to recommend him, I shall be glad to join you again.' It soon became evident that there was general dissatisfaction with Davis of Oregon, and so, to preserve the good will that had prevailed so pleasantly since we had had Harris, an election was called, and the result of it was that Baker of Georgia was chosen. He was splendid! Well, well—after that we had Doolittle, and Hawkins, and McElroy (there was some complaint about McElroy, because he was uncommonly short and thin), and Penrod, and two Smiths, and Bailey (Bailey had a wooden leg, which was clear loss, but he was otherwise good), and an Indian boy, and an organ-grinder, and a gentleman by the name of Buckminster—a poor stick of a vagabond that wasn't any good for company and no account for breakfast. We were glad we got him elected before relief came."

"And so the blessed relief did come at last?"

"Yes, it came one bright, sunny morning, just after election. John Murphy was the choice, and there never was a better, I am willing to testify; but John Murphy came home with us, in the train that came to succor us, and lived to marry the widow Harris—"

"Relict of—"

"Relict of our first choice. He married her, and is happy and respected and prosperous yet. Ah, it was like a novel, sir—it was like a romance. This is my stopping-place, sir; I must bid you goodby. Any time that you can make it convenient to tarry a day or two with me, I shall be glad to have you. I like you, sir; I have conceived an affection for you. I could like you as well as I liked Harris himself, sir. Good day, sir, and a pleasant journey."

He was gone. I never felt so stunned, so distressed, so bewildered in my life. But in my soul I was glad he was gone. With all his gentleness of manner and his soft voice, I shuddered whenever he turned his hungry eye upon me; and when I heard that I had achieved his perilous affection, and that I stood almost with the late Harris in his esteem, my heart fairly stood still!

I was bewildered beyond description. I did not doubt his word; I could not question a single item in a statement so stamped with the earnestness of truth as his; but its dreadful details overpowered me, and threw my thoughts into hopeless confusion. I saw the conductor looking at me. I said, "Who is that man?"

"He was a member of Congress once, and a good one. But he got caught in a snow-drift in the cars, and like to have been starved to death. He got so frost-bitten and frozen up generally, and used up for want of something to eat, that he was sick and out of his head two or three months afterward. He is all right now, only he is a monomaniac, and when he gets on that old subject he never stops till he has eat up that whole car-load of people he talks about. He would have finished the crowd by this time, only he had to get out here. He has got their names as pat as A B C. When he gets them all eat up but himself, he always says: 'Then the hour for the usual election for breakfast having arrived; and there being no opposition, I was duly elected, after which, there being no objections offered, I resigned. Thus I am here.'"

I felt inexpressibly relieved to know that I had only been listening to the harmless vagaries of a madman instead of the genuine experiences of a bloodthirsty cannibal.

39

The Curious Dream

Night before last I had a singular dream. I seemed to be sitting on a doorstep (in no particular city perhaps) ruminating, and the time of night appeared to be about twelve or one o'clock. The weather was balmy and delicious. There was no human sound in the air, not even a footstep. There was no sound of any kind to emphasize the dead stillness, except the occasional hollow barking of a dog in the distance and the fainter answer of a further dog. Presently up the street I heard a bony clack-clacking, and guessed it was the castanets of a serenading party. In a minute more a tall skeleton, hooded, and half clad in a tattered and moldy shroud, whose shreds were flapping about the ribby latticework of its person, swung by me with a stately stride and disappeared in the gray gloom of the starlight. It had a broken and worm-eaten coffin on its shoulder and a bundle of something in its hand. I knew what the clack-clacking was then; it was this party's joints working together, and his elbows knocking against his sides as he walked. I may say I was surprised. Before I could collect my thoughts and enter upon any speculations as to what this apparition might portend, I heard another one coming for I recognized his clack-clack. He had two-thirds of a coffin on his shoulder, and some foot and head boards under his arm. I mightily wanted, to peer under his hood and speak to him, but when he turned and smiled upon me with his cavernous sockets and his projecting grin as he went by, I thought I would not detain him. He was hardly gone when I heard the clacking again, and another one issued from the shadowy half-light. This one was bending under a heavy gravestone, and dragging a shabby coffin after him by a string. When he got to me he gave me a steady look for a moment or two, and then rounded to and backed up to me, saying:

"Ease this down for a fellow, will you?"

I eased the gravestone down till it rested on the ground, and in doing so noticed that it bore the name of 'John Baxter Copmanhurst,' with 'May, 1839,' as the date of his death. Deceased sat wearily down by me, and wiped his os frontis with his major maxillary—chiefly from former habit I judged, for I could not see that he brought away any perspiration.

"It is too bad, too bad," said he, drawing the remnant of the shroud about him and leaning his jaw pensively on his hand. Then he put his left foot up on his knee and fell to scratching his anklebone absently with a rusty nail which he got out of his coffin.

"What is too bad, friend?"

"Oh, everything, everything. I almost wish I never had died."

"You surprise me. Why do you say this? Has anything gone wrong? What is the matter?"

"Matter! Look at this shroud-rags. Look at this gravestone, all battered up. Look at that disgraceful old coffin. All a man's property going to ruin and destruction before his eyes, and ask him if anything is wrong? Fire and brimstone!"

"Calm yourself, calm yourself," I said. "It is too bad—it is certainly too bad, but then I had not supposed that you would much mind such matters situated as you are."

"Well, my dear sir, I do mind them. My pride is hurt, and my comfort is impaired—destroyed, I might say. I will state my case—I will put it to you in such a way that you can comprehend it, if you will let me," said the poor skeleton, tilting the hood of his shroud back, as if he were clearing for action, and thus unconsciously giving himself a jaunty and festive air very much at variance with the grave character of his position in life—so to speak—and in prominent contrast with his distressful mood.

"Proceed," said I.

"I reside in the shameful old graveyard a block or two above you here, in this street—there, now, I just expected that cartilage would let go!—third rib from the bottom, friend, hitch the end of it to my spine with a string, if you have got such a thing about you, though a bit of silver wire is a deal pleasanter, and more durable and becoming, if one keeps it polished—to think of shredding out and going to pieces in this way, just on account of the indifference and neglect of one's posterity!"—and the poor ghost grated his teeth in a way that gave me a wrench and a shiver—for the effect is mightily increased by the absence of muffling flesh and cuticle. "I reside in that old graveyard, and have for these thirty years; and I tell you things are changed since I first laid this old tired frame there, and turned over, and stretched out for a long sleep, with a delicious sense upon me of being done with bother, and grief, and anxiety, and doubt, and fear, forever and ever, and listening with comfortable and increasing satisfaction to the sexton's work, from the startling clatter of his first spadeful on my coffin till it dulled away to the faint patting that shaped the roof of my new home-delicious! My! I wish you could try it tonight!" and out of my reverie deceased fetched me a rattling slap with a bony hand.

"Yes, sir, thirty years ago I laid me down there, and was happy. For it was out in the country then—out in the breezy, flowery, grand old woods, and the lazy winds gossiped with the leaves, and the squirrels capered over us and around us, and the creeping things visited us, and the birds filled the tranquil solitude with music. Ah, it was worth ten years of a man's life to be dead then! Everything was pleasant. I was in a good neighbourhood, for all the dead people that lived near me belonged to the best families in the city. Our posterity appeared to think the world of us. They kept our graves in the very best condition; the fences were always in faultless repair, head-boards were kept painted or whitewashed, and were replaced with new ones as soon as they began to look rusty or decayed; monuments were kept upright, railings intact and bright, the rose-bushes and shrubbery trimmed, trained, and free from blemish, the walks clean and smooth and graveled. But that day is gone by. Our descendants have forgotten us. My grandson lives in a stately house built with money made by these old hands of mine, and I sleep in a neglected grave with invading vermin that gnaw my shroud to build them nests withal! I and friends that lie with me founded and secured the prosperity of this fine city, and the stately bantling of our loves leaves us to rot in a dilapidated cemetery which neighbours curse and strangers scoff at. See the difference between the old time and this—for instance: Our graves are all caved in now; our head-boards have rotted away and tumbled down; our railings reel this way and that, with one foot in the air, after a fashion of unseemly levity; our monuments lean wearily, and our gravestones bow their heads discouraged; there be no adornments any more—no roses, nor shrubs, nor graveled walks, nor anything that is a comfort to the eye; and even the paintless old board fence that did make a show of holding us sacred from companionship with beasts and the defilement of heedless feet, has tottered till it overhangs the street, and only advertises the presence of our dismal resting-place and invites yet more derision to it. And now we cannot hide our poverty and tatters in the friendly woods, for the city has stretched its withering arms abroad and taken us in, and all that remains of the cheer of our old home is the cluster of lugubrious forest trees that stand, bored and weary of a city life, with their feet in our coffins, looking into the hazy distance and wishing they were there. I tell you it is disgraceful!

"You begin to comprehend—you begin to see how it is. While our descendants are living sumptuously on our money, right around us in the city, we have to fight hard to keep skull and bones together. Bless you, there isn't a grave in our cemetery that doesn't leak not one. Every time it rains in the night we have to climb out and roost in the trees and sometimes we are wakened suddenly by the chilly water trickling down the back of our necks. Then I tell you there is a general heaving up of old graves and kicking over of old monuments, and scampering of old skeletons for the trees! Bless me, if you had gone along there some such nights after twelve you might have seen as many as fifteen of us roosting on one limb, with our joints rattling drearily and the wind wheezing through our ribs! Many a time we have perched there for three or four dreary hours, and then come down, stiff and chilled through and drowsy, and borrowed each other's skulls to bail out our graves with—if you will glance up in my mouth now as I tilt my head back, you can see that my head-piece is half full of old dry sediment how top-heavy and stupid it makes me sometimes! Yes, sir, many a time if you had happened to come along just before the dawn you'd have caught us bailing out the graves and hanging our shrouds on the fence to dry. Why, I had an elegant shroud stolen from there one morning—think a party by the name of Smith took it, that resides in a plebeian graveyard over yonder—I think so because the first time I ever saw him he hadn't anything on but a check shirt, and the last time I saw him, which was at a social gathering in the new cemetery, he was the best-dressed corpse in the company—and it is a significant fact that he left when he saw me; and presently an old woman from here missed her coffin—she generally took it with her when she went anywhere, because she was liable to take cold and bring on the spasmodic rheumatism that originally killed her if she exposed herself to the night air much. She was named Hotchkiss—Anna Matilda Hotchkiss—you might know her? She has two upper front teeth, is tall, but a good deal inclined to stoop, one rib on the left side gone, has one shred of rusty hair hanging from the left side of her head, and one little tuft just above and a little forward of her right ear, has her underjaw wired on one side where it had worked loose, small bone of left forearm gone—lost in a fight has a kind of swagger in her gait and a 'gallus' way of going with: her arms akimbo and her nostrils in the air has been pretty free and easy, and is all damaged and battered up till she looks like a queensware crate in ruins—maybe you have met her?"

"God forbid!" I involuntarily ejaculated, for somehow I was not looking for that form of question, and it caught me a little off my guard. But I hastened to make amends for my rudeness, and say, "I simply meant I had not had the honour—for I would not deliberately speak discourteously of a friend of yours. You were saying that you were robbed—and it was a shame, too—but it appears by what is left of the shroud you have on that it was a costly one in its day. How did—"

A most ghastly expression began to develop among the decayed features and shrivelled integuments of my guest's face, and I was beginning to grow uneasy and distressed, when he told me he was only working up a deep, sly smile, with a wink in it, to suggest that about the time he acquired his present garment a ghost in a neighbouring cemetery missed one. This reassured me, but I begged him to confine himself to speech thenceforth, because his facial expression was uncertain. Even with the most elaborate care it was liable to miss fire. Smiling should especially be avoided. What he might honestly consider a shining success was likely to strike me in a very different light. I said I liked to see a skeleton cheerful, even decorously playful, but I did not think smiling was a skeleton's best hold.

"Yes, friend," said the poor skeleton, "the facts are just as I have given them to you. Two of these old graveyards—the one that I resided in and one further along have been deliberately neglected by our descendants of today until there is no occupying them any longer. Aside from the osteological discomfort of it—and that is no light matter this rainy weather—the present state of things is ruinous to property. We have got to move or be content to see our effects wasted away and utterly destroyed.

"Now, you will hardly believe it, but it is true, nevertheless, that there isn't a single coffin in good repair among all my acquaintance—now that is an absolute fact. I do not refer to low people who come in a pine box mounted on an express-wagon, but I am talking about your high-toned, silver-mounted burial-case, your monumental sort, that travel under black plumes at the head of a procession and have choice of cemetery lots—I mean folks like the Jarvises, and the Bledsoes and Burlings, and such. They are all about ruined. The most substantial people in our set, they were. And now look at them—utterly used up and poverty-stricken. One of the Bledsoes actually traded his monument to a late barkeeper for some fresh shavings to put under his head. I tell you it speaks volumes, for there is nothing a corpse takes so much pride in as his monument. He loves to read the inscription. He comes after a while to believe what it says himself, and then you may see him sitting on the fence night after night enjoying it. Epitaphs are cheap, and they do a poor chap a world of good after he is dead, especially if he had hard luck while he was alive. I wish they were used more. Now I don't complain, but confidentially I do think it was a little shabby in my descendants to give me nothing but this old slab of a gravestone—and all the more that there isn't a compliment on it. It used to have:

'GONE TO HIS JUST REWARD'

"On it, and I was proud when I first saw it, but by and by I noticed that whenever an old friend of mine came along he would hook his chin on the railing and pull a long face and read along down till he came to that, and then he would chuckle to himself and walk off, looking satisfied and comfortable. So I scratched it off to get rid of those fools. But a dead man always takes a deal of pride in his monument. Yonder goes half a dozen of the Jarvises now, with the family monument along. And Smithers and some hired specters went by with his awhile ago. Hello, Higgins, goodbye, old friend! That's Meredith Higgins—died in '44—belongs to our set in the cemetery—fine old family—great-grand mother was an Injun—I am on the most familiar terms with him he didn't hear me was the reason he didn't answer me. And I am sorry, too, because I would have liked to introduce you. You would admire him. He is the most disjointed, sway-backed, and generally distorted old skeleton you ever saw, but he is full of fun. When he laughs it sounds like rasping two stones together, and he always starts it off with a cheery screech like raking a nail across a window-pane. Hey, Jones! That is old Columbus Jones—shroud cost four hundred dollars entire trousseau, including monument, twenty-seven hundred. This was in the spring of '26. It was enormous style for those days. Dead people came all the way from the Alleghanies to see his things—the party that occupied the grave next to mine remembers it well.

Now do you see that individual going along with a piece of a head-board under his arm, one leg-bone below his knee gone, and not a thing in the world on? That is Barstow Dalhousie, and next to Columbus Jones he was the most sumptuously outfitted person that ever entered our cemetery. We are all leaving. We cannot tolerate the treatment we are receiving at the hands of our descendants. They open new cemeteries, but they leave us to our ignominy. They mend the streets, but they never mend anything that is about us or belongs to us. Look at that coffin of mine—yet I tell you in its day it was a piece of furniture that would have attracted attention in any drawing-room in this city. You may have it if you want it—I can't afford to repair it. Put a new bottom in her, and part of a new top, and a bit of fresh lining along the left side, and you'll find her about as comfortable as any receptacle of her species you ever tried. No thanks no, don't mention it you have been civil to me, and I would give you all the property I have got before I would seem ungrateful. Now this winding-sheet is a kind of a sweet thing in its way, if you would like to—No? Well, just as you say, but I wished to be fair and liberal there's nothing mean about me. Goodbye, friend, I must be going. I may have a good way to go tonight—don't know. I only know one thing for certain, and that is that I am on the emigrant trail now, and I'll never sleep in that crazy old cemetery again. I will travel till I fiend respectable quarters, if I have to hoof it to New Jersey. All the boys are going. It was decided in public conclave, last night, to emigrate, and by the time the sun rises there won't be a bone left in our old habitations. Such cemeteries may suit my surviving friends, but they do not suit the remains that have the honour to make these remarks. My opinion is the general opinion. If you doubt it, go and see how the departing ghosts upset things before they started. They were almost riotous in their demonstrations of distaste. Hello, here are some of the Bledsoes, and if you will give me a lift with this tombstone I guess I will join company and jog along with them—mighty respectable old family, the Bledsoes, and used to always come out in six-horse hearses and all that sort of thing fifty years ago when I walked these streets in daylight. Goodbye, friend."

And with his gravestone on his shoulder he joined the

grisly procession, dragging his damaged coffin after him, for notwithstanding he pressed it upon me so earnestly, I utterly refused his hospitality. I suppose that for as much as two hours these sad outcasts went clacking by, laden with their dismal effects, and all that time I sat pitying them. One or two of the youngest and least dilapidated among them inquired about midnight trains on the railways, but the rest seemed unacquainted with that mode of travel, and merely asked about common public roads to various towns and cities, some of which are not on the map now, and vanished from it and from the earth as much as thirty years ago, and some few of them never had existed anywhere but on maps, and private ones in real-estate agencies at that. And they asked about the condition of the cemeteries in these towns and cities, and about the reputation the citizens bore as to reverence for the dead.

This whole matter interested me deeply, and likewise compelled my sympathy for these homeless ones. And it all seeming real, and I not knowing it was a dream, I mentioned to one shrouded wanderer an idea that had entered my head to publish an account of this curious and very sorrowful exodus, but said also that I could not describe it truthfully, and just as it occurred, without seeming to trifle with a grave subject and exhibit an irreverence for the dead that would shock and distress their surviving friends. But this bland and stately remnant of a former citizen leaned him far over my gate and whispered in my ear, and said:

"Do not let that disturb you. The community that can stand such graveyards as those we are emigrating from can stand anything a body can say about the neglected and forsaken dead that lie in them."

At that very moment a cock crowed, and the weird procession vanished and left not a shred or a bone behind. I awoke, and found myself lying with my head out of the bed and 'sagging' downward considerably—a position favorable to dreaming dreams with morals in them, maybe, but not poetry.

NOTE—The reader is assured that if the cemeteries in his town are kept in good order, this Dream is not leveled at his town at all, but is leveled particularly and venomously at the next town.

MARY AUSTIN

(1868-1934)

40

The Readjustment

Emma Jeffries had been dead and buried three days. The sister who had come to the funeral had taken Emma's child away with her, and the house was swept and aired; then, when it seemed there was least occasion for it, Emma came back. The neighbour woman who had nursed her was the first to know it. It was about seven of the evening in a mellow gloom: the neighbour woman was sitting on her own stoop with her arms wrapped in her apron, and all at once she found herself going along the street under an urgent sense that Emma needed her. She was half-way dovvp. the block before she recollected that this was impossible, for Mrs. Jeffries was dead and buried; but as soon as die came opposite the house she was aware of what had happened.

It was all open to the summer air; except that it was a little neater, not otherwise than the rest of the street. It was quite dark; but the presence of Emma Jeffries streamed from it and betrayed it more than a candle. It streamed out steadily across the garden, and even as it reached her, mixed with the smell of the damp mignonette, the neighbour woman owned to herself that she had always known Emma would come back.

A sight stranger if she wouldn't, thought the woman who had nursed her. "She wasn't ever one to throw off things easily."

Emma Jeffries had taken death as she had taken everything in life, hard. She had met it with the same bright, surface competency that she had presented to the squalor of the encompassing desertness, to the insuperable commonness of Sim Jeffries, to the affliction of her crippled child; and the intensity of her wordless struggle against it had caught the attention of the townspeople and held it in a shocked curious awe. She was so long a-dying, lying there in that little low house, hearing the abhorred footsteps going about her rooms and the vulgar procedure of the community encroach upon her like the advances of the sand wastes on an imwatered field. For Emma had always wanted things different, wanted them with a fury of intentness that implied off ensiveness in things as they were. And the townspeople had taken offence, the more so because she was not to be surprised in any inaptitude for their own kind of success. Do what you could, you could never catch Emma Jeffries in a wrapper after three o'clock in the afternoon. And she would never talk about the child—in a country where so little ever happened that even trouble was a godsend if it gave you something to talk about. It was reported that she did not even talk to Sim. But there the common resentment got back at her. If she had thought to effect anything with Sim Jeffries against the benumbing spirit of the place, the evasive hopefulness, the large sense of leisure that ungirt the loins, if she still hoped somehow to get away with him to some place for which by her dress, by her manner, she seemed forever and imassailably fit, it was foregone that nothing would come of it. They knew Sim Jeffries better than that. Yet so vivid had been the force of her wordless dissatisfaction that when the fever took her and she went down like a pasteboard figure in the damp, the wonder was that nothing toppled with her. And, as if she too had felt her self indispensable, Emma Jeffries had come back.

The neighbour woman crossed the street, and as she passed the far corner of the garden, Jeffries spoke to her. He had been standing, she did not know how long a time, behind the syringa-bush, and moved even Vith her along the fence imtil they came to the gate. She could see in the dusk that before speaking he wet his lips with his tongue.

"She's in there," he said, at last.

"Emma?"

He nodded. "I been sleeping at the store since—but I thought I'd be more comfortable—as soon as I opened the door there she was."

"Did you see her?"

"No."

"How do you know, then?"

"Don't you know?"

The neighbour felt there was nothing to say to that.

"Come in," he whispered, huskily. They slipped by the rose-tree and the wistaria, and sat down on the porch at the side. A door swung inward behind them. They felt the Presence in the dusk beating like a pulse.

"What do you think she wants?" said Jeffries.

"Do you reckon it's the boy?"

"Like enough."

"He's better off with his aunt. There was no one here to take care of him like his mother wanted." He raised his voice unconsciously with a note of justification, addressing the room behind.

"I am sending fifty dollars a month," he said; "he can go with the best of them."

He went on at length to explain all the advantage that was to come to the boy from living at Pasadena, and the neighbour woman bore him out in it.

"He was glad to go," urged Jeffries to the room. "He said it was what his mother would have wanted."

They were silent then a long time, while the Presence seemed to swell upon them and encroached upon the garden.

Finally, "I gave Ziegler the order for the monument yesterday," Jeffries threw out, appeasingly. "It's to cost three hundred and fifty."

The Presence stirred. The neighbour thought she could fairly see the controlled tolerance with which Emma Jeffries endured the evidence of Sim's ineptitudes.

They sat on helplessly without talking after that until the woman's husband came to the fence and called her.

"Don't go," begged Sim.

"Hush," she said. "Do you want all the town to know? You had naught but good from Emma living, and no call to expect harm from her now. It's natural she should come back—if—if she was lonesome like—in—the place where she's gone to."

"Emma wouldn't come back to this place," Jeffries protested, "without she wanted something."

"Well, then, you've got to find out," said the neighbour woman.

All the next day she saw, whenever she passed the house, that Emma was still there. It was shut and barred, but the Presence lurked behind the folded blinds and fumbled at the doors.

When it was night and the moths began in the columbine imder the windows, it went out and walked in the garden.

Jeffries was waiting at the gate when the neighbour woman came. He sweated with helplessness in the warm dusk, and the Presence brooded upon them like an apprehension that grows by being entertained.

"She wants something," he appealed, "but I can't make out what. Emma knows she is welcome to everything I've got. Everybody knows I've been a good provider."

The neighbour woman remembered suddenly the only time she had ever drawn close to Emma Jeffries touching the boy. They had sat up with it together all one night in some childish ailment, and she had ventured a question. "What does his father think?" And Emma had ttimed her a white, hard face of surpassing dreariness.

"I don't know," she admitted, "he never says."

"There's more than providing," suggested the neighbour woman.

"Yes. There's feeling . . . but she had enough to do to put up with me. I had no call to be troubling her with such." He left off to mop his forehead, and began again.

"Feelings!" he said, "There's times a man gets so wore out with feelings he doesn't have them any more."

He talked, and presently it grew clear to the woman that he

was voiding all the stuff of his life, as if he had sickened on it and was now done. It was a little soul knowing itself and not good to see. What was singular was that the Presence left off walking in the garden, came and caught like a gossamer on the ivy-tree, swayed by the breath of his broken sentences. He talked, and the neighbour woman saw him for once as he saw himself and Emma, snared and floundering in an inexplicable unhappiness. He had been disappointed, too. She had never relished the man he was, and it made him ashamed. That was why he had never gone away, lest he should make her ashamed among her own kind. He was her husband, he could not help that though he was sorry for it. But he could keep the offence where least was made of it. And there was a child—she had wanted a child; but even then he had blundered—begotten a cripple upon her. He blamed himself utterly, searched out the roots of his youth for the answer to that, until the neighbour woman flinched to hear him. But the Presence stayed.

He had never talked to his wife about the child. How should he? There was the fact—the advertisement of his incompetence. And she had never talked to him. That was the one blessed and unassailable memory; that she had spread silence like a balm over his hurt. In return for it he had never gone away. He had resisted her that he might save her from showing among her own kind how poor a man he was.

With every word of this ran the fact of his love for her—as he had loved her, with all the stripes of clean and undeanness. He bared himself as a child without knowing; and the Presence stayed. The talk trailed off at last to the commonplaces of consolation between the retchings of his spirit. The Presence lessened and streamed toward them on the wind of the garden. When it touched them like the warm air of noon that lies sometimes in hollow places after nightfall, the neighbour woman rose and went away.

The next night she did not wait for him. When a rod outside the town—it was a very little one—the burrowing owls whoo-whooedy she hung up her apron and went to talk with Emma Jeffries. The Presence was there, drawn in, lying close. She found the key between the wistaria and the first pillar of the porch, but as soon as she opened the door she felt the chill that might be expected by one intruding on Emma Jeffries in her own house.

"The Lord is my shepherd," said the neighbour woman; it was the first religious phrase that occurred to her; then she said the whole of the psalm and after that a hymn. She had come in through the door and stood with her back to it and her hand upon the knob. Everything was just as Mrs. Jeffries had left it, with the waiting air of a room kept for company.

"Em," she said, boldly, when the chill had abated a little before the sacred words. "Em Jeffries, I've got something to say to you. And you've got to hear," she added with firmness, as the white curtains stirred duskily at the window. "You wouldn't be talked to about your troubles when . . . you were here before; and we humoured you. But now there is Sim to be thought of. I guess you heard what you came for last night, and got good of it.

"Maybe it would have been better if Sim had said things all along instead of hoarding them in his heart, but any way he has said them now. And what I want to say is, if you was staying on with the hope of hearing it again, you'd be making a mistake. You was an uncommon woman, Emma Jeffries, and there didn't none of us understand you very well, nor do you justice maybe; but Sim is only a common man, and I xmderstand him because I'm that way myself.

"And if you think he'll be opening his heart to you every night, or be any different from what he's always been on acount of what's happened, that's a mistake too . . . and in a Kttle while, if you stay, it will be as bad as it always was . . . Men are like that . . . You'd better go now while there's understanding between you." She stood staring into the darkling room that seemed suddenly full of turbulence and denial. It seemed to beat upon her and take her breath, but she held on.

"You've got to go . . . Em . . . and I'm going to stay until you do." She said this with finality, and then began again.

"The Lord is nigh unto them that are of a broken heart," and repeated the passage to the end. Then as the Presence sank before it. "You better go, Emma," persuasively, and again after an interval:

"He shall deliver thee in six troubles, yea, in seven shall no evil touch thee."

. . . The Presence gathered itself and was still. She could make out that it stood over against the opposite comer by the gilt easel with the crayon portrait of the child.

. . . "For thou shalt forget thy misery. Thou shalt remember it as waters that are past," concluded the neighbour woman, as she heard Jeffries on the gravel outside. What the Presence had wrought upon him in the night was visible in his altered mien. He looked more than anything else to be in need of sleep. He had eaten his sorrow, and that was the end of it—as it is with men.

"I came to see if there was anything I could do for you," said the woman, neighbourly, with her hand upon the door. "I don't know as there is," said he; "I'm much obliged, but I don't know as there is."

"You see," whispered the woman over her shoulder, "not even to me." She felt the tug of her heart as the Presence swept past her.

The neighbour went out after that and walked in the ragged street, past the school-house, across the creek below the town, out by the fields, over the headgate, and back by the town again. It was full nine of the clock when she passed the Jeffries house. It looked, except for being a little neater, not other than the rest of the street. The door was open and the lamp was lit; she saw Jeffries, black against it. He sat reading in a book, like a man at ease in his own hotise.

MARY SHELLEY

(1797-1851)

41

Captain Walton's Final Letter

It is past; I am returning to England. I have lost my hopes of utility and glory; I have lost my friend. But I will endeavour to detail these bitter circumstances to you, my dear sister; and while I am wafted towards England and towards you, I will not despond.

September 9th, the ice began to move, and roarings like thunder were heard at a distance as the islands split and cracked in every direction. We were in the most imminent peril, but as we could only remain passive, my chief attention was occupied by my unfortunate guest whose illness increased in such a degree that he was entirely confined to his bed. The ice cracked behind us and was driven with force towards the north; a breeze sprang from the west, and on the 11th the passage towards the south became perfectly free. When the sailors saw this and that their return to their native country was apparently assured, a shout of tumultuous joy broke from them, loud and long-continued. Frankenstein, who was dozing, awoke and asked the cause of the tumult. "They shout," I said, "because they will soon return to England."

"Do you, then, really return?"

"Alas! Yes; I cannot withstand their demands. I cannot lead them unwillingly to danger, and I must return."

"Do so, if you will; but I will not. You may give up your purpose, but mine is assigned to me by Heaven, and I dare not. I am weak, but surely the spirits who assist my vengeance will endow me with sufficient strength." Saying this, he endeavoured to spring from the bed, but the exertion was too great for him; he fell back and fainted.

It was long before he was restored, and I often thought that life was entirely extinct. At length he opened his eyes; he breathed with difficulty and was unable to speak. The surgeon gave him a composing draught and ordered us to leave him undisturbed. In the meantime he told me that my friend had certainly not many hours to live.

His sentence was pronounced, and I could only grieve and be patient. I sat by his bed, watching him; his eyes were closed, and I thought he slept; but presently he called to me in a feeble voice, and bidding me come near, said, "Alas! The strength I relied on is gone; I feel that I shall soon die, and he, my enemy and persecutor, may still be in being. Think not, Walton, that in the last moments of my existence I feel that burning hatred and ardent desire of revenge I once expressed; but I feel myself justified in desiring the death of my adversary. During these last days I have been occupied in examining my past conduct; nor do I find it blamable. In a fit of enthusiastic madness I created a rational creature and was bound towards him to assure, as far as was in my power, his happiness and well-being. This was my duty, but there was another still paramount to that. My duties towards the beings of my own species had greater claims to my attention because they included a greater proportion of happiness or misery. Urged by this view, I refused, and I did right in refusing, to create a companion for the first creature. He showed unparalleled malignity and selfishness in evil; he destroyed my friends; he devoted to destruction beings who possessed exquisite sensations, happiness, and wisdom; nor do I know where this thirst for vengeance may end. Miserable himself that he may render no other wretched, he ought to die. The task of his destruction was mine, but I have failed. When actuated by selfish and vicious motives, I asked you to undertake my unfinished work, and I renew this request now, when I am only induced by reason and virtue.

"Yet I cannot ask you to renounce your country and friends to fulfil this task; and now that you are returning to England, you will have little chance of meeting with him. But the consideration of these points, and the well balancing of what you may esteem your duties, I leave to you; my judgment and ideas are already disturbed by the near approach of death. I dare not ask you to do what I think right, for I may still be misled by passion.

"That he should live to be an instrument of mischief disturbs me; in other respects, this hour, when I momentarily expect my release, is the only happy one which I have enjoyed for several years. The forms of the beloved dead flit before me, and I hasten to their arms. Farewell, Walton! Seek happiness in tranquillity and avoid ambition, even if it be only the apparently innocent one of distinguishing yourself in science and discoveries. Yet why do I say this? I have myself been blasted in these hopes, yet another may succeed."

His voice became fainter as he spoke, and at length, exhausted by his effort, he sank into silence. About half an hour afterwards he attempted again to speak but was unable; he pressed my hand feebly, and his eyes closed for ever, while the irradiation of a gentle smile passed away from his lips.

Margaret, what comment can I make on the untimely extinction of this glorious spirit? What can I say that will enable you to understand the depth of my sorrow? All that I should express would be inadequate and feeble. My tears flow; my mind is overshadowed by a cloud of disappointment. But I journey towards England, and I may there find consolation.

I am interrupted. What do these sounds portend? It is midnight; the breeze blows fairly, and the watch on deck scarcely stir. Again there is a sound as of a human voice, but hoarser; it comes from the cabin where the remains of Frankenstein still lie. I must arise and examine. Good night, my sister.

Great God! what a scene has just taken place! I am yet dizzy with the remembrance of it. I hardly know whether I shall have the power to detail it; yet the tale which I have recorded would be incomplete without this final and wonderful catastrophe.

I entered the cabin where lay the remains of my ill-fated and admirable friend. Over him hung a form which I cannot find words to describe—gigantic in stature, yet uncouth and distorted in its proportions. As he hung over the coffin, his face was concealed by long locks of ragged hair; but one vast hand was extended, in colour and apparent texture like that of a mummy. When he heard the sound of my approach, he ceased to utter exclamations of grief and horror and sprung towards the window. Never did I behold a vision so horrible as his face, of such loathsome yet appalling hideousness. I shut my eyes involuntarily and endeavoured to recollect what were my duties with regard to this destroyer. I called on him to stay.

He paused, looking on me with wonder, and again turning towards the lifeless form of his creator, he seemed to forget my presence, and every feature and gesture seemed instigated by the wildest rage of some uncontrollable passion.

"That is also my victim!" he exclaimed. "In his murder my crimes are consummated; the miserable series of my being is wound to its close! Oh, Frankenstein! Generous and self-devoted being! What does it avail that I now ask thee to pardon me? I, who irretrievably destroyed thee by destroying all thou lovedst. Alas! He is cold, he cannot answer me."

His voice seemed suffocated, and my first impulses, which had suggested to me the duty of obeying the dying request of my friend in destroying his enemy, were now suspended by a mixture of curiosity and compassion. I approached this tremendous being; I dared not again raise my eyes to his face, there was something so scaring and unearthly in his ugliness. I attempted to speak, but the words died away on my lips. The monster continued to utter wild and incoherent self-reproaches. At length I gathered resolution to address him in a pause of the tempest of his passion.

"Your repentance," I said, "is now superfluous. If you had

listened to the voice of conscience and heeded the stings of remorse before you had urged your diabolical vengeance to this extremity, Frankenstein would yet have lived."

"And do you dream?" said the dæmon. "Do you think that I was then dead to agony and remorse? He," he continued, pointing to the corpse, "he suffered not in the consummation of the deed. Oh! Not the ten-thousandth portion of the anguish that was mine during the lingering detail of its execution. A frightful selfishness hurried me on, while my heart was poisoned with remorse. Think you that the groans of Clerval were music to my ears? My heart was fashioned to be susceptible of love and sympathy, and when wrenched by misery to vice and hatred, it did not endure the violence of the change without torture such as you cannot even imagine.

"After the murder of Clerval I returned to Switzerland, heart-broken and overcome. I pitied Frankenstein; my pity amounted to horror; I abhorred myself. But when I discovered that he, the author at once of my existence and of its unspeakable torments, dared to hope for happiness, that while he accumulated wretchedness and despair upon me he sought his own enjoyment in feelings and passions from the indulgence of which I was for ever barred, then impotent envy and bitter indignation filled me with an insatiable thirst for vengeance. I recollected my threat and resolved that it should be accomplished. I knew that I was preparing for myself a deadly torture, but I was the slave, not the master, of an impulse which I detested yet could not disobey. Yet when she died! Nay, then I was not miserable. I had cast off all feeling, subdued all anguish, to riot in the excess of my despair. Evil thenceforth became my good. Urged thus far, I had no choice but to adapt my nature to an element which I had willingly chosen. The completion of my demoniacal design became an insatiable passion. And now it is ended; there is my last victim!"

I was at first touched by the expressions of his misery; yet, when I called to mind what Frankenstein had said of his powers of eloquence and persuasion, and when I again cast my eyes on the lifeless form of my friend, indignation was rekindled within me.

"Wretch!" I said. "It is well that you come here to whine over the desolation that you have made. You throw a torch into a pile of buildings, and when they are consumed, you sit among the ruins and lament the fall. Hypocritical fiend! If he whom you mourn still lived, still would he be the object, again would he become the prey, of your accursed vengeance. It is not pity that you feel; you lament only because the victim of your malignity is withdrawn from your power."

"Oh, it is not thus—not thus," interrupted the being. "Yet such must be the impression conveyed to you by what appears to be the purport of my actions. Yet I seek not a fellow feeling in my misery. No sympathy may I ever find. When I first sought it, it was the love of virtue, the feelings of happiness and affection with which my whole being overflowed, that I wished to be participated. But now that virtue has become to me a shadow, and that happiness and affection are turned into bitter and loathing despair, in what should I seek for sympathy? I am content to suffer alone while my sufferings shall endure; when I die, I am well satisfied that abhorrence and opprobrium should load my memory. Once my fancy was soothed with dreams of virtue, of fame, and of enjoyment. Once I falsely hoped to meet with beings who, pardoning my outward form, would love me for the excellent qualities which I was capable of unfolding. I was nourished with high thoughts of honour and devotion. But now crime has degraded me beneath the meanest animal. No guilt, no mischief, no malignity, no misery, can be found comparable to mine. When I run over the frightful catalogue of my sins, I cannot believe that I am the same creature whose thoughts were once filled with sublime and transcendent visions of the beauty and the majesty of goodness. But it is even so; the fallen angel becomes a malignant devil. Yet even that enemy of God and man had friends and associates in his desolation; I am alone.

"You, who call Frankenstein your friend, seem to have a knowledge of my crimes and his misfortunes. But in the detail which he gave you of them he could not sum up the hours and months of misery which I endured wasting in impotent passions.

For while I destroyed his hopes, I did not satisfy my own desires. They were for ever ardent and craving; still I desired love and fellowship, and I was still spurned. Was there no injustice in this? Am I to be thought the only criminal, when all humankind sinned against me? Why do you not hate Felix, who drove his friend from his door with contumely? Why do you not execrate the rustic who sought to destroy the saviour of his child? Nay, these are virtuous and immaculate beings! I, the miserable and the abandoned, am an abortion, to be spurned at, and kicked, and trampled on. Even now my blood boils at the recollection of this injustice.

"But it is true that I am a wretch. I have murdered the lovely and the helpless; I have strangled the innocent as they slept and grasped to death his throat who never injured me or any other living thing. I have devoted my creator, the select specimen of all that is worthy of love and admiration among men, to misery; I have pursued him even to that irremediable ruin. There he lies, white and cold in death. You hate me, but your abhorrence cannot equal that with which I regard myself. I look on the hands which executed the deed; I think on the heart in which the imagination of it was conceived and long for the moment when these hands will meet my eyes, when that imagination will haunt my thoughts no more.

"Fear not that I shall be the instrument of future mischief. My work is nearly complete. Neither yours nor any man's death is needed to consummate the series of my being and accomplish that which must be done, but it requires my own. Do not think that I shall be slow to perform this sacrifice. I shall quit your vessel on the ice raft which brought me thither and shall seek the most northern extremity of the globe; I shall collect my funeral pile and consume to ashes this miserable frame, that its remains may afford no light to any curious and unhallowed wretch who would create such another as I have been. I shall die. I shall no longer feel the agonies which now consume me or be the prey of feelings unsatisfied, yet unquenched. He is dead who called me into being; and when I shall be no more, the very remembrance of us both will speedily vanish. I shall no longer see the sun or stars or feel the winds play on my cheeks. Light, feeling, and sense will pass away; and in this condition must I find my happiness. Some years ago, when the images which this world affords first opened upon me, when I felt the cheering warmth of summer and heard the rustling of the leaves and the warbling of the birds, and these were all to me, I should have wept to die; now it is my only consolation. Polluted by crimes and torn by the bitterest remorse, where can I find rest but in death?

"Farewell! I leave you, and in you the last of humankind whom these eyes will ever behold. Farewell, Frankenstein! If thou wert yet alive and yet cherished a desire of revenge against me, it would be better satiated in my life than in my destruction. But it was not so; thou didst seek my extinction, that I might not cause greater wretchedness; and if yet, in some mode unknown to me, thou hadst not ceased to think and feel, thou wouldst not desire against me a vengeance greater than that which I feel. Blasted as thou wert, my agony was still superior to thine, for the bitter sting of remorse will not cease to rankle in my wounds until death shall close them for ever.

"But soon," he cried with sad and solemn enthusiasm, "I shall die, and what I now feel be no longer felt. Soon these burning miseries will be extinct. I shall ascend my funeral pile triumphantly and exult in the agony of the torturing flames. The light of that conflagration will fade away; my ashes will be swept into the sea by the winds. My spirit will sleep in peace, or if it thinks, it will not surely think thus. Farewell."

He sprang from the cabin-window as he said this, upon the ice raft which lay close to the vessel. He was soon borne away by the waves and lost in darkness and distance.

O HENRY

(1862-1910)

42

The Furnished Room

Restless, shifting, fugacious as time itself is a certain vast bulk of the population of the red brick district of the lower West Side. Homeless, they have a hundred homes. They flit from furnished room to furnished room, transients forever—transients in abode, transients in heart and mind. They sing 'Home, Sweet Home' in ragtime; they carry their *lares et penates* in a bandbox; their vine is entwined about a picture hat; a rubber plant is their fig tree.

Hence the houses of this district, having had a thousand dwellers, should have a thousand tales to tell, mostly dull ones, no doubt; but it would be strange if there could not be found a ghost or two in the wake of all these vagrant guests.

One evening after dark a young man prowled among these crumbling red mansions, ringing their bells. At the twelfth he rested his lean hand-baggage upon the step and wiped the dust from his hatband and forehead. The bell sounded faint and far away in some remote, hollow depths.

To the door of this, the twelfth house whose bell he had rung, came a housekeeper who made him think of an unwholesome, surfeited worm that had eaten its nut to a hollow shell and now sought to fill the vacancy with edible lodgers.

He asked if there was a room to let.

"Come in," said the housekeeper. Her voice came from her throat; hert hroat seemed lined with fur. "I have the third-floor back, vacant since a week back. Should you wish to look at it?"

The young man followed her up the stairs. A faint light from no particular source mitigated the shadows of the halls. They trod noiselessly upon a stair carpet that its own loom would have forsworn. It seemed to have become vegetable; to have degenerated in that rank, sunless air to lush lichen or spreading moss that grew in patches to the staircase and was viscid under the foot like organic matter. At each turn of the stairs were vacant niches in the wall. Perhaps plants had once been set within them. If so they had died in that foul and tainted air. It may be that statues of the saints had stood there, but it was not difficult to conceive that imps and devils had dragged them forth in the darkness and down to the unholy depths of some furnished pit below.

"This is the room," said the housekeeper, from her furry throat. "It's a nice room. It ain't often vacant. I had some most elegant people in it last summer—no trouble at all, and paid in advance to the minute. The water's at the end of the hall. Sprowls and Mooney kept it three months. They done a vaudeville sketch. Miss B'retta Sprowls—you may have heard of her—Oh, that was just the stage names—right there over the dresser is where the marriage certificate hung, framed. The gas is here, and you see there is plenty of closet room. It's a room everybody likes. It never stays idle long."

"Do you have many theatrical people rooming here?" asked the young man.

"They comes and goes. A good proportion of my lodgers is connected with the theatres. Yes, sir, this is the theatrical district. Actor people never stays long anywhere. I get my share. Yes, they comes and goes."

He engaged the room, paying for a week in advance. He was tired, he said, and would take possession at once. He counted out the money. The room had been made ready, she said, even to towels and water. As the housekeeper moved away he put, for the thousandth time, the question that he carried at the end of his tongue.

"A young girl—Miss Vashner—Miss Eloise Vashner—do you remember such a one among your lodgers? She would be singing on the stage, most likely. A fair girl, of medium height and slender, with reddish, gold hair and a dark mole near her left eyebrow."

"No, I don't remember the name. Them stage people has names they change as often as their rooms. They comes and they goes. No, I don't call that one to mind."

No. Always no. Five months of ceaseless interrogation and the inevitable negative. So much time spent by day in questioning managers, agents, schools and choruses; by night among the audiences of theatres from all-star casts down to music halls so low that he dreaded to find what he most hoped for. He who had loved her best had tried to find her. He was sure that since her disappearance from home this great, water-girt city held her somewhere, but it was like a monstrous quicksand, shifting its particles constantly, with no foundation, its upper granules of today buried tomorrow in ooze and slime.

The furnished room received its latest guest with a first glow of pseudo-hospitality, a hectic, haggard, perfunctory welcome like the specious smile of a demirep. The sophistical comfort came in reflected gleams from the decayed furniture, the ragged brocade upholstery of a couch and two chairs, a foot-wide cheap pier-glass between the two windows, from one or two gilt picture frames and a brass bedstead in a corner.

The guest reclined, inert, upon a chair, while the room, confused in speech as though it were an apartment in Babel, tried to discourse to him of its divers tenantry.

A polychromatic rug like some brilliant-flowered rectangular, tropical islet lay surrounded by a billowy sea of soiled matting. Upon the gay-papered wall were those pictures that pursue the homeless one from house to house—The Huguenot Lovers, The First Quarrel, The Wedding Breakfast, Psyche at the Fountain.

The mantel's chastely severe outline was ingloriously veiled behind some pert drapery drawn rakishly askew like the sashes of the Amazonian ballet. Upon it was some desolate flotsam cast aside by the room's marooned when a lucky sail had borne them to a fresh port—a trifling vase or two, pictures of actresses, a medicine bottle, some stray cards out of a deck.

One by one, as the characters of a cryptograph become explicit, the little signs left by the furnished room's procession of guests developed a significance. The threadbare space in the rug in front of the dresser told that lovely women had marched in the throng. Tiny fingerprints on the wall spoke of little prisoners trying to feel their way to sun and air. A splattered stain, raying like the shadow of a bursting bomb, witnessed where a hurled glass or bottle had splintered with its contents against the wall. Across the pier glass had been scrawled with a diamond in staggering letters the name 'Marie.' It seemed that the succession of dwellers in the furnished room had turned in fury—perhaps tempted beyond forbearance by its garish coldness—and wreaked upon it their passions. The furniture was chipped and bruised; the couch, distorted by bursting springs, seemed a horrible monster that had been slain during the stress of some grotesque convulsion. Some more potent upheaval had cloven a great slice from the marble mantel. Each plank in the floor owned its particular cant and shriek as from a separate and individual agony. It seemed incredible that all this malice and injury had been wrought upon the room by those who had called it for a time their home; and yet it may have been the cheated home instinct surviving blindly, the resentful rage at false household gods that had kindled their wrath. A hut that is our own we can sweep and adorn and cherish.

The young tenant in the chair allowed these thoughts to file, soft-shod, through his mind, while there drifted into the room furnished sounds and furnished scents. He heard in one room a tittering and incontinent, slack laughter; in others the monologue of a scold, the rattling of dice, a lullaby, and one crying dully; above him a banjo tinkled with spirit. Doors banged somewhere; the elevated trains roared intermittently; a cat yowled miserably upon a back fence. And he breathed the breath of the house—a dank savour rather than a smell—a cold, musty effluvium as from underground vaults mingled with the reeking exhalations of linoleum and mildewed and rotten woodwork.

Then, suddenly, as he rested there, the room was filled with the strong, sweet odour of mignonette. It came as upon a single buffet of wind with such sureness and fragrance and emphasis that it almost seemed a living visitant. And the man cried aloud: "What, dear?" as if he had been called, and sprang up and faced about. The rich odour clung to him and wrapped him around. He reached out his arms for it, all his senses for the time confused and commingled. How could one be peremptorily called by an odour? Surely it must have been a sound. But, was it not the sound that had touched, that had caressed him?

"She has been in this room," he cried, and he sprang to wrest from it a token, for he knew he would recognize the smallest thing that had belonged to her or that she had touched. This enveloping scent of mignonette, the odour that she had loved and made her own—whence came it?

The room had been but carelessly set in order. Scattered upon the flimsy dresser scarf were half a dozen hairpins—those discreet, indistinguishable friends of womankind, feminine of gender, infinite of mood and uncommunicative of tense. These he ignored, conscious of their triumphant lack of identity. Ransacking the drawers of the dresser he came upon a discarded, tiny, ragged handkerchief. He pressed it to his face. It was racy and insolent with heliotrope; he hurled it to the floor. In another drawer he found odd buttons, a theatre programme, a pawnbroker's card, two lost marshmallows, a book on the divination of dreams. In the last was a woman's black satin hair bow, which halted him, poised between ice and fire. But the black satin hair bow also is femininity's demure, impersonal, common ornament, and tells no tales.

And then he traversed the room like a hound on the scent, skimming the walls, considering the corners of the bulging matting on his hands and knees, rummaging mantel and tables, the curtains and hangings, the drunken cabinet in the corner, for a visible sign, unable to perceive that she was there beside, around, against, within, above him, clinging to him, wooing him, calling him so poignantly through the finer senses that even his grosser ones became cognizant of the call. Once again he answered loudly: "Yes, dear!" and turned, wild-eyed, to gaze on vacancy, for he could not yet discern form and colour and love and outstretched arms in the odour of mignonette. Oh, God! Whence that odour, and since when have odours had a voice to call? Thus he groped.

He burrowed in crevices and corners, and found corks and cigarettes. These he passed in passive contempt. But once he found in a fold of the matting a half-smoked cigar, and this he ground beneath his heel with a green and trenchant oath. He sifted the room from end to end. He found dreary and ignoble small records of many a peripatetic tenant; but of her whom he sought, and who may have lodged there, and whose spirit seemed to hover there, he found no trace.

And then he thought of the housekeeper.

He ran from the haunted room downstairs and to a door that showed a crack of light. She came out to his knock. He smothered his excitement as best he could.

"Will you tell me, madam," he besought her, "who occupied the room I have before I came?"

"Yes, sir. I can tell you again. 'Twas Sprowls and Mooney, as I said. Miss B'retta Sprowls it was in the theatres, but Missis Mooney she was. My house is well known for respectability. The marriage certificate hung, framed, on a nail over—"

"What kind of a lady was Miss Sprowls—in looks, I mean?"

"Why, black-haired, sir, short, and stout, with a comical face. They left a week ago Tuesday."

"And before they occupied it?"

"Why, there was a single gentleman connected with the draying business. He left owing me a week. Before him was Missis Crowder and her two children, that stayed four months; and back of them was old Mr. Doyle, whose sons paid for him. He kept the room six months. That goes back a year, sir, and further I do not remember."

He thanked her and crept back to his room. The room was dead. The essence that had vivified it was gone. The perfume of mignonette had departed. In its place was the old, stale odour of moldy house furniture, of atmosphere in storage.

The ebbing of his hope drained his faith. He sat staring at the yellow, singing gaslight. Soon he walked to the bed and began to tear the sheets into strips. With the blade of his knife he drove them tightly into every crevice around windows and door. When all was snug and taut he turned out the light, turned the gas full on again and laid himself gratefully upon the bed.

It was Mrs. McCool's night to go with the can for beer. So she fetched it and sat with Mrs. Purdy in one of those subterranean retreats where housekeepers foregather and the worm dieth seldom.

"I rented out my third-floor-back this evening," said Mrs. Purdy, across a fine circle of foam. "A young man took it. He went up to bed two hours ago."

"Now, did ye, Mrs. Purdy, ma'am?" said Mrs. McCool, with intense admiration. "You do be a wonder for rentin' rooms of that kind. And did ye tell him, then?" she concluded in a husky whisper, laden with mystery.

"Rooms," said Mrs. Purdy, in her furriest tones, "are furnished for to rent. I did not tell him, Mrs. McCool."

"'Tis right ye are, ma'am; 'tis by renting rooms we kape alive. Ye have the rale sense for business, ma'am. There be many people will rayjict the rentin' of a room if they be tould a suicide has been after dyin' in the bed of it."

"As you say, we has our living to be making," remarked Mrs. Purdy.

"Yis, ma'am; 'tis true. 'Tis just one wake ago this day I helped ye lay out the third-floor-back. A pretty slip of a colleen she was to be killin' herself wid the gas—a swate little face she had, Mrs. Purdy, ma'am."

"She'd a-been called handsome, as you say," said Mrs. Purdy, assenting but critical, "but for that mole she had a-growin' by her left eyebrow. Do fill up your glass again, Mrs. McCool."

OLIVER ONIONS

(1873-1961)

43

The Rocker

I

There was little need for the swart gipsies to explain, as they stood knee-deep in the snow round the bailiff of the Abbey Farm, what it was that had sent them. The unbroken whiteness of the uplands told that, and, even as they spoke, there came up the hill the dark figures of the farm men with shovels, on their way to dig out the sheep. In the summer, the bailiff would have been the first to call the gipsies vagabonds and roost-robbers; now . . . they had women with them too.

"The hares and foxes were down four days ago, and the liquid-manure pumps like a snow man," the bailiff said . . . "Yes, you can lie in the laithes and welcome—if you can find 'em. Maybe you'll help us find our sheep too—"

The gipsies had done so. Coming back again, they had had some ado to discover the spot where their three caravans made a hummock of white against a broken wall.

The women—they had four women with them—began that afternoon to weave the mats and baskets they hawked from door to door; and in the forenoon of the following day one of them, the black-haired, soft-voiced quean whom the bailiff had heard called Annabel, set her babe in the sling on her back, tucked a bundle of long cane-loops under her oxter, and trudged down between eight-foot walls of snow to the Abbey Farm. She stood in the latticed porch, dark and handsome against the whiteness, and then, advancing, put her head into the great hall-kitchen.

"Has the lady any chairs for the gipsy woman to mend?" she asked in a soft and insinuating voice . . .

They brought her the old chairs; she seated herself on a box in the porch; and there she wove the strips of cane in and out, securing each one with a little wooden peg and a tap of her hammer. The child remained in the sling at her back, taking the breast from time to time over her shoulder; and the silver wedding ring could be seen as she whipped the cane, back and forth.

As she worked, she cast curious glances into the old hall-kitchen. The snow outside cast a pallid, upward light on the heavy ceiling-beams; this was reflected in the polished stone floor; and the children, who at first had shyly stopped their play, seeing the strange woman in the porch—the nearest thing they had seen to gipsies before had been the old itinerant glazier with his frame of glass on his back—resumed it, but still eyed her from time to time. In the ancient walnut chair by the hearth sat the old, old lady who had told them to bring the chairs. Her hair, almost as white as the snow itself, was piled up on her head *à la Marquise*; she was knitting; but now and then she allowed the needle in the little wooden sheath at her waist to lie idle, closed her eyes, and rocked softly in the old walnut chair.

"Ask the woman who is mending the chairs whether she is warm enough there," the old lady said to one of the children; and the child went to the porch with the message.

"Thank you, little missie—thank you, lady dear—Annabel is quite warm," said the soft voice; and the child returned to the play.

It was a childish game of funerals at which the children played. The hand of Death, hovering over the dolls, had singled out Flora, the articulations of whose sawdust body were seams and whose boots were painted on her calves of fibrous plaster. For the greater solemnity, the children had made themselves sweeping trains of the garments of their elders, and those with cropped curls had draped their heads with shawls, the fringes of which they had combed out with their fingers to simulate hair—long hair, such as Sabrina, the eldest, had hanging so low down her back that she could almost sit on it. A cylindrical-bodied horse, convertible (when his flat head came out of its socket) into a locomotive, headed the sad *cortège*; then came the defunct Flora; then came Jack, the raffish sailor doll, with other dolls; and the children followed with hushed whisperings.

The youngest of the children passed the high-backed walnut chair in which the old lady sat. She stopped.

"Aunt Rachel—" she whispered, slowly and gravely opening very wide and closing very tight her eyes.

"Yes, dear?"

"Flora's dead!"

The old lady, when she smiled, did so less with her lips than with her faded cheeks. So sweet was her face that you could not help wondering, when you looked on it, how many men had also looked upon it and loved it. Somehow, you never wondered how many of them had been loved in return.

"I'm so sorry, dear," Aunt Rachel, who in reality was a great-aunt, said.

"What did she die of this time?"

"She died of . . . Brown Titus . . . 'n now she's going to be buried in a grave as little as her bed."

"In a what, dear?"

"As little . . . dread . . . as little as my bed . . . you say it, Sabrina."

"She means, Aunt Rachel, '*Teach me to live that I may dread/The Grave as little as my bed*,'" Sabrina, the eldest, interpreted.

"Ah! . . . But won't you play at cheerful things, dears?"

"Yes, we will, presently, Aunt Rachel; gee up, horse! . . . Shall we go and ask the chair-woman if she's warm enough?"

"Do, dears."

Again the message was taken, and this time it seemed as if Annabel, the gipsy, was not warm enough, for she gathered up her loops of cane and brought the chair she was mending a little way into the hall-kitchen itself. She sat down on the square box they used to cover the sewing machine.

"Thank you, lady dear," she murmured, lifting her handsome almond eyes to Aunt Rachel. Aunt Rachel did not see the long, furtive, curious glance. Her own eyes were closed, as if she was tired; her cheeks were smiling; one of them had dropped a little to one shoulder, as it might have dropped had she held in her arms a babe; and she was rocking, softly, slowly, the rocker of the chair making a little regular noise on the polished floor.

The gipsy woman beckoned to one of the children.

"Tell the lady, when she wakes, that I will tack a strip of felt to the rocker, and then it will make no noise at all," said the low and wheedling voice; and the child retired again.

The interment of Flora proceeded . . .

An hour later Flora had taken up the burden of Life again. It was as Angela, the youngest, was chastising her for some offence, that Sabrina, the eldest, looked with wondering eyes on the babe in the gipsy's sling. She approached on tiptoe.

"May I look at it, please?" she asked timidly.

The gipsy set one shoulder forward, and Sabrina put the shawl gently aside, peering at the dusky brown morsel within.

"Sometime, perhaps—if I'm very careful—"

Sabrina ventured diffidently, "—if I'm *very* careful—may I hold it?"

Before replying, the gipsy once more turned her almond eyes towards Aunt Rachel's chair. Aunt Rachel had been awakened for the conclusion of Flora's funeral, but her eyes were closed again now, and once more her cheek was dropped in that tender suggestive little gesture, and she rocked. But you could see that she was not properly asleep . . . It was, somehow, less to Sabrina, still peering at the babe in the sling, than to Aunt Rachel, apparently asleep, that the gipsy seemed to reply.

"You'll know some day, little missis, that a wean knows its own pair of arms," her seductive voice came.

And Aunt Rachel heard. She opened her eyes with a start.

The little regular noise of the rocker ceased. She turned her head quickly; tremulously she began to knit again; and, as her eyes rested on the sidelong eyes of the gipsy woman, there was an expression in them that almost resembled fright.

II

They began to deck the great hall-kitchen for Christmas, but the snow still lay thick over hill and valley, and the gipsies' caravans remained by the broken wall where the drifts had overtaken them. Though all the chairs were mended, Annabel still came daily to the farm, sat on the box they used to cover the sewing machine, and wove mats. As she wove them, Aunt Rachel knitted, and from time to time fragments of talk passed between the two women. It was always the white-haired lady who spoke first, and Annabel made all sorts of salutes and obeisances with her eyes before replying.

"I have not seen your husband," Aunt Rachel said to Annabel one day. (The children at the other end of the apartment had converted a chest into an altar, and were solemnising the nuptials of the resurrected Flora and Jack, the raffish sailor-doll.)

Annabel made roving play with her eyes. "He is up at the caravans, lady dear," she replied. "Is there anything Annabel can bid him do?"

"Nothing, thank you," said Aunt Rachel.

For a minute the gipsy watched Aunt Rachel, and then she got up from the sewing machine box and crossed the floor. She leaned so close towards her that she had to put up a hand to steady the babe at her back.

"Lady dear," she murmured with irresistible softness, "your husband died, didn't he?"

On Aunt Rachel's finger was a ring, but it was not a wedding ring. It was a hoop of pearls.

"I have never had a husband," she said.

The gipsy glanced at the ring. "Then that is—?"

"That is a betrothal ring," Aunt Rachel replied.

"Ah! . . ." said Annabel.

Then, after a minute, she drew still closer. Her eyes were fixed on Aunt Rachel's, and the insinuating voice was very low.

"Ah! . . . And did *it* die too, lady dear?"

Again came that quick, half-affrighted look into Aunt Rachel's face. Her eyes avoided those of the gipsy, sought them, and avoided them again.

"Did what die?" she asked slowly and guardedly . . .

The child at the gipsy's back did not need suck; nevertheless, Annabel's fingers worked at her bosom, and she moved the sling. As the child settled, Annabel gave Aunt Rachel a long look.

"Why do you rock?" she asked slowly.

Aunt Rachel was trembling. She did not reply. In a voice soft as sliding water the gipsy continued:

"Lady dear, we are a strange folk to you, and even among us there are those who shuffle the pack of cards and read the palm when silver has been put upon it, knowing nothing . . . But some of us *see*—some of us *see*."

It was more than a minute before Aunt Rachel spoke.

"You are a woman, and you have your babe at your breast now . . . Every woman sees the thing you speak of."

But the gipsy shook her head. "You speak of seeing with the heart. I speak of eyes—these eyes."

Again came a long pause. Aunt Rachel had given a little start, but had become quiet again. When at last she spoke it was in a voice scarcely audible.

"That cannot be. I know what you mean, but it cannot be . . . He died on the eve of his wedding. For my bridal clothes they made me black garments instead. It is long ago, and now I wear neither black nor white, but—" her hands made a gesture. Aunt Rachel always dressed as if to suit a sorrow that Time had deprived of bitterness, in such a tender and fleecy grey as one sees in the mists that lie like lawn over hedgerow and copse early of a midsummer's morning. "Therefore," she resumed, "your heart may see, but your eyes cannot see that which never was."

But there came a sudden note of masterfulness into the gipsy's voice.

"With my eyes—*these* eyes," she repeated, pointing to them.

Aunt Rachel kept her own eyes obstinately on her knitting needles. "None except I have seen it. It is not to be seen," she said.

The gipsy sat suddenly erect.

"It is not so. Keep still in your chair," she ordered, "and I will tell you when—"

It was a curious thing that followed. As if all the will went out of her, Aunt Rachel sat very still; and presently her hands fluttered and dropped. The gipsy sat with her own hands folded over the mat on her knees. Several minutes passed; then, slowly, once more that sweetest of smiles stole over Aunt Rachel's cheeks. Once more her head dropped. Her hands moved. Noiselessly on the rockers that the gipsy had padded with felt the chair began to rock. Annabel lifted one hand.

"*Dovo se li*," she said. "It is there."

Aunt Rachel did not appear to hear her. With that ineffable smile still on her face, she rocked . . .

Then, after some minutes, there crossed her face such a look as visits the face of one who, waking from sleep, strains his faculties to recapture some blissful and vanishing vision . . .

"*Jal*—it is gone," said the gipsy woman.

Aunt Rachel opened her eyes again. She repeated dully after Annabel:

"It is gone."

"Ghosts," the gipsy whispered presently, "are of the dead. Therefore it must have lived."

But again Aunt Rachel shook her head. "It never lived."

"You were young, and beautiful? . . ."

Still the shake of the head. "He died on the eve of his wedding. They took my white garments away and gave me black ones. How then could it have lived?"

"Without the kiss, no . . . But sometimes a woman will lie through her life, and at the graveside still will lie . . . Tell me the truth."

But they were the same words that Aunt Rachel repeated: "He died on the eve of his wedding; they took away my wedding garments . . ." From her lips a lie could hardly issue. The gipsy's face became grave . . .

She broke another long silence.

"I believe," she said at last. "It is a new kind—but no more wonderful than the other. The other I have seen, now I have seen this also. Tell me, does it come to any other chair?"

"It was his chair; he died in it," said Aunt Rachel.

"And you—shall you die in it?"

"As God wills."

"Has . . . *other life* . . . visited it long?"

"Many years; but it is always small; it never grows."

"To their mothers babes never grow. They remain ever babes . . . None other has ever seen it?"

"Except yourself, none. I sit here; presently it creeps into my arms; it is small and warm; I rock, and then… it goes."

"Would it come to another chair?"

"I cannot tell. I think not. It was his chair."

Annabel mused. At the other end of the room Flora was now bestowed on Jack, the disreputable sailor. The gipsy's eyes rested on the bridal party . . .

"Yet another might see it—"

"None has."

"No; but yet . . . The door does not always shut behind us suddenly. Perhaps one who has toddled but a step or two over the threshold might, by looking back, catch a glimpse . . . What is the name of the smallest one?"

"Angela."

"That means 'angel' . . . Look, the doll who died yesterday is now being married . . . It may be that Life has not yet sealed the little one's eyes. Will you let Annabel ask her if she sees what it is you hold in your arms?"

Again the voice was soft and wheedling . . .

"No, Annabel," said Aunt Rachel faintly.

"Will you rock again?"

Aunt Rachel made no reply.

"Rock . . ." urged the cajoling voice.

But Aunt Rachel only turned the betrothal ring on her finger. Over at the altar Jack was leering at his new-made bride, past decency; and little Angela held the wooden horse's head, which had parted from its body.

"Rock, and comfort yourself—" tempted the voice.

Then slowly Aunt Rachel rose from her chair.

"No, Annabel," she said gently. "You should not have spoken. When the snow melts you will go, and come no more; why then did you speak? It was mine. It was not meant to be seen by another. I no longer want it. Please go."

The swarthy woman turned her almond eyes on her once more.

"You cannot live without it," she said as she also rose . . .

And as Jack and his bride left the church on the reheaded horse, Aunt Rachel walked with hanging head from the apartment.

III

Thenceforward, as day followed day, Aunt Rachel rocked no more; and with the packing and partial melting of the snow the gipsies up at the caravans judged it time to be off about their business. It was on the morning of Christmas Eve that they came down in a body to the Abbey Farm to express their thanks to those who had befriended them; but the bailiff was not there. He and the farm men had ceased work, and were down at the church, practising the carols. Only Aunt Rachel sat, still and knitting, in the black walnut chair; and the children played on the floor.

A night in the toy-box had apparently bred discontent between Jack and Flora—or perhaps they sought to keep their countenances before the world; at any rate, they sat on opposite sides of the room, Jack keeping boon company with the lead soldiers, his spouse reposing, her lead-balanced eyes closed, in the broken clockwork motor-car. With the air of performing some vaguely momentous ritual, the children were kissing one another beneath the bunch of mistletoe that hung from the centre beam. In the intervals of kissing they told one another in whispers that Aunt Rachel was not very well, and Angela woke Flora to tell her that Aunt Rachel had Brown Titus also.

"Stay you here; I will give the lady dear our thanks," said Annabel to the group of gipsies gathered about the porch; and she entered the great hall-kitchen. She approached the chair in which Aunt Rachel sat.

There was obeisance in the bend of her body, but command in her long almond eyes, as she spoke.

"Lady dear, you must rock or you cannot live."

Aunt Rachel did not look up from her work.

"Rocking, I should not live long," she replied.

"We are leaving you."

"All leave me."

"Annabel fears she has taken away your comfort."

"Only for a little while. The door closes behind us, but it opens again."

"But for that little time, rock—"

Aunt Rachel shook her head.

"No. It is finished. Another has seen . . . Say goodbye to your companions; they are very welcome to what they have had; and God speed you."

"They thank you, lady dear . . . Will you not forget that Annabel saw, and rock?"

"No more."

Annabel stooped and kissed the hand that bore the betrothal hoop of pearls. The other hand Aunt Rachel placed for a moment upon the smoky head of the babe in the sling. It trembled as it rested there, but the tremor passed, and Annabel, turning once at the porch, gave her a last look. Then she departed with her companions.

That afternoon, Jack and Flora had shaken down to wedlock as married folk should, and sat together before the board spread with the dolls' tea-things. The pallid light in the great hall-kitchen faded; the candles were lighted; and then the children, first borrowing the stockings of their elders to hang at the bed's foot, were packed off early—for it was the custom to bring them down again at midnight for the carols. Aunt Rachel had their good-night kisses, not as she had them every night, but with the special ceremony of the mistletoe.

Other folk, grown folk, sat with Aunt Rachel that evening; but the old walnut chair did not move upon its rockers. There was merry talk, but Aunt Rachel took no part in it. The board was spread with ale and cheese and spiced loaf for the carol-singers; and the time drew near for their coming.

When at midnight, faintly on the air from the church below, there came the chiming of Christmas morning, all bestirred themselves.

"They'll be here in a few minutes," they said; "somebody go and bring the children down;" and within a very little while subdued noises were heard outside, and the lifting of the latch of the yard gate. The children were in their nightgowns, hardly fully awake; a low voice outside was heard giving orders; and then there arose on the night the carol.

"Hush!" they said to the wondering children; "listen! . . ."

It was the Cherry Tree Carol that rose outside, of how sweet Mary, the Queen of Galilee, besought Joseph to pluck the cherries for her Babe, and Joseph refused; and the voices of the singers, that had begun hesitatingly, grew strong and loud and free.

". . . and Joseph wouldn't pluck the cherries," somebody was whispering to the tiny Angela . . .

"'Mary said to Cherry Tree,
'Bow down to my knee,
That I may pluck cherries
For my Babe and me.'"

the carollers sang; and "Now listen, darling," the one who held Angela murmured . . .

"'The uppermost spray then
Bowed down to her knee;
'Thus you may see, Joseph,
These cherries are for me.'

"'O, eat your cherries, Mary,
Give them your Babe now;
O, eat your cherries, Mary,
That grew upon the bough.'"

The little Angela, within the arms that held her, murmured, "It's the gipsies, isn't it, mother?"

"No, darling. The gipsies have gone. It's the carol-singers, singing because Jesus was born."

"But, mother . . . it *is* the gipsies, isn't it? . . . 'Cos look . . ."

"Look where?"

"At Aunt Rachel, mother . . . The gipsy woman wouldn't go without her little baby, would she?"

"No, she wouldn't do that."

"Then has she *lent* it to Aunt Rachel, like I lend my new toys sometimes?"

The mother glanced across at Aunt Rachel, and then gathered the night-gowned figure more closely.

"The darling's only half awake," she murmured . . . "Poor Aunt Rachel's sleepy too . . ."

Aunt Rachel, her head dropped, her hands lightly folded as if about some shape that none saw but herself, her face again ineffable with that sweet and peaceful smile, was once more rocking softly in her chair.

OSCAR WILDE

(1854-1900)

44

The Sphinx Without a Secret

One afternoon I was sitting outside the Cafe de la Paix, watching the splendour and shabbiness of Parisian life, and wondering over my vermouth at the strange panorama of pride and poverty that was passing before me, when I heard some one call my name. I turned round, and saw Lord Murchison. We had not met since we had been at college together, nearly ten years before, so I was delighted to come across him again, and we shook hands warmly. At Oxford we had been great friends. I had liked him immensely, he was so handsome, so high-spirited, and so honourable. We used to say of him that he would be the best of fellows, if he did not always speak the truth, but I think we really admired him all the more for his frankness. I found him a good deal changed. He looked anxious and puzzled, and seemed to be in doubt about something. I felt it could not be modern scepticism, for Murchison was the stoutest of Tories, and believed in the Pentateuch as firmly as he believed in the House of Peers; so I concluded that it was a woman, and asked him if he was married yet.

"I don't understand women well enough," he answered.

"My dear Gerald," I said, "women are meant to be loved, not to be understood."

"I cannot love where I cannot trust," he replied.

"I believe you have a mystery in your life, Gerald," I exclaimed; "tell me about it."

"Let us go for a drive," he answered, "it is too crowded here. No, not a yellow carriage, any other colour—there, that dark green one will do;" and in a few moments we were trotting down the boulevard in the direction of the Madeleine.

"Where shall we go to?" I said.

"Oh, anywhere you like!" he answered—"to the restaurant in the Bois; we will dine there, and you shall tell me all about yourself."

"I want to hear about you first," I said. "Tell me your mystery."

He took from his pocket a little silver-clasped morocco case, and handed it to me. I opened it. Inside there was the photograph of a woman. She was tall and slight, and strangely picturesque with her large vague eyes and loosened hair. She looked like a clairvoyante, and was wrapped in rich furs.

"What do you think of that face?" he said; "is it truthful?"

I examined it carefully. It seemed to me the face of some one who had a secret, but whether that secret was good or evil I could not say. Its beauty was a beauty moulded out of many mysteries—the beauty, in fact, which is psychological, not plastic—and the faint smile that just played across the lips was far too subtle to be really sweet.

"Well," he cried impatiently, "what do you say?"

"She is the Gioconda in sables," I answered. "Let me know all about her."

"Not now," he said; "after dinner," and began to talk of other things.

When the waiter brought us our coffee and cigarettes I reminded Gerald of his promise. He rose from his seat, walked two or three times up and down the room, and, sinking into an armchair, told me the following story:—

"One evening," he said, "I was walking down Bond Street about five o'clock. There was a terrific crush of carriages, and the traffic was almost stopped. Close to the pavement was standing a little yellow brougham, which, for some reason or other, attracted my attention. As I passed by there looked out from it the face I showed you this afternoon. It fascinated me immediately. All that night I kept thinking of it, and all the next day. I wandered up and down that wretched Row, peering into every carriage, and waiting for the yellow brougham; but I could not find ma belle inconnue, and at last I began to think she was merely a dream. About a week afterwards I was dining with Madame de Rastail. Dinner was for eight o'clock; but at half-past eight we were still waiting in the drawing-room. Finally the servant threw open the door, and announced Lady Alroy. It was the woman I had been looking for. She came in very slowly, looking like a moonbeam in grey lace, and, to my intense delight, I was asked to take her in to dinner. After we had sat down, I remarked quite innocently, 'I think I caught sight of you in Bond Street some time ago, Lady Alroy.' She grew very pale, and said to me in a low voice, 'Pray do not talk so loud; you may be overheard.' I felt miserable at having made such a bad beginning, and plunged recklessly into the subject of the French plays. She spoke very little, always in the same low musical voice, and seemed as if she was afraid of some one listening. I fell passionately, stupidly in love, and the indefinable atmosphere of mystery that surrounded her excited my most ardent curiosity. When she was going away, which she did very soon after dinner, I asked her if I might call and see her. She hesitated for a moment, glanced round to see if any one was near us, and then said, 'Yes; tomorrow at a quarter to five.' I begged Madame de Rastail to tell me about her; but all that I could learn was that she was a widow with a beautiful house in Park Lane, and as some scientific bore began a dissertation on widows, as exemplifying the survival of the matrimonially fittest, I left and went home.

"The next day I arrived at Park Lane punctual to the moment, but was told by the butler that Lady Alroy had just gone out. I went down to the club quite unhappy and very much puzzled, and after long consideration wrote her a letter, asking if I might be allowed to try my chance some other afternoon. I had no answer for several days, but at last I got a little note saying she would be at home on Sunday at four and with this extraordinary postscript: 'Please do not write to me here again; I will explain when I see you.' On Sunday she received me, and was perfectly charming; but when I was going away she begged of me, if I ever had occasion to write to her again, to address my letter to 'Mrs. Knox, care of Whittaker's Library, Green Street.' 'There are reasons,' she said, 'why I cannot receive letters in my own house.'

"All through the season I saw a great deal of her, and the atmosphere of mystery never left her. Sometimes I thought that she was in the power of some man, but she looked so unapproachable, that I could not believe it. It was really very difficult for me to come to any conclusion, for she was like one of those strange crystals that one sees in museums, which are at one moment clear, and at another clouded. At last I determined to ask her to be my wife: I was sick and tired of the incessant secrecy that she imposed on all my visits, and on the few letters I sent her. I wrote to her at the library to ask her if she could see me the following Monday at six. She answered yes, and I was in the seventh heaven of delight. I was infatuated with her: in spite of the mystery, I thought then—in consequence of it, I see now. No; it was the woman herself I loved. The mystery troubled me, maddened me. Why did chance put me in its track?"

"You discovered it, then?" I cried.

"I fear so," he answered. "You can judge for yourself."

"When Monday came round I went to lunch with my uncle, and about four o'clock found myself in the Marylebone Road. My uncle, you know, lives in Regent's Park. I wanted to get to Piccadilly, and took a short cut through a lot of shabby little streets. Suddenly I saw in front of me Lady Alroy, deeply veiled and walking very fast. On coming to the last house in the street, she went up the steps, took out a latch-key, and let herself in. 'Here is the mystery,' I said to myself; and I hurried on and examined the house. It seemed a sort of place for letting lodgings. On the doorstep lay her handkerchief, which she had dropped. I picked it up and put it in my pocket. Then I began to consider what I should do. I came to the conclusion that I had no right to spy on her, and I drove down to the club. At six I called to see her. She was lying on a sofa, in a tea-gown of silver tissue looped up by some strange moonstones that she always wore. She was looking quite lovely. 'I am so glad to see you,' she said; 'I have not been out all day.' I stared at her in amazement, and pulling the handkerchief out of my pocket, handed it to her. 'You dropped this in Cumnor Street this afternoon, Lady Alroy,' I said very calmly. She looked at me in terror but made no attempt to take the handkerchief. 'What were you doing there?' I asked. 'What right have you to question me?' she answered. 'The right of a man who loves you,' I replied; 'I came here to ask you to be my wife.' She hid her face in her hands, and burst into floods of tears. 'You must tell me,' I continued. She stood up, and, looking me straight in the face, said, 'Lord Murchison, there is nothing to tell you.'—'You went to meet some one,' I cried; 'this is your mystery.' She grew dreadfully white, and said, 'I went to meet no one.'—'Can't you tell the truth?' I exclaimed. 'I have told it,' she replied. I was mad, frantic; I don't know what I said, but I said terrible things to her. Finally I rushed out of the house. She wrote me a letter the next day; I sent it back unopened, and started for Norway with Alan Colville. After a month I came back, and the first thing I saw in the Morning Post was the death of Lady Alroy. She had caught a chill at the Opera, and had died in five days of congestion of the lungs. I shut myself up and saw no one. I had loved her so much, I had loved her so madly. Good God! how I had loved that woman!"

"You went to the street, to the house in it?" I said.

"Yes," he answered.

"One day I went to Cumnor Street. I could not help it; I was tortured with doubt. I knocked at the door, and a respectable-looking woman opened it to me. I asked her if she had any rooms to let. 'Well, sir,' she replied, 'the drawing-rooms are supposed to be let; but I have not seen the lady for three months, and as rent is owing on them, you can have them.'—'Is this the lady?' I said, showing the photograph. 'That's her, sure enough,' she exclaimed; 'and when is she coming back, sir?'—'The lady is dead,' I replied.

'Oh sir, I hope not!' said the woman; 'she was my best lodger. She paid me three guineas a week merely to sit in my drawing-rooms now and then.' 'She met someone here?' I said; but the woman assured me that it was not so, that she always came alone, and saw no one. 'What on earth did she do here?' I cried. 'She simply sat in the drawing-room, sir, reading books, and sometimes had tea,' the woman answered. I did not know what to say, so I gave her a sovereign and went away. Now, what do you think it all meant? You don't believe the woman was telling the truth?"

"I do."

"Then why did Lady Alroy go there?"

"My dear Gerald," I answered, "Lady Alroy was simply a woman with a mania for mystery. She took these rooms for the pleasure of going there with her veil down, and imagining she was a heroine. She had a passion for secrecy, but she herself was merely a Sphinx without a secret."

"Do you really think so?"

"I am sure of it," I replied.

He took out the morocco case, opened it, and looked at the photograph. "I wonder?" he said at last.

RICHARD MIDDLETON

(1882-1911)

45

On the Brighton Road

Slowly the sun had climbed up the hard white downs, till it broke with little of the mysterious ritual of dawn upon a sparkling world of snow. There had been a hard frost during the night, and the birds, who hopped about here and there with scant tolerance of life, left no trace of their passage on the silver pavements. In places the sheltered caverns of the hedges broke the monotony of the whiteness that had fallen upon the coloured earth, and overhead the sky melted from orange to deep blue, from deep blue to a blue so pale that it suggested a thin paper screen rather than illimitable space. Across the level fields there came a cold, silent wind which blew a fine dust of snow from the trees, but hardly stirred the crested hedges. Once above the skyline, the sun seemed to climb more quickly, and as it rose higher it began to give out a heat that blended with the keenness of the wind.

It may have been this strange alternation of heat and cold that disturbed the tramp in his dreams, for he struggled tor a moment with the snow that covered him, like a man who finds himself twisted uncomfortably in the bed-clothes, and then sat up with staring, questioning eyes. "Lord! I thought I was in bed," he said to himself as he took in the vacant landscape, "and all the while I was out here." He stretched his limbs, and, rising carefully to his feet, shook the snow off his body. As he did so the wind set him shivering, and he knew that his bed had been warm.

"Come, I feel pretty fit," he thought. "I suppose I am lucky to wake at all in this. Or unlucky—it isn't much of a business to come back to." He looked up and saw the downs shining against the blue, like the Alps on a picture-postcard. "That means another forty miles or so, I suppose," he continued grimly. "Lord knows what I did yesterday. Walked till I was done, and now I'm only about twelve miles from Brighton. Damn the snow, damn Brighton, damn everything!" The sun crept higher and higher, and he started walking patiently along the road with his back turned to the hills.

"Am I glad or sorry that it was only sleep that took me, glad or sorry, glad or sorry?" His thoughts seemed to arrange themselves in a metrical accompaniment to the steady thud of his footsteps, and he hardly sought an answer to his question. It was good enough to walk to.

Presently, when three milestones had loitered past, he overtook a boy who was stooping to light a cigarette. He wore no overcoat, and looked unspeakably fragile against the snow, "Are you on the road, guv'nor?" asked the boy huskily as he passed.

"I think I am," the tramp said.

"Oh! then I'll come a bit of the way with you if you don't walk too fast. It's bit lonesome walking this time of day."

The tramp nodded his head, and the boy started limping along by his side.

"I'm eighteen," he said casually. "I bet you thought I was younger."

"Fifteen, I'd have said."

"You'd have backed a loser. Eighteen last August, and I've been on the road six years. I ran away from home five times when I was a little 'un, and the police took me back each time. Very good to me, the police was. Now I haven't got a home to run away from."

"Nor have I," the tramp said calmly.

"Oh, I can see what you are," the boy panted; "you're a gentleman come down. It's harder for you than for me." The tramp glanced at the limping, feeble figure and lessened his pace.

"I haven't been at it as long as you have," he admitted.

"No, I could tell that by the way you walk. You haven't got tired yet. Perhaps you expect something at the other end?"

The tramp reflected for a moment. "I don't know," he said bitterly, "I'm always expecting things."

"You'll grow out of that;" the boy commented. "It's warmer in London, but it's harder to come by grub. There isn't much in it really."

"Still, there's the chance of meeting somebody there who will understand—"

"Country people are better," the boy interrupted. "Last night I took a lease of a barn for nothing and slept with the cows, and this morning the farmer routed me out and gave me tea and toke because I was so little. Of course, I score there; but in London, soup on the Embankment at night, and all the rest of the time coppers moving you on."

"I dropped by the roadside last night and slept where I fell. It's a wonder I didn't die," the tramp said. The boy looked at him sharply.

"How did you know you didn't?" he said.

"I don't see it," the tramp said, after a pause.

"I tell you," the boy said hoarsely, "people like us can't get away from this sort of thing if we want to. Always hungry and thirsty and dog-tired and walking all the while. And yet if anyone offers me a nice home and work my stomach feels sick. Do I look strong? I know I'm little for my age, but I've been knocking about like this for six years, and do you think I'm not dead? I was drowned bathing at Margate, and I was killed by a gypsy with a spike; he knocked my head and yet I'm walking along here now, walking to London to walk away from it again, because I can't help it. Dead! I tell you we can't get away if we want to."

The boy broke off in a fit of coughing, and the tramp paused while he recovered.

"You'd better borrow my coat for a bit, Tommy," he said, "your cough's pretty bad."

"You go to hell!" the boy said fiercely, puffing at his cigarette; "I'm all right. I was telling you about the road. You haven't got down to it yet, but you'll find out presently. We're all dead, all of us who're on it, and we're all tired, yet somehow we can't leave it. There's nice smells in the summer, dust and hay and the wind smack in your face on a hot day—and it's nice waking up in the wet grass on a fine morning. I don't know, I don't know—" he lurched forward suddenly, and the tramp caught him in his arms.

"I'm sick," the boy whispered—"sick."

The tramp looked up and down the road, but he could see no houses or any sign of help. Yet even as he supported the boy doubtfully in the middle of the road a motor car suddenly flashed in the middle distance, and came smoothly through the snow.

"What's the trouble?" said the driver quietly as he pulled up. "I'm a doctor." He looked at the boy keenly and listened to his strained breathing.

"Pneumonia," he commented. "I'll give him a lift to the infirmary, and you, too, if you like."

The tramp thought of the workhouse and shook his head "I'd rather walk," he said.

The boy winked faintly as they lifted him into the car.

"I'll meet you beyond Reigate," he murmured to the tramp. "You'll see." And the car vanished along the white road.

All the morning the tramp splashed through the thawing snow, but at midday he begged some bread at a cottage door and crept into a lonely barn to eat it. It was warm in there, and after his meal he fell asleep among the hay. It was dark when he woke, and started trudging once more through the slushy roads.

Two miles beyond Reigate a figure, a fragile figure, slipped out of the darkness to meet him.

"On the road, guv'nor?" said a husky voice. "Then I'll come a bit of the way with you if you don't walk too fast. It's a bit lonesome walking this time of day."

"But the pneumonia!" cried the tramp, aghast.

"I died at Crawley this morning," said the boy.

RUDYARD KIPLING

(1865-1936)

46

My Own True Ghost Story

As I came through the Desert thus
it was—As I came through the Desert.
—*The City of Dreadful Night*

Somewhere in the Other World, where there are books and pictures and plays and shop windows to look at, and thousands of men who spend their lives in building up all four, lives a gentleman who writes real stories about the real insides of people; and his name is Mr. Walter Besant. But he will insist upon treating his ghosts—he has published half a workshopful of them—with levity. He makes his ghost-seers talk familiarly, and, in some cases, flirt outrageously, with the phantoms. You may treat anything, from a Viceroy to a Vernacular Paper, with levity; but you must behave reverently toward a ghost, and particularly an Indian one.

There are, in this land, ghosts who take the form of fat, cold, pobby corpses, and hide in trees near the roadside till a traveller passes. Then they drop upon his neck and remain. There are also terrible ghosts of women who have died in child-bed. These wander along the pathways at dusk, or hide in the crops near a village, and call seductively. But to answer their call is death in this world and the next. Their feet are turned backward that all sober men may recognize them. There are ghosts of little children who have been thrown into wells. These haunt well curbs and the fringes of jungles, and wail under the stars, or catch women by the wrist and beg to be taken up and carried. These and the corpse ghosts, however, are only vernacular articles and do not attack Sahibs. No native ghost has yet been authentically reported to have frightened an Englishman; but many English ghosts have scared the life out of both white and black.

Nearly every other Station owns a ghost. There are said to be two at Simla, not counting the woman who blows the bellows at Syree dâk-bungalow on the Old Road; Mussoorie has a house haunted of a very lively Thing; a White Lady is supposed to do night-watchman round a house in Lahore; Dalhousie says that one of her houses 'repeats' on autumn evenings all the incidents of a horrible horse-and-precipice accident; Murree has a merry ghost, and, now that she has been swept by cholera, will have room for a sorrowful one; there are Officers' Quarters in Mian Mir whose doors open without reason, and whose furniture is guaranteed to creak, not with the heat of June but with the weight of Invisibles who come to lounge in the chairs; Peshawur possesses houses that none will willingly rent; and there is something—not fever—wrong with a big bungalow in Allahabad. The older Provinces simply bristle with haunted houses, and march phantom armies along their main thoroughfares.

Some of the dâk-bungalows on the Grand Trunk Road have handy little cemeteries in their compound—witnesses to the 'changes and chances of this mortal life' in the days when men drove from Calcutta to the Northwest. These bungalows are objectionable places to put up in. They are generally very old, always dirty, while the *khansamah* is as ancient as the bungalow. He either chatters senilely, or falls into the long trances of age. In both moods he is useless. If you get angry with him, he refers to some Sahib dead and buried these thirty years, and says that when he was in that Sahib's service not a *khansamah* in the Province could touch him. Then he jabbers and mows and trembles and fidgets among the dishes, and you repent of your irritation.

In these dâk-bungalows, ghosts are most likely to be found, and when found, they should be made a note of. Not long ago it was my business to live in dâk-bungalows. I never inhabited the same house for three nights running, and grew to be learned in the breed. I lived in Government-built ones with red brick walls and rail ceilings, an inventory of the furniture posted in every room, and an excited snake at the threshold to give welcome. I lived in 'converted' ones—old houses officiating as dâk-bungalows—where nothing was in its proper place and there wasn't even a fowl for dinner. I lived in second-hand palaces where the wind blew through open-work marble tracery just as uncomfortably as through a broken pane. I lived in dâk-bungalows where the last entry in the visitors' book was fifteen months old, and where they slashed off the curry-kid's head with a sword. It was my good luck to meet all sorts of men, from sober travelling missionaries and deserters flying from British Regiments, to drunken loafers who threw whisky bottles at all who passed; and my still greater good fortune just to escape a maternity case. Seeing that a fair proportion of the tragedy of our lives out here acted itself in dâk-bungalows, I wondered that I had met no ghosts. A ghost that would voluntarily hang about a dâk-bungalow would be mad of course; but so many men have died mad in dâk-bungalows that there must be a fair percentage of lunatic ghosts.

In due time I found my ghost, or ghosts rather, for there were two of them. Up till that hour I had sympathized with Mr. Besant's method of handling them, as shown in 'The Strange Case of Mr. Lucraft and Other Stories.' I am now in the Opposition.

We will call the bungalow Katmal dâk-bungalow. But THAT was the smallest part of the horror. A man with a sensitive hide has no right to sleep in dâk-bungalows. He should marry. Katmal dâk-bungalow was old and rotten and unrepaired. The floor was of worn brick, the walls were filthy, and the windows were nearly black with grime. It stood on a bypath largely used by native Sub-Deputy Assistants of all kinds, from Finance to Forests; but real

Sahibs were rare. The *khansamah*, who was nearly bent double with old age, said so.

When I arrived, there was a fitful, undecided rain on the face of the land, accompanied by a restless wind, and every gust made a noise like the rattling of dry bones in the stiff toddy palms outside. The *khansamah* completely lost his head on my arrival. He had served a Sahib once. Did I know that Sahib? He gave me the name of a well-known man who has been buried for more than a quarter of a century, and showed me an ancient daguerreotype of that man in his prehistoric youth. I had seen a steel engraving of him at the head of a double volume of Memoirs a month before, and I felt ancient beyond telling.

The day shut in and the *khansamah* went to get me food. He did not go through the pretense of calling it "*khana*"—man's victuals. He said "*ratub*," and that means, among other things, "grub"—dog's rations. There was no insult in his choice of the term. He had forgotten the other word, I suppose.

While he was cutting up the dead bodies of animals, I settled myself down, after exploring the dâk-bungalow. There were three rooms, beside my own, which was a corner kennel, each giving into the other through dingy white doors fastened with long iron bars. The bungalow was a very solid one, but the partition walls of the rooms were almost jerry-built in their flimsiness. Every step or bang of a trunk echoed from my room down the other three, and every footfall came back tremulously from the far walls. For this reason I shut the door. There were no lamps—only candles in long glass shades. An oil wick was set in the bathroom.

For bleak, unadulterated misery that dâk-bungalow was the worst of the many that I had ever set foot in. There was no fireplace, and the windows would not open; so a brazier of charcoal would have been useless. The rain and the wind splashed and gurgled and moaned round the house, and the toddy palms rattled and roared. Half a dozen jackals went through the compound singing, and a hyena stood afar off and mocked them. A hyena would convince a Sadducee of the Resurrection of the Dead—the worst sort of Dead. Then came the *ratub*—a curious meal, half native and half

English in composition—with the old *khansamah* babbling behind my chair about dead and gone English people, and the wind-blown candles playing shadow-bo-peep with the bed and the mosquito-curtains. It was just the sort of dinner and evening to make a man think of every single one of his past sins, and of all the others that he intended to commit if he lived.

Sleep, for several hundred reasons, was not easy. The lamp in the bath-room threw the most absurd shadows into the room, and the wind was beginning to talk nonsense.

Just when the reasons were drowsy with blood-sucking I heard the regular—"Let-us-take-and-heave-him-over" grunt of doolie-bearers in the compound. First one doolie came in, then a second, and then a third. I heard the doolies dumped on the ground, and the shutter in front of my door shook. "That's some one trying to come in," I said. But no one spoke, and I persuaded myself that it was the gusty wind. The shutter of the room next to mine was attacked, flung back, and the inner door opened. "That's some Sub-Deputy Assistant," I said, "and he has brought his friends with him. Now they'll talk and spit and smoke for an hour."

But there were no voices and no footsteps. No one was putting his luggage into the next room. The door shut, and I thanked Providence that I was to be left in peace. But I was curious to know where the doolies had gone. I got out of bed and looked into the darkness. There was never a sign of a doolie. Just as I was getting into bed again, I heard, in the next room, the sound that no man in his senses can possibly mistake—the whir of a billiard ball down the length of the slates when the striker is stringing for break. No other sound is like it. A minute afterwards there was another whir, and I got into bed. I was not frightened—indeed I was not. I was very curious to know what had become of the doolies. I jumped into bed for that reason.

Next minute I heard the double click of a cannon and my hair sat up. It is a mistake to say that hair stands up. The skin of the head tightens and you can feel a faint, prickly, bristling all over the scalp. That is the hair sitting up.

There was a whir and a click, and both sounds could only have been made by one thing—a billiard ball. I argued the matter out at great length with myself; and the more I argued the less probable it seemed that one bed, one table, and two chairs—all the furniture of the room next to mine—could so exactly duplicate the sounds of a game of billiards. After another cannon, a three-cushion one to judge by the whir, I argued no more. I had found my ghost and would have given worlds to have escaped from that dâk-bungalow. I listened, and with each listen the game grew clearer. There was whir on whir and click on click. Sometimes there was a double click and a whir and another click. Beyond any sort of doubt, people were playing billiards in the next room. And the next room was not big enough to hold a billiard table!

Between the pauses of the wind I heard the game go forward—stroke after stroke. I tried to believe that I could not hear voices; but that attempt was a failure.

Do you know what fear is? Not ordinary fear of insult, injury or death, but abject, quivering dread of something that you cannot see—fear that dries the inside of the mouth and half of the throat—fear that makes you sweat on the palms of the hands, and gulp in order to keep the uvula at work? This is a fine Fear—a great cowardice, and must be felt to be appreciated. The very improbability of billiards in a dâk-bungalow proved the reality of the thing. No man—drunk or sober—could imagine a game at billiards, or invent the spitting crack of a 'screw-cannon.'

A severe course of dâk-bungalows has this disadvantage—it breeds infinite credulity. If a man said to a confirmed dâk-bungalow-haunter:—"There is a corpse in the next room, and there's a mad girl in the next but one, and the woman and man on that camel have just eloped from a place sixty miles away," the hearer would not disbelieve because he would know that nothing is too wild, grotesque, or horrible to happen in a dâk-bungalow.

This credulity, unfortunately, extends to ghosts. A rational person fresh from his own house would have turned on his side and slept. I did not. So surely as I was given up as a bad carcass by the scores of things in the bed because the bulk of my blood was in my heart, so surely did I hear every stroke of a long game at billiards played in the echoing room behind the iron-barred door. My dominant fear was that the players might want a marker. It was an absurd fear; because creatures who could play in the dark would be above such superfluities. I only know that that was my terror; and it was real.

After a long, long while the game stopped, and the door banged. I slept because I was dead tired. Otherwise I should have preferred to have kept awake. Not for everything in Asia would I have dropped the door-bar and peered into the dark of the next room.

When the morning came, I considered that I had done well and wisely, and inquired for the means of departure.

"By the way, *khansamah*," I said, "what were those three doolies doing in my compound in the night?"

"There were no doolies," said the *khansamah*.

I went into the next room and the daylight streamed through the open door. I was immensely brave. I would, at that hour, have played Black Pool with the owner of the big Black Pool down below.

"Has this place always been a dâk-bungalow?" I asked.

"No," said the *khansamah*. "Ten or twenty years ago, I have forgotten how long, it was a billiard room."

"A how much?"

"A billiard room for the Sahibs who built the Railway. I was *khansamah* then in the big house where all the Railway-Sahibs lived, and I used to come across with brandy-*shrab*. These three rooms were all one, and they held a big table on which the Sahibs played every evening. But the Sahibs are all dead now, and the Railway runs, you say, nearly to Kabul."

"Do you remember anything about the Sahibs?"

"It is long ago, but I remember that one Sahib, a fat man and always angry, was playing here one night, and he said to me:—'Mangal Khan, brandy-*pani do*,' and I filled the glass, and he bent over the table to strike, and his head fell lower and lower till it hit the table, and his spectacles came off, and when we—the Sahibs and I myself—ran to lift him. He was dead. I helped to carry him out. Aha, he was a strong Sahib! But he is dead and I, old Mangal Khan, am still living, by your favour."

That was more than enough! I had my ghost—a firsthand, authenticated article. I would write to the Society for Psychical Research—I would paralyze the Empire with the news! But I would, first of all, put eighty miles of assessed crop land between myself and that dâk-bungalow before nightfall. The Society might send their regular agent to investigate later on.

I went into my own room and prepared to pack after noting down the facts of the case. As I smoked I heard the game begin again—with a miss in balk this time, for the whir was a short one.

The door was open and I could see into the room. *Click—click!* That was a cannon. I entered the room without fear, for there was sunlight within and a fresh breeze without. The unseen game was going on at a tremendous rate. And well it might, when a restless little rat was running to and fro inside the dingy ceiling-cloth, and a piece of loose window-sash was making fifty breaks off the window-bolt as it shook in the breeze!

Impossible to mistake the sound of billiard balls! Impossible to mistake the whir of a ball over the slate! But I was to be excused. Even when I shut my enlightened eyes the sound was marvelously like that of a fast game.

Entered angrily the faithful partner of my sorrows, Kadir Baksh.

"This bungalow is very bad and low-caste! No wonder the Presence was disturbed and is speckled. Three sets of doolie-bearers came to the bungalow late last night when I was sleeping outside, and said that it was their custom to rest in the rooms set apart for the English people! What honor has the *khansamah*? They tried to enter, but I told them to go. No wonder, if these *Oorias* have been here, that the Presence is sorely spotted. It is shame, and the work of a dirty man!"

Kadir Baksh did not say that he had taken from each gang two annas for rent in advance, and then, beyond my earshot, had beaten them with the big green umbrella whose use I could never before divine. But Kadir Baksh has no notions of morality.

There was an interview with the *khansamah*, but as he promptly lost his head, wrath gave place to pity, and pity led to a long conversation, in the course of which he put the fat Engineer-Sahib's tragic death in three separate stations—two of them fifty miles away. The third shift was to Calcutta, and there the Sahib died while driving a dogcart.

If I had encouraged him the *khansamah* would have wandered all through Bengal with his corpse.

I did not go away as soon as I intended. I stayed for the night, while the wind and the rat and the sash and the window-bolt played a ding-dong 'hundred and fifty up.' Then the wind ran out and the billiards stopped, and I felt that I had ruined my one genuine, hall-marked ghost story.

Had I only stopped at the proper time, I could have made *anything* out of it.

That was the bitterest thought of all.

W F HARVEY

(1885-1937)

47

August Heat

Phenistone Road, Clapham, August 20th, 190—

I have had what I believe to be the most remarkable day in my life, and while the events are still fresh in my mind, I wish to put them down on paper as clearly as possible.

Let me say at the outset that my name is James Clarence Withencroft.

I am forty years old, in perfect health, never having known a day's illness.

By profession I am an artist, not a very successful one, but I earn enough money by my black-and—white work to satisfy my necessary wants.

My only near relative, a sister, died five years ago, so that I am independent. I breakfasted this morning at nine, and after glancing through the morning paper I lighted my pipe and proceeded to let my mind wander in the hope that I might chance upon some subject for my pencil.

The room, though door and windows were open, was oppressively hot, and I had just made up my mind that the coolest and most comfortable place in the neighbourhood would be the deep end of the public swimming bath, when the idea came.

I began to draw. So intent was I on my work that I left my lunch untouched, only stopping work when the clock of St. Jude's struck four.

The final result, for a hurried sketch, was, I felt sure, the best thing I had done. It showed a criminal in the dock immediately after the judge had pronounced sentence. The man was fat—enormously fat. The flesh hung in rolls about his chin; it creased his huge, stumpy neck. He was clean shaven (perhaps I should say a few days before he must have been clean shaven) and almost bald. He stood in the dock, his short, clumsy fingers clasping the rail, looking straight in front of him. The feeling that his expression conveyed was not so much one of horror as of utter, absolute collapse.

There seemed nothing in the man strong enough to sustain that mountain of flesh.

I rolled up the sketch, and without quite knowing why, placed it in my pocket. Then with the rare sense of happiness which the knowledge of a good thing well done gives, I left the house.

I believe that I set out with the idea of calling upon Trenton, for I remember walking along Lytton Street and turning to the right along Gilchrist Road at the bottom of the hill where the men were at work on the new tram lines.

From there onwards I have only the vaguest recollection of where I went. The one thing of which I was fully conscious was the awful heat, that came up from the dusty asphalt pavement as an almost palpable wave. I longed for the thunder promised by the great banks of copper-coloured cloud that hung low over the western sky.

I must have walked five or six miles, when a small boy roused me from my reverie by asking the time.

It was twenty minutes to seven.

When he left me I began to take stock of my bearings. I found myself standing before a gate that led into a yard bordered by a strip of thirsty earth, where there were flowers, purple stock and scarlet geranium. Above the entrance was a board with the inscription—

CHS. ATKINSON. MONUMENTAL MASON.
WORKER IN ENGLISH AND ITALIAN MARBLES

From the yard itself came a cheery whistle, the noise of hammer blows, and the cold sound of steel meeting stone.

A sudden impulse made me enter.

A man was sitting with his back towards me, busy at work on a slab of curiously veined marble. He turned round as he heard my steps and I stopped short.

It was the man I had been drawing, whose portrait lay in my pocket.

He sat there, huge and elephantine, the sweat pouring from his scalp, which he wiped with a red silk handkerchief. But though the face was the same, the expression was absolutely different.

He greeted me smiling, as if we were old friends, and shook my hand.

I apologised for my intrusion.

"Everything is hot and glary outside," I said. "This seems an oasis in the wilderness."

"I don't know about the oasis," he replied, "but it certainly is hot, as hot as hell. Take a seat, sir!"

He pointed to the end of the gravestone on which he was at work, and I sat down.

"That's a beautiful piece of stone you've got hold of," I said.

He shook his head. "In a way it is," he answered; "the surface here is as fine as anything you could wish, but there's a big flaw at the back, though I don't expect you'd ever notice it. I could never make really a good job of a bit of marble like that. It would be all right in the summer like this; it wouldn't mind the blasted heat. But wait till the winter comes. There's nothing quite like frost to find out the weak points in stone."

"Then what's it for?" I asked.

The man burst out laughing.

"You'd hardly believe me if I was to tell you it's for an exhibition, but it's the truth. Artists have exhibitions: so do grocers and butchers; we have them too. All the latest little things in headstones, you know."

He went on to talk of marbles, which sort best withstood wind and rain, and which were easiest to work; then of his garden and a new sort of carnation he had bought. At the end of every other minute he would drop his tools, wipe his shining head, and curse the heat.

I said little, for I felt uneasy. There was something unnatural, uncanny, in meeting this man.

I tried at first to persuade myself that I had seen him before, that his face, unknown to me, had found a place in some out-of-the-way corner of my memory, but I knew that I was practising little more than a plausible piece of self-deception.

Mr. Atkinson finished his work, spat on the ground, and got up with a sigh of relief.

"There! what do you think of that?" he said, with an air of evident pride. The inscription which I read for the first time was this—

SACRED TO THE MEMORY
OF
JAMES CLARENCE WITHENCROFT.
BORN JAN. 18TH, 1860.
HE PASSED AWAY VERY SUDDENLY
ON AUGUST 20TH, 190—

"In the midst of life we are in death."

For some time I sat in silence. Then a cold shudder ran down my spine. I asked him where he had seen the name.

"Oh, I didn't see it anywhere," replied Mr. Atkinson. "I wanted some name, and I put down the first that came into my head. Why do you want to know?"

"It's a strange coincidence, but it happens to be mine." He gave a long, low whistle.

"And the dates?"

"I can only answer for one of them, and that's correct."

"It's a rum go!" he said.

But he knew less than I did. I told him of my morning's work. I took the sketch from my pocket and showed it to him. As he looked, the expression of his face altered until it became more and more like that of the man I had drawn.

"And it was only the day before yesterday," he said, "that I told Maria there were no such things as ghosts!"

Neither of us had seen a ghost, but I knew what he meant.

"You probably heard my name," I said.

"And you must have seen me somewhere and have forgotten it! Were you at Clacton-on-Sea last July?"

I had never been to Clacton in my life. We were silent for some time. We were both looking at the same thing, the two dates on the gravestone, and one was right.

"Come inside and have some supper," said Mr. Atkinson.

His wife was a cheerful little woman, with the flaky red cheeks of the country-bred. Her husband introduced me as a friend of his who was an artist. The result was unfortunate, for after the sardines and watercress had been removed, she brought out a Doré Bible, and I had to sit and express my admiration for nearly half an hour.

I went outside, and found Atkinson sitting on the gravestone smoking.

We resumed the conversation at the point we had left off. "You must excuse my asking," I said, "but do you know of anything you've done for which you could be put on trial?"

He shook his head. "I'm not a bankrupt, the business is prosperous enough. Three years ago I gave turkeys to some of the guardians at Christmas, but that's all I can think of. And they were small ones, too," he added as an afterthought.

He got up, fetched a can from the porch, and began to water the flowers. "Twice a day regular in the hot weather," he said, "and then the heat sometimes gets the better of the delicate ones. And ferns, good Lord! they could never stand it. Where do you live?"

I told him my address. It would take an hour's quick walk to get back home.

"It's like this," he said. "We'll look at the matter straight. If you go back home tonight, you take your chance of accidents. A cart may run over you, and there's always banana skins and orange peel, to say nothing of fallen ladders."

He spoke of the improbable with an intense seriousness that would have been laughable six hours before. But I did not laugh.

"The best thing we can do," he continued, "is for you to stay here till twelve o'clock. We'll go upstairs and smoke, it may be cooler inside."

To my surprise I agreed.

We are sitting now in a long, low room beneath the eaves. Atkinson has sent his wife to bed. He himself is busy sharpening some tools at a little oilstone, smoking one of my cigars the while.

The air seems charged with thunder. I am writing this at a shaky table before the open window.

The leg is cracked, and Atkinson, who seems a handy man with his tools, is going to mend it as soon as he has finished putting an edge on his chisel.

It is after eleven now. I shall be gone in less than an hour.

But the heat is stifling.

It is enough to send a man mad.

W W JACOBS

(1863-1943)

48

The Monkey's Paw

I

Without, the night was cold and wet, but in the small parlour of Laburnum villa the blinds were drawn and the fire burned brightly. Father and son were at chess; the former, who possessed ideas about the game involving radical chances, putting his king into such sharp and unnecessary perils that it even provoked comment from the white-haired old lady knitting placidly by the fire.

"Hark at the wind," said Mr. White, who, having seen a fatal mistake after it was too late, was amiably desirous of preventing his son from seeing it.

"I'm listening," said the latter grimly surveying the board as he stretched out his hand. "Check."

"I should hardly think that he's come tonight," said his father, with his hand poised over the board.

"Mate," replied the son.

"That's the worst of living so far out," balled Mr. White with sudden and unlooked-for violence; "Of all the beastly, slushy, out of the way places to live in, this is the worst. Path's a bog, and the road's a torrent. I don't know what people are thinking about. I suppose because only two houses in the road are let, they think it doesn't matter."

"Never mind, dear," said his wife soothingly; "perhaps you'll win the next one."

Mr. White looked up sharply, just in time to intercept a knowing glance between mother and son. the words died away on his lips, and he hid a guilty grin in his thin grey beard.

"There he is," said Herbert White as the gate banged to loudly and heavy footsteps came toward the door.

The old man rose with hospitable haste and opening the door, was heard condoling with the new arrival. The new arrival also condoled with himself, so that Mrs. White said, "Tut, tut!" and coughed gently as her husband entered the room followed by a tall, burly man, beady of eye and rubicund of visage.

"Sergeant-Major Morris," he said, introducing him.

The Sergeant-Major took hands and taking the proffered seat by the fire, watched contentedly as his host got out whiskey and tumblers and stood a small copper kettle on the fire.

At the third glass his eyes got brighter, and he began to talk, the little family circle regarding with eager interest this visitor from distant parts, as he squared his broad shoulders in the chair and spoke of wild scenes and doughty deeds; of wars and plagues and strange peoples.

"Twenty-one years of it," said Mr. White, nodding at his wife and son. "When he went away he was a slip of a youth in the warehouse. Now look at him."

"He don't look to have taken much harm," said Mrs. White politely.

"I'd like to go to India myself," said the old man, "just to look around a bit, you know."

"Better where you are," said the Sergeant-Major, shaking his head. He put down the empty glass and sighning softly, shook it again.

"I should like to see those old temples and fakirs and jugglers," said the old man. "What was that that you started telling me the other day about a monkey's paw or something, Morris?"

"Nothing." said the soldier hastily. "Leastways, nothing worth hearing."

"Monkey's paw?" said Mrs. White curiously.

"Well, it's just a bit of what you might call magic, perhaps." said the Sergeant-Major off-handedly.

His three listeners leaned forward eagerly. The visitor absent-mindedly put his empty glass to his lips and then set it down again. His host filled it for him again.

"To look at," said the Sergeant-Major, fumbling in his pocket, "it's just an ordinary little paw, dried to a mummy."

He took something out of his pocket and proffered it. Mrs. White drew back with a grimace, but her son, taking it, examined it curiously.

"And what is there special about it?" inquired Mr. White as he took it from his son, and having examined it, placed it upon the table.

"It had a spell put on it by an old Fakir," said the Sergeant-Major, "a very holy man. He wanted to show that fate ruled people's lives, and that those who interfered with it did so to their sorrow. He put a spell on it so that three separate men could each have three wishes from it."

His manners were so impressive that his hearers were conscious that their light laughter had jarred somewhat.

"Well, why don't you have three, sir?" said Herbert White cleverly.

The soldier regarded him the way that middle age is wont to regard presumptuous youth. "I have," he said quietly, and his blotchy face whitened.

"And did you really have the three wishes granted?" asked Mrs. White.

"I did," said the sergeant-major, and his glass tapped against his strong teeth.

"And has anybody else wished?" persisted the old lady.

"The first man had his three wishes. Yes," was the reply, "I don't know what the first two were, but the third was for death. That's how I got the paw."

His tones were so grave that a hush fell upon the group.

"If you've had your three wishes it's no good to you now then Morris," said the old man at last. "What do you keep it for?"

The soldier shook his head. "Fancy I suppose," he said slowly. "I did have some idea of selling it, but I don't think I will. It has caused me enough mischief already. Besides, people won't buy. They think it's a fairy tale, some of them; and those who do think anything of it want to try it first and pay me afterward."

"If you could have another three wishes," said the old man, eyeing him keenly, "would you have them?"

"I don't know," said the other. "I don't know."

He took the paw, and dangling it between his forefinger and thumb, suddenly threw it upon the fire. White, with a slight cry, stooped down and snatched it off.

"Better let it burn," said the soldier solemnly.

"If you don't want it Morris," said the other, "give it to me."

"I won't." said his friend doggedly. "I threw it on the fire. If you keep it, don't blame me for what happens. Pitch it on the fire like a sensible man."

The other shook his head and examined his possession closely. "How do you do it?" he inquired.

"Hold it up in your right hand, and wish aloud," said the Sergeant-Major, "But I warn you of the consequences."

"Sounds like the 'Arabian Nights'," said Mrs. White, as she rose and began to set the supper. "Don't you think you might wish for four pairs of hands for me."

Her husband drew the talisman from his pocket, and all three burst into laughter as the Seargent-Major, with a look of alarm on his face, caught him by the arm.

"If you must wish," he said gruffly, "wish for something sensible."

Mr. White dropped it back in his pocket, and placing chairs, motioned his friend to the table. In the business of supper the talisman was partly forgotten, and afterward the three sat listening in an enthralled fashion to a second installment of the soldier's adventures in India.

"If the tale about the monkey's paw is not more truthful than those he has been telling us," said Herbert, as the door closed behind their guest, just in time to catch the last train, "we shan't make much out of it."

"Did you give anything for it, father?" inquired Mrs. White, regarding her husband closely.

"A trifle," said he, colouring slightly, "He didn't want it, but I made him take it. And he pressed me again to throw it away."

"Likely," said Herbert, with pretended horror. "Why, we're going to be rich, and famous, and happy. Wish to be an emperor, father, to begin with; then you can't be henpecked."

He darted around the table, pursued by the maligned Mrs. White armed with an antimacassar.

Mr. White took the paw from his pocket and eyed it dubiously. "I don't know what to wish for, and that's a fact," he said slowly. "It seems to me I've got all I want."

"If you only cleared the house, you'd be quite happy, wouldn't you!" said Herbert, with his hand on his shoulder. "Well, wish for two hundred pounds, then; that'll just do it."

His father, smiling shamefacedly at his own credulity, held up the talisman, as his son, with a solemn face, somewhat marred by a wink at his mother, sat down and struck a few impressive chords.

"I wish for two hundred pounds," said the old man distinctly.

A fine crash from the piano greeted his words, interrupted by a shuddering cry from the old man. His wife and son ran toward him.

"It moved," he cried, with a glance of disgust at the object as it lay on the floor. "As I wished, it twisted in my hand like a snake."

"Well, I don't see the money," said his son, as he picked it up and placed it on the table, "and I bet I never shall."

"It must have been your fancy, father," said his wife, regarding him anxiously.

He shook his head. "Never mind, though; there's no harm done, but it gave me a shock all the same."

They sat down by the fire again while the two men finished their pipes. Outside, the wind was higher than ever, and the old man started nervously at the sound of a door banging upstairs. A silence unusual and depressing settled on all three, which lasted until the old couple rose to retire for the rest of the night.

"I expect you'll find the cash tied up in a big bag in the middle of your bed," said Herbert, as he bade them good night, "and something horrible squatting on top of your wardrobe watching you as you pocket your ill-gotten gains."

He sat alone in the darkness, gazing at the dying fire, and seeing faces in it. The last was so horrible and so simian that he gazed at it in amazement. It got so vivid that, with a little uneasy laugh, he felt on the table for a glass containing a little water to throw over it. His hand grasped the monkey's paw, and with a little shiver he wiped his hand on his coat and went up to bed.

II

In the brightness of the wintry sun next morning as it streamed over the breakfast table he laughed at his fears. There was an air of prosaic wholesomeness about the room which it had lacked on the previous night, and the dirty, shriveled little paw was pitched on the side-board with a carelessness which betokened no great belief in its virtues.

"I suppose all old soldiers are the same," said Mrs. White. "The idea of our listening to such nonsense! How could wishes be granted in these days? And if they could, how could two hundred pounds hurt you, father?"

"Might drop on his head from the sky," said the frivolous Herbert.

"Morris said the things happened so naturally," said his father, "that you might if you so wished attribute it to coincidence."

"Well don't break into the money before I come back," said Herbert as he rose from the table. "I'm afraid it'll turn you into a mean, avaricious man, and we shall have to disown you."

His mother laughed, and following him to the door, watched him down the road; and returning to the breakfast table, was very happy at the expense of her husband's credulity. All of which did not prevent her from scurrying to the door at the postman's knock, nor prevent her from referring somewhat shortly to retired Sergeant-Majors of bibulous habits when she found that the post brought a tailor's bill.

"Herbert will have some more of his funny remarks, I expect, when he comes home," she said as they sat at dinner.

"I dare say," said Mr. White, pouring himself out some beer; "but for all that, the thing moved in my hand; that I'll swear to."

"You thought it did," said the old lady soothingly.

"I say it did," replied the other. "There was no thought about it; I had just—What's the matter?"

His wife made no reply. She was watching the mysterious movements of a man outside, who, peering in an undecided fashion at the house, appeared to be trying to make up his mind to enter. In mental connexion with the two hundred pounds, she noticed that the stranger was well dressed, and wore a silk hat of glossy newness. Three times he paused at the gate, and then walked on again. The fourth time he stood with his hand upon it, and then with sudden resolution flung it open and walked up the path. Mrs. White at the same moment placed her hands behind her, and hurriedly unfastening the strings of her apron, put that useful article of apparel beneath the cushion of her chair.

She brought the stranger, who seemed ill at ease, into the room. He gazed at her furtively, and listened in a preoccupied fashion as the old lady apologized for the appearance of the room, and her husband's coat, a garment which he usually reserved for the garden. She then waited as patiently as her sex would permit for him to broach his business, but he was at first strangely silent.

"I—was asked to call," he said at last, and stooped and picked a piece of cotton from his trousers. "I come from 'Maw and Meggins.'"

The old lady started. "Is anything the matter?" she asked breathlessly. "Has anything happened to Herbert? What is it? What is it?"

Her husband interposed. "There there mother," he said hastily. "Sit down, and don't jump to conclusions. You've not brought bad news, I'm sure sir," and eyed the other wistfully.

"I'm sorry—" began the visitor.

"Is he hurt?" demanded the mother wildly.

The visitor bowed in assent. "Badly hurt," he said quietly, "but he is not in any pain."

"Oh thank God!" said the old woman, clasping her hands. "Thank God for that! Thank—"

She broke off as the sinister meaning of the assurance dawned on her and she saw the awful confirmation of her fears in the others averted face. She caught her breath, and turning to her slower-witted husband, laid her trembling hand on his. There was a long silence.

"He was caught in the machinery," said the visitor at length in a low voice.

"Caught in the machinery," repeated Mr. White, in a dazed fashion, "yes."

He sat staring out the window, and taking his wife's hand between his own, pressed it as he had been wont to do in their old courting days nearly forty years before.

"He was the only one left to us," he said, turning gently to the visitor. "It is hard."

The other coughed, and rising, walked slowly to the window. "The firm wishes me to convey their sincere sympathy with you in your great loss," he said, without looking round. "I beg that you will understand I am only their servant and merely obeying orders."

There was no reply; the old woman's face was white, her eyes staring, and her breath inaudible; on the husband's face was a look such as his friend the sergeant might have carried into his first action.

"I was to say that Maw and Meggins disclaim all responsibility," continued the other. "They admit no liability at all, but in consideration of your son's services, they wish to present you with a certain sum as compensation."

Mr. White dropped his wife's hand, and rising to his feet, gazed with a look of horror at his visitor. His dry lips shaped the words, "How much?"

"Two hundred pounds," was the answer.

Unconscious of his wife's shriek, the old man smiled faintly, put out his hands like a sightless man, and dropped, a senseless heap, to the floor.

III

In the huge new cemetery, some two miles distant, the old people buried their dead, and came back to the house steeped in shadows and silence. It was all over so quickly that at first they could hardly realize it, and remained in a state of expectation as though of something else to happen—something else which was to lighten this load, too heavy for old hearts to bear.

But the days passed, and expectations gave way to resignation—the hopeless resignation of the old, sometimes mis-called apathy. Sometimes they hardly exchanged a word, for now they had nothing to talk about, and their days were long to weariness.

It was about a week after that the old man, waking suddenly in the night, stretched out his hand and found himself alone. The room was in darkness, and the sound of subdued weeping came from the window. He raised himself in bed and listened.

"Come back," he said tenderly. "You will be cold."

"It is colder for my son," said the old woman, and wept afresh.

The sounds of her sobs died away on his ears. The bed was warm, and his eyes heavy with sleep. He dozed fitfully, and then slept until a sudden wild cry from his wife awoke him with a start.

"THE PAW!" she cried wildly. "THE MONKEY'S PAW!"

He started up in alarm. "Where? Where is it? What's the matter?"

She came stumbling across the room toward him. "I want it," she said quietly. "You've not destroyed it?"

"It's in the parlour, on the bracket," he replied, marveling. "Why?"

She cried and laughed together, and bending over, kissed his cheek.

"I only just thought of it," she said hysterically. "Why didn't I think of it before? Why didn't you think of it?"

"Think of what?" he questioned.

"The other two wishes," she replied rapidly. "We've only had one."

"Was not that enough?" he demanded fiercely.

"No," she cried triumphantly; "We'll have one more. Go down and get it quickly, and wish our boy alive again."

The man sat in bed and flung the bedclothes from his quaking limbs."Good God, you are mad!" he cried aghast. "Get it," she panted; "get it quickly, and wish—Oh my boy, my boy!"

Her husband struck a match and lit the candle. "Get back to bed," he said unsteadily. "You don't know what you are saying."

"We had the first wish granted," said the old woman, feverishly; "why not the second?"

"A coincidence," stammered the old man.

"Go get it and wish," cried his wife, quivering with excitement.

The old man turned and regarded her, and his voice shook. "He has been dead ten days, and besides he—I would not tell you else, but—I could only recognize him by his clothing. If he was too terrible for you to see then, how now?"

"Bring him back," cried the old woman, and dragged him towards the door. "Do you think I fear the child I have nursed?"

He went down in the darkness, and felt his way to the parlour, and then to the mantlepiece. The talisman was in its place, and a horrible fear that the unspoken wish might bring his mutilated son before him ere he could escape from the room seized up on him, and he caught his breath as he found that he had lost the direction of the door. His brow cold with sweat, he felt his way round the table, and groped along the wall until he found himself in the small passage with the unwholesome thing in his hand.

Even his wife's face seemed changed as he entered the room. It was white and expectant, and to his fears seemed to have an unnatural look upon it. He was afraid of her.

"WISH!" she cried in a strong voice.

"It is foolish and wicked," he faltered.

"WISH!" repeated his wife.

He raised his hand. "I wish my son alive again."

The talisman fell to the floor, and he regarded it fearfully. Then he sank trembling into a chair as the old woman, with burning eyes, walked to the window and raised the blind.

He sat until he was chilled with the cold, glancing occasionally at the figure of the old woman peering through the window. The candle-end, which had burned below the rim of the china candlestick, was throwing pulsating shadows on the ceiling and walls, until with a flicker larger than the rest, it expired. The old man, with an unspeakable sense of relief at the failure of the talisman, crept back back to his bed, and a minute afterward the old woman came silently and apathetically beside him.

Neither spoke, but sat silently listening to the ticking of the clock. A stair creaked, and a squeaky mouse scurried noisily through the wall. The darkness was oppressive, and after lying for some time screwing up his courage, he took the box of matches, and striking one, went downstairs for a candle.

At the foot of the stairs the match went out, and he paused to strike another; and at the same moment a knock came so quiet and stealthy as to be scarcely audible, sounded on the front door.

The matches fell from his hand and spilled in the passage. He stood motionless, his breath suspended until the knock was repeated. Then he turned and fled swiftly back to his room, and closed the door behind him. A third knock sounded through the house.

"WHAT'S THAT?" cried the old woman, starting up.

"A rat," said the old man in shaking tones—"a rat. It passed me on the stairs."

His wife sat up in bed listening. A loud knock resounded through the house.

"It's Herbert!"

She ran to the door, but her husband was before her, and catching her by the arm, held her tightly.

"What are you going to do?" he whispered hoarsely.

"It's my boy; it's Herbert!" she cried, struggling mechanically. "I forgot it was two miles away. What are you holding me for? Let go. I must open the door."

"For God's sake don't let it in," cried the old man, trembling.

"You're afraid of your own son," she cried struggling. "Let me go. I'm coming, Herbert; I'm coming."

There was another knock, and another. The old woman with a sudden wrench broke free and ran from the room. Her husband followed to the landing, and called after her appealingly as she hurried downstairs. He heard the chain rattle back and the bolt drawn slowly and stiffly from the socket. Then the old woman's voice, strained and panting.

"The bolt," she cried loudly. "Come down. I can't reach it."

But her husband was on his hands and knees groping wildly on the floor in search of the paw. If only he could find it before the thing outside got in. A perfect fusillade of knocks reverberated through the house, and he heard the scraping of a chair as his wife put it down in the passage against the door. He heard the creaking of the bolt as it came slowly back, and at the same moment he found the monkey's paw, and frantically breathed his third and last wish.

The knocking ceased suddenly, although the echoes of it were still in the house. He heard the chair drawn back, and the door opened. A cold wind rushed up the staircase, and a long loud wail of disappointment and misery from his wife gave him the courage to run down to her side, and then to the gate beyond. The street lamp flickering opposite shone on a quiet and deserted road.

WASHINGTON IRVING

(1783-1859)

49

The Adventure of the German Student

On a stormy night, in the tempestuous times of the French Revolution, a young German was returning to his lodgings, at a late hour, across the old part of Paris. The lightning gleamed, and the loud claps of thunder rattled through the lofty narrow streets—but I should first tell you something about this young German.

Gottfried Wolfgang was a young man of good family. He had studied for some time at Göttingen, but being of a visionary and enthusiastic character, he had wandered into those wild and speculative doctrines which have so often bewildered German students. His secluded life, his intense application, and the singular nature of his studies, had an effect on both mind and body. His health was impaired; his imagination diseased. He had been indulging in fanciful speculations on spiritual essences, until, like Swedenborg, he had an ideal world of his own around him. He took up a notion, I do not know from what cause, that there was an evil influence hanging over him; an evil genius or spirit seeking to ensnare him and ensure his perdition. Such an idea working on his melancholy temperament produced the most gloomy effects. He became haggard and desponding.

His friends discovered the mental malady preying upon him, and determined that the best cure was a change of scene; he was sent, therefore, to finish his studies amidst the splendours and gayeties of Paris.

Wolfgang arrived at Paris at the breaking out of the revolution. The popular delirium at first caught his enthusiastic mind, and he was captivated by the political and philosophical theories of the day: but the scenes of blood which followed shocked his sensitive nature, disgusted him with society and the world, and made him more than ever a recluse. He shut himself up in a solitary apartment in the Pays Latin, the quarter of students. There, in a gloomy street not far from the monastic walls of the Sorbonne, he pursued his favorite speculations. Sometimes he spend hours together in the great libraries of Paris, those catacombs of departed authors, rummaging among their hoards of dusty and obsolete works in quest of food for his unhealthy appetite. He was, in a manner, a literary ghoul, feeding in the charnel-house of decayed literature.

Wolfgang, thought solitary and recluse, was of an ardent temperament, but for a time it operated merely upon his imagination. He was too shy and ignorant of the world to make any advances to the fair, but he was a passionate admirer of female beauty, and in his lonely chamber would often lose himself in reveries on forms and faces which he had seen, and his fancy would deck out images of loveliness far surpassing the reality.

While his mind was in this excited and sublimated state, a dream produced an extraordinary effect upon him. It was of a female face of transcendent beauty. So strong was the impression made, that he dreamt of it again and again. It haunted his thoughts by day, his slumbers by night; in fine, he became passionately enamored of this shadow of a dream. This lasted so long that it became one of those fixed ideas which haunt the minds of melancholy men, and are at times mistaken for madness.

Such was Gottfried Wolfgang, and such his situation at the time I mentioned. He was returning home late on stormy night, through some of the old and gloomy streets of the Marais, the ancient part of Paris. The loud claps of thunder rattled among the high houses of the narrow streets. He came to the Place de Grève, the square, where public executions are performed. The lightning quivered about the pinnacles of the ancient Hôtel de Ville, and shed flickering gleams over the open space in front. As Wolfgang was crossing the square, he shrank back with horror at finding himself close by the guillotine. It was the height of the reign of terror, when this dreadful instrument of death stood ever ready, and its scaffold was continually running with the blood of the virtuous and the brave. It had that very day been actively employed in the work of carnage, and there it stood in grim array, amidst a silent and sleeping city, waiting for fresh victims.

Wolfgang's heart sickened within him, and he was turning shuddering from the horrible engine, when he beheld a shadowy form, cowering as it were at the foot of the steps which led up to the scaffold. A succession of vivid flashes of lightning revealed it more distinctly. It was a female figure, dressed in black. She was seated on one of the lower steps of the scaffold, leaning forward, her face hid in her lap; and her long dishevelled tresses hanging to the ground, streaming with the rain which fell in torrents. Wolfgang paused. There was something awful in this solitary monument of woe. The female had the appearance of being above the common order. He knew the times to be full of vicissitude, and that many a fair head, which had once been pillowed on down, now wandered houseless. Perhaps this was some poor mourner whom the dreadful axe had rendered desolate, and who sat here heart-broken on the strand of existence, from which all that was dear to her had been launched into eternity.

He approached, and addressed her in the accents of sympathy. She raised her head and gazed wildly at him. What was his astonishment at beholding, by the bright glare of the lighting, the very face which had haunted him in his dreams. It was pale and disconsolate, but ravishingly beautiful.

Trembling with violent and conflicting emotions, Wolfgang again accosted her. He spoke something of her being exposed at such an hour of the night, and to the fury of such a storm, and offered to conduct her to her friends. She pointed to the guillotine with a gesture of dreadful signification.

"I have no friend on earth!" said she.

"But you have a home," said Wolfgang.

"Yes—in the grave!"

The heart of the student melted at the words.

"If a stranger dare make an offer," said he, "without danger of being misunderstood, I would offer my humble dwelling as a shelter; myself as a devoted friend. I am friendless myself in Paris, and a stranger in the land; but if my life could be of service, it is at your disposal, and should be sacrificed before harm or indignity should come to you."

There was an honest earnestness in the young man's manner that had its effect. His foreign accent, too, was in his favor; it showed him not to be a hackneyed inhabitant of Paris. Indeed, there is an eloquence in true enthusiasm that is not to be doubted. The homeless stranger confided herself implicitly to the protection of the student.

He supported her faltering steps across the Pont Neuf, and by the place where the statue of Henry the Fourth had been overthrown by the populace. The storm had abated, and the thunder rumbled at a distance. All Paris was quiet; that great volcano of human passion slumbered for a while, to gather fresh strength for the next day's eruption. The student conducted his charge through the ancient streets of the Pays Latin, and by the dusky walls of the Sorbonne, to the great dingy hotel which he inhabited. The old portress who admitted them stared with surprise at the unusual sight of the melancholy Wolfgang, with a female companion.

On entering his apartment, the student, for the first time, blushed at the scantiness and indifference of his dwelling. He had but one chamber—an old-fashioned saloon—heavily carved, and fantastically furnished with the remains of former magnificence, for it was one of those hotels in the quarter nobility. It was lumbered with books and papers, and all the usual apparatus of a student, and his bed stood in a recess at one end.

When lights were brought, and Wolfgang had a better

opportunity of contemplating the stranger, he was more than ever intoxicated by her beauty. Her face was pale, but of a dazzling fairness, set off by a profusion of raven hair that hung clustering about it. Her eyes were large and brilliant, with a singular expression approaching almost to wildness. As far as her black dress permitted her shape to be seen, it was of perfect symmetry. Her whole appearance was highly striking, though she was dressed in the simplest style. The only thing approaching to an ornament which she wore, was a broad black band round her neck, clasped by diamonds.

The perplexity now commenced with the student how to dispose of the helpless being thus thrown upon his protection. He thought of abandoning his chamber to her, and seeking shelter for himself elsewhere. Still he was so fascinated by her charms, there seemed to be such a spell upon his thoughts and senses, that he could not tear himself from her presence. Her manner, too, was singular and unaccountable. She spoke no more of the guillotine. Her grief had abated. The attentions of the student had first won her confidence, and then, apparently, her heart. She was evidently an enthusiast like himself, and enthusiasts soon understand each other.

In the infatuation of the moment, Wolfgang avowed his passion for her. He told her the story of his mysterious dream, and how she had possessed his heart before he had even seen her. She was strangely affected by his recital, and acknowledge to have felt an impulse towards him equally unaccountable. It was the time for wild theory and wild actions. Old prejudices and superstitions were done away; everything was under the sway of the 'Goddess of Reason.' Among other rubbish of the old times, the forms and ceremonies of marriage began to be considered superfluous bonds for honourable minds. Social compact were the vogue. Wolfgang was too much of theorist not to be tainted by the liberal doctrines of the day.

"Why should we separate?" said he: "our heart are united; in the eye of reason and honour we are as one. What need is there of sordid forms to bind high soul together?"

The stranger listened with emotion: she had evidently received illumination at the same school.

"You have no home nor family," continued he: "Let me be everything to you, or rather let us be everything to one another. if form is necessary, form shall be observed—there is my hand. I pledge myself to you forever."

"Forever?" said the stranger, solemnly.

"Forever!" repeated Wolfgang.

The stranger clasped the hand extended to her: "Then I am yours," murmured she, and sank upon his bosom.

The next morning the student left his bride sleeping, and sallied forth at an early hour to seek more spacious apartments suitable to the change in his situation. When he returned, he found the stranger lying with her head hanging over the bed, and one arm thrown over it. He spoke to her, but received no reply. He advanced to awaken her from her uneasy posture. On taking her hand, it was cold—there was no pulsation—her face was pallid and ghastly. In a word, she was a corpse.

Horrified and frantic, he alarmed the house. A scene of confusion ensued. The police was summoned. As the officer of police entered the room, he started back on beholding the corpse.

"Great heaven!" cried he, "how did this woman come here?"

"Do you know anything about her?" said Wolfgang eagerly.

"Do I?" exclaimed the officer: "she was guillotined yesterday."

He stepped forward; undid the black collar round the neck of the corpse, and the head rolled on the floor!

The student burst into a frenzy. "The fiend! the fiend has gained possession of me!" shrieked he; "I am lost forever."

They tried to soothe him, but in vain. He was possessed with the frightful belief that an evil spirit had reanimated the dead body to ensnare him. He went distracted, and died in a mad-house.

Here the old gentleman with the haunted head finished his narrative.

"And is this really a fact?" said the inquisitive gentleman.

"A fact not to be doubted," replied the other. "I had it from the best authority. The student told it me himself. I saw him in a mad-house in Paris."

50

The Adventure of My Aunt

My aunt was a lady of large frame, strong mind, and great resolution; she was what might be termed a very manly woman. My uncle was a thin, puny little man, very meek and acquiescent, and no match for my aunt. It was observed that he dwindled and dwindled gradually away, from the day of his marriage. His wife's powerful mind was too much for him; it wore him out. My aunt, however, took all possible care of him, had half the doctors in town to prescribe for him, made him take all their prescriptions, *willy nilly*, and dosed him with physic enough to cure a whole hospital. All was in vain. My uncle grew worse and worse the more dosing and nursing he underwent, until in the end he added another to the long list of matrimonial victims, who have been killed with kindness.

"And was it his ghost that appeared to her?" asked the inquisitive gentleman, who had questioned the former storyteller.

"You shall hear," replied the narrator:—My aunt took on mightily for the death of her poor dear husband! Perhaps she felt some compunction at having given him so much physic, and nursed him into his grave. At any rate, she did all that a widow could do to honor his memory. She spared no expense in either the quantity or quality of her mourning weeds; she wore a miniature of him about her neck, as large as a little sun dial; and she had a full-length portrait of him always hanging in her bed chamber. All the world extolled her conduct to the skies; and it was determined, that a woman who behaved so well to the memory of one husband, deserved soon to get another.

It was not long after this that she went to take up her residence in an old country seat in Derbyshire, which had long been in the care of merely a steward and housekeeper. She took most of her servants with her, intending to make it her principal abode. The house stood in a lonely, wild part of the country among the gray Derbyshire hills; with a murderer hanging in chains on a bleak height in full view.

The servants from town were half frightened out of their wits, at the idea of living in such a dismal, pagan-looking place; especially when they got together in the servants' hall in the evening, and compared notes on all the hobgoblin stories they had picked up in the course of the day. They were afraid to venture alone about the forlorn black-looking chambers. My ladies' maid, who was troubled with nerves, declared she could never sleep alone in such a "gashly, rummaging old building;" and the footman, who was a kind-hearted young fellow, did all in his power to cheer her up.

My aunt, herself, seemed to be struck with the lonely appearance of the house. Before she went to bed, therefore, she examined well the fastenings of the doors and windows, locked up the plate with her own hands, and carried the keys, together with a little box of money and jewels, to her own room; for she was a notable woman, and always saw to all things herself. Having put the keys under her pillow, and dismissed her maid, she sat by her toilet arranging her hair; for, being, in spite of her grief for my uncle, rather a buxom widow, she was a little particular about her person. She sat for a little while looking at her face in the glass, first on one side, then on the other, as ladies are apt to do, when they would ascertain if they have been in good looks; for a roystering country squire of the neighborhood, with whom she had flirted when a girl, had called that day to welcome her to the country.

All of a sudden she thought she heard something move behind her. She Looked hastily round, but there was nothing to be seen. Nothing but the grimly painted portrait of her poor dear man, which had been hung against the wall. She gave a heavy sigh to his memory, as she was accustomed to do, whenever she spoke of him in company; and went on adjusting her nightdress. Her sigh was re-echoed; or answered by a long-drawn breath. She looked round again, but no one was to be seen. She ascribed these sounds to the wind, oozing through the rat holes of the old mansion; and proceeded leisurely to put her hair in papers, when, all at once, she thought she perceived one of the eyes of the portrait move.

"The back of her head being towards it!" said the story-teller with the ruined head, giving a knowing wink on the sound side of his visage—"good!"

"Yes, sir!" replied drily the narrator, "her back being towards the portrait, but her eye fixed on its reflection in the glass."

Well, as I was saying, she perceived one of the eyes of the portrait move. So strange a circumstance, as you may well suppose, gave her a sudden shock. To assure herself cautiously of the fact, she put one hand to her forehead, as if rubbing it; peeped through her fingers, and moved the candle with the other hand. The light of the taper gleamed on the eye, and was reflected from it. She was sure it moved. Nay, more, it seemed to give her a wink, as she had sometimes known her husband to do when living! It struck a momentary chill to her heart; for she was a lone woman, and felt herself fearfully situated.

The chill was but transient. My aunt, who was almost as resolute a personage as your uncle, sir, (turning to the old story-teller,) became instantly calm and collected. She went on adjusting her dress. She even hummed a favorite air, and did not make a single false note. She casually overturned a dressing box; took a candle and picked up the articles leisurely, one by one, from the floor, pursued a rolling pin-cushion that was making the best of its way under the bed; then opened the door; looked for an instant into the corridor, as if in doubt whether to go; and then walked quietly out.

She hastened down-stairs, ordered the servants to arm themselves with the first weapons that came to hand, placed herself at their head, and returned almost immediately.

Her hastily levied army presented a formidable force. The steward had a rusty blunderbuss; the coachman a loaded whip; the footman a pair of horse pistols; the cook a huge chopping knife, and the butler a bottle in each hand. My aunt led the van with a red-hot poker; and, in my opinion, she was the most formidable of the party. The waiting maid brought up the rear, dreading to stay alone in the servants' hall, smelling to a broken bottle of volatile salts, and expressing her terror of the ghosteses.

"Ghosts!" said my aunt resolutely, "I'll singe their whiskers for them!"

They entered the chamber. All was still and undisturbed as when she left it. They approached the portrait of my uncle.

"Pull me down that picture!" cried my aunt.

A heavy groan, and a sound like the chattering of teeth, was heard from the portrait. The servants shrunk back. The maid uttered a faint shriek, and clung to the footman.

"Instantly!" added my aunt, with a stamp of the foot.

The picture was pulled down, and from a recess behind it, in which had formerly stood a clock, they hauled forth a round-shouldered, black-bearded varlet, with a knife as long as my arm, but trembling all over like an aspen leaf.

"Well, and who was he? No ghost, I suppose!" said the inquisitive gentleman.

"A knight of the post," replied the narrator, "who had been smitten with the worth of the wealthy widow; or rather a marauding Tarquin, who had stolen into her chamber to violate her purse and rifle her strong box when all the house should be asleep. In plain terms," continued he, "the vagabond was a loose idle fellow of the neighborhood, who had once been a servant in the house, and had been employed to assist in arranging it for the reception of its mistress. He confessed that he had contrived his hiding-place for his nefarious purposes, and had borrowed an eye from the portrait by way of a reconnoitering hole."

"And what did they do with him—did they hang him?" resumed the questioner.

"Hang him?—how could they?" exclaimed a beetle-browed barrister, with a hawk's nose—"the offence was not capital—no robbery nor assault had been committed—no forcible entry or breaking into the premises—"

"My aunt," said the narrator, "was a woman of spirit, and apt to take the law into her own hands. She had her own notions of cleanliness also. She ordered the fellow to be drawn through the horsepond to cleanse away all offences, and then to be well rubbed down with an oaken towel."

"And what became of him afterwards?" said the inquisitive gentleman.

"I do not exactly know—I believe he was sent on a voyage of improvement to Botany Bay."

"And your aunt—" said the inquisitive gentleman—"I'll warrant she took care to make her maid sleep in the room with her after that."

"No, sir, she did better—she gave her hand shortly after to the roystering squire; for she used to observe it was a dismal thing for a woman to sleep alone in the country."

"She was right," observed the inquisitive gentleman, nodding his head sagaciously—"but I am sorry they did not hang that fellow."

It was agreed on all hands that the last narrator had brought his tale to the most satisfactory conclusion; though a country clergyman present regretted that the uncle and aunt, who figured in the different stories, had not been married together. They certainly would have been well matched.

"But I don't see, after all," said the inquisitive gentleman, "that there was any ghost in this last story."

"Oh, if it's ghosts you want, honey," cried the Irish captain of dragoons, "if it's ghosts you want, you shall have a whole regiment of them. And since these gentlemen have been giving the adventures of their uncles and aunts, faith and I'll e'en give you a chapter too, out of my own family history."